Starving Hearts

by

Janine Mendenhall

HERITAGE BEACON
FICTION

STARVING HEARTS BY JANINE MENDENHALL
Published by Heritage Beacon Fiction
an imprint of Lighthouse Publishing of the Carolinas
2333 Barton Oaks Dr., Raleigh, NC, 27614

ISBN: 978-1-938499-84-5
Copyright © 2016 by Janine Mendenhall
Cover design by Elaina Lee
Interior design by AtriTeX Technologies P Ltd

Available in print from your local bookstore, online, or from the publisher at:
www.lighthousepublishingofthecarolinas.com

For more information on this book and the author visit: www.janinemendenhall.com

All rights reserved. Non-commercial interests may reproduce portions of this book without the express written permission of Lighthouse Publishing of the Carolinas, provided the text does not exceed 500 words. When reproducing text from this book, include the following credit line: "*Starving Hearts* by Janine Mendenhall published by Heritage Beacon Fiction. Used by permission."

Commercial interests: No part of this publication may be reproduced in any form, stored in a retrieval system, or transmitted in any form by any means—electronic, photocopy, recording, or otherwise—without prior written permission of the publisher, except as provided by the United States of America copyright law.

This is a work of fiction. Names, characters, and incidents are all products of the author's imagination or are used for fictional purposes. Any mentioned brand names, places, and trademarks remain the property of their respective owners, bear no association with the author or the publisher, and are used for fictional purposes only.

Scripture quotations from The Authorized (King James) Version. Rights in the Authorized Version in the United Kingdom are vested in the Crown. Reproduced by permission of the Crown's patentee, Cambridge University Press.

Brought to you by the creative team at Lighthouse Publishing of the Carolinas:
Eddie Jones, Ann Tatlock, Amberlyn Dwinnell, Brian Cross, Paige Boggs

Library of Congress Cataloging-in-Publication Data
Mendenhall, Janine.
Starving Hearts / Janine Mendenhall 1st ed.

Praise for *Starving Hearts*

A historically rich tale that appeals to the imagination while tugging on the heartstrings, immersing you in the world of Georgian England with all its vices and virtues. *Starving Hearts* is a memorable debut!

~ **Laura Frantz**
Author of *The Mistress of Tall Acre*

In *Starving Hearts*, Janine Mendenhall skillfully draws readers into the romance, history, and adventure of 18th-century England as she immerses them into the world of wealth and deception.

~ **Pam Johnson**
Freelance editor for Steven James (the Patrick Bowers series) and Donald Brobst (*The Ghost of Africa*)

In *Starving Hearts*, Janine Mendenhall transports the reader to 18th-century England as the characters maneuver high society, struggling with family secrets, romance, and the ethics and politics of the African slave trade. An engaging, thoughtful debut.

~ **Susanne Dietz**
Author of *One Word From You: Austen in Austin, Volume I* and *My Heart Belongs in Ruby City, Idaho*

Starving Hearts is the kind of book that makes you want to stay up all night to finish it. It has its share of intrigue, adventure, romance, and historical authenticity, while still bearing a beautiful Christian witness. While reading it, I was continually amazed that this was the work of a first-time author, much less my dear friend and colleague. It left me thirsty for more from her – more about these characters, and more of this amazingly well-thought-out plot. Keep writing, Janine!

~ **Beverly (Haack) Ohlendorf**
Pastor's wife and middle school ESL teacher

As both her editor and an avid recreational reader, I fell in love with Janine and her book. It is written in a refreshingly vintage tone with an engaging modern pace that will appeal to any *Downton Abbey* or Jane Austen follower. Her characters became dear friends I was loath to part with when I finished reading. During the editing process, I told Janine that I had managed to tear through her first 18 chapters in the evenings. My main problem was discovering I didn't have the rest of her book at the time!

~ **Amberlyn Dwinnell**
Professional Editor

Acknowledgments

How can one ever truly acknowledge her Maker?

Words cannot fully express how grateful I am to my Savior, Jesus Christ, for His indescribable gift. He has also directed every step of my writing and publishing process, especially the vital one when He led my wonderful editor to find *Starving Hearts*—which had already been rejected—at the bottom of an email stack.

That being said, I would also like to recognize the brilliant team at Lighthouse Publishing of the Carolinas. It's likely I'll never meet you, but I'm so grateful for everything you've done to make my book the finest it can be and for giving me the opportunity to share the Light in its pages.

As far as my loved ones go, I have the same "maker-acknowledgement" challenges.

There are so many of you that I see a family & friend tree reaching from Downey, CA to Hickory, NC and to so many places in between, I'm amazed. And, "I thank my God every time I remember you . . . because of your (love and) partnership in the gospel." Phil. 1:3-5 As far as my writing goes, suffice it to say, soon after Pastor Don came to our church, I asked him to read a manuscript. Later, he returned it with a note saying: "good writing is primarily good rewriting. Write, then rewrite and rewrite and rewrite and rewrite." So I've been doing that ever since.

This brings me to the group of wonderful, professional writers whom I met at the Blue Ridge Mountains Christian Writers Conference, the Autumn in the Mountains Novelist Retreat, and the Novel Writing Intensive offered by Steven James and his excellent assistant. Not only could I never have done this without you, I still have that little DELETE key magnet I received when I learned an even more significant lesson than REWRITE.

Finally, I must acknowledge those who are closer to home.

To my wonderful friends at school and church: You've made me into the writer I am because you kept saying: "Yes, I'd love to read it," and that kept me dreaming up new things to write. LG buddies: Your prayers and encouragement have helped me move forward too—which brings me to the most important people of my life.

Tom, Todd, Scott, Katelyn, Lacey, and Jonathan: You are the true heroes and heroines. There are few, if any, husbands and teenage children who would entertain the "Will you read this?" question as many times as you have. And, I know of no others who would patiently assist me with my technological challenges for free. Most importantly, you've supported me through the countless hours of writing and rewriting. Therefore, you are my earthly makers.

Finally, Tom, my dearest love, how can I ever thank you for what you've sacrificed to make my dream of becoming a writer reality, except to pray . . .

May my life and my writing testify to God's great mercy and love to and through *Starving Hearts*—everywhere.

Prologue

Betherton Hall
Staffordshire, England
24 August 1793

If she met the right person, Miss Annette Chetwynd supposed he would see her shattered heart in her eyes. She blinked and brushed a tear away. Now was not the time for such gloom. This was her garden party—Aunt Claire's, actually. But it was her first adult event, and she had been dreaming of it for weeks. Might the young gentlemen admire her? Would the ladies think her clever? She sighed.

None of that mattered any longer.

"Miss Chetwynd, niece of Mrs. Claire Betherton, is it?"

Concealing her misery behind a gracious smile, she turned to find the Reverend Sharpe's wife, an older matron decked in pearls and an ostrich feather hat, evaluating her through a pair of gold-rimmed spectacles.

"It is, indeed," Annette responded.

"Well then, you should know . . ."

As the cleric's wife droned on, Annette speculated about how many slaves she would free if she could snatch those pearls and that hat. She shivered, sickened at the thought, and forced herself to be more attentive. After what seemed a reasonable amount of time, she began extracting herself from the one-sided conversation.

"Indeed, Mrs. Sharpe, it is most unfortunate that while Bach is appropriate for the occasion, the quartet is not performing to your standards. I shall advise Aunt Claire of your concern. In the meantime, enjoy some more champagne. Good day."

For the better part of the afternoon, Annette had been choking back words as she roved around the maze of linen-covered tables. Now, all she wanted to do was run and hide, or scream. To be frank, if she heard one more bit of—

"Mr. Betherton's estate is failing; everyone knows it."

"Poor Claire, and how unfortunate for her dear Sylvia."

"'Tis unlikely she'll land a husband of any distinction now, not after three Seasons."

"Has it been that long?"

Annette's fingers curled into fists. Gossip: even as society's best gorged themselves on cucumber sandwiches and lemon tarts prepared for Aunt's birthday, they stirred it with glee. And, oh how they mocked people. Mr. William

Wilberforce, the leader of the anti-slave trade movement and one of the few politicians Annette respected, was at the top of their list this afternoon.

She took a deep breath and moved away from the ladies. Eight, seven, six, five, four, three . . . Exhaling, Annette flexed her fingers. She mustn't dwell on the negatives so much. The event was not entirely without hope, after all.

Mr. Peter Adsley was in attendance.

Annette glided around the tables toward the edge of the awning where a small platform stood. Was he still here? She stepped onto the platform to see if she could find him.

Mr. Adsley, the crowd's only saving grace, was a singular gentleman with disheveled brown hair and dark maple eyes. He had defended Mr. Wilberforce's efforts at every turn, and his passion for abolishing the slave trade was unmistakable. Annette stood on her tiptoes and surveyed the party one last time. She could have listened to him for hours. Only, it appeared he had already excused himself.

Had he gone inside, or to the stables perhaps? His windswept locks and drooping cravat hinted that a horse, rather than a carriage, may have been his means of transportation. An early departure, however, might give the impression he wished to avoid further confrontation, and surely, he would never desire that—not after a stand like his.

Annette smiled. Mr. Adsley was a noteworthy speaker.

The sky darkened, and Annette looked up. The sun was playing hide and seek behind some churning clouds. Her eyes drifted over the green and up the hill to the chapel. Mr. Adsley might be there. Despite the distant location, it was not uncommon for guests to make the trek simply to view the stained glass. She certainly enjoyed it.

Annette straightened her shoulders. In fact, the moment she could escape, she would visit the chapel herself.

Suddenly, thunder rumbled, and the entire company froze. Then, in one accord, their heads tilted back and their mouths dropped open in a most awkward manner. Even the stringed quartet ceased its Bach and listened to the grumbling clouds. With wary eyes, the crowd assessed the rigging and the hole in the top of the large tent. Annette followed their worried stares upward.

Nervous whispers rippled across the silence. No doubt they remarked on Aunt's poor planning, though she had arranged for both outdoor and indoor eventualities.

A moment later, lightning struck, and chaos broke loose. Ladies leaped from their chairs and hastened across the expansive lawn to Betherton Hall. Gentlemen tottered beside them, balancing parasols and plates of food while the servants grabbed trays laden with tiny cakes, china plates, and crystal glasses—whether they were full of champagne or not—before the footmen made off with the tables.

"Annette, to the house at once!" Mother shouted. "Or you will catch your death."

She turned to respond, but Mrs. Chetwynd was already weaving around chairs on her way to join the others. As soon as the assembly was settled inside, the celebration—not to mention the malicious talk—would most certainly resume. Aunt was always mindful of her guests. Annette, on the other hand, wanted nothing more to do with them.

She smiled up at the thunderous sky. This was her opportunity to escape. She glanced at the frilly cloud of guests floating toward the house; then lifted her lacy gown to her knees and took off running in the opposite direction to the stone chapel on the hill.

Laughing, she raced up the steps and leaned against a marble pillar to catch her breath and watch the last guests scurrying in the back door of Betherton Hall. She was just about to congratulate herself when—

"The young Miss Annette Chetwynd, is it?" A masculine voice startled her.

"Yes?" She whipped around.

"Sir Steven Likebridge, at your service." He bowed.

"Dear me." Her heart skipped a beat. Sir Likebridge was a fine-looking gentleman with a black wig. She wiped her cheeks and smoothed her wet curls.

"If you are not careful, you could fall ill in this weather. May I accompany you inside?" He offered his arm.

Her heart tried crawling into her throat, but she swallowed it into place. Where had he been during the party? And how odd, a gentleman with tan skin. Travel, perhaps?

"You have nothing to fear of me. I am a guest of the neighboring Adsley family, friends of your uncle and aunt, I believe. Surely you know them."

Why was he here?

"You refuse my assistance?"

Annette found her voice. "I know of the family, but have no need of your help. Now, if you will excuse me—"

A chuckle purred in his chest. "I suppose you think yourself quite the independent young lady." He reached toward her bosom, and she jumped back.

Heavens!

"Forgive me." He bowed again, but his voice was flat. His icy gray eyes held no warmth. "I did not mean to startle you. I merely noticed your brooch, one of Josiah Wedgwood's anti-slavery medallions, if I am not mistaken. How did you come by it?"

She glanced down at the badge displayed to the left of her heart, which jerked about in her chest. "Mr. Wedgwood ga . . . gave it to my father. He had it set—"

"'Tis nicely done. Tell me, what age are you, Miss Chetwynd? Sixteen? Seventeen? Not too young to join Wilberforce's movement, evidently. I suppose you are part of the protest as well. Have you stopped taking sugar in your tea like so many other girls have?"

Her stomach sank. Why must he persist?

"Please, no more questions, sir." She backed around the column, placing it between them. "Won't you go to the house with the other guests, and leave me to my prayers?" She could hardly get the words out.

"You will need them."

Brazen scound—!

Suddenly, he was beside her, laughing. "You bid me leave in this deluge? How unkind of you. *I* could catch a cold."

Chills sped down her back, even as the rain pelted it with needles.

He held out his hand. "Come, let us call a truce. Your gown is soaked. I shall help you inside, and all will be well."

Annette glanced over her shoulder at the Hall. Her throat tightened. It was so far away, and by now, everyone was gathered in the grand salon at the front of the house where the other feast was laid out. If she ran, he would surely catch her. No one would know a thing about it.

"Pl . . . Please, sir. I can go inside by myself." Had he noticed the tremor threatening her voice? "You shall remain here under the portico, and I will say nothing of this matter to Father."

"Your father is not here, Miss Chetwynd. You are traveling with your mother only."

Dizziness washed over her. Lord, no, *please*, not another spell. It had been weeks since her last one, and she had eaten only an hour ago. The faintness should not be coming now.

"Come, Miss Chetwynd, your hand. You have grown quite pale."

She stared at his hand. It seemed to flicker and shift like a wave. But she did not take it.

"Enough of this madness. You're coming with me." His fingers clamped around her wrist, and he dragged her from behind the column. She started to scream, but he covered her mouth. "And you shall remain quiet, or it will go all the worse for you."

Yellow and white stars exploded in front of her eyes as the cigar stench of his breath overwhelmed her.

The next thing she knew, he was shoving her through the chapel door. Suffocating pressure choked her breath away, even as the pews reeled in front of her. She tried to free herself from his grasp, but her foot caught in her gown, and she started to fall. Latching onto a pew, she caught herself, but he wrenched her free.

"Shame on you, Miss Chetwynd." His hot breath hissed against her cheek. "You appeared to be innocent at your aunt's party. Yet, here you are alone and tempting me thus."

"Release me. I beg you."

"Begging does not suit you."

"What are you—?"

"You needn't distress yourself. I am perfectly adept where ladies are concerned."

"I have no idea . . . ." A haze obscured her vision, and the weight of her head was suddenly too much for her neck to bear.

"There is no need to pretend, Miss Chetwynd. I fully appreciate your . . . appetite, shall we say?"

With that, he locked his arm around her upper back, hooked his foot behind her knee, and collapsed her backward onto the floor. With one hand, he held her wrists in a vice grip above her head and began nosing at her neck like a foraging pig.

"Stop! You're hurting me!" She tried to kick, but his weight was heavy upon her.

Suddenly, another imposing voice: "On your feet, man!"

Determined footsteps beat the wood floor. For an instant, Annette glimpsed a man with dark hair over her assailant's shoulder. Then Sir Likebridge was gone, his weight heaved clean away from her body. She was free, but still she could not move.

Sprawled in the center aisle, she tried to focus on the wooden crossbeams of the ceiling, but darkness was closing in. She recognized clamor of some sort: a heated exchange; the scraping noise of pews being shoved around; and . . . punches? The potent thuds came from such a distance that she was uncertain. Then all went quiet.

"Miss?" Someone, a man, was shaking her now, rubbing her hands and arms, even patting her face. But it seemed so unreal. She was barely certain she felt it.

"Please, miss, listen to me." Her head was being lifted. He grasped her shoulders and raised her to a sitting position. "You must open your eyes, please."

She opened her eyes, or tried to. The indistinct image of her rescuer's face and his dark hair appeared. He was speaking to her, but she so wanted to sleep.

"Stay with me, my lady."

She felt his warm palm against her cheek.

"You must not sleep."

She leaned into his hand, attempting to turn onto her side, but . . .

Strong, yet gentle hands slid under her knees. He gathered her close, and she came to rest cradled against a wall of warmth. A soothing sway put her heart at ease as she drifted into a void where the scent of sandalwood soap bathed the darkness.

※

"Get up, me girl. Wake up!"

Annette became mildly aware of her nurse calling. *Ouch!* Lucy's slap stung.

"Get the smelling salts!" Lucy grasped her by the chin. "Breathe in, child."

She obeyed. "Uhhh!" *What a foul stench.*

"Go on then, take it in, me girl. It will help."

Annette attempted to squirm away from the reeking odor, but someone else held her head in place. Next, she felt a cup against her lips.

"Here now, drink this up." The cool rush of liquid flooded her mouth and dribbled down her chin. She swallowed.

"Ah, yes." *Sugar water. Thank you.*

Some minutes later, Annette heard joy in her dear nurse's voice. "Look, Mistress, she's comin' 'round."

"I can see that, Miss Haack."

⁂

Later that evening when Annette was sufficiently recovered, Mother's questions began.

"Who was it? What did he do to you?"

Annette squeezed her eyes shut and tried to think. "It was Sir Likebr—"

"—Did you let him—? Did he touch you?"

Yes, he touched me, obviously! Tears flooded her cheeks. *But you . . . You just implied I am to blame.*

"NO!" Annette gulped back a sob. "The other man stopped him before . . . befo—"

"Well, who was the *other* man, and what did he—?"

"—I don't *know!*"

By the end of the interrogation, Annette's freedom was revoked: no more visits to the chapel, no morning walks, and no riding, whether here at Betherton Hall or back at home. If she wanted to go anywhere, Lucy must never leave her side. Ever!

Annette was too overwhelmed to care. All she wanted was Mother's assurance that she would never see or hear of the fiend again. Mrs. Chetwynd agreed that was best, and she would personally see him immediately dispatched from the estate. And that was precisely what Annette believed Mother would do.

Chapter 1
The Confrontation

Betherton Hall
Staffordshire, England
27 February 1795

"*You think yourself quite the independent young lady . . . independent young lady . . . independent. . . Ha, ha, ha.*" His wicked laugh echoed as Annette writhed in the dark. Her hands were useless against his weight.

"*Shame on you for tempting me thus.*" His cheek scraped her neck and his mouth . . .

Her heart thrashed and lungs burned.

Suddenly, a scream tore the curtain of darkness, and she bolted upright. Pulling the coverlet to her chin, she scanned the room. She was at home—in her chamber at Betherton Hall, rather. But that was nearly the same thing, since they practically lived here when Papá was away. The scream had been hers.

Her hands fell heavy on the bed, and the pounding in her ears began to subside. It was only a dream, another dream. She straightened her shoulders and stretched, then slid off the bed and walked to the window.

She had chosen to take a short rest before Cousin Sylvia's ball, and this was what she got. Was that beastly man now to plague both her evening and afternoon rest? Why must he? And where was her savior in these wretched nightmares?

She plopped down on the window seat cushion and gazed across the green. There, at the top of the hill, stood the lonely chapel. She touched her fingertips to the cool glass. Their warmth fogged her view, but not the indistinct memory of her champion. Just over eighteen months ago, he had rescued her. Yet, he never appeared in her dreams. Who was he? Where was he now?

That day, after the assault, he had delivered her, soaking wet and unconscious, to the kitchen door. She knew that much from Lucy. The servants were in such an uproar over the guests' transition into the house, they simply took Annette and called for her nurse. When someone finally thought to thank him for saving her, he was gone.

Now, all that remained of him was the blurred image of dark hair, the scent of sandalwood soap, and the warmth of his hand cradling her cheek. Annette raised her hand to that cheek. She would never forget what little she had left of him. If only she could find him.

Uncle and Aunt had made inquiries throughout the entire district, but no one had responded. Locating him was hopeless, apparently. But every time she visited, she thought perhaps she would find—

The mantle clock chimed, and Annette jumped. *Gracious! Half past four: nearly time to dress.* And she must speak with Mother.

Regardless of how desperately she wished to find her savior, she must focus on the chaperon issue first.

Once again, she would go to Mother and attempt to free herself of Lucy. She was determined to obtain some freedom—just a bit, and only for tonight— so she could . . .

This evening she truly desired to converse, and she could manage that with any sensible gentleman willing to listen.

She and a dance partner could speak in front of the entire assembly during a minuet, and no one would care. Couples did it all the time. But if Lucy kept her distance, Annette and her companion could stroll about and share more freely without interruption.

How she longed for . . . No, the gnawing sense of emptiness and loss was far more severe. With Papá away for so long and her brother, Gerald, gone to university, she *yearned* for someone with whom to share her thoughts. The slave trade or Mr. Wilberforce's recent activities in Parliament intrigued her, but any intellectual subject would do.

Chatter amongst the ladies about the latest fashion or the most eligible bachelor could be interesting for a time, a very brief time. But it simply did not suffice. She was starving for rational, sensible—masculine—company, *his* companionship, actually. He seemed so attentive.

Therefore, the chaperon issue was her highest priority, and she must act soon.

A glimmer of white caught her eye. The waning winter sunlight transformed her ball gown into a shimmering waterfall of silk cascading down the side of the full-length mirror on which it hung. If only it could help her secure the attention of a gentleman inclined to intelligent conversation rather than flirting.

She looked out the window at the chapel on the hill. Ha! Amiable conversation with a gentleman other than Father or Gerald—and without a chaperon—that would be a miracle indeed, after what had happened.

Perhaps she should petition God for this necessity. *But*—never mind. She could at least try.

Annette closed her eyes. Darkness. Nothing, except . . .

Oh!

What a dreadful thought, especially with Papá being such a devout Christian! He would be so disappointed. She opened her eyes and looked at nothing.

Nevertheless, she had her doubts about God. For instance, if He truly existed, what interest could He possibly have in her affairs? She was no one special. Could Papá ever appreciate such misgivings, or would her lack of faith hurt him?

Enough! Annette left her window seat and strode to the chamber door. She needn't waste more time. She began rehearsing her argument. A direct approach was best.

Cousin Sylvia's birthday presented the perfect occasion to meet new people right there at Betherton Hall. Lucy could observe from a distance. If there were any concerns, Mother would be close at hand. Uncle and Aunt would be there too. It was a solid start.

She opened the door and jumped back. "Lucy!"

"And who else would it be?" She barged in with the laundry and planted it beside the dresser. "But never mind. Your mother wants you in the music room."

"Did she say why?"

"And since when would she do that?"

"Never. I was only hoping—"

"Ah, sweet girl, come now." Lucy held out her substantial arms. "You're always so hopeful." Annette snuggled in for a hug and received a kiss atop her head. "Now off with you, before she gets to that pianoforte. She'll forget she even called, if she does."

"Indeed. I shall be back soon."

Annette darted along the hall to the staircase and down to the main level. Her clicking boot heels echoed across the black and white checkered floor of the grand salon. Pausing at a mirror, she checked the froth of honey-colored curls framing her face and smoothed her peacock-green day dress. It set off her eyes perfectly. Mother, fashion devotee as she was, would certainly approve. If only she would consent to this bit of freedom.

The door to the music room loomed in front of her. Should she attempt another prayer? Papá would.

Her shoulders slumped, and she bowed her head. *God, if it is not too much trouble* ... She stopped. This was all wrong. If He did exist, it would be no trouble at all. But He was not about to respond just because she called. Why should He?

She lifted her chin. She could do this on her own. Facing Mother by herself was nothing new. Annette took a deep breath, exhaled, and knocked.

"Enter." Mother answered from within.

⚔

Skirting the pianoforte that graced the center of the room, Annette went to the chaise near the window where Mrs. Chetwynd was reclining.

"Hello, Mother. I see I have found you at ease."

Mrs. Chetwynd stopped rolling a strand of pearls across her fingers and sat up. "You have. Preparations for the ball are complete, our gowns are pressed and ready, and there is time for me to play the pianoforte. Then we have only to dress before the festivities begin. Tell me, has Miss Haack found something suitable to wear?"

"She has a dress. But I would rather she did not escort me this evening."

Mother stood up and sailed past Annette, leaving the scent of roses in her wake.

"Speak up, child. I did not hear you."

"Mother—" Annette hesitated, gathering her thoughts as she followed. "Can we not explore the matter of my chaperon?"

"You make it sound as though it were up for negotiation."

"I would only like some freedom for tonight. Permit me to attend Sylvia's ball without Miss Haack at my side. I am eighteen, and—"

"Old enough to be free and independent; is that it?"

"I only ask that Miss Haack maintain some distance." You have seen how she—"

"Watches you?" Mother raised her left eyebrow. "She is your chaperon. What do you expect?"

"I was going to say how she gets underfoot."

"So you no longer care for her?"

"That is not true. I only wanted—"

"No." Mother turned and rubbed her chin, deep in thought. Calculating? What was she thinking? Planting her fists firmly on her waist, Mother returned with a fierce gaze. "My decision remains unchanged. No chaperon, no ball. And do not ask again. You know what could happen."

"But Miss Haack will be there, as will you and Uncle and Aunt. Please, Mother, with everyone present, I thought I—"

"—Could find that extraordinary being you described some weeks ago? The charitable gentleman, who will overlook your faults and rescue you from the prison in which you believe you live?"

Annette blinked and swallowed hard.

"What makes you think he would have you? You are hideously opinionated, and you've an unnatural appetite for knowledge no respectable lady has any right to indulge. Heaven forgive me for allowing your father to educate you like a son. No man will abide your opinions. The fact you have them is a detriment."

"That is unreasonable."

"Unreasonable? You know nothing of the word." Mother's eyes flickered, then she gazed out the window. "Your father is all mercy and kindness."

"But I need—"

"Hold your tongue and listen." She snapped back from the mysterious lapse. "What you need is to come to your senses regarding a Season and finding a good match."

"You mean allowing myself to be auctioned off to the highest bidder?"

"How dare you?"

"Would the metaphor of a breeding mare suit better?" Annette shuddered inside. Had she really said that?

"Insolent child! You know naught of the process."

"And I haven't the slightest interest in finding out."

"Well, it is high time you start. Otherwise, you might as well accept Sir Steven Likebridge, if he would take you."

Air evaporated from Annette's lungs, and her head started to swim—but not because of her health. It was that loathsome name.

"No other man in his right mind would consider you with your clever new ideas, sharp tongue, and . . . Need I mention your condition?"

Gripping the back of the chair beside her, Annette forced out the question, "Have you forgotten what he tried to do?"

"Forgotten? With all your sniveling, how could I? It was everything I could do to keep you from ruining us both with that episode. It is good I did what I did, or we would all be lost."

Tears threatened to spill, but Annette refused to give Mother the satisfaction of knowing it.

"What did you do, Mother?" She grounded out the question.

"It is none of your concern. But speaking of breeding mares, you could only hope to have the privilege of bearing Sir Likebridge's children. He has a title."

"Title or no, I refuse to be bound to such a beast. Or to any other man who supposes any female will suffice as long as she has a healthy dowry and can produce sons."

"Be that as it may, my decision is final. Miss Haack will be your constant companion during the entire ball or you will not attend. Now, good afternoon."

Mother sat down at the pianoforte and punctuated her closing statement with a chord, the one she always practiced before her cherished Bach and his French Suites.

※

Closing the door—though Annette would rather have slammed it—she exited in time to wipe the single tear trickling down her cheek. She leaned against the wall, closed her eyes, and clenched her teeth.

Mother always twisted things. Insulting Annette with her own image of the ideal gentleman, a treasure Annette had revealed in confidence; and, insinuating she no longer cared for Lucy! Dreadful. And that while broaching the topic of marriage to . . . to that brute! How could she even speak of him?

Annette paused. What else could Mother have done? Ousting him was a necessity, a generosity rather. She might have had him arrested. But why speak of it now? Did she resent that action? Or worse, did she blame her own daughter for having to take it?

Nausea bubbled up from the pit of her stomach as his cold gray eyes materialized in her thoughts. The foul rake, she would sooner marry a highwayman or . . . or even a slave trader than allow herself to become attached to Sir Steven Likebridge.

Declining to squander another moment on either Mother or memories, Annette wiped her eyes on her sleeve and forced the nausea back down into its shadowy reservoir. She would find another way to speak with a proper gentleman about issues that truly mattered.

Annette started up the stairs.

Wait. In a matter of seconds, Lucy would wheedle out the details of this wretched meeting. Then they would both be crying, and if Lucy suspected anything about her desire for freedom . . . *Dear!* She hated to think how it would hurt her friend.

The floor-to-ceiling windows to her right caught her attention: the second-floor gallery. *Splendid.* Or was it part of the construction area Aunt Claire had put off limits last week?

She continued up the stairs and looked into the gallery. Good. The renovation area was further down the hall. She could just sit and study her favorite painting. That would help clear her mind. Perhaps she would work on her sketch some more.

A smile pulled at her lips; she could not help it.

Chapter 2
Savior

Annette tried to ignore Mother's rudeness, but her early comment about Papá kept ricocheting in her thoughts.

True, he was "all mercy and kindness." He always had been. But why mention it? And that look? Mother almost seemed sad. The word "unreasonable" seemed to disturb her. Why?

Annette glanced at the full-length portrait of a gray-haired gentleman dressed in a fine red hunting coat and crisp white breeches. She stopped.

He was her grandfather, Sir Clarence Alexander, a baronet, and father to both Mother and Aunt Claire. Shortly after he died, Aunt Claire had the painting moved here. Annette's home at Chesterfield held no such portrait. Apparently, Mother had a falling out with Sir Alexander before she married Father, though Annette knew nothing more of the circumstances. Neither of her parents ever spoke of it.

Was Sir Alexander very unreasonable with Mother when she was a girl compared to how Papá was with her? Annette sat down in her regular chair across from the painting and tried to find the answer.

Over the years, she had spent hours—no, months of hours—in this very chair, analyzing the artist's use of color, his nearly-invisible brush strokes, and his technique with oils. Her newest interest was in determining how he had captured the life in the three hounds seated at Grandfather's feet. Their eyes glistened, and they literally seemed to drool as they awaited his next command. But she never imagined the portrait held secrets about Mother's relationship with her father, Annette's grandfather.

Annette stood up. Speculating about Mother's youth would not change her. Annette had come up to visit her gentleman.

She peered over the balcony rail onto the grand salon. Servants carried trays of crystal glasses back and forth across the checkered floor. Glancing up and down the corridor, she confirmed no one was watching; then she slipped into the curtained alcove a few steps away. This favorite little nook held the painting of the man who reminded Annette of her rescuer, what little she could remember of him.

Lifting the seat of the cushioned bench—the trusty hiding spot she visited almost daily—across from the masterpiece, she took out a pencil and her private sketchbook, a secret sketch diary, as it were, that held her dreams.

Seating herself, Annette gazed at the dark-haired man in the painting. He was a laborer of sorts, or so his clothing seemed to say, and he was kneeling at the feet of a noblewoman adorned in courtly apparel and a powdered wig. But Annette did not care about his low position or lack of wealth. This unassuming man was the image of her ideal.

She remembered his dark hair and powerful voice. His strong, warm hands holding her with reverence were still very real to Annette. The man in this painting extended his hand toward his lady with the same care she sensed in her savior. His handsome features and loving expression did the rest.

She opened her sketchbook to her drawing of him. After a week's worth of work, it was nearly complete. Adjusting the book on her lap, she rested her elbow on one knee and gazed at him a while longer.

Some minutes later, oblivious to all else in the world except the details of his adoring face, Annette went to work.

Her initial lines enhanced his noble forehead. With each stroke, those expressive eyes and their arched brows emerged more perfectly from the page. Shadows contouring his handsome nose appeared to summon forth a living breath, and she willed her pencil to capture every nuance of his suppliant lips.

Suddenly, a cacophony of shattering glass and a large serving tray hitting the floor in the downstairs salon startled her. Her hand jerked, and the sketchbook slid from her lap.

Scrambling to retrieve it, she flipped open to his face and stared. A heavy charcoal line marred his upper lip. She clenched her teeth. There was not enough time to fix it now. Tomorrow afternoon was out of the question too. They would be packing for Sunday's departure home.

She tucked her pencil behind her ear and turned her sketchbook this way and that. Tonight's ball could wait. She must correct this mistake while she could.

Digging an eraser out of her pocket, she positioned it above the scar and started to make her move. Then she stopped.

Downstairs, Mother's voice thundered. Then Aunt Claire and the housekeeper joined the conflict, making it impossible to concentrate.

"Oh, for Heaven's sake!"

Closing her sketchbook, Annette pushed the bench back against the wall, kissed her fingertips, and tapped her painted love's cheek. "Farewell, kind sir." With that, she left for a more peaceful haven.

At the far end of the gallery, she entered the deserted renovation area. Honestly, at the moment, she could not care less that it was off limits.

Opening the door of the first room she reached, Annette stepped in and lurched to a halt.

Chapter 3
Calculating

Cousin Sylvia, who was shifting the end of a leather sofa, shrieked and dropped it on her foot. Groaning, she freed her toes and crumpled onto the ottoman.

"Oh, Syl!?" Annette set her sketchbook on a table and rushed in.

"Quick, close the door."

"Can I get—?"

"Just close the door and be quiet."

Annette swallowed her next comment, closed the door, and seated herself in the wing-backed chair beside the sofa. Averting her eyes, she studied the carved marble fireplace as a means of subduing her shock.

Ordinarily, Sylvia was a gentle spirit who demonstrated more patience than any lady of Annette's acquaintance. The fact that today was her twenty-sixth birthday did not even seem to intimidate her. But she had never been sharp before.

"Forgive me." Her forehead wrinkled as she massaged her toes. "That was most ill-mannered. Give me a moment, I shall explain. In the meantime, what of this study? It is quite elegant, is it not?"

Annette admired the forest green velvet curtains, the rich walnut paneling, and the fine leather sofa. But her gaze settled on the extensive collection of leather-bound volumes organized on the floor-to-ceiling shelves flanking the fireplace.

"Remarkable, especially the books. Might I browse through them later?"

"Certainly."

Annette glanced at Sylvia's foot. "Will you be able to dance?"

"The pain has lessened. If I soak it while Martha does my hair, I suspect all will be well."

"Good. But tell me, why are you here? Aunt Claire declared the area off-limits."

"I could ask the same of you."

"Except you know I care little for rules."

Sylvia gave a sidelong grin. At times, she too was inclined to question boundaries.

"At least tell me how they finished so soon. The other rooms are far from ready."

"Two of my friends on staff and I put it back together. But you mustn't tell Mamma. If she found out . . ."

"Why should I?"

"My apologies. I know you would not."

"So why did you do it?"

Sylvia leaned closer. "Do you recall Mamma's garden party? We had it back in . . . Let me see, when was it?"

"Aunt Claire's fiftieth birthday was on the twenty-fourth of August, about eighteen months ago."

"How did you—?"

"Never mind. Do continue."

"Right then. Do you remember the two gentlemen with whom we dined that afternoon? My neighbors' sons. Mr. Richard Adsley was the redhead. He is quite the avid conversationalist, while his brother, Mr. . . . ."

Annette's mind reeled. Mr. Richard Adsley was one of the self-absorbed . . . Well, she would rather not say. But she remembered his profound ignorance regarding the slave trade. It would have hastened her departure from the party had the storm not struck. Come to think of it, had Aunt Claire not warned her to avoid his advances, if they occurred? Though heir to his father's massive estate, apparently he was a known rake in Caverswall.

Annette's stomach churned.

"Nettie, are you well?" Her cousin grasped her hand. "Look at me, dearest. Is everything all right? Do you need something to eat? You looked as though you were about to—"

"Faint? No, I was just a bit distracted." Annette brushed away her cousin's concern. "As long as I eat regularly, the spells are in check. It has been weeks since the last one. But tell me, what have the Adsley brothers to do with the guest study?"

Another thought struck her. *Heavens, there are two of them! No . . . Yes, but wait. Was he not the man who—?* Suddenly, her heart began to gallop.

"Well . . ." Sylvia looked away; then she faced Annette. "Mr. Adsley, the second son—"

"—Did he speak against the slave trade?" Annette's heart somersaulted as the image of her gentle, dark-haired laborer from the painting fleeted across her memory. It reminded her of Mr. Adsley, who had dark hair. *Could he be the One?* Dear, how could she have forgotten him?

"Now that I think of it, I believe he did. Leave it to you to remember such a thing."

"What do you expect? I fancy the topic. But go on. I should not have interrupted."

"So as I was saying, I suspect Peter will have need of this study after dinner."

Annette's heart dropped. Sylvia used Mr. Adsley's Christian name, a privilege strictly prohibited, unless the lady had a very close connection to the gentleman. Had they a secret understanding?

"Does he not dance?"

"He does. However, after Father makes his announcement, Peter will want ... Hold a moment. Why are you so interested in him?"

"Me, interested? You brought him up."

"I apologize." Sylvia's eyes shifted to the fireplace then back again. "But things are so complicated."

"Perhaps I can help." *Since I would give anything to renew my acquaintance with him.*

"Thank you, but the matter will be settled soon."

Annette studied Sylvia as she folded and unfolded her hands. She was hiding something. Annette could tell, but she hesitated to pry, lest she reveal her own secret.

Sylvia cleared her throat. "Let me say this, and then we shall put it to rest."

"As you wish."

"Peter has just returned from a journey. This study is perfectly situated away from the celebration so he can retire if he desires to escape the noise."

"I understand," Annette responded, though she understood nothing. A giddy sensation pulled at her heart. If he was here, and she could manage to get away from Lucy . . . Mother's chaperon rule would be of no consequence. Dare she speak with him? Oh, but what would he think of her?

"Nettie? Distracted again?"

"No, just thinking. But what matters is your foot. How is it?"

Sylvia stood up and wiggled her toes. "I shall survive, and what of you? Does your mother still require Miss Haack to escort you?"

"Please, do not remind me."

Sylvia draped her arm around Annette's shoulders and huddled her close. "I am sorry, truly I am."

Suddenly, her eyes brightened, and she grabbed Annette's hand.

"What? Why are you looking so—?"

"—Nettie!"

"Yes?"

"I have the perfect solace gift for you." A smile stretched across her lips, and Annette gave a doubtful glance.

"No, no. I do!" Sylvia could hardly contain herself. "Nothing serious, mind you, just a little something to explore later this evening. If you forgo the dancing after dinner."

Annette eyed her cousin.

"You enjoy investigating architecture of manor houses, do you not?"

"At times."

"Come then. You must see the secret passage this study offers."

Sylvia dragged her to the far corner of the room. She pressed a carved wooden rosette on the wall, and a wood panel clicked open.

"Remarkable." Annette peered inside. "Where does it lead?"

"To the guest chamber next door. It has a similar rigged panel."

Goose bumps prickled Annette's arms as she brushed aside the cobwebs and entered the cool passageway. Seconds later, she pushed open another door that revealed the neighboring suite with its sheet-covered furnishings and stark, glaring windows. Annette secured the secret door, and in a few steps she was back with Sylvia.

"Exciting!" Her heart leaped with joy. As unseemly as it was—she could never speak of it to anyone, not even Sylvia—her new idea had taken hold, and this secret passage was just the thing to fulfill it. "How did you find it?"

"Father showed me when I was a child."

"I wonder what it was used for."

"A gentlemen seeking a midnight rendezvous with his lady, no doubt." Sylvia wiggled her eyebrows.

Did she suspect? Heavens, if she did and was offering . . . What an appalling pair they were! But Annette could never ask. That would be worse.

Pursing her lips into a little circle, Annette adopted the shaky voice of an old matron. "Miss Betherton! Well-bred ladies of your circle never speak of such improprieties. It's scandalous, I say, simply scandalous."

They both broke down laughing.

"Shhh. Oh, please, we mustn't be so loud."

"I know." Annette rubbed both sides of her jaw right below her ears. She had not laughed so hard in a long time, and it felt good.

After a few minutes, Annette and Sylvia wiped their blissful tears.

"Well," Sylvia spoke first. "Clandestine meetings or not, we must ready ourselves for my ball. And who knows, I might be able to switch the seating so you can dine beside Peter. He was a favorite of yours, was he not?"

Yet again, Sylvia called Mr. Adsley by his given name. But there mustn't be anything more than friendship between them, or else why would she offer to adjust his seat?

"I suppose. But he seemed rather less sociable."

"Yes, not for want of interest in people, though. He is simply more reflective by nature."

"A reasonable enough answer." She must calm herself, or Sylvia might suspect something. "Can you really change the seating?"

"It is my birthday, after all."

"Point taken."

"Come then; we must get dressed." Sylvia opened the door and peeked into the hall. "The way is clear. Our guest study secret is safe."

"Indeed, it is." Her heart pounded as she grabbed her sketchbook. Was she desperate enough to go through with her plan? And what if he was there? And, if he was the One . . . Lord, she could hardly bear to think of it!

Chapter 4

The Plan

Caverswall Manor
Staffordshire, England
27 February 1795

Mr. Peter Adsley stopped fumbling with his cravat.

"Giles, if you please, I need your assistance," he called to his manservant and kept mumbling. "I've about as much skill tying cravats as—" A crisp, white handkerchief peeking out of the top dresser drawer caught his eye. "—as I have embroidering hankies." He took out the cloth and inspected the delicately stitched initials Mary Hope had embroidered in the corner. *Amazing.*

"At your service, sir." The old servant answered as he shuffled across the richly appointed bedchamber.

"So you're takin' up your sister's sewin' now, are ya?" Giles's eyes twinkled as his expert fingers went to work on the misshapen knot.

"Absolutely not." Peter felt a smile tugging at his lips as he folded the handkerchief and stuck it in his waistcoat pocket. "I suffer enough pricking about my anti-slave trade sentiments without taking one of Mary Hope's needles in hand."

"Trouble with your father again, sir? Or be it your brother this time?"

"Father." Peter's spirit dropped. "Earlier today, he was fuming about the Bethertons losing two more ships to a horde of French pirates. He holds William Wilberforce and his followers responsible, though I cannot see the connection."

"Does he now?"

"To be sure. He called me and my abolitionist friends, and I quote, 'a bunch of slave-lovin' dreamers meddling in matters we don't understand.'"

"Ah well, that be your father."

"Regrettably."

"He owns a shippin' company though, and he built up this here fine estate with spoils he took from the *Carnatic* in '71 when he was privateerin' with old Peter Baker. He must know somethin'."

"My point, exactly. He has been exercising his *right* of *free* enterprise for decades, so he should have no trouble freeing other men to exercise theirs. You know him. You have been here for years."

"Indeed. Your father took me on in '67."

13

"Then you must agree. He, of all people, should understand that fighting against freedom is a losing battle."

"Can't say much about that, sir. But have a look at that cravat." Giles gestured to the dresser mirror.

Peter glanced. "Thank you. It is perfect, but would you stop with the formal address? I've said you needn't use it with me."

"I s'ppose ya did—" The servant gave a sheepish grin. "—as *you* well know, but some of us be set in our ways."

"I expect you are right. But comfort is no excuse for delaying progress, especially when people's liberty and lives are at stake."

"Ya don't have to remind me o' that, son, and ya needn't worry neither. The tide'll be turnin'. You'll see. In the meantime, stop your frettin' and enjoy the party. Perchance the dancin' will lift your spirits."

"Actually, I have something far more *engaging* in mind." Peter smiled. He may not be as socially adept as his brother, but he enjoyed word play and given his plan for the evening, the word had the perfect double meaning.

"Sounds promisin'. What is it, if ya do not mind me askin'?" Giles's eyes twinkled.

"I have decided I should like to wed this summer."

"Mercy me, 'tis a bit *aearly* for that. Ya are but four and twenty, still a lad."

"I will be five and twenty in June, and I have been thinking about it for quite some time. Richard has been working more with Father and . . ."

His smile melted away. As the second son, he would not inherit anything unless his older brother chose to grant him a gift, as if that would ever happen. He brushed off his discouragement, though. "And I look forward to moving on with my life."

"Sounds to me like runnin' away."

"No. I merely wish to start my ministry, and I would like a wife with whom to share it. Now that I have secured the position at St. John's in Buxton, I can afford to marry and have a family of my own . . . God willing, of course."

"Just like—" Giles stopped. For a few seconds his eyes gazed at another time and place. Peter studied Giles's expression in the mirror. Until this moment, he had never seen his valet disturbed about anything, but something had changed.

"Giles?"

"Yes?" Peter turned to face his man.

"Are you well?"

"As ever I could be. But forgive me, sir. I didn't mean to be driftin' like that. I was only thinkin' of me daughter." His eyes glistened. "And her gettin' all carried away with them romantic notions, then endin' up . . ."

Odd, Giles had never mentioned having a daughter.

"But it doesn't matter, me boy. She's with God now. And all this to say, undertakin' a marriage be a serious thing."

"Indeed, it is."

"Well then, let me get your coat, and ya can be on your way." The manservant shuffled toward the closet. "Ya better get to work on that mop o' yours," he called over his shoulder. "It's goin' wild again."

Peter eyed the clump of dark curls falling across his forehead and tried to smooth it back. "I will get this mane cut yet," he muttered as he pulled the blue satin ribbon from his queue. Rubbing his cheeks and chin, he leaned toward the mirror. Giles had just seen to his shave after tea, but a slight shadow was already forming. Another nuisance. He glanced at the mantel clock and sighed. There was nothing to be done now so he grabbed his brush and started in on his hair.

"The Lord's Word instructs a young man to marry," Peter called to Giles. "And she could help me with my ministry at the parish. So I am going to propose tonight."

"Heaven help ya, me boy!" Giles chuckled as he reentered Peter's chamber carrying a sable cutaway dress coat. "And who's to be the fortunate lady?"

"Miss Sylvia Betherton."

All at once, Giles started coughing. The poor man rushed to the side of the bed, tossed the coat across it, and then hunched over and gave in to wheezing.

"Here Giles, let me have you sit."

The old servant mumbled something unintelligible as Peter guided him to a chair near the fire. Peter poured some wine from the service on the end table. "Drink this."

Giles took a few sips, cleared his throat, and inhaled a shallow breath.

"Are you better, my friend? Can I get you anything else?" Peter leaned over him anxiously.

"Blasted closet dust could choke a horse," Giles grumbled. "I'll take it up with the housekeeper."

"Hold a while. Do not get up yet."

"I need to help ya on with your coat."

"I can do it myself."

"Sure ya can. Them thin-cut sleeves slide right up your burly arms like butter on toast, do they?"

"Giles—"

"Let me alone, me boy. I'll be fine." He shuffled over to the bed and retrieved the evening coat. "But you're goin' to be late if we don't hurry. Now, on with your coat, sir."

"As you wish." Peter shoved his muscled arms into the narrow sleeves. "Well, have you nothing to say about me proposing to Miss Betherton?"

"No, sir."

"Come now, you could at least wish me joy."

"If that's what ya want, ya have my deepest regards, sir."

"Giles, a moment ago we were speaking freely. Then you had a coughing fit over dust I have never seen, and now this formality again. What is wrong?"

"Nothin'." Giles snatched the coat brush from the dresser and began brushing. "But if you'll pardon me for askin', be it not more typical to wait for happy returns 'til after the lady accepts?"

"Undoubtedly. However, Miss Betherton and I have known each other since we were children. She has been aware of my desire to marry and start my own life for some time. She even encouraged me to apply for the living at St. John's. Now that I have obtained it, I am certain she will accept me."

"Sounds right enough."

"Hold with brushing, Giles." Peter faced his man. "I have complete confidence in you. If something is amiss, you must tell me."

"Sorry for pesterin' ya so, but are ya sure of the lady's feelin's?"

"Should I be in doubt of her affection?"

"I'm just askin'."

"Are you certain? I have been away making arrangements at the parish. If there is something I have missed—"

"No, but there's been some talk."

"What kind of talk?"

"'Tis nothin', only perhaps there might be another suitor."

"Another suitor, in the last two weeks? She has not had any suitors for the last two years. Who is it?"

"That's what I mean by talk. No one knows, only there's been some tales spreadin'."

"They must not mean much. I just saw her yesterday when I got back, and she did not mention it. Is there nothing more you can tell me?"

"No, sir," he said. But his eyes said otherwise.

"Well, if you ever need to tell me something, please feel free to be direct. And you started with the 'sir' again."

"I will, s — I mean, me boy."

"I would be most grateful. Now, what of the rest of the family? Have Mother and Mary Hope left for the ball yet?"

"They have, with your father and brother right before I came up. Now, if you'll excuse me, I'll see to your coach."

"Thank you. I shall be down shortly."

"Very good, sir," Giles responded, then closed the door before Peter could comment.

⁂

Peter rested his elbow on his dresser and frowned at his reflection. What a muddle. Arguments with Father over the slave trade, his intended proposal to Miss Betherton, and now the prospect of another suitor. How frustrating. But he wanted the matter of a wife settled so he could move on with his life.

Nevertheless, Miss Betherton was a year and a half his senior, almost a spinster and . . . Well, she was rather plain, not exactly the wife he had anticipated.

Peter studied the depths of dark eyes, and then bowed in shame.

Must his carnal nature forever taunt him? Why must a lady's physical appearance be such a concern? Admiring the color of one's hair, another's eyes, or still another's delicate hands, it was nearly a compulsion.

He closed his eyes. He must get control of this aspect of his person.

Forgive me this fault, Lord, and help me to content myself with her inner beauty and friendship. Neither age nor appearance matters in these.

Peter raised his head and glared at himself, attempting to stare down his hunger for . . . for nothing! He turned away with another heavy sigh and massaged his forehead. *Lord. Help me! She is kind, and those other things are nothing but fleeting treasures.*

Finally, he straightened his shoulders and adjusted his coat.

Though he did not love Miss Betherton with the passion of great poetry, he would proceed. Once they were wed, his affection would grow. Was that not what so many said? Besides, finding another suitable lady, who also met his exact preferences, seemed too daunting a task, especially in view of his status as a second son with so little to offer.

His eyes darkened for a second, and he swallowed hard. Had he been the first . . .

No! He forbade himself to think about it. Richard's inheritance of the entire estate and shipping company was not his concern. Starting his new ministry with a godly wife was his primary goal, and Miss Betherton was the best choice.

Adjusting his evening coat again, Peter willed himself to move to the door. He had made his decision. He would propose tonight, and she would accept him. Then his life would begin, and all would be well.

Chapter 5
Shock

Betherton Hall
Staffordshire, England
27 February 1795

Peter checked his pocket watch and rubbed his chin. Two hours had passed since he set out to propose, but he still had not had the chance. He slipped his watch back into his waistcoat pocket and scanned the people seated around him at the banquet table.

All evening, these elegantly-clad guests had so bombarded Miss Betherton with greetings he could scarcely speak to her, let alone ask for a private audience. And now, instead of sitting beside her at dinner—as was his custom—Richard received that honor while he sat halfway down the table from her. Peter ground his teeth.

Yet, he mustn't worry. All would be well. He started to reach for his wine glass.

Suddenly, the Reverend Sharpe, who was seated to his left, exploded with coughing. For pity's sake, the man had been wheezing his way through the first two courses. Was he now to choke?

"Reverend!" Peter rested his hand on the man's back. "Are you well, sir?"

The gentleman nodded vigorously while coughing into his curled fist, then he cleared his throat and reached for his glass. After four generous swallows, he held it up to signal a footman. Then he leaned close and whispered, "Yes, indeedy, son. I'm quite well, so long as my cup runneth over." He grinned.

Peter grimaced and turned away, only to find his gaze drawn to the enchanting creature seated to his right.

The candlelight glow of her porcelain skin combined with the halo of curls crowning her head and trailing along her neck gave her a nether-worldly appearance he was helpless to resist. He sighed with satisfaction. She was a sort of consolation gift for all his trouble.

Wait! Peter forced himself to look down at his empty soup dish. Yes. It would do for the moment. He mustn't indulge himself too much. Miss Betherton was to be his wife. Besides, he could not very well address this young lady. Earlier, when they were first seated, and she introduced herself, he was so taken with her crystal eyes that he forgot her name.

19

A footman removed his dish. He reached for a roll, buttered it, and took a bite. He glanced at the centerpiece but chanced to catch a glimpse of her hand and forearm as she set down her glass. What grace.

Perhaps it would be wise to practice a polite dialogue. As a new pastor, he would need to engage a variety of people—whether or not he knew their names—in many different arenas, including assemblies and balls like this one. The least he could do was attempt some light table talk.

"The Hall looks magnificent tonight," he ventured. "And this banquet . . . Mrs. Betherton has outdone herself."

"She has, indeed." She responded with such a charming smile, Peter believed he may successfully manage more conversation, despite the fact he had forgotten her name.

"So tell me, Miss—"He coughed through his memory slip and took some wine. "Excuse me." He cleared his throat. "So how are you acquainted with the family?"

"Mr. and Mrs. Betherton are my uncle and aunt."

"What a surprise." Peter's heart sank. His comment seemed rather dull. "I mean . . . what a pleasant happenstance. They are my neighbors."

"Consequently, despite your age and sophistication, you are dutifully engaging me in conversation? How very noble of you."

Peter reached for his glass and took another sip while peering at her from over the rim. Age? Sophistication? Did she think him so old and stuffy? He set his glass down and pulled at his cravat. It seemed rather tight around his neck.

"I see I have put you on edge. Can you forgive me?" Ah, that charming, dimpled smile again. She addressed him with such ease, and she was so poised and clever and . . . and vaguely familiar. Yes, familiar. Had they met before?

"I can and do," he responded.

"Very good then. From now on, I shall limit myself to comments on the food, the weather, and the size of the party."

"I was attempting to do the same, and you see where it got me."

"Yes." She smiled then took a bite of food. As she chewed, the smile played at her rosebud lips. She swallowed, then reached for her glass. "Hmm . . . So what of the wine; is it not delicious?" She swirled her glass beneath her nose, and closing her eyes, inhaled its aroma. "It has a rich bouquet of blackberries, red currants, and do I detect a hint of . . . What do you guess?" She slanted a shifty-eyed grin at him, almost daring him to guess.

He raised his glass to get the scent. "Is it cinnamon, or . . . no, cloves perhaps? I am no connoisseur."

"Neither am I." Her eyes sparkled. "But do let's pretend we are."

He laughed.

Why had he not noticed her before? She was so . . . unique. And somehow he knew her or had seen her. But he could not think where, not while she was sitting right here and speaking with him.

As the banquet continued, he became less anxious about engaging in small talk but more mindful of the nagging sensation a buried memory makes when thrusting itself forward.

Suddenly, Peter noticed guests leaving. Had the meal concluded so soon? He glanced up and down the table and around the room for Miss Betherton. There she was, some twenty feet away on the other side of the table. And she was alone. Now was his chance!

He got to his feet. "If you will excuse me, Miss . . . I must leave now." The light faded from her eyes. "But, make no mistake, it was a pleasure to dine with you." She moved to stand, and he pulled back her chair.

"The pleasure was mine, sir. As a dance would be, if you cared to ask."

"Well . . . ah, perhaps later." The room grew unexpectedly warm, and he pulled at his collar. "I must go now. Good evening." He bowed, and then headed for Miss Betherton.

Weaving through the crowd, he was nearly there when . . .

"May I have your attention, please?" Miss Betherton's father, who was tapping a fork against a glass and calling for another toast, intercepted her and proceeded to the center of the ballroom. "Your attention, please. I have a very special announcement."

Peter stopped. Mr. Betherton had already given his daughter's birthday toast, yet what were a few more minutes of waiting if it pleased her father? But he was rather elated.

As a rule, Mr. Phillip Betherton was a solemn person, especially of late since it had been given out that he was on the brink of financial destruction. Not through some fault of his own, of course. Any estate subjected to as many decades of loss as his had been was destined for failure.

Even so, at this moment he was a changed man. His face was alight with smiles as the servants hastened to deliver champagne to the audience gathering around him and Miss Betherton under the crystal chandelier.

"I would be a deplorable host if I failed to inform this dignified company of my daughter's good fortune."

Excited whispers volleyed about. Across the circle of guests, Miss Betherton met Peter's gaze with a teary smile while suspicion gnawed in Peter's chest. It almost seemed as though her father were preparing to declare an engage—

No, Lord, it could not be. She would have told me.

Time seemed to grind to a crushing halt as Peter watched Mr. Betherton raise his glass.

"I will have you know, my most esteemed guests, that I love my daughter very much. And because of that, I am extremely proud to offer a toast to Mr. Richard Adsley of Caverswall Manor, who has agreed to take her on as wife."

A wave of pleasure rippled through the crowd.

"To Mr. Richard Adsley, my future son-in-law."

"Engaged to Richard?" Peter gasped. *How? He cares nothing for her.*

The shadow of horror that crossed Miss Betherton's face reached through Peter's eyes and seared his memory. *Good Heavens, had she heard him?* At that exact moment, her champagne glass slid from her fingers and hit the floor.

A shattering silence arrested the entire company as Peter stared at her. The pendulum of the long case clock on the other side of the grand salon echoed as it marked off the seconds. Tick. Tick. Tick. Not a murmur. Miss Betherton blinked and brushed the corner of her eye with her gloved hand. Peter raked his fingers through his hair. He must maintain composure. Humiliating himself or Miss Betherton by making a scene would not do.

"That calls for another toast!" Mechanically lifting his glass, Peter spoke up in his richest, pastoral voice and threw in a broad smile to go with it. "To Miss Betherton, though she cannot keep hold of her glass, she's the only lady to secure my brother's faithful attendance. May she keep him as close to home as she is close to our hearts."

Richard emerged from the clapping crowd and stood beside Miss Betherton.

"Thank you, brother, but not so fast. Footman, another champagne for Miss Betherton," he called, and a liveried man with a silver tray appeared beside him. "Here you are, my dear." Richard handed her a glass. "Now, my friends, another toast to my fiancée."

The crowd relaxed.

"To Miss Betherton. Her generous spirit has captured my heart."

The audience clapped and chattered their approval as Richard drained his glass. Then he kissed Miss Betherton's hand and tucked it around his elbow.

"Now for some dancing!"

The music commenced, and he escorted her to the opposite side of the salon as guests dispersed to find their dancing partners. Only Peter remained under the chandelier.

"May I be of assistance, sir?"

"Pardon?"

A footman standing beside the two servants, who were tidying up the broken glass, questioned Peter. "Would you care for more to drink, or perhaps directions to a quieter room?"

"Oh. Yes, thank you. I would like to retire for a while."

"There is a newly renovated guest study available. Would that suit?"

"Very well."

"This way then." The footman exited the salon, ascended the staircase, and walked through the gallery to the study. "Here we are, sir." He opened the door and stepped back for Peter to enter. "The room is at your disposal."

An inviting blaze danced behind the grate. Warm orange and gold hues skipped along the paneled walls, over the leather sofa, and across the chair facing the fireplace.

"Brandy and wine are on the side table by the window. May I assist you with something else, sir?"

"No, thank you."

"Excellent." The servant bowed and approached the fireplace, noting the red velvet cord, which hung to its right. "If a need arises, pull this chime, and someone will attend you."

"I am most grateful."

"At your service, sir." The servant bowed and left the room.

Peter took off his coat and laid it over the wing-backed chair facing the fireplace; then he slumped onto the sofa. Stretching across the full length of the cushions, he folded his hands behind his head and looked up at the painted fresco ceiling.

Shadows played with cherubs dancing amongst the clouds, but Peter was not interested in their games. He closed his eyes and tried to collect his thoughts, but the terrible look on Miss Betherton's face kept besieging them.

"Lord, how could this happen? I had everything planned." The plea burst from his lips.

"As disappointing as it seems, your brother got to her first," a feminine voice responded.

Chapter 6

Mystified

"Who's there?" Peter sprang to his feet so fast, the sofa scraped the floor.

"You needn't worry. 'Tis only I."

He stared at what appeared to be the glimmering apparition of a young lady. She dragged her fingers along the edge of the large desk as she moved toward him.

"Forgive me if I startled you. But I could not resist answering your prayer, if only for a bit of comic relief. Surely, you understand."

But he did not.

"Besides, who's to say a divine designer—or God, depending on your beliefs—could not use me to speak on His behalf?" She perched on the arm of the wing-backed chair beside him.

It was she, the beauty from dinner! Firelight glittered in her eyes.

"I must go." He reached over her to retrieve his coat.

"Why?"

"What do you mean?"

"Must you leave so soon? I had hoped to speak with you more." Her eyes widened. "But no one saw me enter, I am certain of it."

"You desire further conversation here, and without a chaperon?" *What could possibly merit such a peril?*

"Yes."

"Why?"

Her shoulders sank.

"I beg your pardon, Miss . . ." *Ah! Her name!* "But your reputation . . . the risk! And we exhausted every suitable topic at dinner."

"Indeed." Her gaze dropped to the floor. She seemed so lost. "Father and I, even Gerald and I, debate. But they're—" She looked up at him through misty crystal eyes. "'Tis so very difficult to share a truly noteworthy conversation amidst a crowd."

She had a point.

"Any meaningful subject will do: the slave trade, perhaps; William Wilberforce's work in Parliament, even religious philosophy." Her voice cracked. "Peculiar topics for a young lady, I know. But I have no one else with whom to discuss them, and I miss—"

She darted off her chair, turned her back, and bowed her head.

Peter's heart twisted with the anguish she was attempting to conceal. A most startling and powerful desire to comfort her, even protect her, surged within him.

Remaining here alone with her would be . . . Actually, her reputation was in peril this very moment, and he could lose his parish if someone found them. Yet, how extraordinary for her to reveal such a delicate, personal matter! And how appealing to experience these unguarded moments.

As the firelight danced across her shoulders and glistened in her honey-colored curls, his resolve weakened. And that memory! He really must know who she was.

His heart skipped a beat. Her hair! Those unusual, reddish-gold curls! For an instant, he recognized them, but the memory faded when she turned around.

"So will you stay?"

"Are you absolutely sure no one knows?"

Her face brightened. "I am."

Despite his better judgment, Peter dropped to the edge of the sofa. "Yes, but only for a little while." He must resolve the question of a former acquaintance with her.

"Here, let me take your coat." She held out her hands. "It will wrinkle if you do not lay it out."

"Thank you." Peter gave it over, and she breezed past him.

Closing his eyes, he took a deep breath and tried to concentrate. He must try to remember where they had met. It was no simple task, though, not with her enthralling citrus fragrance wreaking havoc on his senses.

"It is orange blossom. Father had it made in Paris."

Peter's eyes flew open as she reseated herself in front of him.

"You needn't be bothered, though. Many of my acquaintances have attempted to decipher my perfume. The scent is one of those familiar, yet challenging-to-identify fragrances, at least until you know what it is. Perfect, is it not? Exactly like oranges."

'Familiar, yet challenging-to-identify.' Lord, what was her name?

"Now, speaking of perfection, was not my timing perfect? I answered your prayer about what happened to your plan with a clear and forthright response at the precise moment you hoped to receive one."

"Who are you, and how did you get in here?" Peter surprised himself with the directness of his questions, but it did not seem to worry her. Why should it, with her unguarded nature and perfect perfume, not to mention her ability to answer prayers? Blunt questions should be of little concern to her.

"I am Miss Betherton's cousin, as well you know, and I entered through the door."

Peter followed her gesture toward the back corner of the room. Shadows jostled and bounced across a paneled wall. There was no sign of a door. He knitted his brows and turned back to her but lost himself in her luminous eyes and unrelenting smile. She was so lovely and free . . . No, more like unfettered, and her lips looked like—

Stop this. His rational side instantly prevailed over such errant thoughts. She lacked proper reserve; every word she said—every move she made—was unsettling, nerve-racking and . . . thrilling, actually.

Lord, help me. "I do apologize, but I must leave now. If you will excuse me, I cannot impose any longer." He stood up.

"Don't be ridiculous, Mr. Adsley. I followed you here." She gazed up at him, then stood up. "Be seated, please. The study is yours. Clearly, Miss Betherton was wise to prepare it on your behalf. Events of the evening have most decidedly turned against you."

Now there was an understatement if ever one existed. *What?* "Hold a moment, if you please."

"Yes?"

"Do me the kindness of explaining what you mean by that."

"Sylvia told me you might have need of some rest after dinner, but that is not true, is it? You had something to ask her, did you not? At least it appeared to me that you did."

Peter coughed and pulled at his collar. Had he been so obvious?

"Forgive me, please. My curiosity overwhelmed me. I shall take my leave now." She walked away.

No, please. You must stay. I believe we have met, and I . . . Well, I would like to know you . . . Ah! Wrong word! "Wait. You needn't go."

She stopped.

"I would be obliged if you stayed," Peter added.

When she turned around, the surprise on her face was palpable. "Are you certain?"

"Yes, but I could use some quiet. It *has* been a rather taxing day."

She returned to her chair. "Take as long as you need. I am content to study the flames."

Peter seated himself on the sofa and bowed his head in his hands. His plan was in shambles, and now this free-spirited, young lady—Miss Betherton's cousin, no less—asked about his failed proposal, not to mention the other surprising list of topics. And, he mustn't forget that former acquaintance. Perhaps she remembered him. Could that be why she engaged him so freely? Yet, why had she not spoken of it?

Father in Heaven, I cannot imagine what you have in mind, but I thought— Scripture flashed in Peter's mind. *"My thoughts are not your thoughts, saith the LORD."*

Yes, but you know my desire for a godly wife, and I was convinced Miss Betherton was she. Now this stunning creature . . . I can scarcely look at her without going adrift. Lord, I have asked so little of you, why can you not give me a wife?

Ashamed of his outburst, Peter bowed lower, digging his fingers into his scalp. His desire for intimacy with a woman taunted him so. "Forgive me this wretched flaw, and for my impatience," he whispered.

"As you wish," she answered. "Though it only seems natural, given your taxing day and my presence here."

Peter straightened up. *Lord, have mercy!* Her impeccable timing again, and with such a blameless smile! He raked his fingers through his hair. Yet, she knew nothing of her effect on him, hopefully. If he was to remain near her, he must brace himself, and keep it that way.

"So, will you tell me why you wished to speak with my cousin?"

Curiosity first, of course. He sighed. "What of the slave trade, Wilberforce, and religious philosophy?"

"Agreeable topics, to be sure." The dimple in her left cheek deepened. "We can discuss them next."

Evidently, this naïve little temptress was taking far more pleasure in their situation than she ought. He must act to remedy that right now.

"Then I should like to know how we became dinner companions, since I typically sit beside Miss Betherton."

Her eyes widened. "Yes, uh . . . Of course. But there is not much to tell. Your place was set beside my cousin's, until I . . . My goodness, how I do go on."

"Indeed."

"Well, you heard Uncle Phillip's announcement. It was only fitting for your brother to be seated beside my cousin. As a result, you ended up sitting further down the table."

"And remarkably close to you, I might add." He also added the smile Miss Betherton always called so dashing.

"Yes, I rather enjoyed studying your—"

"My what? Pray tell."

She blinked, and her eyes darted away. Ha! He had her now. But to what purpose? He need not press her so.

"Do forgive me," he added. "You needn't answer that."

Her look of relief satisfied him.

"But a moment ago you asked me why I wished to speak with your cousin. Why do you suppose?"

"To propose?" Was the forlorn answer.

The sad slant of her brow, he recognized it. Yet from where? And how to determine that? "Yes, but why such a pitiful tone? I should think you would be glad of it."

"Do you love her?"

It was Peter's turn for pathetic silence. "I must go now." He grabbed his coat and headed toward the fireplace. "It was a pleasure to speak with you."

"On the contrary, I make you uneasy, and that cannot bring you much pleasure. And you did not answer my question."

He turned back. "Your cousin is a friend."

She stood up. "So you would sacrifice yourself for your friend?" As if in appeal, she extended her hand to him. "However eccentric you may think . . ."

He skimmed the graceful line of her outstretched arm, and his heart lurched into a gallop. He permitted his gaze to drift along her neck and across her cheeks. It came to rest on her lips, those delicate . . . A wave of heat surged through his chest, and his throat went dry. For Heaven's sake, he must manage himself better. What was she saying?

". . . poor judge of character. It takes a very courageous man to make such a sacrifice. It may not be for the best, however." She glanced at her outstretched hand, as if seeing it for the first time, and quickly withdrew it behind her, offering him a surprised, if not awkward grin. "Might I share some advice with you?"

"What makes you think it would be of interest to me?"

"I cannot tell, but Father taught me that it keeps one's heart in the right place. Perhaps it will help you temper your loss of Sylvia since you sought to marry her for the wrong reason."

What right had she to make that judgment? Yet, how could he be angry when she was right?

She gazed up at him in rather an expectant manner. Ah, such divine innocence and intellect combined. And her orange blossom scent again. He inhaled deeply. What color were those incredible eyes? It was a challenge to determine, especially with her rosebud lips distracting him. His gaze drifted down her delicate neck to the gauzy white material hovering at her smooth shoulder. What would it be like to touch . . . ?

Peter's thoughts exploded! He had touched her! Saints alive! She was the young lady from the chapel, alive. Praise Heaven! He shoved his hands in his pockets lest he scare her with rejoicing.

He had saved her! How long had it been? A year and a half or so? He always wondered what had happened to her. She seemed nearly dead by the time he got her to the house. And the rain: it was terrible! Yet, here she was, grown up, beautiful, and alive!

"Mr. Adsley, you are positively glowing, like you've witnessed a miracle."

"Perhaps I have." His heart rattled like a cracked carriage wheel. But he mustn't frighten her, not after her previous ordeal.

"So do you want to tell me about it?"

Firm voice; deep breath; maintain self-control, but be kind. "I would rather not."

"'Tis your choice. I believe you could still benefit from Papá's advice, though."

"Go on then. Tell me."

"Splendid. Mind you, it is from the Scriptures."

"Even better."

"'To obey is better than sacrifices.'" She tilted her head. "So are you being obedient or are you simply martyring yourself for another good cause?"

Chapter 7
Questions

The question ripped through him, striking him with silence.
Perhaps God was using her to make a point, after all. Obviously He was, or she would not be here now. And Peter knew exactly why.

The truth was, Peter had chosen Miss Betherton because she provided a swift solution for his want. No doubt a marriage would have benefited her too, as old as she was. But had he shown any faith in God's provision?

"Mr. Adsley, please do not be angry with me." She grasped his arm, and he looked down at her hand. Then their eyes met. "I meant no offense, sir."

"I took none. But you are quick to give your opinions."

"I am, much to Mother's despair." The sparkle in her eyes vanished as her hand slipped from his arm. "But Father provided me with an education, the same any son would receive. So I am accustomed to sharing them."

"You must enjoy an uncommonly frank relationship with your father."

"I do." She smiled a little. "But I shall go now. Good evening, Mr. Adsley." She curtsied. "I am delighted to have made your acquaintance."

And I am so very pleased to see you are alive. "Yes. As am I yours. Very well then, good night." He would ask Miss Betherton her name at the earliest possible moment.

Moving along the wall to the back corner of the room, she ran her hand along the carved chair rail as if searching for something. Peter followed.

"What are you doing?"

"Leaving." A previously invisible door clicked open. "This is the door I used to access the study, remember?"

"Oh. Ah . . . but why . . . why are you here? That is to say, why are you not dancing with the other young ladies? It is your cousin's birthday, after all."

"Mother's silly fancy: she never débuted in society, so she desires that dubious honor for me. And she refuses to let me go anywhere—including Uncle's ballroom—without my chaperon, at least until I've had a Season." The charming smile, in nearly all its glory, returned. "Thank you for this conversation tonight. It was a pleasure I shall not soon forget."

"Without a doubt! And I . . ."

He stepped forward, but she disappeared behind the paneled door, which clicked back into place before he reached it. He listened against the wall. Nothing.

He felt along the chair rail and smiled when he found a carved rosette with a loose center, a button of sorts. He started to press but thought better of it. Following her would be most unseemly—as if their whole interaction had been anything less—and if he found her, what then?

Peter walked over to the window. He took out his handkerchief, mopped his forehead, and then shoved the cloth back into his pocket. So her mother required an escort. It was no wonder. But she had evaded that expectation. He smiled. It seemed just like her—at least from what he learned of her tonight—to resist such a restriction. She was also opposed to having a Season; rare, but again, not surprising.

His thoughts darkened, and his hands curled into fists. Was that why she asked if he loved her cousin? Was she afraid of being condemned to a loveless match? A Season could mean but one thing: arranged marriage, certainly a desirable match for the highest bidder. But what of her feelings?

Merciful Heaven! Was she so desperate for love—or at least the knowledge of it—that she would ask a man why he proposed? Had no one taught her of love? Her father must have. He certainly taught her about the difference between obedience and sacrifices.

"So are you being obedient or are you simply martyring yourself for another good cause?" Yes. It was highly probable he would be hearing her question for some time: weeks, months, perhaps even years.

However, what kind of parents could toy with a daughter's life by parading her about for a Season while forbidding her to dance at her cousin's birthday? It made no sense. At least with slaves—as horrendous as the idea was to him—their owners believed they were only animals, so buying and selling them was expected.

Buying and selling! Miss Betherton and her father's ailing estate came to mind. What sort of arrangement had Father and dear brother Richard reached with Mr. Betherton in that calamitous agreement?

It was one thing for Peter to marry Miss Betherton, despite his lack of passion for her. She was his friend, and he would have treasured her as such, anticipating love would grow between them. Richard was a different man entirely. He loved only himself, and his wine. God help Miss Betherton. Richard did not even respect her, but would end up taking advantage of her.

Peter's thoughts rushed back to Miss Betherton's cousin. Would she too be bound to a man who cared nothing for her? Or worse yet, to one whom she loathed?

I must, at least, attempt to stop Sylvia's marriage to Richard.

Peter strode across the room and tugged on the velvet cord to summon assistance. Within seconds, a knock sounded at the door.

"Call for my coach, if you please. I shall follow immediately."

"Yes, sir."

Before exiting the study, Peter glanced back at the corner of the room where his lovely dinner companion had slipped away. *Be gracious, Lord. Allow that her match be made for love.*

In the wee hours of the morning, when Peter finally crawled into bed, he prayed for strength to confront his father and Richard. He must dissuade the loggerheads from this marriage scheme. Not for his own sake, of course. If Miss Betherton preferred to marry someone else, that was her prerogative. He would find another lady. But she did not deserve to be bound to Richard.

Peter stared at the carved plaster ceiling as he lay in bed. He pictured Miss Betherton's young cousin and the mischievous stars dancing in her eyes. He must speak to Miss Betherton about her. And what was this, having the study set up for him? Had she also advised her cousin to meet him there?

Peter rolled onto his side and stared at the orange glow emanating from the fireplace. She was alive!

He thought back to that fateful evening.

After he left Betherton Hall, Father sent him posthaste to Liverpool to manage a complicated situation—one of Richard's making—because Richard had too much to drink at Mrs. Betherton's garden party.

A month later, when Peter finally returned, he said nothing of the girl. Though he often wondered what had happened to her, he could hardly ask. Appearing overly curious about a girl could give the family—his and hers—the wrong impression, or they might suspect him of some wrongdoing, since she was so ill. And he certainly did not want to involve himself with the other wretched blackguard. If he ever saw him again . . .

Peter did not care to think about what he would do then. All he knew was that it was a good thing he had been there to save Miss Betherton's cousin or she might not be here today.

Trying to find a comfortable position, he sat up, fluffed his pillow, and re-situated himself under the blankets. Still, her voice resonated in his thoughts.

"Are you being obedient or simply martyring yourself for another good cause?"

A single candle flickered beside Annette. Golden tendrils of hair fell across her page; she tucked them behind her ear and kept drawing.

Oh saints or fate, destiny, God, who or whatever ye be, please save Mr. Adsley for me.

She chanted the erroneous little rhyme over and over as her pencil flew across the page, sketching a line here and shadowing there, summoning forth Mr. Adsley's likeness from the canvas of her memory.

He had dark hair. Earlier today, Sylvia had confirmed he was at the garden party. And oh, he was so kind, even when she asked about his proposal! What man would ever entertain such a question? She had surprised herself asking it. And he had spoken against the slave trade at the party, but then he left early. She remembered now. Ever since the nightmares . . . Well, she had only ever dwelt on the horrid event.

But Mr. Adsley was good, and kind, and . . . Well, he must be the one! He had to be her savior!

After several minutes of feverish work, Annette set her pencil down. She took half of the jam-covered roll waiting on a plate beside her water cup and studied the foundation of her new masterpiece. She smiled as she savored her treat.

She had captured Mr. Adsley—on paper, at least.

His modest air of confidence appeared in his strong jaw and in the solid arch of his brows. The dark curl falling across his forehead supplied his handsome, yet boyish charm, and his chiseled lips added a hint of the debonair. She took another bite of her sweet roll. The sketch was an excellent start.

"If it is any consolation, Mr. Adsley," she said as she licked her thumb, "now that Sylvia is taken, I would be honored to be your wife."

The words sounded as hollow as the possibility, but Annette felt better for having said them. She popped the last bit of roll in her mouth and flipped back a few pages to her loving laborer's picture, the man in her favorite painting whom she believed looked like her savior. Her eye was drawn to the charcoal scar on his lip. In the last-minute excitement with Sylvia about Mr. Adsley's seating change, she had forgotten about it. And now there was no time to fix it.

She sighed. Perhaps it did not matter since she had Mr. Adsley.

She closed her eyes and tried to picture her champion, but the image was still unclear. Annette opened her eyes and, interlacing her fingers, stretched her arms in front of her, then leaned her head back and yawned. It had been a wonderful day.

Unlacing her fingers, she closed her sketchbook, drank the last bit of water, and blew out her candle. She stashed her drawings under the mattress—as a precaution against any probing eyes—then she hopped into bed.

Oh, saints or fate, destiny, God, who or whatever ye be, please—

"No, I must do better, for Papá's sake, at least." She looked out the window at the crescent moon. "God, I know I have no right to ask; I am not even certain you are there. But if you really are, could you please save Mr. Adsley for me? And can you tell me if he is the man who rescued me?

Chapter 8

Hostilities

Caverswall Manor
Staffordshire, England
28 February 1795

A blazing fire raged against the damp coolness of the weather, but it did nothing to break the ice in the Adsley family dining room. Servants set out a luncheon of turnip soup, roast beef, rice pilaf, cranberry-orange salad, and gingerbread cakes on the sideboard. Peter added another spoonful of rice to his plate, served himself some salad, then seated himself to the left of his father, who was at the head of the table. He bowed his head for a brief prayer. Afterward, he began cutting his roast beef. The click of his knife against his china plate was the only sound in the room, besides the crackling fire.

"Well, little brother, what happened last night?" Richard mocked from across the table. "Miss Bether . . . no, Sylvia. Now that she's mine, I'll use her given name. At any rate, she was saving a dance for you, but you were nowhere to be found."

"You do not love her, Richard."

"What has love to do with anything?"

"You should not marry her. There is no affection between you."

"Affection is not essential." He gave a derisive chuckle. "Indeed. If I had any feelings for her, they might curtail my appetite for—"

"Richard!" Mr. Adsley's knife clattered against his plate.

"I know, Father. Indecent comments will not be tolerated."

"Peter." His father leveled a cool stare at him. "If you wanted her for yourself, you should have spoken sooner."

"Had I known Richard had designs on her, I would have," Peter spoke to his brother. "So what possessed you to propose while I was away? You have never shown any interest before. In fact, you have only ever criticized me for befriending her."

"Had you been home, you might have known my aim," Richard said, taking a gulp of wine.

Peter frowned. The only aim Richard ever had was finding his next drink and a woman to go with it. All of Caverswall was littered with the broken relics of his conquests.

"Speaking of aim," Richard continued, "of all the idiotic things to do, you became a clergyman? What kind of career is that? I'll wager you won't even get the full tithe. I would've bought a commission in the Army. Even a naval officer would command more attention than you will receive, and they both have better wages."

"I have no interest in wealth or recognition."

"Perhaps you should."

"My employment is none of your concern. I want to discuss your sudden decision to marry Miss Betherton. Can you explain it? She has no dowry to speak of, and she knows your reputation. You know she cannot want this."

"I wouldn't be so sure about that if I were you. Besides, as Father said, if you wanted her for yourself, you should have told him. We only finished the initial arrangements . . . What was it Father, five days ago? If you had returned sooner, things might have been different. But oh, yes, tardiness has always been your defeat, has it not, Pete?" Richard lifted his glass and drank some more. "But you needn't worry. Sylvia will suffer far less pain than our poor mother endured on your behalf."

Richard's words stung, but Peter refused to yield. For years, he had been developing defenses against such tactics.

No one else knew it, but once, when he and Richard were boys, they were playing in the servants' quarters and overheard two women discussing their mother's death. It was a forbidden topic; even their father refused to speak of his first wife since her death just two hours after Peter's birth. Consequently, whenever anyone dropped the least bit of information about her, Peter and Richard listened with thirsty ears.

And since that fateful day, Richard had made it his life's work to remind Peter of the servant's agonizing words: *"If it hadn't been for how long the young Master Peter, poor babe, took in comin', she might a lived."*

"Enough, Richard," Mr. Adsley growled. "Have done with this, and leave your brother's choice of career to him." Then he turned to Peter. "Mr. Betherton has signed the initial agreements, and with our help, his finances will soon be in order. I am confident Miss Betherton is relieved to know that by doing her duty, she has rescued her parents from certain disaster."

"Duty is not the point. Miss Betherton should have a choice in marriage. Heaven knows she hasn't one in anything else. Your property is extensive, Father. You mustn't allow him to prey on her."

"Presumptuous boy!" The china plates and silverware jumped and chattered when Mr. Adsley's fist hit the table. "You know nothing of my estate."

"Well said, Father." Richard slowly clapped his hands. "Peter doesn't care a wit about your property nor its workings. He just wants to write sermons. And now that Wilberforce has lost the slavery issue, he's starting a movement to free our oppressed daughters and wives. Right, Pete? Let the lady choose? Balderdash. The only choice that woman has is marriage to me—with all the freedom it will afford her and her family—or poverty. Which do you think she wants for her dear Mum and Da?"

"She would not have chosen you. And why would you want her, anyway?"

"It matters naught, because I'll have her." Richard emptied his glass in one great swallow. "Do you suppose she'll breed a healthy son? If she can't, I might as well call the whole thing off and let her rot."

"You are a vicious fiend." *And some day you will pay for that irreverence with a surplus of interest.*

"Well, you are a parsimonious—"

"Cease this squabbling!" Mr. Adsley glared at Richard. Then he turned to Peter. "Our appointment with the solicitors is set. In a fortnight, Betherton, your brother, and I will complete negotiations in Liverpool. The ladies will accompany us as well. There will be no retractions, Peter. You will abide by this decision, or I will leave you to your precious parish without so much as a shilling. In addition, you are to have no contact with Miss Betherton from now until the wedding two months hence, or your monthly allowance is dust."

Mr. Adsley wiped his mouth with his napkin and stood from the table. "Richard, you have had too much to drink. Get upstairs and ring for some coffee."

"Can I have the new maid serve it? She looks like she could—"

"Silence. Your vulgarities make me sick."

"Then send a footman," Richard retorted. But Mr. Adsley left without looking back.

Richard plucked a bite of gingerbread from his plate and sucked it from between his fingers. Then he wiped his hands on his napkin and tossed it on his chair.

"Well, Pete, that settles it." Richard strutted toward the door. "I'll let you know how it goes with the new maid." He smirked and walked out.

Peter moved his untouched plate away, and folding his hands in front of him, rested his forehead on them. Someday Richard would pay.

Chapter 9

Adversary

At the Port of Falmouth in
Trelawney, Jamaica
5 March 1795

It was auction day in Port Falmouth. Rattling wagons clanked along the dusty road. Dock workers loaded ships with huge crates and barrels of supplies while crowds swarmed the town square. Bidding would start in less than a half hour, and Mr. Slike, who was also known as Sir Steven Likebridge when he was home in England, was quite satisfied with himself.

He leaned against a gnarled tree beside a large covered stockade, sharpening his knife. Then he took aim at a target painted on the side of a shed some twenty-five feet away and threw it. The blade whizzed through the air and landed dead center. Casually bending down, he pulled another blade from his right boot and cast it with lightning speed.

"So, Mr. Slike, my golden-haired genius. . ." A pungent cigar stench wafted over his shoulder. "On the mark as usual, I see."

He raked his fingers through his sun-bleached hair, pasted on a smile, and turned to greet one of his preferred clients. "Good day to you too, Colonel Fontaine. How are you this fine morning?"

"Right as the best, but it's gettin' mighty hot out here." The aging gentleman removed his straw hat and fanned himself. "And I'd like to get on with my business, if you're not too busy with that pastime o' yours."

Slike glanced past his client. A ravenous pack of buyers circled the platform in front of the stockade, but he could not resist closing another deal before the public sale began.

"Too busy for you? Never. What did you have in mind?"

"I hear ya got some fine-lookin' breeders in this shipment."

Slike's gray eyes gleamed as he rubbed his beard. "I might have something along those lines, if you have the coin."

"Don't fret the money. You know I got it." Colonel Fontaine blew cigar smoke out the side of his mouth. "Recall that black mammoth you brought me a couple trips back?"

"I do."

"Well, Goliath—that's what I call him—has settled in real nice, he has, and I was thinkin' I'd like to set him up as a stud." A sinister grin slithered across his lips. "So I'm in the market for some of your finest breedin' stock."

"I keep the exceptional specimens for my more selective clients in here." Slike sauntered over to the shed, collected his knives, and returned them to their respective hiding places on his person. "They are some of the finest I have seen in a while: sturdy, shapely, and first-rate coloring, but they are going to cost you."

"Doesn't bother me. It's the long-term investment I'm considerin'. Gotta have the best for my boy. Once he's mated with 'em, sellin' the progeny'll more than cover my expenses."

Slike unlocked the rickety door and held it open. "In that case, have a look around. See what tickles your fancy."

Fontaine took a few steps into the dingy enclosure. Slike followed, and they both paused. Sunlight seeped through the cracks in the plank siding, but it took a few seconds for one's eyes to adjust.

"Check the stall on the right first."

"Don't mind if I do."

Slike always held back so buyers could give his exhibits their full attention. When the colonel let out a low whistle, the bottom half of the slave trader's face cracked into a reptilian smirk. He was quite proud of this particular display.

The Negro woman was arranged in a standing position with her arms and legs stretched wide. Her wrists and ankles were held apart by ropes tied to the sides of the stall so she could not move while buyers examined her. There was no doubt she would arouse interest.

After another minute, Slike stepped forward.

"That's some fine lookin' female flesh ya got there." The colonel sucked on his cigar and let out the smoke. "Don't know how you manage keepin' 'em so lusty and fresh after six thousand miles across the sea, but she's definitely got my attention. Are the others as good as this one?"

"See for yourself. I will wait while you browse."

The colonel spent the next quarter of an hour inspecting each of the four women Slike had available.

"Well now, looky here—" Fontaine called from the far corner of the shed.

Oh no, Lani! Steven heard scuffling noises and crunching straw. Without delay, he rushed back. "What is it?"

"How about this one? What'll you take for her?"

Steven's stomach turned. The colonel held the cinnamon-cheeked woman Steven had grown to care about in a headlock, and he was pointing his pistol at her belly.

"Caught her rummagin' behind those crates. She musta gotten loose somehow." Fontaine's eyes glistened like the droplets of sweat forming on his wrinkled forehead. "My, but she's a fine one, she is."

Lani struggled, but he tightened his arm around her throat.

"Steady there, girl, I'm not gonna hurt you."

Her eyes pleaded as she tilted her head sideways, gasping for air. Steven stared. They had become friends. More than friends, actually. Though she spoke little English, they had come to understand each other. He had told her to hide in the back until he could find her a better place. But she must not have understood this time.

"You are awfully quiet, son. Does she mean somethin' to you? She's a bit plump in the belly, you know."

Steven's eyes dropped to Lani's midsection, then jumped to her syrupy, caramel eyes.

"Ah, don't let it bother you too much. It wouldn't be the first time one o' these heathen banshees stole a decent, God-fearin' man's heart." The colonel's face turned nostalgic. "I, myself, once had . . ." He cleared his throat. "Anyway, don't need to bother you with that. So how much will you take for this one, young man?"

Steven's mouth went dry.

"I asked how much you'll take for her, son."

No response.

"Well, I'll be da—"

"It is likely we both will, Fontaine, but not on her account." Steven spat out the words as he reached for a knife. "She is not for sale."

"Easy there, son, no need for trouble. Everything's gonna be just fine. Now put the blade away, and take your girl." Fontaine gently pushed her towards him.

She clasped his hand, kissing it and weeping as he pocketed his knife.

But then the doubts began.

He had no idea what to do with her, and if there was a child . . . His throat tightened. He could feel the droplets of sweat trickling down his back and sides. No matter how much he wanted to keep Lani, Steven knew it was impossible. He had a life back in England, and there was his mother and little Charlie to think of.

"Do you have a place for her, son?" Colonel Fontaine spoke in a calm voice. "Life's pretty rough at sea. Maybe you were thinkin' o' puttin' her up somewhere in the country once you got home. It's not easy, but it's been done." He paused. "Ah, don't know what you'll think o' this, but what if I keep her for you? I'll treat her real well. She'll have the best care, and when you're in port, you can visit."

Steven loathed himself as he pulled his hands away from Lani. But Fontaine was right. England was no place to keep her. Someone might see her. People watched his every move. And if they found her . . . Well, that would be the end of Sir Steven Likebridge.

"Tell you what. I'll house your girl for you, and if she's carryin', I'll see that she keeps the pup. Then, if things change, you can have 'em both. I won't even charge you extra."

Heartsick, Steven looked at his client and looked at Lani. He saw no other way. Forcing aside his feelings and stuffing his humanity down into the darkest corner of his soul, Steven crushed his longings the same way he had so many times before.

Mother and little Charlie were his main concern. Everything he did was for them. Life had been that way for as long as he could remember—and it must continue to be—now that the end was in sight.

"If there's a child, she keeps it, and they both get the best you have until I come back."

"You have my word." Colonel Fontaine extended his hand and they shook. "Just name your price."

"You'll get a total for the entire purchase once you've made your selections."

"Excellent. I'll take another look around while you finish your business here." He nodded toward Lani then walked away.

With tears trickling down her cinnamon cheeks, Lani wrapped her arms around Steven. He attempted to unlatch her hands from his neck, but she became frantic. Even as he tried to explain, she clutched at him and cried louder. She didn't understand him, or perhaps she knew too well. Whatever the case, he could no longer take it. With hell's fires burning in the hollow of his very soul, Steven shoved her away with all his might.

"Stop! You're his now."

She slammed against the wall and collapsed to the floor, but that did not stop her. Scrambling to right herself, with hands outstretched and tears flooding her cheeks, she came to him on her knees.

"Lani be Steven's. Lani Steven's friend."

His knees melted, and he—

"You know, Mr. Slike, we could use a man like you down here."

Lani fled to the corner as Colonel Fontaine, who seemed to have appeared from nowhere, caught Steven by the shoulders and maneuvered him toward the front of the shed. "You'd be great at managin' the plantation over at New Hope. What do ya say to growin' sugarcane? I could put in a good word for you. The owner'll be down from England in a few months. Then you could stay."

Slike cleared his throat. "With all due respect, Colonel, it is a nice offer, but I have my eye on something far more substantial."

"What could be bigger than runnin' a plantation? From what I understand, you're a nobody back home, and they don't make it in Liverpool. Down here there aren't so many rules."

"I appreciate what you are saying, but I plan to take over my father's estate."

"Worth that much, huh? Bet you got your eye on a rich little filly to go with it then."

"In point of fact, my father is very rich, but adding more by way of a dowry never hurt a man." Slike's lips bent into an empty smile. "Her mother's already in my pocket."

"Doubtless with all your schemin' and plannin' you've got the whole thing worked out."

"That I do, Colonel."

"Well then, I'm happy to be of service by keepin' your girl."

"I appreciate it. Now, which of these other fine females do you want? The rest are going on the auction block."

Chapter 10
Revelation

Caverswall Manor
Staffordshire, England
13 March 1795

The day had finally arrived. Peter stood outside the ladies' coach saying his last good-byes to his stepmother and Mary Hope. They were off to Liverpool with the Bethertons.

"I shall miss you, Peter." His sister leaned across their mother. "But I have been looking forward to this visit. Wilberforce's supporters are giving tours of slave ships in Merseyside harbor, and Sylvia and I plan to take one."

"You will do no such thing."

She scooted to the opposite side of the coach and looked out the window.

"Listen to me, Mary Hope. This is a tour for your soon-to-be sister's pleasure, and you must help her with the trousseau. No errands of mercy at the workhouses. No visits to the Stanley Tower prison, and absolutely no traipsing about on some putrid, vermin-infested slave ship! Mother, see to this, please!"

"I dare say there will be ample opportunity for you to see one yourself, with the way things are going for Wilberforce now."

Peter stared at his mother.

"Forgive me, but you know it is true."

"Doubtless. But give me your word you will protect Sylvia."

"I will." She raised her voice. "There will be plenty of dress fittings, teas in proper tea houses, and dances at public assemblies, perhaps a visit to the opera as well."

"Sylvia is already engaged, Mama. She no longer needs such things," Mary Hope responded.

"I was not thinking of Sylvia, dear."

"What?"

"Never mind, sweetheart."

"But we were planning to attend a meeting of the Bluestockings."

"You two know enough about the rights of women already," Mrs. Adsley quipped.

"Mother!"

45

"I'm only teasing. But this is the one chance I will get to go to Liverpool with a bride in mind, since you do not care to wed. Therefore, we need to emphasize Sylvia's status as a new bride, not an intellectual. Now, get yourself situated. It is going to be a long trip."

"As you wish, Mama, but we are still going to a meeting."

His stepmother turned back to Peter and spoke in a serious whisper. "I have something for you, Peter, but you must remain composed."

"What is it?"

"I found this in your father's bureau." She handed him a folded letter. The handwriting sobered him.

"Thank you." He glanced at his father and brother, who were mounting their horses a few paces down the drive, and tucked it into his inner coat pocket.

"When you finish, return it to his top left drawer. He will never know the difference. And Peter, though you may not think so, your father has your best interests at heart."

Peter looked into his stepmother's loving eyes but made no comment.

"Very well, son." Her voice brightened. "Give me a kiss, and we shall be off."

"Safe journey, Mother." He gave her a peck on the cheek.

"Good-bye, Peter," Mary Hope chimed in. "Enjoy your time as Master of Caverswall."

"I will. Remember what I said."

"All right. But we are still attending a lecture with some Bluestockings."

"You would not be my sister if you did not." Peter smiled as he stepped away from the coach and signaled the driver. The conveyance lurched forward, and Peter waved as they cleared the large circle drive. His father, who was riding at the head of the small procession, gave his usual salute and headed down the road. Only Richard lagged behind.

"So, little brother," he jeered from his horse as it pranced in front of Peter. "While I am gone, you may finally have your chance."

"Is that so?"

"Remember our luncheon discussion with Father about my imminent marriage to Sylvia the afternoon following her birthday celebration?" Peter nodded. "Then you must also recall my desire to know our enticing new chambermaid better. That being said, with all the arrangements for this trip, I haven't had time to further that acquaintance. However, I have spoken to Arlene, and she assures me she wouldn't mind if you stood in on my behalf, if you catch my meaning."

Peter clenched his teeth. "Can you, for once, exercise some personal restraint and conduct yourself as a proper gentleman?"

Richard threw back his head and laughed. "Agreed, if, upon my return, Arlene tells me you were successful at being a man." Then he kicked his horse's sides and galloped away. At the end of the drive, he waved to Peter and shouted, "Enjoy!"

"Forgive me, Lord, but I would like nothing better than to show him what it means to be a man."

Peter strode into the library, sat down in a chair beside the fire, and took Miss Betherton's letter from his pocket.

28 February 1795

Peter sighed. She wrote a fortnight ago, and fourteen days had passed without an answer. What must she think of him? She knew nothing of Father's ruling against his having any contact with her. And now that everyone was off to Liverpool, it probably did not matter.

Peter continued reading.

> *Mr. Adsley, Peter, my dear friend,*
>
> *I pray this letter finds you in your usual forbearing spirit, both because I violate convention by writing it, and because I have made a dreadful mistake by choosing not to inform you of my engagement.*
>
> *Without doubt, it is difficult to comprehend, but I pray you will indulge me. I wish to explain how it all came about. For I fear my impending marriage to your brother presses you most dreadfully, and I cannot bear the thought of having disappointed you so.*
>
> *Despite the many rumors about him, I have agreed to marry Richard, Lord willing, after the banns have been read, on Sunday the 10th day of May. Yet hold a moment, lest you think I have lost my senses. All is not as it seems. There is a larger plan at work, and I praise God for giving me the strength to seize this opportunity.*
>
> *Peter, you know me to be a very sensible soul, one who cherishes no illusions about her circumstances. You must also know—for I am convinced it is the talk of all society—that regardless of my father's best efforts to avoid it, his estate is soon to foreclose.*
>
> *But I could not allow that to happen. Consequently, I decided—as you so often have encouraged me—to assert myself.*
>
> *In order to help my family, I chose to take my stand beside your brother as his wife, for I had no knowledge of any other possibilities, and opportunities have been few.*
>
> *As you are so painfully aware, he is the principal heir to your father's fortune, and his resources will save my father's estate. Richard will also help me fulfill my own personal hopes. I had almost resigned myself to living out my days as a childless spinster. However, because of this arrangement, children might yet be within my grasp.*

"Ah Sylvia, I could have given you children." Peter sighed. "And Father might have helped your family as a wedding gift to us."

> *Please do not attempt to deter me, Peter. There is far too much at stake. And do not think ill of your brother or father. No matter what their faults, the truth is, none of this was their doing. It was all mine.*
>
> *Without my parents' knowledge and with no pressure from your family—for certainly your father and brother were as astonished by my offer as I was by their kind reception of it—I presented myself and my poor encumbered inheritance as a business venture.*
>
> *You must believe me. My own dear parents have no knowledge of this arrangement. They understand your brother's proposal to be the natural outgrowth of a young man's coming to maturity, and it must remain this way. Do you understand?*
>
> *Forgive me, friend, but you also would know nothing of this plan, except for the look I saw on your face when my father made the announcement. Was it despair or anger? Have I offended you so terribly?*
>
> *I pray it is not so, but forgive me if I have. And, will you allow me this additional question? (After all I have said, I have little to lose in the asking.)*
>
> *Throughout the evening, I knew you wanted to see me. But every time I attempted to break away, my efforts were thwarted. What did you want of me?*
>
> *I do not mean to be presumptuous, but if you wished to propose, you have my deepest gratitude. I cherished no hope of such an offer from you. Our friendship was blessing enough. But if you sought to speak to me for some lesser purpose than love—say for example, to gain a companion for your new ministry—then I defy you and pray God's deliverance of your own restless heart.*

Peter's jaw muscles worked. "She knows me too well."

> *Dear friend, no matter how much you long for that true empathy of souls one finds in a marriage blessed of God, you must not settle for someone who merely allows you to be comfortable. He did not design you for such an ordinary existence. You must find a wife whose passion for life ignites your own fervent soul.*

"Without a doubt."

> *And, on a final intrusive note—forgive this terrible transition, but my paper runs short of space—I understand from my young cousin, Miss Annette . . . "*

"Annette, so that is her name." Peter smiled.

> *. . . my young cousin, Miss Annette Chetwynd, whom you met in the study last night, that you are . . . How did she put it? 'A cautious and conventional sort of gentleman.' I do hope you were not too put off by her. For one so young, she is a rare and zealous conversationalist, is she not? (She is also an avid Wilberforce supporter. Did you speak with her of that?)*
>
> *I hope you can forgive the . . . irregular nature (I know it is far worse, but I trusted you to act appropriately) of the meeting. In view of her mother's tiresome rule and suspecting how you might react to Father's announcement, I could think of no other way for you to meet her. Did all go well? You must tell me sometime.*
>
> *I shall end my letter now. Mother is calling. I'm ever blessed with the honor of your friendship and forgiveness.*
>
> *With my sincerest thanks, your soon-to-be sister,*
>
> *Sylvia*

Peter rubbed the bridge of his nose. Sylvia's decision to marry Richard bothered him, but she had chosen to take a stand for her family. How could he dislike her for that?

And as far as the secret little rendezvous with her maddening cousin . . . "Annette," he whispered. What mischief was she about, throwing them together like that? It was a terrible risk and manifestly improper. He smiled. But it was not wholly unpleasant.

Peter stood and headed for the door. He must return the letter to its place.

Chapter 11

Homecoming

Liverpool
Merseyside, England
14 April 1795

Drawing heavily on his cigar, Slike reclined in a large, copper bathing tub—the only extravagance he permitted himself, besides the wardrobe he used to play Sir Steven Likebridge. Every last shilling he earned went directly to his plan, and now he had enough to execute it.

As he blew smoke rings and watched them vanish into the steamy air, he almost smiled. For twenty-seven years, he had called this musty hole above the King's Wharf Ale House his home. He gazed up at the cracked plaster ceiling. That would all be changing soon.

Numbers, calculations, and the details of his plan cycled in his mind. He had amassed a fortune—selling slaves, mainly. His earliest employment as ladies' esquire, which Steven had maintained only to help Mother, was no longer necessary. Profits ranging between two hundred fifty and three hundred percent per slave had secured him his wealth, and he was going to use it for her again. Blimey, his most recent trip alone had brought twenty-five percent more than usual, including the private sales to Colonel Fontaine.

Suddenly, chills bristled along his neck and over his shoulders. He winced. Concentrate. It would pass. He mustn't yield.

Take a deep breath. There now, hold and count: One . . . two . . . three . . . four . . . Mother's soft voice echoed in his thoughts. *Keep holding as long as you can; then let go. And again.* He inhaled. *One . . . two . . .*

The wave of panic and guilt over what he had done to Lani slipped away, back into the darkness, and Steven stared at his feet, unsure why these emotions overwhelmed him. Then it started again.

Cold chills. Shortness of breath. Fire burning in his throat. But he had missed his opportunity for counting. Grasping the side of the tub, he rose up, and leaning over, spat out his cigar, and gagged. Boiling nausea erupted from his stomach.

More coughing, gagging, and spasms racked his body; then came the tears.

White-knuckled and shaking, Steven slid down into the tub. Guilt, that relentless parasite that daily burrowed deeper into his heart, had torn into a nerve.

A knock sounded at the outer door. "Ready for your shave now, sir?"

"Go away."

Folding his arms over his chest, he closed his eyes and sank beneath the cloudy water. Bubbles gurgled in his ears, and all was quiet. Beautiful. He could listen to silence for hours.

Traitor. Betrayer. Judas . . . the stain is forever. You sold Lani, your friend, just like your father betrayed your mother. You'll never be clean.

He opened his eyes and, with rippling vision, viewed the cracked plaster ceiling from a fish's perspective. *Judas hung himself; I need only to breathe and be free.*

A hammering noise and the pressure grew stronger. He squeezed his eyes shut and ground his teeth, attempting to block it out, but the pounding intensified. His lungs hurt. Panic. Desperation. The noise would not stop.

Breathe and get away. It will be a clean break.

But what of Mother and Little Charlie?

"QUIET!" Bursting forth, Steven inhaled a massive breath. Crazed, he wiped his dripping hair off his bearded face, clamped his hands around his head, and squeezed with all his might. But the pulsing still persisted.

Wait. He took another deep breath and analyzed the pounding. It was changing now, slowing, and it was no longer inside his head. The outer door, someone was knocking.

"Jackson, answer that!" Slike shouted, and the guilt slunk back into its hole in his heart.

"Right away, sir," his man called. Seconds later, Jackson peeked around the door. "It's a message for you, sir."

"Well, give it to me then."

"Here it is, sir." Jackson's voice quaked as much as his twig of an arm did when he held out the wrinkled paper. Slike eyed him and took the note.

"I'll shave myself. See to my clothes. I expect to be ready within the hour."

"Yes, sir." He turned to leave.

"Hold. Have you posted the letter I wrote this morning?"

"The one to Mr. William Chetwynd of Chesterfield in Devonshire?"

"Was there another?"

"No, sir. I mean yes, sir. I posted the letter. The 'no' was for—"

"Enough." Slike waved him away. "Leave me."

As he read the mangled note, Slike smiled. So the man who had sired him was dining at the Water Street Inn this afternoon. And he would have Richard, Likebridge's old school mate, with him. How convenient. It certainly paid to keep watchdogs about. Over the years, they had provided Slike with so much information, he already felt like part of his father's family, and the inn was just around the corner from the Town Hall, not so far from Mother's place.

Slike tossed the note into the fire and reached for his towel. It was time to become Sir Steven Likebridge.

Fifty-two minutes later, Slike found himself transformed into the clean-shaven Sir Steven Likebridge, sporting his lion-headed walking stick as he strolled down Castle Street. Sir Likebridge glanced at his reflection in a flower shop window and ran his hand over his smooth cheeks. It was good to be rid of the beard. And his black Club wig? Well, it lent him a more conservative air than his natural blond hair. He adjusted his top hat. Sir Steven Likebridge had returned.

He tipped his reflection a nod and entered the shop. A tinkling bell announced his presence as he sauntered around the colorful buckets of nature and up to the counter. There was one more thing he needed before he visited Mother and little Charlie.

"Good afternoon, sir." The buxom shop girl, who was arranging a bouquet, fluttered her eyelashes and smiled. "And what can I be gettin' you today?"

He liked the provocative little flourish in her voice.

"Cornflowers, please."

"I'd guess a fine gentleman like yourself to be choosin' roses or violets. Fine ladies in your circle don't care much about cornflowers, do they? It's a lady you're buyin' for isn't it?"

"Indeed, it is." He felt half of a smile bending his lips. "And she loves cornflowers."

"Then cornflowers i'tis."

She squeezed around the counter, brushing against him. Less than a minute later, she returned with a bunch of the humble, blue dainties and handed them to him. Then, she took an expectant position behind the counter, placing her largest assets well within his view.

"Is there anything else you'd be wantin' today, sir?"

"Thank you, my dear, but not now." He laid five shillings on the counter.

She gazed up at him in awe. "That's enough for a pound o' chocolate."

He allowed the tip of his right pointer finger to whisper along the inside of her wrist. "Perhaps we can share it later this evening," he said. Then he left the flower shop.

Share an evening, indeed! Without warning, Lani's image flashed in his thoughts, and the cornflowers slipped from his fingers. He took off his hat and leaned against a brick storefront. His stomach protested.

There was nothing I could do to help you, Lani, not yet. Mother and Charlie must come first.

Steven repeated his rationalization—once, twice, three more times, and Lani faded away. Then he straightened his shoulders, put on his hat, and headed to Lord Street, leaving the flowers in the dirt. Mother and Charlie would have to wait too. Steven needed a drink.

As he walked up the street, his eyes blurred. Tears came as readily now as they had fifteen years ago on that terrible night when he had found his mother beaten and lying on the floor of their shabby upstairs dwelling. She was barely breathing. And Charlie, only six at the time, was curled up under the bed, whimpering like a puppy.

But back then, no matter what he vowed or how hard he worked in the shipping yards by day and behind closed doors at night, Steven could not save her or his little brother from poverty and pain.

A strong breeze rustled through the trees as the sun dipped behind some clouds.

I know, Ma!

It had been some while since he had visited her. But it had taken all these years to save up for his plan. She needn't wait much longer, though. Ma and Charlie would be home with him in their grand country house soon enough.

Wind whipped the dead leaves around Steven's feet as he proceeded up the street. *Don't worry. The plan is flawless, and I'm ready to claim what's ours.*

He shoved his hands into his pockets and burrowed his chin into his coat. Steven could never forgive the man who sired him. Mother was only a chambermaid in Caverswall while the man she served was the young master, according to the daily catechism Abigail Likebridge had borne into her young son's head. Her evidence of their attachment was a gold watch she had saved for Steven as proof of his parentage.

He took out his watch and examined the coin-like charm that dangled from its chain. On the front side, it bore the image of a dog's head. He flipped it over and scrutinized the engraved initials—C.A. for Mr. Charles Adsley, his mother's traitor.

I am the firstborn son of Mr. Charles Adsley of Caverswall Manor. I was born on the first of April in the year of our Lord, 1767. I am the firstborn son of Mr. Charles Adsley . . . He slipped the watch into his waistcoat pocket and continued repeating his litany.

At the corner of Castle Street and Lord Street, the sky released what seemed to be a million tears. Slike waved down a coach and ordered the driver to the Water Street Inn, where he would find his half-brother, his father, and that drink he wanted.

He smiled. It had helped to develop a relationship with Richard while they attended Oriel College of Oxford. Carousing in dark alleys and shady game halls was great sport for them. Likebridge had also done an exceptional job of acquainting his brother with the distinctive pleasures of strong drink and women—all part of his master plan. He smiled.

Some minutes later, the coach pulled up in front of the Water Street Inn. Likebridge got out, tossed the driver a coin, and went inside. He had hardly removed his hat to shake off the rain when he heard a slightly slurred, yet very familiar, voice.

"I say there, Likebridge, is that you, Old Chap?" He turned to observe Richard Adsley setting his glass down and stepping away from the window seat he had occupied.

Chapter 12

Reunion

Chesterfield of Taddington
Derbyshire, England, the Peak District northeast of Caverswall
2 May 1795

Ensconced in her favorite window seat, amidst an array of abolitionist pamphlets and open books, Annette sat reading the most recent news page she could find.

Oh, dear. Wilberforce losing support in Parliament; French Directoire armies plundering Europe; slavery, politics, and war . . . It was all so vexing, and still she had no one with whom to discuss it.

She set the paper aside, leaned her forehead against the window pane, and watched her breath fogging up the glass.

Papá's journey to Cornwall was taking entirely too long. A new china clay for his business in fine tableware could not be so important, not when she needed him. And Gerald had been gone so long, she could hardly remember his last visit.

Her eyes drifted from the window, and she began rummaging through her discarded articles. Her sketchbook was buried somewhere.

There! She pulled it out. Studying Mr. Adsley would help take her mind off things. A smile tugged at her lips as she leafed through the pages, eight sketches in all since that night in the study.

Whatever would he think of her sketching him? She giggled, then sighed.

He would be as flabbergasted as he was in this drawing where she had captured him nearly flying off the sofa when she first entered. She traced her fingers along his cheek.

He would never see her sketches, so what harm could come of it?

In the next sketch, he was brooding. In the one after that, he was trying to hide a smile behind that mask of austere distain. But it was not working. She could read his face like a book. If only she could see him again. She rolled her eyes. Of course, she would see him at Sylvia's wedding. His brother was marrying her, after all.

She flipped pages between her loving laborer, the image of her savior from her favorite painting, and Mr. Adsley. Could he be the man who rescued her?

They had had such an engaging conversation in the study that night; at least it was to her. If Mr. Adsley was her savior, would it not be a miracle?

Annette sketched a couple lines and shaded the curls on his forehead, but her effort was half-hearted and slow.

Oh, where was Papá? She had so much to tell him, and Sylvia's wedding was only eight days away. If he did not get home soon, they would miss each other again, and she would have to wait to see him until their annual pilgrimage to Liverpool.

Closing her sketchbook, Annette drifted over to the rolling library ladder. She climbed to the top and stashed her drawings between two atlases on the highest shelf. One could never be too careful with Mother poking about.

Shimmying down, Annette plopped in the window seat and glanced out the window again. A movement caught her eye. Holding her breath, she strained to see a single horseman riding far out on the horizon.

"Oh, Papá!" A flurry of papers cascaded into the air as Annette darted out of the library. She bolted along the corridor and flew down the grand staircase.

"Annette, stop this instant!" Her mother's sharp voice halted Annette in her tracks. "One must never rush. It is unfitting."

"But Papá is home."

"That is no excuse for running about like a savage. You are a lady with the promise of many suitors." She slid an envelope into her pocket.

"Mother, please. I asked you not to speak of—"

"Silence. I will have no interruptions from you. Now observe my example."

Trying to contain her impatience, Annette watched as Mrs. Chetwynd raised her chin and, with back ramrod straight, sashayed across the polished wood floor to the entryway. "That is how a proper young lady is to walk. Now, go back up those stairs and demonstrate."

It took every shred of Annette's willpower to ascend and descend the stairs in an appropriate fashion, but she managed it.

"Better. Now, find your place outside. And mind you, I shall never see or hear of such an infraction again, or you will go back to practice with Master Coppenheim."

"That will not be necessary, Mother."

"Splendid."

A footman opened the door, and they moved outside where the entire household had assembled on the drive to greet the master. Annette scanned the line for Miss Haack but found her brother instead.

She quickened her pace. "Oh, Gerald, you are home too!" She hugged him.

"Yes. I arrived an hour ago, not knowing Father was behind me. However, I shall be in my grave straight away unless you loosen your arms from my neck."

She laughed and released him. "You exaggerate, as usual. But why not write and say you were coming? How long will you stay?"

"For a few days. Do calm yourself before Mother starts her clucking."

"She already has," Annette sighed. "Oh, but look, Papá is just coming up the drive." She clasped her hands to prevent herself from clapping. "He's here! You're both here, finally!"

Mr. William Chetwynd waved as his horse cantered up the drive.

Annette fidgeted.

He dismounted and tossed the reins to a groom, briefly greeting each member of the staff and sending them on their way. He was moving rather slowly, but he seemed well enough. When he reached Annette's mother, he greeted her with a kiss on the hand; then he turned to Gerald and offered his hand.

"Are you well, son?"

"I am, Father. We must talk later, though. This elfin creature beside me," he nodded at Annette, "can hardly wait. Brace yourself. She nearly throttled me a minute ago."

"Is that so?"

"It is. I will see to your horse with the groom. We shall speak after dinner."

"Many thanks, Gerald." Annette's father clapped Gerald on the back as he left.

"Oh, Papá, you are home." Annette rushed into his arms, closed her eyes, and inhaled his familiar cherry tobacco scent. It was mixed with linseed oil and miles of riding, but she didn't care.

"Ah, my sweet, 'tis so good to see you again," he whispered.

"I have missed you so, Papá." Tears gathered in her eyes. "It has been too long this time."

"I know. And my goodness, how you smell . . . "

"Of all the awful things to say!" Annette held Father at arm's length.

"Like my favorite orange blossom perfume, I was about to say." His eyes twinkled, and he laughed. "What did you think, my mischievous little poppet?"

"You are terrible!" She smoothed his coat lapels.

"Nevertheless, it appears you have grown taller in my absence."

Bantering with her father over her diminutive form of five feet three inches was always a source of pleasure.

"But why did you take so long? Mother has been most wearisome." She stepped away and spoke louder. "You missed Cousin Sylvia's ball as well. And what of our trip to Caverswall, for her wedding? I wrote you about it but never received a reply. It is the tenth of May, and after that we have our trip to Liverpool."

"Come, come, poppet. So many questions! Of course, we will attend the wedding. And I plan to go to Liverpool, as usual. I have already reserved our rooms at The Dove on the road to Buxton. And you will be visiting the beautiful glade you love to paint. But that is not 'til June."

"I am sorry, Papá."

"You needn't be, child. It has been a long time." Her father touched her cheek. "Now, as to the reason I was late ..." He reached into his breast pocket and pulled out a small brown package. "It took a while to get you this."

"Thank you!"

"Perhaps you should wait, Mr. Chetwynd," Annette's mother broke into the reunion. "The parlor is more suitable for opening gifts."

"Thank you, Mrs. Chetwynd." The twinkle in her father's eye dulled for a second. "But I have waited for some days to see her open this, and would not delay a moment longer."

"Certainly. I was only thinking of your health and the long journey."

"I am quite all right." Mr. Chetwynd turned back to his daughter. "Well, open it! See if it pleases you."

Annette smiled as she removed the brown paper wrapping from the small box and discovered inside an oval-shaped, gold locket on a long gold chain. She opened it and found a miniature silhouette of Papá inside.

Her eyes blurred as she inspected the fine cuts of his distinguished profile. "It is perfect, Papá."

"I had it made in London by John Miers. Do you know of him? He is said to be the best."

"Yes, I have heard of his work." She closed the locket, looped the chain over her head, and snuggled into his arms. "Thank you, Papá. I shall cherish it forever."

"I knew you would." He hugged her again and whispered into her hair. "I love you, my child, more than life itself. Remember that. I shall always love you."

"I know, Papá." She brushed away a tear and stood on her toes to kiss his cheek.

"Now off you go. Get your sketches ready. I want to see what you have been up to. And your journals. What have you been reading: Wollstonecraft, or perhaps something of Wilberforce's? What about your study of the Scriptures? Have you made any headway on the doctrine of God's sovereignty?"

"Yes to everything, generally." She tossed a smile over her shoulder as she took out her handkerchief and walked toward the stairs.

"Annette, your manners." Her mother's warning tone grated on her nerves.

"Yes, Mother." She returned to her father and gave him a proper curtsey, then flew up the stairs and disappeared behind the entry door.

⚜

"Wife, you needn't pressure our daughter. She is gracious and respectful and knows well when to use formalities. You've seen to that most effectively."

"But I have such plans for her, and there is the possibility of a suitor."

"Really?"

"Yes, and he has a title."

"A title, indeed? You know my feelings about that. 'Tis all so much pompous twaddle. Our daughter will do well enough without conniving to catch a husband."

"But he is a gentleman, Sir Steven Likebridge. And he has written a letter." Mrs. Chetwynd took it out of her pocket and handed to her husband. "I received it only yesterday."

"Thank you." Mr. Chetwynd stuffed the letter in his riding coat pocket.

"Will you not read it?"

"Later, my dear. Let us go inside. I would like to bathe, and here comes Gerald again." He motioned to Gerald to come up. "Mrs. Chetwynd, order a bath and call for some tea if you will, my dear."

"Yes, of course."

"Thank you." He turned to his son. "Come, Gerald, tell me about your studies. Are you nearly finished?"

"I will have graduated by year's end."

"Very good then. Now, what do they say about Parliament's dim view of Wilberforce fighting the slave trade? Is it trouble with France?"

Chapter 13
Reprimand

Caverswall Manor
Staffordshire, England
4 May 1795

Dark clouds gathered on the horizon, but Peter wanted to see the prospect of his father's estate one last time before his family returned from Liverpool. At the crest of the hill, he reined in his black stallion, Archangel, and studied the panorama below.

A patchwork quilt of farmland dotted with tenants' houses and newly planted fields surrounded the Manor, its stables, and the outbuildings. The adjoining Betherton land reflected the same picturesque scene. He knitted his brows. Richard would inherit all of it. Yet, however disappointed Peter might be, he was not resentful. He knew little of managing an estate and wanted even less to do with the associated financial affairs. That was the heir's job.

Even so, Peter would miss Caverswall and its people. They were a kind lot who had farmed the land for generations. They deserved a landlord who would take care of them. And therein lay the issue.

Inasmuch as Richard pretended to care about the people of Caverswall, Peter knew he did not, not really. His brother craved city life. For weeks, he stayed in London or Liverpool with little or no contact with anyone here. Peter also suspected he had run up excessive debts.

Three times in the last six months, their father had increased Richard's stipend. Peter knew, because each time he did, their father asked him if he wanted more. Naturally, Peter declined, knowing it came from the pockets of their tenants. But that did not stop Richard.

Richard's drinking had also increased, or perhaps it only seemed that way. Whatever the case, Peter knew—as did Mr. Betherton and every landowner—these shortcomings, if left unchecked, could decimate an estate, especially in these challenging times.

Suddenly, lightning split the heavens. Archangel reared up on his hind legs.

"Ho, there, boy!" Clamping his knees tight, Peter leaned forward and spoke into the frightened horse's ear. "Easy does it, Archie."

The sky, now an ocean of boiling clouds, rumbled and pitched with the wind. Peter glanced at the panoramic scene once more, a bittersweet good-bye, and gave the command.

"Giddy up, Archie. Gallop a pace."

🔺

Fear ripened in the stable's musty air as the wind howled through the rafters, scattering pigeons to opposite corners of the building.

"Get up 'n pull yourself t'gether." Richard spat the words as he adjusted his trousers. "Dull, button-nosed spinster," he mumbled. "Never should've agreed to this."

Getting to her feet, Miss Betherton brushed the hay off her skirts.

"Listen here—" He grabbed her by the chin and pulled her close. "You pitiful ..." She recoiled from his alcohol breath. "Look at me when I'm talkin' to you! This is what ya wanted, isn't it? And come Sunday you'll be gettin' it doin' your duty when I please, as I please, until ya produce a son, or the whole thing's off. Annulment, as per our contract. R'member?" His cold green eyes perused her face. "And stay quiet 'bout this little ... tête-à-tête of ours, or you'll regret it." He released her chin. "Now, turn around. Straw's in your hair."

She did, and he pulled.

"Ouch, that hurts!"

"Keep your mouth shut 'r I'll . . . "

🔺

Another angry talon slashed the sky, loosing a torrent of rain as Archangel rounded the corner of the stable and halted at the door. No sooner had Peter vaulted from his horse to open the gloomy shelter, than Archangel was inside, and Peter found himself fighting the wind to secure the door again.

But what was this? Peter found two grays—they looked like Betherton's—still saddled and eating hay from the crib. Where were the grooms? Archangel tossed his head, jangling his reigns and stamping his front hoofs.

"Say there, groomsmen, step forward," Peter called. A muffled noise came from his left, a dog perhaps. Weather like this always bothered the hounds. "Patience, Archie." Peter patted his horse's neck. "I will see where they are."

He made his way into the dimness, glancing into the first two stalls as he went. Nothing.

Suddenly, Richard emerged from the third stall.

"Hello, li'l brother, monstrous weather out there, wouldn't ya say?"

"Infernal pest!" Peter jumped. "You heard me calling. Why leap out at me thus?" He adjusted his coat. "And what are you doing here? Where are the grooms?"

Thunder burst overhead, shaking the entire building and deafening Peter to everything except the cry Miss Betherton made as she burst from the same stall

Richard had occupied. Strands of her typically neat hairstyle hung over her ears, and her disheveled pelisse was buttoned wrong.

"I sent 'em inside." Scorn dripped from Richard's words, and he leveled a disgusted look in Sylvia's direction. "Unfortunately, it's too cold for a good ride now. Don't you agree, Sylvia?" Richard snaked his arm around Miss Betherton's waist and pulled her to his side. She averted her face. "But things'll be warmin' up soon enough, won't they, my dear?"

"Say, Pete, what of our agreement regardin' the new little chambermaid, Arlene? Shall I go 'n have a word with her?"

"What have you done, Richard?"

"I said I dismissed the stablemen."

"Richard."

"Ah Pete, why so negative? She's my wife now. Can't I have a bit—?"

"The ceremony is not until Sunday."

"Who cares when the paperwork's done?"

Peter's jaw muscles tightened as he studied Miss Betherton's face. Dirt streaks on her cheeks and her disheveled appearance told him all he needed to know.

"I care."

"Go'n the house, woman." Richard grabbed Miss Betherton's riding coat, which hung on a peg outside the stall, and dumped it over her shoulders.

Anger boiled inside Peter. He clenched his fists and stepped toward Richard.

"No, Peter!" With hands raised and fingers spread wide, Miss Betherton rushed forward. "Please, nothing happened."

Richard lunged and, catching her by her hair, dragged her backward. "What do ya think you're doin'?"

She cried out, clutching at his wrist. "Oww!"

"Shut your trap," Richard hissed as he pulled her face around to his. "I told ya to get inside. Now move!"

Peter watched in what appeared to be slow motion as his brother attempted to shove Miss Betherton toward the exit but instead smacked her head-first into the large center post supporting the roof.

Her pitiful cry broke as she hit; then she fell to the floor in a silent heap.

White-hot fury exploded behind Peter's eyes. He bolted at Richard, grabbed him by the shirt, and landed his fist full force on his brother's cheek. The drunken swine toppled backward and smashed against the stable wall.

Peter rushed to Miss Betherton and cautiously turned her over. Blood oozed from her forehead, and she was unconscious. Peter rested her head in the straw and marched back to Richard. Seizing him by the collar, Peter heaved him to his feet.

"You disgraceful beast! If I ever see or hear of you treating her with such contempt—"

"What're ya gonna do, li'l brother?"

"If I even suspect she is not—"

"Come on, Pastor, le' me hear ya say it. Are ya gonna kill me like Cain did Abel?"

Rage took over, and Peter slammed his fist into Richard's jaw, landing him hard against the stable a second time. He rushed into the stall and, planting his knee on Richard's chest, grabbed him by the throat.

"You filthy lecher." Peter forced Richard down into the stable muck. "You do not deserve the breath you were given."

Richard clawed and kicked as a drowning man, but Peter did not relent. Pent up rage from years of insults flowed down through his fingers as his brother's face turned purple. Peter had had enough.

"Thou shalt not kill." The command echoed in Peter's soul, instantly giving him pause.

Gasping for air and coughing, Richard rolled onto his side as Peter stared. *Lord, I could have killed him, my own brother. I would have killed him.*

Yet, how many innocent women had suffered at Richard's hand, and now Miss Betherton too? And how many insults had Peter suffered, even since childhood? Richard was a shameful beast, an utter disgrace.

Peter watched as his brother, who had finally begun to catch his breath, rolled over and looked up.

"Why not finish the job, an' give us both some peace?" His gravelly whisper struck a chord in Peter's heart.

"It is not my place." Peter stood. "But take this warning. No harm comes to her, ever again. Do you understand?"

Peter studied his brother's glistening eyes. Finally, Richard grunted and rolled away from Peter, curling up with his face against the wall.

Peter rushed to Miss Betherton and knelt beside her to examine the angry cut on her temple. Quickly untucking his shirt, he tore off a strip of linen and wrapped it around her head in a bandage of sorts. Gathering her up in her riding coat, he lifted her from the ground. He freed the heavy wood bolt of the stable door with his elbow and pushed it open with his boot. Then he rushed out into the storm.

Chapter 14

Intelligence

Chesterfield of Taddington
Derbyshire, England
4 May 1795

After supper, Mrs. Chetwynd spied her husband in the drawing room, sitting by the fireplace and reading. Perhaps this was her chance to broach the subject of Sir Likebridge's letter again. Of course, she already knew its general content. Likebridge had written two letters, actually: one for her, which she had already read, and a formal letter of introduction for Mr. Chetwynd, which she had given him upon his arrival.

She smiled to herself. Sir Steven Likebridge had kept his end of the bargain they had made eighteen months ago at the garden party—to stay away from Annette until she was closer to marriageable age. Now, it was her turn to deliver her daughter.

"Good evening, Mr. Chetwynd." She seated herself in the chair opposite his. "Are you satisfied with the news?"

"What?" He glanced up from the page. "Oh, yes, supper was splendid, my dear."

Mrs. Chetwynd sighed. "It is a rather dull evening with the stormy weather. What say you to a game of cards?"

"I am rather occupied at the moment. You may favor me with some music, however. One never tires of Bach or Mozart."

"It would be my pleasure. Yet, I must speak with you on a matter of grave import."

He looked over his paper at her. "Is it our daughter's health? Has she been ill again?"

"No, she manages herself well enough. I cannot remember the last time she fainted."

"Very good. But what else is it?"

"Our niece's wedding. We are leaving for Caverswall on Wednesday, as you know."

"Ah yes, that reminds me." Mr. Chetwynd folded his paper and set it on the end table. "The letter you gave me, I must look at it again." He pulled it out of his inner coat pocket and studied its contents. "Apparently, the gentleman who wrote, Sir Steven Likebridge, has some connection with your sister and her neighbors, the Adsleys."

"Really?"

"Indeed. It says here... Let me find the part... Yes, this is it. He says he is lately home from travels in the Colonies—the United States and the surrounding islands, that is—and he wants to speak with me regarding our trade in fine china. Apparently, our product has made an impact over there, and he is interested in my business. But no, that is not the part."

Mr. Chetwynd studied the letter again. "Ah, here it is. He says he will be out to Caverswell from Liverpool this week for a friend who is getting married on the tenth of May, and wonders if he might meet here at Chesterfield after he has finished with his visit there."

Her husband's eyes sparkled as he spoke. "What with our niece being married on the tenth of May, it sounds as if this Sir Likebridge may be acquainted with our future nephew, Mr. Richard Adsley. What do you think?"

"How very extraordinary."

"The world grows ever smaller, wife. Knowing how wretched the roads are around here, I believe he will be quite relieved if I meet him at the wedding. Won't that be a surprise?"

"No suitor then?" Mrs. Chetwynd smoothed the armrest of her chair.

"Suitor? What do you mean?"

"Well, I thought perhaps the letter was from a—"

"I see. But I told you not to worry. Our daughter will do well enough without meddling."

"I am sure you are right." Mrs. Chetwynd took out her handkerchief. "But Annette hardly has any opportunity to meet anyone out here in the country."

"Do not distress yourself. There is no hurry. In fact, I will tell you what." He perused the letter again. "This Sir Steven Likebridge says he has been in trade these last ten years since he was eighteen. That makes him of an age to consider marriage. Therefore, after I have met him, if I deem him a fitting suitor, I will allow that Annette be introduced to him at our niece's celebration. Will that do, Mrs. Chetwynd?"

"Would you?"

"Yes, but only if he is the proper sort of Christian gentleman and one with reasonable enough intelligence, otherwise she will not have him."

"Thank you. It is most kind of you, Mr. Chetwynd."

"'Tis only an introduction, nothing more. She is too young to marry, and I will not have her wed where she does not love."

"I understand." Mrs. Chetwynd stood up. "Now for some music. Which piece would you prefer, Mr. Chetwynd?"

"Whatever you choose. Bach, perhaps."

Chapter 15

Turmoil

Betherton Hall
Staffordshire, England
8 May 1795

Annette and her mother and a few of the neighborhood's leading ladies and gentlemen, who joined them for the weekend, were out of doors exploring the grounds.

"Happily, the weather is cooperative today," Mrs. Chetwynd commented.

"Yes. Sylvia picked a beautiful time for a wedding."

"She has always had a sense for such things. Look there, your father is out and about today too."

Some distance ahead and moving toward them were Mr. Chetwynd and another gentleman. It was so good to have him home. She started to call out to him and wave, but stopped herself. The consequence of such a breach of etiquette right in front of Mother would be far more trouble than the greeting was worth. She would simply have to wait.

"He looks very well today," Annette said.

"Indeed. He told me he was very grateful for a restful sleep. He is also quite eager about his meeting with the gentleman beside him."

"Why? Who is he?" Annette looked to see if she recognized the man, but she did not. His black hair and brown skin gave him the look of . . .

They drew closer to the men.

"Father's companion has the look of a travel—"

Suddenly, her stomach lurched. She would never forget the tan skin and those cold gray eyes. "Oh dear . . . Mother—" She stared at Mrs. Chetwynd. "It's Sir Likebri—"

Mother's grip tightened around Annette's upper arm. "Yes, it is, and you will restrain yourself directly. Do I make myself clear?"

Her knees weakened, and she felt her head beginning to swim. "But you said I would never see him again. Mother, you said—"

"Stop this at once! Look around. Everyone is here. All of your aunt's guests are out, and they are watching. If you do not control yourself, your father will be ruined, and we will be the laughingstock of society."

"Remove your hand." Annette felt sparks flying from her eyes as she glared at the woman beside her. "Or you will find yourself at the center of their undivided attention."

Mrs. Chetwynd released her hold and casually continued strolling. To the outside world, it must have seemed they had merely shared a pleasant little secret as mothers and daughters often do.

"You would never do a thing to hurt your father."

"My father would approve of my behavior, especially after I tell him you believe maintaining an image for society is more important than maintaining my dignity."

"I have no control over where a man can and cannot appear."

"True. But this is your sister's and her husband's home. I should think they would have control over who comes and goes, especially after what happened the last time he was here. Therefore, I should not see him here, should I?"

Mrs. Chetwynd did not answer.

"Now, for Father's sake, I will control myself. But after this wretched little social necessity is over, I am telling him everything I know about that man and your part in this debacle. Then we will let him decide what is to be done."

"You wouldn't."

"You think not?" Annette whispered through a pleasant smile she put into place as Father and Sir Steven Likebridge approached. "Then you shall see."

"Hello, Father. The weather is glorious today, is it not?"

"It is, indeed. My new acquaintance, Sir Steven Likebridge, and I were just saying how good it is to be out after such a terrible wet season. They say it has been the worst on record." He turned to his wife. "Mrs. Chetwynd, I see the sunshine is a blessing to you as well."

"It is."

"Let me introduce Sir Steven Likebridge. He is rather interested in your favorite china pattern, *Summer Meadow*. Apparently, they cannot keep enough of it on the shelves for our American buyers."

"Yes, of course." She tipped her head and offered her hand. "It is a pleasure to meet you, Sir Likebridge."

"The pleasure is mine, Mrs. Chetwynd."

The sadistic reptile bowed over Mother's hand.

"Annette—" Father offered her his wonderful smile, but for obvious reasons, she could not enjoy it. "Make the acquaintance of Sir Steven Likebridge."

"Sir." She curtsied, but did not offer her hand.

"Your father speaks highly of you, Miss Chetwynd."

"Thank you," she responded as she looked at his boots. Then she turned to the dearest man in her life. "It is rather warm, Father, and I have failed to bring my parasol. Would it be too much of a disappointment if I went inside?"

"Certainly not. We are speaking on matters of business, anyway."

"Thank you, Father. Then, if you will excuse me." Annette curtsied again, refusing even to make eye contact with Father's companion.

"I would never wish to be the cause of any discomfort to you, Miss Chetwynd."

She cringed at the lying wretch's comment.

"I am to the house now, Mother, if you care to walk with me."

"Certainly, dearest," Mrs. Chetwynd acquiesced, but Annette could tell she was not happy. "Good day, husband and Sir Likebridge. Perhaps we shall see you at supper."

"I would be honored," Sir Likebridge responded, and Annette started walking. Mother was beside her in an instant.

"That went well enough, did it not?" Mrs. Chetwynd spoke as they made their way to the Hall. "So you needn't mention our misunderstanding to your father."

"Misunderstanding? Is that what you call it?"

"I am only concerned for his health. I would not want him to have an apoplexy over something I resolved many, many months ago."

"If you resolved it—" Annette worked to keep her rage at bay. "Why did my own dear father just formally introduce me to the rake who assaulted me on this very estate? It is utterly revolting!"

"How could I know of your father's business? He is gone often, and he tells me nothing."

Annette stopped walking. "What mother would allow this to happen to her daughter? You should have worked harder to discover his plans."

"I promise I will speak to your father about Sir Likebridge at the earliest possible moment. But we need not spoil his weekend. He has just now begun to rest well. And there is your cousin's wedding to consider. Need we mention it now, with all the festivities?"

Annette studied her mother's eyes. They appeared to be filled with legitimate concern, and her observations seemed reasonable enough.

"I understand Father's need for rest. But you must guarantee that after this weekend, I shall never lay eyes on the scoundrel again. This is imperative, Mother. Do you promise?"

"I will."

"I never even want to hear of him again."

"You have my word. I will take care of the matter."

"Then it's settled." Annette started walking. She felt a bit more secure, but her light-headedness was still skulking in the shadows. "It has been a while since I ate, and I am—"

"Is it your health?"

Annette knitted her brows and slanted a look as they reached the back entry of the Hall. "You needn't start on that, Mother. I have it under control."

"Splendid, child."

Annette glared.

"My apologies. You are no longer a child."

"Indeed."

"Well, off you go then. See if Miss Haack has reserved some of those wonderful oranges from the breakfast. I am going to play the pianoforte."

"Thank you, Mother. I will."

Chapter 16

The Sacrifice

St. Peter's Church
Staffordshire, England
10 May 1795

Peter slumped against the wall of his trunk-laden coach, feeling every bump and shudder it made as it hobbled along the muddy road to church. Today, Sylvia would marry his brother, and soon after the ceremony, Peter planned to leave for Buxton. However, the reality of what Richard had done in the stable was taking its toll.

Peter took off his hat and began circling it between his hands. Should he expose Richard? Miss Betherton's reputation would most certainly be damaged, if he did. In that case, he could marry her. But she wanted this marriage to Richard. She and her family needed it.

His father's voice echoed in his mind: *"... exercise self-control or I'll leave you to your precious parish without a single shilling."*

What would become of Sylvia as Richard's wife? Would he treat her well? What of being a good father to her children? What about when he was drunk?

"If you wanted her for yourself, you should have spoken sooner," his father had said. Why had Peter delayed?

He set his hat down and raked his fingers through his hair. The memory of the two serving women gossiping about his mother's death those many years ago flashed before him.

"If it hadn't been for how long the young Master Peter, poor babe, were in comin', she might a lived."

"Lord, if I had not been so late, Mother . . . and now Miss Betherton. God, this is my fault. If I had not been so late ..."

Peter stopped. He must collect his thoughts. He glanced up at the sky. Dark clouds threatened the weak morning sun, and a heavy mist thickened the air.

"Would you have me give up my ministry for her?"

Annette's words—her father's dictum, that is—came to mind. *"Are you being obedient or simply martyring yourself for another good cause?"*

"Lord, what a circumstance." Peter took out his handkerchief and mopped his forehead. "I do not even know her. Nevertheless, she influences me."

And it was true. Since he had discovered Annette's name from Sylvia's letter, her dazzling eyes and enchanting smile intruded at the most inopportune moments. Peter was not displeased though. In fact, he rather looked forward to seeing her again today, despite her bluntness.

If only he could resolve himself on this matter of Sylvia's marriage.

Pocketing his handkerchief, Peter checked his watch. It was ten of nine. Slipping it back in his waistcoat pocket, he glanced out the window again. Whitewashed houses with their thatched roofs dotted the landscape, offering a sense of peaceful routine and consistency. If only he could remember what that was like.

Peter bowed his head. *Parish or not, Lord, Miss Betherton is my friend, and I cannot permit my brother to hurt her. So I will protest this marriage, and if Father disowns me, I will have nothing else, except the Army. Oh, Lord, please allow me to keep my ministry.*

"Even so, if you have a different plan—though I cannot imagine what could be more important than going into the Church—I pray . . . He raked his fingers through his hair again. "Lord, this makes no sense to me." He folded his hands and looked out the window at the pasture lands. Then he sighed. "But, I pray you will thwart my plan if that is for the best."

⚜

The footman opened the coach door, and Peter stepped out. He rotated his shoulders, then donned his hat and entered the back door of the chapel. Slipping into the back center aisle pew, he added his rich baritone voice to the opening hymn.

The service progressed from the hymn directly into a prayer, during which Peter looked down at his hands, which were curled into fists. He flexed his fingers, leaned his head from side to side, and sat down after the prayer.

Flickering candles and feeble rays of sunlight fought the chapel's gloom, while a daunting mix of Caverswall's best situated themselves into the pews. Richard and Miss Betherton stepped up to the altar, and the crowd grew silent. The Reverend Sharpe—that red-faced barrel of a man whose labored breathing involved his entire body—waddled forward, adjusted his spectacles, and wheezed out the opening lines.

"Dearly beloved ... *wheeze* ... we are gathered together ..."

As he droned on, the same army of thoughts revolted in Peter's mind.

"... honorable among all men—and therefore is not by any to be ... taken in hand, unadvisedly, lightly, or wantonly, to satisfy men's carnal lusts ..."

Peter's back and neck muscles went taut. He rolled his shoulders and pulled at his collar. His time was coming next.

"... if any man can show any just cause, why they may not lawfully be joined together, let him now speak, or else hereafter forever hold his peace."

Peter took a deep breath, stood up, and cleared his throat.

"I have something to say."

Silence like a cottony fog absorbed every breath in the room. The Reverend Sharpe, Richard, Peter's father, his stepmother, Mary Hope, and the rest of the gathering—except Miss Betherton, who continued to face forward—turned with mouths agape to stare at Peter.

Choking down his heart, Peter willed himself to speak. If he maintained the ascetic, self-assured English gentleman stance his father displayed, no one would ever suspect that he would give anything to escape this scene.

"This marriage is—"

"A most splendid arrangement!" Miss Betherton said in a loud voice as she swung around to face the group. All eyes whipped back to her. "And I'm delighted that you, my soon-to-be brother-in-law, are so anxious to extend your congratulations. However, it is customary to hold them until after the ceremony. If you please, sir."

Despite her pleasant tone, Miss Betherton's eyes pleaded.

With an edgy rustle, the crowd turned back to Peter.

His heart pounded in his chest as he gripped the back of the pew in front of him. *My Lord, she has spoken up again. Is it as I requested, you are thwarting my plan?*

Peter had to think. If he did not respond in kind with jovial banter, her efforts to preclude his intrusion would be ruined. He had to act fast, trusting that this wedding, as distasteful as it was to him, was meant to be.

"Since that is the case, dear sister, let us make haste. I, and no doubt my brother, have no wish to stand on ceremony." He forced a smile and tipped his head to her. "Do excuse my impatience." He played to the audience hoping for mercy. "But one begins to anticipate upcoming festivities after sitting in these pews, even for the shortest time."

The building itself seemed to heave a sigh as a few muffled snickers and bits of gossip scuffled around the room. Miss Betherton and Richard turned back to the reverend and the guests began re-situating themselves.

Thank God, Peter had made it through that twisted affair without too much trouble, at least for now.

"An amusing interlude ..." Reverend Sharpe quipped as he adjusted his spectacles. "But do let us continue." He nodded to the groom, then turned to Miss Betherton. "Wilt thou have this man to be thy wedded husband?"

Miss Betherton must have given the expected answer, but Peter was no longer listening. His exhausted mind drifted from the ceremony into a mindless exploration of the guests on the opposite side of the T-shaped room.

He noted a cool, sidelong glance here and a few raised eyebrows there, but everyone was focused on the ceremony—everyone except a young lady with honey-colored curls spiraling along her cheeks. She sat forward in her pew, peering at him from across the room.

There was a pleasing contrast between her porcelain cheeks, the golden curls, and the rich burgundy and white trim of her pelisse. She wore ...

It was she! Annette, Miss Betherton's cousin! Peter shifted his eyes away from her and back again. His heart started beating faster, and he yielded another look in her direction.

She smiled and inclined her head.

Peter looked down at his nails for a few seconds, then glanced at the candles and out the murky windows. Lightning flashed outside, and raindrops started tapping at the glass.

God forgive him. Here he sat at Sylvia's wedding ceremony, which he had just attempted to protest, and now he was distracting himself with her cousin! From the corner of his eye, Peter could see Annette's resolute form almost willing him to look at her again—waiting, as it were, for acknowledgement. He adjusted his position in the pew and nonchalantly looked her way.

Her smile brightened, and his heart skipped a beat. Then, without warning, she sat back in her pew, or was drawn backward. The movement was rather abrupt.

Peter leaned his elbow on the end of the pew and tilted his head to get a better look. To her right sat a matronly woman, most likely her mother, considering her furrowed brows and the disapproving frown on her lips. On her left sat a polished, black-haired gentleman of some thirty years, Peter figured. Who was he?

His copper-tanned skin hinted at long-term travel, or perhaps a naval career. Might he be another cousin, or maybe Annette's older brother? She had spoken of an older brother away at university. Yet, there was no apparent camaraderie between Annette and the gentleman. Now that he thought about it, the gentleman looked rather severe, and Annette seemed somewhat ill at ease beside him.

"Who giveth this woman to be married to this man?" The question jolted Peter back.

"Her mother and I do." Mr. Betherton's gruff voice sounded from the front pew, and it was finished. Miss Betherton had sold herself to Richard in order to save her father's estate.

Peter bowed his head, which for the moment seemed to pound with dismay.

Lord, it is obvious my plan was wrong. He paused. *Forgive my self-centeredness. I have not forgotten Miss Betherton. I pray you would be with her. Yet, would you allow that Miss Chetwynd be in your plan for me?*

Peter slowly raised his head. His neck muscles were really beginning to bother him now. He rolled his shoulders and tilted his head from side to side attempting to loosen the tension in them. He must remain focused until this was over; then he would attempt to gain a formal introduction to Miss Chetwynd.

Chapter 17
Good-byes

Outside, raindrops sputtered from the sky. But the guests did not seem to mind. Caught up in the excitement, the festive group poured from the chapel, carrying Peter right along with it. When the bride and groom emerged from the vestry, joyous well-wishers shouted congratulations and threw flower petals.

Bells rang, streamers danced, and a haze enveloped Peter's mind as he watched Richard towing the new Mrs. Adsley down the steps to the carriage. Richard handed her into the coach drawn by four white horses in flowered harnesses, chomping at their bits and stamping their hooves. Then he climbed onto the drivers' bench and began tossing gold coins into the air.

Instantly, the crowd flocked around the coach. Sylvia waved through the open coach window as thunder rumbled again. The phrase "lamb to slaughter" flashed in Peter's thoughts, and pressing forward into the crowd, he stretched out his hand above all the rest.

Sylvia caught it, and for a second, the world stood still.

"Good-bye, Peter," she said as the tears slid down her cheeks. "Be happy for us both."

Trying to prolong his hold on her gloved hand a moment longer, Peter took a few steps next to the coach as it lurched forward. But her fingers slipped away.

Just then, Richard leaned down from beside the driver.

"It's over, little brother. You've lost again. Now, why don't you get along to that little parish of yours? There's nothing for you here." Then he opened the coach door, climbed inside, and closed the window.

Lightning flashed, and in a matter of seconds, a deluge broke forth.

A few desperate souls scavenged for neglected coins, but most people took cover. Peter, however, stood in the middle of the road and watched them drive away.

"Again, Lord, please keep her safe," he whispered, even as the dull pain behind his eyes clamored for attention.

When the coach disappeared from view, he turned around and all but collided with his father.

"Hold a moment, sir. I will have a word with you." His father's dark eyes sparked from beneath his bushy gray brows. He held the silver handle of his umbrella firmly in his black-gloved hand, but he did not offer Peter any coverage.

"It is fortunate you have such a friend in that young woman. Two syllables more and you would have ruined your entire situation."

Rain dribbled from the edge of Peter's hat, even as a sickening throb hammered behind his temples and a fist of anger surged in the pit of his stomach. But he maintained his composure.

"I was blessed to enjoy her friendship, Father. Now she is his. Do me the favor of seeing that he does not destroy her. Will you?"

With that, Peter turned away from Mr. Adsley and trudged up the muddy road to his coach. When his driver opened the door, Peter threw in his hat and climbed inside.

Bile stung his throat, and the pain in his temples and behind his eyes had migrated to the top of his head.

"To St. John's in Buxton," Peter snapped, and the door clicked shut. Within seconds, the coach staggered forward. Then closing his eyes, Peter leaned his head back against the cushioned seat and massaged his head with both hands.

Depending on the weather and road conditions, the journey to his new parish could take anywhere between three and four hours, a terrible predicament in view of this disastrous headache.

He reached for the window curtains, intending to block the light, but a flash of burgundy and white caught his eye, and he looked out.

"Oh no," he groaned. "Annette."

Amidst the commotion, his anger, the rain, and this wretched headache, he had forgotten her. He raised his fist to pound the ceiling of the coach ordering his driver to halt, but stopped himself.

No matter how curious he was, he could not just run over to speak with her, not here and now. Paying her any particular attention, especially in this situation, would be extremely improper. And the rain was worsening, as was the throbbing in his head.

He sighed and allowed his fist to drop, but quickly opened the window so he could see her more clearly, at least for a few seconds.

Despite the showers—he corrected himself, more likely because of them—she stood on the cobblestone path beside the church with her arms spread wide and her blissful face raised toward heaven. Her plumed bonnet drooped, her curls were limp, and the hem of her white gown was muddy. But there was no mistaking her enthusiasm.

A mournful smile crept over his lips. He would have to wait for her a while longer.

Suddenly, the young lady lowered her face from the sky and met Peter's gaze with a forlorn smile. It must have matched Peter's. She did not seem so wholly discouraged, though. In fact, she stepped into the shelter of the church's eaves and, raising one graceful, white-gloved hand as if offering some form of benediction, she called out, "Godspeed, until we meet again."

Peter shuddered. He should not have been able to hear her through the rain, yet as if they were joined by some inexplicable link, her words came to him.

He raised his hand in acknowledgement. "So be it." *My mysterious angel.*

And thus he remained watching her until the same sea-weathered gentleman who sat beside her in church came around the corner.

He must have called her—lucky him—because she immediately turned in his direction. But when he offered her his arm, Peter saw her refuse it. He offered it again, more strenuously the second time. She hesitated, but then took it.

Who was he, and what claim had he in her life? Peter did not like the look of him, nor the idea of another man . . . Did they have an understanding? What of her Season? Had it begun?

Before the gentleman could lead her out of sight, she looked back over her shoulder and waved to Peter again. Then the coach turned, and Peter lost sight of her.

He closed the window and drew the curtains. *Another missed opportunity, and another man.* He never should have allowed himself to get carried away with the crowd. Even the interaction with Father was useless.

He loosened his cravat, slumped back against the cushion, and closed his eyes against the pounding headache and sense of loss. But somewhere inside his web of despair, Peter could hear his mysterious angel whispering.

"Godspeed, Mr. Adsley, until we meet again."

Chapter 18

Counterfeit

"I do not need your assistance." Annette could hardly conceal her contempt for Sir Likebridge. His presence, not to mention that he had seated himself beside her in church, was beyond her comprehension. Yet there he was at breakfast, fawning over Mother and conversing with Father.

"I disagree."

"That is irrelevant. Now, release my hand."

"I doubt your mother would desire it. You are a sight to behold in that damp gown."

Annette watched his eyes rove to her bodice and further down where they rested long enough to stir up the dark reservoir of nausea in the pit of her stomach.

"And if she were to discover you were dancing in the mud and throwing yourself at that man, I am certain she would not approve."

"How dare you speak, after . . . ? I will tell my father what you did at once."

"Will you, Miss Chetwynd? My understanding is that he is not well. Even this morning you might have told him, but for the fact that he said he slept so very poorly, you remained quiet. Is that not true?"

Annette knitted her brow.

"The truth is your dear Papá has been unwell since his most recent trip to Bristol, if I am not mistaken."

A chill sped down her spine.

"And you wish to disturb him with some petty complaint against me, his newest partner?"

Annette wilted. Since the moment she saw him today, she had been pondering what happened when Mother sent him packing. The question plagued her now too.

"No, Miss Chetwynd, you will do nothing of the kind. And from now on, you will conduct yourself in a more amiable and proper manner, or your mother will hear of the scene I just beheld. Is that clear?"

"Tell her what you wish. I care naught." She tried to control the tremor in her voice. "You are nothing to me. And when my father is better, I am going to tell him all about you."

A laugh rumbled deep inside his chest. "I admire your spirit, Miss Chetwynd." Then he stopped their progress, and fixed her with an icy stare. "But you will remain quiet. Have you not wondered why, after our less than successful beginning, I have been welcomed back into your life?"

Her heart pounded in her ears, and fear gripped her throat. Although he seemed to expect a response, she could not answer. His words were suffocating her.

"Well, perhaps you should ask your mother. And if you claim any religious faith, you may also wish to pray for your father. It might be that he needs One more powerful to look after him. He is no longer the man he once was, and it would be a shame if something were to distress him overmuch. Do you comprehend my meaning, Miss Chetwynd?"

Annette could only nod her head as terror's talons squeezed the very life from her.

"Why certainly you do. Oh yes, and there is the matter of your upcoming trip to Liverpool. I am fully aware of the annual family outing to Liverpool. I had my men look into it. Your first stop is in Buxton at The Dove Inn. Without a doubt, you and your mother will be perfectly safe. But do you suppose your father will manage? What of all the highwaymen on the roads? One can never tell what might happen these days."

Annette's knees were melting.

"My dear young lady, you are pale and shivering." He slipped out of his frock coat and put his arm around her shoulders. "Please, take my coat and permit me to give you some support." He draped the coat over her and drew her to his side. "You seem a bit uneasy with this conversation, but I am confident you shall bear your new understanding of my position well enough, once you are used to it. We all learn to do what we must, do we not?"

For a moment, his eyes seemed to soften. "Is that better? Answer me like the affable young lady I know you to be."

"I need a moment," Annette whispered as he propelled her towards the group gathered under the roof at the back of the church.

"I am pleased to hear it. You needn't fear a thing from me. Your father will be fine, unless the Almighty chooses differently. Your mother is another story, however. By the look on her face, she desires particular satisfaction." He sighed. "I shall do my best."

"Why Sir Likebridge, many thanks for attending my daughter." Mother masked her annoyance in syrupy sweetness. "At times she forgets herself."

"It was not as bad as that."

Annette glanced up at him.

"I found her beside the church saying good-bye to a friend."

"As you can see, sir, she is a caring soul."

"More than you know, I am certain." He nodded to Annette and smiled.

"Will you be joining us for the wedding feast, Sir Likebridge?"

"Alas, I cannot, Mrs. Chetwynd. I have a previous engagement." He bowed over her hand. "I do apologize, but so goes the life of a man of business."

"'Tis a shame. You would have made an excellent addition to our party."

"Truly, you exaggerate." He turned to Annette. "But it would be my pleasure to call on you at Chesterfield, Miss Chetwynd."

"That is most kind of you, sir," she responded on cue and with such authenticity that even he must have been surprised.

"Until then, you may keep my coat. I have plenty more from which to choose."

"She would be honored," Mother interjected.

"Then, I bid you good day, ladies." Likebridge bowed again.

"Good day and safe journey," Mother called as he strode away, and Annette tried to keep from being sick.

⚔

Mrs. Chetwynd, like the numerous women Steven had served in his youth, had played right into his hand, and it offended his few remaining sensibilities. In fact, part of him loathed how he had used her and all the other women over the years. Mrs. Chetwynd's fault, however, was not enough to deter Likebridge from taking the riches she offered—her daughter, in this case. So, he brought his disgust to heel and signaled his coach driver to come.

When the coach pulled up, he quickly unlatched the door and climbed inside. Once situated, he began reviewing his exchange with the ladies.

The daggers in Mrs. Elizabeth Chetwynd's eyes bothered him. But it served the little chit right for dancing in the rain and drawing Adsley's attention like that. The last thing he needed was for the second Adsley son to develop an interest in her.

It was not that he cared about the man or the young miss, though she had blossomed quite nicely since he had last seen her. It was her dowry that caught his eye. The money pot was so large, a man looking to enter society would be a fool to overlook it. Moreover, Mrs. Chetwynd had made it abundantly clear—eighteen months ago at the Betherton garden party—that his only option was to accept their quiet arrangement or she would publicize his mishap with her daughter.

Likebridge smiled. It had taken him six months to research the Chetwynd family and to plan the attack on that girl so her mother would believe she was doing him a favor. (The beating he received from that cleric, or whoever he was, the same day was not part of his plan, but it still worked out.) Everything in his plan was developing exactly as it should. By the end of the year, he would have his estate, and he would marry Miss Chetwynd to double his wealth.

Marry Miss Chetwynd to double his . . . betrayal. Steven rested his elbows on his knees and bowed his head into his hands as the image of Lani crawling to him on her knees with her arms outstretched in that dark hut with Colonel Fontaine appeared before him.

Lani twice betrayed. Betrayer . . . betrayed, just like Mother . . . I'm betraying her again.

"No!" Steven shook his head. "Mother and Charlie are first. I cannot change that."

He pulled the curtain aside. Where was he? How much longer until he reached the inn? He beat the roof of the coach with his fist, but the noise was lost in the pounding rain. He closed his eyes and leaned against the seat cushion. He must get control of himself. His plan was nearly complete. He must put Lani aside to avenge Mother. He had no other engagement besides his appointment with Mr. Charles Adsley's destiny. Nothing would move him from his purpose. He repeated these facts over and over until the coach stopped at the inn in the next village where he had reserved a room.

Chapter 19

Ridiculous Women

St. John's Parish, Buxton
Derbyshire, England
9 June 1795

Peter wiped his forehead, planted his heel on the back of the spade, and dug in for the next shovelful of dirt. Balancing his pastoral responsibilities while toiling in a field each day was no small task. The work was invigorating, however, not to mention profitable. Soon it would help offset the expense of maintaining his new life and the small staff included with his parish.

A cow supplied milk, cream, cheese, and butter. His chickens gave plenty of eggs. As soon as he finished clearing this plot, which he was carving out of the underbrush behind the stable, it would produce vegetables. Then he would be able to support a wife.

A wife. Lord, how he wanted her here now. Having someone to manage his household while he wrote sermons would be so helpful. She could also call on the ladies. The unanticipated challenges of being an eligible bachelor were beginning to test his patience.

"Good morning, Mr. *Aaa*dsley." The shrill voice of an enthusiastic matron jarred his nerves, but he glanced toward her. "The weather's quite lovely, is it not?" she called as she wiggled the rusty iron latch on the courtyard gate.

Lord help him. *Mistress Hoot Owl* and her daughters had just come 'round an hour ago! It was not her actual name, of course. Peter could not remember it at the moment. But her large blinking eyes, pinched lips, and round face reminded him of an owl. She was waving a white handkerchief and hushing her daughters as they squeezed in beside her. Peter sent up a prayer and nodded. Thank Heaven he had locked the gate.

"What's that you say, Mr. Adsley? I could not quite hear you."

Peter forced the shovel into the dirt so it would stand alone and dusted off his hands. "Nothing, madam. I was praying."

Her gloved hand shot up to cover her mouth, and she started blinking like a hoot owl. Oh no, ruffled feathers. Peter pasted on a smile. "But the weather is comfortable, and you ladies look as charming as a spring morning."

"Why thank you, Mr. Adsley," Mistress Hoot Owl preened.

"You are quite welcome. I must get on with my work now. A pleasant stroll to you." He bowed and reached for his spade.

"But it was our intention—" Another voice chimed in, but was cut off by a third one.

"We want to know if you are attending the assembly tonight."

Peter turned to watch their peculiar display.

"You ruined everything, Penelope!" The shorter daughter hissed as she stamped her foot and began pouting. Frowning, Penelope elbowed her sister, and Mistress Hoot Owl's face puckered and turned beet red. All the while, her white handkerchief flailed about in double time as the matron attempted to hustle her daughters away.

"Good day to you, ladies," Peter called.

He dug deep into the dirt for another load. *Ridiculous ladies! Husband-hunters on the prowl, more like. Forgive my impatience, Lord, but surely other bachelors are about. Could not the ladies pursue them instead?*

Suddenly, Miss Chetwynd's face invaded Peter's thoughts. He lost his footing, then his balance. Miss Chetwynd's eyes twinkled all the more and her impish little grin appeared. She was laughing at him, something she would likely do if she was here. Peter smiled.

He bent to retrieve his spade, but paused. Surveying the ten rows of dark furrowed earth that lay ready to be seeded, he decided it was time for a break. He stalked over to a dilapidated bench under the poplars. Stretching out and crossing his legs, he interlaced his fingers behind his head and closed his eyes to savor the memory of Miss Chetwynd. He imagined himself running his fingers along her smooth cheek as she smiled up at him.

Hold. His conscience ended the reverie. Dwelling on her outward appearance told him nothing of her heart. Was she even the sort of lady to be a pastor's wife? Analyzing sermons, discussing philosophy—or the slave trade—certainly posed no challenge. But had she a passion for sharing God's love? What of the stamina required for managing a household while supporting a congregation? A life of ministry, as Peter was discovering, was not easy, and it was unlikely she had experience serving. How could she? For pity's sake, Peter hadn't any either, not really. Making the rounds for Caverswall tenants was different. They were like family to him.

Family. Lord willing, he and Miss Ch—well, whoever his wife was to be—would have children . . .

Peter forced himself to stop the carousel of thoughts he had been considering since last he had seen her. He had no time for them now. He needn't wait much longer to discover the truth, either.

Three days hence, he would return to Caverswall for Richard's twenty-seventh birthday. Mother had written to ask specifically, and he could not disappoint her. While he was home, he would speak to Sylvia regarding her cousin. In the meantime, he must finish this garden and seed the plot before Friday.

Peter sat up, stretched, and inhaled deeply.

"Eghh!" Dirt, sweat, and the stench of the stable muck he had been using to fertilize his garden permeated him, and he was hungry.

Peter glanced to the back of the property. Hidden in the woods behind the parish was an enticing pool, one of the healing springs for which Buxton was so famous. He had seen it last week when he was out riding Archangel. A dip in that pool and some food was just the thing.

He reached for the luncheon bundle his housekeeper had made and . . .

Housekeeper? Goodness! Here she came now, traipsing across his newly furrowed garden. Why should she be here? He jogged over to the elderly lady.

"Mrs. Striklin, please, you needn't have come all this way."

"I have a letter for you, sir, and there's a messenger 'waitin' your response." Her voice trembled as she extended a wrinkled paper in a shaking hand.

"Thank you." Peter stuffed the folded page in his pocket and took the woman's hand. "But please, let me escort you back."

"I can walk on me own." She pushed his hand away.

"All right, but be careful. Please."

"Enough of your fussin'. I've been walkin' a mite longer than you, and I think I've got it down by now."

"Yes, of course."

"Just read your letter and come back to the house afore that messenger boy starts causin' trouble."

"I will as soon as I can, Mrs. Striklin."

His housekeeper did not respond. She was making her way back across his furrows.

Peter took out the letter and glanced at the handwriting. It was his father's. Odd. What could he want that could not wait 'til Friday?

Peter broke the seal and read. He blinked and reread the page.

Effective immediately, you are relieved of your pastoral responsibilities at Buxton. Return home at once.

Chapter 20

Betrayal

Approaching Buxton, near St. John's Parish
Derbyshire, England
9 June 1795

Anger-tinted fear simmered behind Annette's composed face. Every muscle in her back, shoulders, and neck was strung so tightly she could hardly move as the coach bounced along the pitted road.

Why had she allowed Mother to explain away Sir Likebridge's original assault? If only she had told Father the day he introduced them at Sylvia's wedding. She could have refused to meet him and answered questions after the fact. That would have saved her this present anguish.

Now, here they were—mother, father, daughter, and Lucy—lurching down the mountain road from Chesterfield to Buxton on their annual journey to Liverpool, while Mother chattered on about Sir Likebridge as if he were a prince. But Annette could do nothing to stop it. She must act cordial, or he would find out. Likely his men were right behind them or along the road somewhere.

Had the rake told them to kill Papá? Were they watching this very moment? Was Sir Likebridge waiting for them at The Dove? Annette was not certain, but the choking terror mixed with rage against Mother was very real indeed.

Annette looked over at her father and chomped down on her tongue. His gray head rocked back and forth as he leaned against the wall of the coach and looked out the window. His skin had a greenish tint. If she drudged up all the sordid details of the garden party— of the entire wretched affair—here in the coach with Lucy, Papá might succumb to an apoplexy. And who knew what Mother would do?

She leaned her head against her side of the coach and willed her ears not to hear her mother's relentless worship of the beast.

God, where are you?

Until this very instant, she had not thought of Him. But it seemed that He should know about this if He cared as much as Papá said He did.

God, please help me. I am afraid, and I know naught what to do. Please, I need you.

White plaster houses with thatched roofs appeared along the road. They would reach Buxton's Dove Inn soon enough. Then, she would be free, at least for a little while.

"So, my beautiful canary . . . " Annette glanced up from the brushes and paints she was unpacking to see Papá peeking in the door of the humble upstairs chamber she and Lucy would share. "Off for some painting, I see."

"Yes. But I am no songbird, not after today's ride."

"Do not contradict me, child, especially while wearing that yellow frock."

"Yes, Papá."

"Come now, give me a little peck." He offered his cheek, which still appeared to have a rather greenish tint, and she came to him. "I am going to rest before supper."

"Are you well, Papá?" She studied his glassy eyes. Their familiar twinkle had faded. "Shall I call for a physician?"

"No, no 'tis nothing. Only I could do with some rest and quiet, after being jolted about while listening to your mother's prattle." A grin played at his weathered smile.

"Indeed. But why let her go on? One word from you would have silenced her."

"Ah, little poppet, you mustn't fret. Sometimes, it is best to let her talk. Be assured, though, you need not marry where you do not love. I will not permit it."

"Thank you, Papá. Now, rest yourself before the next round."

"Rest indeed, but there will be no more rounds. Your Mother has had her say; next, the Lord will have His way. You can be certain of it." With that, he kissed Annette on the forehead and headed down the hall, trudging slowly.

"Sleep well, Papá."

"I will, dear girl."

"Now see there, Miss Canary." Miss Haack drew Annette's attention. "Your Papá will look after you, no matter what that mother of yours says."

"I know . . . " Annette picked up her shoulder bag with her secret sketchbook inside, slipped the strap over her head, and turned toward the door.

"And where might you be going?" Mrs. Chetwynd stormed into the room, forcing Annette to step back.

"I am . . . We could use a walk, Mother."

"To where?"

"The forest glade. I visit it every year. Miss Haack and I are going to explore again," Annette answered, emphasizing that her chaperon was going along.

"Make certain you take some food. It would be most inconvenient to go wandering around the grove trying to retrieve you if you faint." Mrs. Chetwynd turned to Lucy. "Miss Haack, keep an eye on her. She is nothing unless I can vouch—"

Annette felt fire shoot through her chest. "Vouch for what, Mother?"

Mrs. Chetwynd's face went red. "You will not speak to me thus."

"Indeed. I will not speak with you." Annette attempted to push past her mother, but Mrs. Chetwynd blocked her from leaving.

"Your father has done you a great disservice, young lady. I am merely attempting to remedy it."

"By lying to me?" Annette pushed her mother to the side and stormed out of the room.

"Well, he has a title and . . ." were the last words Annette heard as she lifted her canary skirt, then flew down the narrow staircase and out into the afternoon sunlight.

Tears streaming down her cheeks, she ran toward the forest.

⚔

"Make haste, Lucy! Go after her!"

"Right away, Mistress. Just let me get these things."

"Hurry. She must not be left alone."

"Yes, Mistress." Lucy grabbed the easel and canvas. The palette, brushes, and paints were already secured in the bag she had strapped across her back.

In a sort of dance—first right, then left—Mrs. Chetwynd attempted to move around Lucy, but there was not enough space.

"Forgive me, Madam. But if you'll step to your left, I'll be on my way."

Mrs. Chetwynd's cold eyes flickered. "Very well. But you must hurry. If you do not find her within the next quarter of an hour, come back so we can send a footman to locate her. Everything is lost if I cannot guarantee her reputation. Now, find her."

"Yes, Mrs. Chetwynd." Lucy curtsied and was out the door.

Chapter 21
Found

Peter read his father's message for the third time, then crumpled the page and shoved it in his pocket. He raked his fingers through his hair and started pacing.

Dispatched from ministry? How on earth? What could he possibly have done, or failed to do, that merited such drastic action?

He headed toward the stable, striding through the underbrush at the edge of the field. He would speak to his father's messenger this minute. Father had no right to—

Without warning, Peter's foot caught on a hidden obstacle, and he was launched forward into a fall. Stifling a curse, he caught himself, but the maneuver did nothing to improve his patience. Whipping around to find the offending object, Peter groped through the undergrowth and discovered an old ale jug half buried in the dirt. Grabbing it by the neck, he heaved it up and hurled it against the stable wall.

The explosion of pottery shattering against the plaster wall of the parish stable and Peter's angry roar sent a flock of sparrows into frenzied flight. When the rustle of their flapping wings faded, Peter thought he heard the faint, yet unmistakable sound of a woman crying—wailing actually.

He stopped and listened. His anger was instantly replaced with apprehension. Had some danger befallen Mistress Hoot Owl and her daughters?

He heard the noise again. It was most definitely a woman's cry, and it seemed to be coming from the woods at the back of the property. He must attempt to help.

Running toward the sound, in one fluid movement, Peter swung himself over a split-rail fence and kept going. Flying over a fallen tree trunk and ducking around branches, he rushed forward. Large ferns and other bushes surrounded the area so he could not see her, but if he followed her cry, she should not be too hard to locate.

He paused to listen again, but could scarcely hear for the thunder of his pulse pounding in his ears. Moving ahead, Peter startled a flock of quail that burst from the grass. The jittery birds circled in the trees, their terrified chirps overwhelming her cries.

"God, help me find her."

Some yards ahead, he glimpsed a splash of bright yellow and stopped to get a better look. Stepping closer, he concealed himself beside an ancient oak tree.

Looking out from the shadows, Peter spied a young lady in a bright yellow dress, down on her hands and knees in the glen. The vivid fabric lay in a rumpled mass around her, and she was sobbing.

Thankfully, she did not appear to be suffering any physical pain. But how peculiar. Were there not other more convenient places for a lady to voice her anguish?

Peter scanned the area. Nothing seemed amiss. But she was alone. What had befallen her? Had she lost something? Was she ill?

Peter leaned against the tree's gnarled trunk and studied the scene as she wiped her tears and arranged herself in a sitting position with her back to him, just a few steps away from a marble bench. Golden shafts of light illuminated the swaying grasses. Tiny dandelion seeds floated on the delicate haze that enveloped the natural arena. A cheerful stream emptied into a crystal pool, and it dawned on him that this picturesque amphitheater overlooked the healing spring where he had intended to bathe. What an amazing coincidence, though he did not believe in such a thing. But back to the task at hand.

He studied the young lady. Bright dress, elegant coiffure: clearly, she was not one of Mistress Hoot Owl's party. Nor was she a village girl. He would have noticed her before. Nevertheless, what she was doing out in the woods, crying?

Peter allowed his eyes to peruse her a while longer.

Apparently, she had taken a book out of her bag and was reading now, though it was impossible to tell with her back to him. Gossamer strands of golden hair gently played along her neck. His gaze drifted to the exposed skin of her upper back, producing unexpected warmth in his chest. Then his heart flipped, and he could hardly draw breath.

He knew her! Lord, it was she, Miss Chetwynd! Or at least he thought it was.

Peter leaned forward, attempting to analyze and match every detail of this young lady's person with those cherished features that haunted his memory.

Surely, this girl was Miss Chetwynd. Yet how? She lived in—

Peter thought for a moment. She must have been visiting for Sylvia's birthday. Could Buxton be her home? Yet, if Buxton was her home, where was her chaperon? No worthy companion would leave a young lady like her unattended. And what terrible grief had she to bear all alone?

He rubbed his chin. Had he stumbled upon a tryst gone wrong? He shook his head, hating himself for thinking it. But he could not exclude the idea, not entirely, not after their first meeting in the guest study at Sylvia's house.

Peter clenched his teeth and looked at her again. Why was she here alone? Whatever the reason, Peter must know.

Abandoning his hiding place, Peter stepped into the clearing and walked up behind her. She turned abruptly and gave a sharp cry, attempting to scuttle to her feet and dropping her book. Then she started to run, except her foot caught in her tangled gown and she flailed forward.

Peter lunged ahead, caught her around the waist, and drew her back against his chest, effectively thwarting the fall. He was about to congratulate himself on sparing her a possible injury when she started kicking and screaming.

His first reaction was to drop her like a clawing cat. But if he did, she might truly hurt herself. So he tightened his arms around her, put one hand over her mouth, and leaning his cheek against her head, spoke into her ear.

"Please, Miss Chetwynd, cease your kicking." He felt her tense in his arms. "Please, my dear lady, I mean you no harm."

She stiffened in his arms and quieted herself.

"Thank you. It was not my intent to startle you. But I heard you crying."

He felt her relax against his chest.

"I will remove my hand, but you must remain quiet. Since I heard your screams, they may have alerted someone else . . . And I hate to think of it, actually, but do you understand what could happen if we are discovered? It would go very poorly for us."

She nodded her head and murmured consent. He loosened his arms, but all coherent thought seemed to crumble as he did. Those golden curls so soft against his cheek and her delicious orange fragrance enveloped him.

"Mr. Adsley? Mr. Adsley, of Caverswall Manor, is it truly you?"

He gazed into her luminous eyes and tried to speak, but no words came. She swayed a little herself, and Peter automatically drew her closer.

"You are here," she whispered.

With their faces a breath apart, he drank in every detail of her. Even with red splotches and tear-streaked cheeks, she was stunning.

"Dear me, sir." She crinkled her nose as she pushed away from him. "Have you been mucking out a barn?"

Still he could not speak.

She lowered her eyes to the front of her dress, and Peter followed her gaze to the grass stains and mud smears covering it. She glanced back up at him and blushed. "It appears that I am no better off. Now, if you will excuse me. You have caught me quite . . . Well, rather at a bad time."

Her brows tilted in a mournful arch. Then she made for the bench, stumbling to its edge and burying her face in her arms.

↟

Surveying his own appearance, Peter raked his fingers through his wild mane, which was falling out of its queue, and stared at his dust-covered shirt and trousers. Even his fingernails were blackened. Merciful heaven, what must she think of him, mucking out a barn. It was far worse than that.

Seating himself on the bench, Peter looked down at the honey-colored curls along her neck. "Please, I did not mean to be so rude. I had hoped . . . It's only that . . ." He took a deep breath. "Please, Miss Chetwynd, you mustn't start crying again."

She did not respond.

Peter dug into his pocket for a handkerchief and muddled on as best he could. "Here, will you not take this? It is not much, but the gesture should account for something." Still no answer.

He reached out to touch her bowed head but pulled his hand back just in time. The plaintive sound of a lady crying—her crying—crushed his very soul. How he wanted to help, but he could do no more here, now. He bowed his head. *I am helpless against her tears. Lord, will you not soothe her distress?*

Tilting his head from side to side and stretching his neck muscles, he continued praying for her. When he finally opened his eyes, he found Miss Chetwynd watching him.

"Thank you," she sniffed as she cautiously pulled the handkerchief from his fingers. "'Tis a bit dusty, but it will serve the purpose very well." With that, she began making muffled little trumpet noises as she used it to blow her nose—right there in front of him.

Feeling rather uneasy, Peter looked for some other employment besides studying every detail of the living Miss Chetwynd. He noticed her book. It lay open and face-down in the grass, so he stepped over to pick it up. As Peter stood up, he glanced at the page, and then his head began swimming.

Utterly flabbergasted, he stared at the drawing in front of him. He flipped to the next page, the next, and the page after that. Looking up from her sketchbook, Peter's eyes collided with Miss Chetwynd's, and the book slid from his grasp.

"I suppose I must be the one to apologize now," she said with a sheepish grin. "I am sorry for sketching you without permission, and I regret you had no warning about my work. But how could I have known you would find it? No one has seen, not even Miss Haack."

"Miss Haack?" Peter could hardly comprehend what she was saying, let alone remember a Miss Haack, whoever she was.

"Miss Haack is my companion. Years ago she was my nurse."

In as many years as Peter could remember, he had never experienced any nervous complaints of the stomach or weakness of the knees, but if he did not get back to that bench that instant, he was certain he would drop where he stood. So he sat down.

"My sketches are rather good likenesses, would you not agree?"

Peter stared as she retrieved her sketchbook and re-situated herself on the grass. She smiled once she was settled.

"Please, say no more."

"As you wish. I shall study my sketches while you collect your thoughts."

He bowed his forehead into his hand. The situation was inconceivable. Here she was alone with him, again, and in a forest, no less. And she had drawn at least eight perfect sketched images of him. Circumstances could hardly be any worse. Strike that; things could be far worse.

"Lord, what am I to do?" he whispered.

"You could accept my apology." Her voice flowed over him like warm bathwater. "'Tis your Christian duty to do so, is it not?"

Something rumbled in his chest. He raised his face and, with brows knitted, attempted to show his dismay. His effort proved ineffective, however. As soon as their eyes met, his heart, if not his face, softened. Peter stood up and started pacing.

"I am sorry, Mr. Adsley, truly I am. It was wrong of me to place you in such a complicated situation and use you this way. But I could not help it."

Use him? Lord, if she only knew.

He stopped pacing and looked down at her. Was it Providence? Had the Lord something in mind by bringing them together once more? Peter seated himself on the bench. "It's of no consequence. You needn't apologize." How he wanted to take her hands in his and tell her how many times he had thought of her since their last missed encounter. Oh, how he wanted to ask all of his questions, but he didn't.

"You needn't be dishonest again. I have upset you, as it seems I am in the habit of doing."

"'Dishonest again'? What do you mean?"

"You were not being truthful when you said my sketches were of no consequence. They worry you. You dismissed me the same way when you told me you were pleased to meet me on that first night, though you could hardly wait to escape me. I am grateful for your indulgence, Mr. Adsley, but I anticipate the day you will allow yourself to speak more freely." Her mesmerizing eyes sparkled and her lips tilted into a perfect smile. "Now tell me, why must you do anything?"

"What?"

"I presume you were just praying about what you must do now that you have seen my drawings. So I asked why you must take action of any sort." Stray honey-colored curls danced along her creamy cheeks, and orange blossoms taunted his senses.

"Your drawings are rather disturbing." In fact, many things about her were disturbing, and they all befuddled Peter. Yet, he felt a certain partiality for her intrepid behavior. If truth be told, he would be disappointed if she were more predictable. She had a genuine passion for life he had to admire, even if it worried him.

"Disturbing to you, perhaps. I take great pleasure in them. But why must you do something? They never bothered you before."

He raised his eyebrow. "I knew nothing of them before."

"And now that you do, they have become indecent or improper? I do not understand how your knowledge of them could make them so."

Torn between captivation and shock, Peter watched her put the sketchbook back inside her bag and slip the strap over her head. Then she looked up at him again.

"I told you, no one else knows about them. And they never will."

"Indeed."

"You do not trust me?"

"That is not the issue."

She held her hands out to him. "Please, will you help me up? I would prefer discussing the issue, as you call it, in a more equitable location, say perhaps on the bench beside you rather than kneeling at your feet?"

"Yes, of course." Peter choked back a laugh, but paused when he saw how filthy his hands were. "But . . . "

She glanced at her own hands, and then smiled. "You needn't worry; mine are nearly as bad. In fact, we are both a wretched jumble, but it matters naught. I would rather be at your side than at your feet."

"Without a doubt," he answered as he stood up and took her hands, lifting her nearly weightless form to her feet. Then he froze.

A tingling sensation raced through his fingertips and up his arms. Her skin was like silk beneath his thumbs. He attempted to clear a lump that had formed in his throat, but the heat radiating from her touch made it nearly impossible to remember how. So he simply stood there, holding her hands and gazing down into her eyes.

"Mr. Adsley? I say, Mr. Adsley, may I have my hands back now?" Her eyes twinkled as she smiled, but before he could think of how to release his grasp, there was another disturbance.

"My lady, Miss Chetwynd, what goes on here?" The shout came from his left.

Peter jumped and shot a glance that way, only to find a rather large woman with a cumbersome bag slung over her shoulder barreling toward them. Peter's stomach turned.

"Do not worry, 'tis only Lucy," she whispered through a smile. "All will be well; I promise." He felt the gentle pressure of her fingers squeezing his. Then she slid her hands away from him and stepped back.

Chapter 22
Captivated

'*Do not worry. All will be well?*' How could he not? The entire situation was one worry atop the next, and it kept getting worse. A man could not be alone with a young lady unless he were proposing. And this Lucy, her missing chaperon, presumably, had seen him holding the young lady's bare hands.

"Where have you been, dear? I've been looking for you everywhere." She rushed between them and encircled her charge with two substantial arms. "Are you hurt?"

"No." She tried to escape her chaperon's clutches. "Please, nothing is wrong, Lucy."

"That's not the way I see it." The chaperon eyed Peter. "What happened to your dress?" She took Annette's face in her hands. "And your face?" She licked her thumb and started rubbing at the dirt smudges. "You mustn't run off like that. Your mother is—"

"Stop niggling, Lucy. You are my companion, not my nurse, and there is a gentleman present."

"A fact of which I am well aware." She threw Peter a look that might have crumbled a statue's frozen smile, and Peter knew he must act immediately to content this chaperon or Mistress Hoot Owl's constant annoyances would be the least of his concerns.

"Pardon me, madam. Since the young lady's well-being has been established, let me apologize for these inconvenient circumstances." He paused to measure the effect. Good, at least he had gained Lucy's attention. "I am Mr. Adsley, the new pastor at St. John's."

"Pastor?" Miss Chetwynd stared at Peter. "When did that happen?"

He smiled. For once, he had caught her off guard. "I believe it was settled in eternity, but I moved here to St. John's last month after your cousin's wedding. You saw me leaving. Remember?"

"I do, but I never thought you were a pastor."

"Does that present some difficulty?"

"No, I simply had no idea—"

"Be that as it may, my dear—" Her chaperon interrupted. "Pastor Adsley was attempting to persuade me that I have nothing over which to worry. May he continue now?"

Annette gazed at her nurse for a second. "Yes, yes, of course. But Lucy, he is a pastor."

"Yes, I am, and as I was about to say, while I was furrowing out my garden, I heard a commotion, a woman crying, actually, and I ran as quickly as I could to see if I might be of assistance." He glanced down at his filthy work clothes. "Do forgive my unusual attire, but I thought it best to hurry." He turned to his eager little artist and noted her mischievous eyes laughing again. "I hope there is no permanent damage."

"Thank you, Mr. Adsley. As for my dress, let us simply say my maid has been known to work miracles."

"Indeed?" He stifled his smile. How could she do this to him? One moment his nerves trembled and he was frayed with apprehension; the next he was filled with delight.

"She most certainly does. Now for introductions: this is my companion, Miss Haack."

It is a pleasure to make your acquaintances." He bowed, and Miss Haack grunted.

"Now, if I may be so bold, Miss Chetwynd, why were you so distressed when I found you?"

"We must get back now." Miss Haack spoke up. "Your mother will be worried."

"I will escort you to wherever you are going, Miss Haack. Miss Chetwynd may tell us her story as we walk, if you please."

"Certainly, I will be happy to explain," Annette interjected, but Miss Haack did not look too pleased.

"You should also be aware, Mr. Adsley, since you are a pastor, I am counting on you for some spiritual guidance."

Give her spiritual guidance? At the moment, he was not even sure how to resolve his own troubles, let alone help with hers.

"Is there some problem, Mr. Adsley?"

"Yes. What? Oh ... I mean no. There is nothing wrong."

"You seem a bit distracted."

"Forgive me. Please continue." He pushed a branch out of the pathway to make more room for them to pass.

"Certainly. I was about to explain that I was coming to paint this beautiful little grove of yours while the light was still good. You see, Miss Haack has brought my easel and painting supplies with her." She gestured to her companion's burdens. "But then I became so distraught over a quandary into which I had stumbled that I rushed into the forest ... for some privacy."

"Is there something with which I may help?"

She laid her hand on his arm. "I haven't the least desire to discuss it now, but when I do, I will consult you."

"As you wish, but—" *Heaven help me, I want to know everything about you.*

"Do let us continue walking. It is getting cooler, and you must hear the rest of my story." She removed her hand and continued down the path. He matched his steps to hers.

"Now, as I was about to say, I heard a fearsome noise, a man's tormented howl, if you will, and a loud crash. It frightened me, so I started to run, but then I tripped and fell into some mud. You found me shortly thereafter."

Peter offered her his hand so she could step over a branch that was lying across the pathway. He assisted Miss Haack as well.

"Really Mr. Adsley, as a pastor, you must know the man who cried out so pitifully. Without a doubt. He is already under your care, is he not?"

"Yes, Miss Chetwynd, I am well acquainted with him."

"I am glad of it. He seems much in need of your care, as I was before you entered the glade and helped me realize that all would be well." She turned to her chaperon. "The rest of my story is quite simple, Lucy. You came up, we had our introductions, and now we are walking back. Is that clear, Lucy?"

Peter noted the slightest bit of an authoritarian tone in Miss Chetwynd's voice.

"So it would seem." Her chaperon sighed.

"Well, I am sorry for your ... accident, but I am glad to have been of service, ladies."

As much as Peter would like to have relayed his own story, it would be most unfitting. And since it appeared that he had survived the chaperon's scrutiny, he did not want to risk more.

Just then Miss Chetwynd lost her footing. Peter quickly caught her around the waist.

"Thank you, Mr. Adsley," she sighed. Her lashes fluttered, and her face grew pale. "As you can see, I am quite all right. Despite my present clumsiness, however, I haven't any trouble dancing."

"It is very fortunate, Miss Chetwynd, that you can dance. I am certain many a gentleman would be sorely disappointed if you could not."

She gave him a rueful little smile and swayed toward him.

At this juncture, Miss Haack interjected, "We are most grateful for your assistance, Mr. Adsley. But this is our road. I will take Miss Chetwynd from this point. We are quite capable of continuing on our own." Her eyes sharpened, and Peter promptly released Miss Chetwynd into her arms. But he did not like the idea. She seemed terribly weak, and he feared for her safety.

"Just a moment, Lucy. I am not finished." Miss Chetwynd leaned her forehead against her companion's. "Please, I need a few more minutes with him."

"But what am I to do with you? I can tell you have not eaten. And what of this pastor? Who is he?"

"Please, 'tis just for a minute or two."

"Did you bring your comfits?"

Annette shook her head.

"No? Then I should take you home this instant."

"Lucy, please. I know you have them with you. Give me one."

"Here then." Miss Haack dug in her pocket and handed Annette something, which she immediately ate. "Now lean on this tree for a bit, and let it do its work. But it will not last long. So be quick."

"Thank you, Lucy."

"Mr. Adsley—" Miss Haack's voice was firm. "If you will, I need your assistance."

"Absolutely. How may I be of service?"

"Help me off with these painting things. You can carry them for me."

"Yes, of course." He took the easel and bag from Miss Haack.

"Now, see that you stand beside her. If she starts to faint, help her sit down. I will be over there by the hedge." She gestured a short distance down the road.

"Certainly. Is there anything else?"

"No. She should be fine, but do not waste her time." With that, she walked away.

He placed his hand on the tree Miss Chetwynd was leaning against, and stepped closer to her. She was so beautiful and vulnerable. He had the deepest desire to whisk her away and keep her safe forever.

"What are you thinking, Mr. Adsley?" She looked up at him and smiled. Her right cheek bulged with the sweet she was eating. "You seem to have left me for another world."

"No, it is nothing of the kind, but I apologize." He could not tell her, not now and not here. He must get to know her better. Yet, he was so pleased he could hardly speak.

"I accept your apology. And see—just as I told you—I am well. Now, back to the topic of spiritual guidance, do you recall?"

"I do. But you if you are ill, you needn't speak of it."

"I am fine."

"But you—"

"Please, sir." Her eyes were desperate. "It is a simple matter. If I go too long between meals, I faint. That is all. And I have it under control."

Suddenly, a bolt of lightning exploded in his thoughts. This must be what had happened to her when he rescued her from that wretched swine in the chapel. "Are you under a physician's care?" His tone was too sharp, and she drooped.

Suddenly, he had the overwhelming desire to comfort her, to take her in his arms and hold her. But he fought the urge. Miss Haack would never tolerate such familiarity, and in all honesty, he hardly knew Miss Chetwynd, not the way he must if she was to be his wife.

Probing the depths of her crystal blue eyes, he spoke. "Forgive me. That was a most ill-mannered question, but I find I am quite anxious about your health."

"You needn't be. The sugar comfit will hold me for now. But, please, you must listen."

Peter could hardly think straight, let alone listen. However, her coloring had improved, and her speech sounded sharper.

"I will do my best, though you have given me quite a fright."

"It seems I am in the habit of doing that too." She grinned.

"So you are."

"Now, about that unfortunate man who cried out, you must assure me that you will consult with him. He needs your guidance and that of the Almighty, if He will involve Himself."

Peter flinched. Did she just question God's interest in humanity? Or was it that the unfortunate man would not want to involve himself with God? Peter studied her eyes and her lips, and the thought faded.

"I will, Miss Chetwynd. You have my word." Peter looked over to Miss Haack, who was intently studying a blossom. "But what of the sketchbook and the drawings?"

"I promise I will keep them safe." She patted her bag.

"Splendid. Though I am uncertain as to how that reflects on your chaperon's skill as a watchful companion."

"I thought you would be happy for her . . . liberality."

"I am," he whispered, and she giggled. "But what if you faint, and she finds the drawings?"

"They are safe. You must trust me."

Peter yielded with a heavy sigh. "All right. You have won, but please keep them hidden. Neither of us can afford to have them discovered."

"As you wish."

He leaned forward slightly and inhaled her orange blossom scent. *What would it be like to kiss her?*

"I see you are finished," Miss Haack said, and Peter jerked back to find the chaperon eyeing him. "We must leave now. You may keep the paint supplies at the parsonage until our footman comes, Mr. Adsley. I'll dispatch him as soon as I can."

"Yes, of course, Miss Haack." Peter bowed. "I am pleased to have made your acquaintances."

"As we are at having made yours." Miss Chetwynd smiled as she looped elbows with her companion. Then Miss Haack whisked her away.

In keeping with her usual enthusiasm, Miss Chetwynd looked back over her shoulder and smiled before they disappeared from view.

Suddenly, it occurred to Peter that he had not asked where Miss Chetwynd lived. He took a couple steps after them but stopped. Was it wise for him to seek her out? Would her boldness and lack of reserve make for a proper pastor's wife? And what of her comment about God's willingness to involve Himself? Who knew what she meant by it? Hopefully, she was referring to the man's refusal to involve himself with God. And what of her illness, if it could be called such? She faded so quickly. Apparently, it only happened if she went too far between meals. That could happen to anyone. He had so many questions.

Peter would wait, for now, but as soon as her footman came for her painting supplies, Peter would find out where they lived. For that matter, he could ask his housekeeper or the cook about the Chetwynds. They were bound to know where the family resided.

Peter lifted Miss Haack's bag with the easel, canvas, and paint supplies and headed back toward his parish's stable. He would leave her things with John, his stable hand, and then he would bathe and prepare to meet her footman.

Suddenly, Peter's musings came to a grinding halt, and the terrible message from Father rang in his head. He had been relieved of this parish and was commanded to return home at once. Had Mrs. Striklin said there was a messenger waiting too?

Well, Peter would send him right back to his father with a simple answer: NO. Peter had no intention of leaving his parish, especially since Miss Chetwynd was here.

Chapter 23

Strategy

The Dove Inn, Buxton
Derbyshire, England
9 June 1795

"Ssst. Annette, you mustn't turn around. 'Tis not fitting to look back." Miss Haack pulled Annette to the side of the lane. "You are not listening to me."

"I heard every word you said, Lucy. But I cannot help it. Mr. Adsley is such a singular gentleman. Did you not see how kind he was?"

"I did, but that is not the problem."

"But I am eighteen. I can—"

"Your age is not my concern either." Miss Haack huffed. "You ran away with little if any consideration for your health or safety. I followed as quickly as I could, after begging your mother for the privilege. Then, when I found you, you were covered in mud and holding hands with a young man who looked every bit the part of a common farmer, with wild hair falling about his face and dirt covering him from head to foot. What was I to think? That he was the pastor coming to admire your sketches? And what of your condition? If I hadn't had that comfit, what would have happened?"

"I would have managed eating some berries or something."

"But you were alone with him."

"I already told you what happened, Lucy."

"And you were not presenting the appropriate, modest reserve. 'A young lady is not to speak with a man. But if it's unavoidable, she must not betray any inclination toward him.' Yet, you spoke with him like he was a brother. If your mother finds out … Goodness, I can hardly think of it. And what of Sir Likebridge? He does have a title and wealth. Perhaps his original intentions were honor—"

"I detest the very thought of him."

"But your mother, she has such great plans and—"

"Forget her plans! I'll not have him! Now, let's get to the inn. We will have some tea and forget the whole matter. Mother needn't know a thing about it. And if she asks, let me explain."

"All right. But you must be more careful. One can never tell about men."

"And *you* mustn't worry so much. Mr. Adsley is a pastor, after all."

"He's still a man."

Annette sighed. "Yes, but I need something to eat, and I must change my gown before Mother sees it. Have you any suggestions on how we might resolve that problem?"

🠕

As they walked, Miss Haack planned a quick ascent to their cramped chamber by way of the servants' stairs in the kitchen while Annette entertained a far more risky endeavor.

When they reached the inn, they ducked in the back door. Lucy made her way around a massive wood table laden with assorted cooking utensils and food in various stages of preparation for the evening meal, grabbed an orange from a fruit basket, and headed for the servants' staircase while Annette trailed behind, hoping to find Martin. He was a footman who had, over the years, become a co-conspirator in the plethora of amusing diversions Annette had dreamed up, including the guest-room rescue Miss Betherton had arranged for Peter months ago, the night of Sylvia's birthday celebration.

"Martin," Miss Haack snapped. "You should be packing."

He jumped to attention, and the scullery maid with whom he had been chatting darted back to the fireplace. "Right away, mum."

Lucy started up the stairs, mumbling as she went. Annette signaled Martin to wait.

"Lucy, I will be up soon. I am thirsty."

Miss Haack stopped her ascent up the narrow staircase. "I'll get some milk for you."

"No, Lucy. You are halfway up. Martin is here. He can see to it; then I will send him packing." She tried to hold a straight face as she played with words. "Martin, will you fetch me some ice too, please?" Annette added.

"Well, come up as soon as you are finished," Miss Haack responded as she continued up the stairs. "We do not need anyone else seeing you in that dress."

Martin whispered to Annette, "Is there a plan afoot, Miss, or did you really want the ice?"

"Yes. I have an idea, but see to the iced-milk for now. I will wait on the bench outside the kitchen door."

"At your service, Miss." He eyed her dress and smiled.

"Do not be too long; Miss Haack will be back any moment. She forgot to tell you about an errand she has for you."

"Right away, Miss." He grabbed a mug and headed outside to the icehouse.

Annette followed Martin out and glanced around the courtyard—no people, only chickens and geese clucking and pecking about. She sat down on the bench and slipped her sketchbook halfway out of her satchel, then peeked inside. Flipping through the pages, she reached the one she wanted and carefully tore it out before slipping the book back in her bag. She dug out her pencil, scribbled a line in the lower right corner of the drawing, and studied the sketch for a moment. Satisfied, she carefully rolled it up, pulled a white ribbon from her curls, and tied the scroll closed, first in a knot, and then a bow.

"Your iced-milk, Miss." Martin stepped up and smiled as he extended the mug to her.

"Thank you." She took a few swallows.

"And how else may I assist you?"

"Miss Haack will ask you to retrieve my paints from the church down the road—St. John's. When you go, please see that Mr. Adsley, the pastor, gets this." She handed him the scroll. "It is of particular import that he receive it privately. Do you understand?"

"Certainly, Miss." He carefully placed the scroll inside his livery. "I'll see that it's done, and quietly too."

"You are always so helpful, Martin. What would I do without you?"

"However I can serve, Miss." He bowed and turned to leave. But at the same moment, Miss Haack came out the door.

"Martin, where do you think you're going?"

"Pardon, Miss Haack, but I'm off to packing as you instructed."

"Good. But a moment please. I remembered an errand I have for you."

Annette swallowed her last bit of milk and stood up. "I am going upstairs, Lucy."

"Go ahead. I'll be right there. In the meantime, I have your orange wedges waiting."

Annette mouthed the words "thank you" to Martin behind Miss Haack's back. "Thank you, I will eat them now."

Chapter 24

Inventions

The squeaky wooden door of their cluttered upstairs chamber swung open, and Mrs. Chetwynd swept into the space for the second time today. Miss Haack rushed forward to catch the teetering washbowl before it hit the floor, and Annette ducked behind the screen in the corner, snatching her blue day dress as she went.

"Mother, what are you doing here?" Annette screeched.

"Saints above, Annette, cease this banshee noise," her mother snapped. "What is going on with this running about?" Shifting her eyes to Miss Haack, she continued. "Marcus—or Martin, whatever his name is—the footman, was wandering outside when he should have been packing. He said *you* sent him to the church for Annette's paints. Why are they there?"

"Yes, Mrs. Chetwynd." Miss Haack hesitated. "As you know, I followed Annette, and—"

"It is my fault, Mother," Annette called from behind the screen as she finished adjusting the blue day dress into which she had slipped and kicked the muddy yellow dress back into the corner. "After I recovered from our . . . discussion, I found the glade I mentioned. It was overlooking a beautiful pool, and there was a golden haze—"

"To the point, Annette. What is this business about going to church?"

"We did not go to church. After Miss Haack found me, we took a walk and during the walk . . ."

Annette glanced at the orange wedges Miss Haack had prepared. Her mother hated to be reminded of Annette's infirmity. It was the one flaw that could cost Mrs. Chetwynd her dream of a superior match for Annette, and they both knew it. So if Annette invented just the right story, she would be rid of her mother.

"I felt a little faint."

"What do you mean?" Her mother's brows knitted together. "Did you forget—?"

"It was nothing, Mother. Lucy had a snack for me. I was fine. Then we started back here. But it was too hard for her to carry everything, so when we came upon the pastor, who was also out for a walk, Miss Haack asked him to keep my things until she could send Martin to fetch them back. He said he would, and then we came up here so I could rest before supper." Annette pasted on a particularly sappy smile. "I was just about to have an orange." She offered the plate to her mother. "Would you like one?"

"No."

"I apologize for having screamed when you came in, but I was changing. And I am sorry that I ran away. It was wrong of me, and I will not do it again." Annette popped an orange slice into her mouth and began chewing.

"Well, that is for certain. There is too much at stake for such recklessness. Have I not always insisted that you keep a fruit or other sweet with you? Annette, I am exceedingly disappointed. Do not you understand a husband might count your ailment as a flaw of breeding? He could cast you off for fear of it tainting his heir? And how will you ever manage an entire household if you cannot even care for yourself? Your husband's happiness and comfort—indeed, that of the entire family—will depend wholly upon you and your ability to maintain a home."

Anger boiled inside Annette, but she knew she must watch her wording and tone, or all would be lost. "So we are going to act as if my ailment does not exist?"

"Not exactly. To put it simply, when the right man comes along, you will inform him of your predicament in such a way as to lessen its significance, since you are in good health, and it does not make any difference when you manage it properly. Then you will prove you have it under control by not fainting, and he will never even notice."

"I understand." Annette adopted the most humble, remorseful daughter stance she could assume—anything to be rid of her mother right now. "And I promise I will carry some refreshment with me at all times."

"Make certain you do, or I will have to devise a way to manage it myself."

Mrs. Chetwynd turned to Lucy. "See that she does, Miss Haack. If you cannot, plenty of other effective chaperons are up to the task. I need only ask."

"Yes, Madam."

"Now get some rest before dinner, Annette. And Lucy, when that footman returns, make certain those brushes, paints, and whatever other paraphernalia she has are packed. We are leaving early tomorrow morning, so there is not much time."

"I'll see to it, Mrs. Chetwynd." Miss Haack curtsied, and Annette's mother left the room.

Annette held her breath as she listened to her footsteps fading down the stairs. When they were far enough away, the flood of tears broke, and she rushed into Miss Haack's arms.

"How could she say those things?" Annette sobbed. Miss Haack took out her handkerchief for Annette, and held her close, rocking her and caressing her hair.

"She never should have, dearest. You are a fine, healthy young lady, and you are doing very well taking care of yourself."

After some minutes, Annette began to regain her composure. "Thank you, Lucy." She blew her nose. "But sometimes I just cannot control it. She is so hard and cold. How could poor Papá ever have chosen her?"

"You know your father. There must have been a very good reason or he never would have."

"Thank you, Lucy."

"Ah, 'tis nothing. I've known your mother for many years. Sometimes she doesn't realize what she's saying. You need to remember that, my girl, and stay strong. Any gentleman would be enchanted with you, no matter about the fainting. Look at that Pastor Adsley. He could not keep his eyes off of you, though you would not stop talking." Miss Haack chuckled. "And he knows about as much as there is to know about your illness, but it didn't bother him. Actually, he was even more attentive when he saw you needed his help."

"He was a perfect gentleman." Annette ate another one of her orange segments.

"Yes." Lucy patted Annette's cheek and smiled. "But just now, your story was not exactly truthful, and he's a pastor. Remember?"

"But it served its purpose."

"True. However, a pastor's wife . . ."

"I understand, and I will be more mindful of it." Annette hugged her confidant.

"We must both be more careful in all things, my girl. Just because you did not faint this time, does not mean you will not some other day."

"I know. Thank you for looking after me."

"And I appreciate your helping me with your mother."

Annette sat up. "If I was more reserved, I could not have ousted her as soon as I did."

"But if you weren't such a little varmint, we would not have been in trouble in the first place."

"Yes, but then we would not have met Mr. Adsley, I mean Pastor Adsley."

Lucy stood up and waddled around behind the screen. She came out with the canary dress hanging over her arm. "Finish up your oranges, and take a rest. I will take care of this dress with your miracle-working laundress, whoever that is."

"All right." Annette smiled.

After Miss Haack exited the room, Annette reached for her art bag on the floor by the dressing table. She was going to hide the sketchbook when a crumpled piece of white fabric on the ground by the screen caught her eye, and she picked it up.

His handkerchief. She smiled as she remembered stuffing it into her bodice when he was not looking. It must have fallen out when she changed dresses. She popped the last orange slice in her mouth and lay down on the bed to examine her treasure. Now she must add theft to her list of sins. How could she ever be a pastor's wife?

Fingering the delicate black stitches, she studied his scripted monogram. Then she clasped his handkerchief to her heart, closed her eyes, and summoned his image in her mind. Long dark hair, sun-warmed cheeks with the shadow of a beard darkening his jaw, and rich maple eyes—he looked just like the man in her favorite painting at Betherton Hall.

Then she frowned. Would he care if she had fainting spells? He was all manners and attentiveness when she stumbled on the pathway. But would his manners be so amiable if he suspected his children might be tainted by her disease?

Annette could feel tears welling up from deep in her soul, but she held her breath and wiped her face with Peter's handkerchief. She refused to cry over this. He did not like it when she cried. Instead, she reached for the gold chain around her neck and followed its links down to the gold locket her father had given her. She opened it and studied his profile.

"Oh, Papá, why must it be so hard? Could not a man just love me for who I am and not worry so much about my faults? You do not love me any less for them."

She closed the locket and kissed it. Then she wrapped it in Mr. Adsley's handkerchief and clutched her treasures close.

He had said he was most concerned about her health while he was leaning close beside her under the tree. It did not seem like he cared for her any less. In fact, after yielding to her promise to keep the sketches secret, it seemed like he wanted to kiss her.

"But Lord, he's a pastor. How shall I ever manage?" She sat up in bed. "And he lives in Buxton, but now I am going to Liverpool. I should have written our address on the sketch I sent him. Oh, how could I have missed that?"

Annette looked out the window. The magnificent late afternoon sky was streaked with golden pinks, oranges, and rich purples as the sun fought to keep its place above the horizon.

"Lord, how can I fix this?" She paused and started again in a more reverent tone. "God, forgive that disrespectful start, but I have another favor to ask." Annette's heart sank, and she stopped again. She closed her eyes and collected her thoughts; then she continued.

"God, I know You are the Creator of the Universe, and I am such a faithless and peevish creature. I have doubted You and wandered away from You since Sir Likebridge . . . Well, You know what he tried to do. And I am furious he is here again now. I want You to know I will not marry him. But that is another story I will tell You later.

"Today, I manipulated the truth, which is lying; I allowed my anger to direct my actions, and I just remembered that when I was speaking with Mr. Adsl—Pastor Adsley, that is—I insulted You by insinuating You do not involve yourself with humanity. Please forgive me, and prevent him from knowing that I did it. I too often speak without thinking, and I dishonor You by doing so. But You have been so kind to me by letting me see Pastor Adsley again. Thank You. I am very grateful, and I am not just saying that because Mr. Adsley is Your servant. I truly mean it.

"Now, here is my request. I hope You will permit it, but I will understand if You do not. I would likely make the worst pastor's wife in the whole of England anyway. But would You please allow Pastor Adsley to find me again? I will devise a plan to read and study the Scriptures as much as I do my other studies, just as Father asks, if You do. Thank You and Amen."

Annette lay down again. *God, do You think he will like the sketch I sent him?* She re-situated herself on the bed, and then lay very still. *Well, he would not throw it away, would he? Not after today, I hope.* She rolled her eyes and sighed. *Propriety. Of course, I should have thought of that.* "Please, God, do not let him throw my sketch away either. He might need it someday."

Chapter 25

Temptation

St. John's Parish, Buxton
Derbyshire, England
9 June 1795

Peter deposited Miss Chetwynd's paint supplies in the barn with John, his stable hand. He had every intention of telling John he wished to speak with Miss Chetwynd's footman when he came by and every intention of going back to the glade to clean himself up, but the words and plans fled when he heard his housekeeper screeching like a flustered goose.

"What in the name of beetle-headed beggars is that woman up to now?" John mumbled.

"We had better see," Peter responded, and both men headed out of the barn.

"I'm gonna find me a good switch and tan your hide, you good-for-nothin' little …" Mrs. Striklin fumed.

"Please, I meant nothing by it." A young lad whimpered as the housekeeper clutched him by the back of the collar and marched him toward the wood pile.

"Mrs. Striklin, if you please, what is going on here?"

"Pastor, I caught this little thief, the messenger boy I told you about earlier, in me pantry tryin' to pinch one o' cook's fresh beef pies."

Peter looked down at the messenger's beleaguered face. He could not have been more than twelve years old, and his dirt-smeared cheeks, drooping eyelids, and bloodshot eyes spoke of fatigue.

"Well, release him. It is obvious he will not get away from us now." Peter spoke to the boy. "It is getting late, young man. Have you had anything to eat since this morning?"

"No, sir."

"And he reeks to high heaven."

"Mrs. Striklin, that is quite enough. The boy needs food. And have Cook heat some water. We both need a good bath."

"Cook's busy. She hasn't any time for the likes of him. If he wants a bath, he can use the pond."

Peter nodded at John, who tipped his head toward the barn and backed away from the situation.

"Unacceptable, Mrs. Striklin. This boy is my guest, and either you or Cook must see to his needs, or I will have to find a more accommodating staff."

Peter hated having to take a high hand with his housekeeper, but if she was unwilling to fulfill the simplest of requests on behalf of a helpless child, how could he keep her?

"Well, it hasn't ever been done before, takin' in a common messenger boy, and never heard tell of such a boy gettin' a hot bath in a tub as if he were one of the gentry."

"I appreciate your concern, but I am making an exception. In fact, if Cook's too busy with the meal, I will boil the water myself."

"No, 'tis not your business. No pastor boils water when he ought to be writin' sermons. I'll see to the boy's meal and bath, but he better not be causin' me any more trouble."

Peter glanced down at the boy. "Well, son, can you manage that?"

"Yes, sir, Mr. Adsley."

"There you have it, Mrs. Striklin. Now ready a meal for both of us, if you please. We will be in shortly."

The old woman eyed the boy up and down, then eyed Peter. "All right, but don't be takin' too long 'bout it." She turned her back and headed for the kitchen, muttering along the way.

Peter turned to the messenger. "Now, my boy, tell me your name and more about your business here at St. John's."

"I be Arnold, sir, at your service."

"It's good to know you, Arnold." Peter extended his hand to the boy, and he shook it. "And I hear you've had quite a ride today."

"That I did. Took me almost four hours on horseback to get here, and now I have to explain that you are needed back home immediately. A coach is coming to fetch you tomorrow."

"Many thanks. I'm indebted to you, Arnold. Do you know why I'm needed at home?"

"No, sir, but they wanted me to be sure you got the message."

"Well, I did."

🙢

After his bath and halfway through dinner, Peter realized he had forgotten to speak to John about Miss Chetwynd's footman.

"If you'll excuse me, Arnold—" Peter stood from his seat. "I need to step outside."

"Yes, sir," Arnold mumbled as he shoveled another spoonful of beef pie into his mouth.

When Peter stepped out of the parsonage, it was dark. He headed to the barn, where light was seeping through the cracks of the door. Perhaps he could still meet Miss Chetwynd's footman.

"Hello in there. John, are you still about?"

"Yes, sir."

"Has a footman stopped by to pick up those things I left before all the ruckus?"

Starving Hearts

"Yes, sir, he did, 'bout fifteen minutes ago, I'd say."

"Did you know the man—I mean, recognize him?"

"Can't say that I did. But he told me to give you this." John picked up a scroll tied with a white ribbon and handed it to Peter. His heart skipped a beat as a whiff of orange blossom scent tickled his nose.

"Seems like you might'a snagged yourself another *follower*." John grinned.

"Thank you, John."

"Anytime."

"And you are certain you did not recognize the footman?"

"That's right."

"Good evening then." Peter stopped at the barn door. "Oh and I almost forgot—"

"Goin' riding early tomorrow, sir?"

"Yes."

"Archangel'll be ready by seven, as usual."

"Splendid. Well, good night." Peter exited the barn.

"G'night, sir, and pleasant readin' to ya," John called after him.

Peter held the scroll to his nose and inhaled the rich citrus scent. His heart beat a little faster, and he hastened across the courtyard to the parsonage. Picking up a candleholder, he lit the candle from the kitchen fireplace and stepped down the hall to his study. Once inside the room, he set the candleholder on the corner of his desk and sat down. He closed his eyes, inhaled the scroll's sweet perfume again, and pictured Miss Chetwynd's face as he held her in his arms that afternoon.

Opening his eyes, Peter began to pull the ribbon but suddenly tossed the scroll away as if it was a hot ember. It rolled across his desk and settled at the base of the candleholder.

What was he thinking? A single man could not receive a letter from a young lady. And she—sending it in the first place—had committed another breach of proper etiquette. He must not open it. He should give it back, or better yet, he should get rid of it.

He scooted back from his desk, closed his eyes, and massaged his temples. It had been a miraculous day. He had found her again, and they had spoken at length.

Lord, I cannot think it right to open this letter; nor should I entertain any amiable thoughts about receiving it, but I ...

Peter stopped rubbing his forehead and stared at the scroll. He abruptly stood from his desk, walked across the room, and locked the door to his study. When he returned to his chair, he took a deep breath and slowly released a heavy sigh.

Forgive me, if it is a sin, but I cannot resist. I must know her thoughts.

Then, he gently loosened the bow and began working on the knot, but his clumsy fingers fumbled with the delicate ribbon, and he could not undo it fast enough. Quickly digging in his desk drawer, Peter found a letter opener and cut the ribbon. Carefully unrolling the page, he spread it out on the desk in front of him.

A sharp breath caught in his chest. He blinked hard and leaned closer. A tremor ran through his fingers as he held his breath and stared in amazement.

Miss Chetwynd had not written a letter. It was something far more dangerous, and infinitely more dear.

Golden candlelight spilled over a perfect replica of Miss Chetwynd herself. She had drawn her own portrait, which now gazed up at him with sparkling eyes. The dimple beneath the left corner of her mouth seemed to deepen, and a hint of her teeth showed through the delicately parted lips of her enigmatic smile. And there was someone else.

The shadow of a faceless man hovered behind her. His shoulders and cravat were drawn, but only the sketched outline of his face and hair appeared. And in the lower right corner of the page, another treasure. She had signed the drawing.

He held the page closer and studied her delicate script. "From Annette Marie Chetwynd for her pastor, Mr. Adsley," he whispered. And at that exact moment, something inside of him righted itself. He set the portrait aside, rested his elbows on his desk, and bowed his head.

God, she places herself under my control with this drawing, and I will never give her secret away. But if someone discovers her sketches, we could ... My Lord, I hate to think of it. Nevertheless, I pray for wisdom. What would You have me do next?

'Why must you do anything?' Her voice echoed in his thoughts.

Of course, Annette would remind me of that, but what do You say? Good heavens, now I am calling her by her Christian name.

His gaze drifted down to her portrait again. *But what am I to do? I cannot deny she is fascinating and beautiful. But what of this fainting?* Another thought surfaced. *And what of her faith?*

Her lively manner and natural bent towards questioning and exploring a topic appealed to him. Her passion for life showed in her conversation, and . . . This very afternoon, however, had she not made some statement about God's lack of interest in humanity?

Peter closed his eyes and tried to remember what she said, but he could not. All he knew was that he could not determine exactly what she believed. There must be some reason for their paths crossing, however. Goodness knows he had not sought her out.

Lord, I am drawn to her. If it pleases You, give me an opportunity to see her and to learn if she is committed to You. And give me patience."

Peter rolled up the scroll, took out his wax, and sealed it. As much as he wanted to study her more, he must not yield to that temptation. He would return it to her after he spoke with her father to obtain permission to call again.

↟

That night, a barrage of scenes and questions plagued Peter's dreams.

"*He needs your guidance and that of the Almighty, if He'll involve Himself.*"

"*Who's to say a divine designer—or God, depending on your beliefs—could not use me if it served His purpose?*"

"*You are relieved of your responsibilities. Return home at once. Your patron will see to a replacement.*"

"*Why must you do anything?*"

"*Godspeed, Mr. Adsley, until we meet again.*"

Chapter 26

Thwarted

Peter dismounted and headed for the back door of the parsonage, tossing Archangel's reins to his stable hand as he went.

"Can you saddle him with my bags, John? I will be out in a quarter of an hour."

"Yes, sir."

Peter stepped through the back door. His firm steps echoed on the wood floors as he moved down the hall to his study. Closing the door firmly behind him, he took Miss Chetwynd's scroll out of his coat pocket, laid it on his desk, and planted himself in the wing-backed chair facing the window.

The entire morning had been a disheartening waste of time. And, as usual, things had not gone as Peter expected. He looked at his pocket watch, half past two. If he hoped to reach Caverswall before dusk, he needed to leave soon. He slipped his watch back into his pocket and pondered his day thus far.

His father's coach arrived early, so he had to attend to young Arnold's departure back to Caverswall before he could speak to Mrs. Striklin and Cook about the Chetwynd family's residence. When he finally asked, neither one knew anything about them. After that, Peter rode to town to see if anyone there could help him locate the Chetwynds. No one could. In point of fact, no one had heard of any Chetwynd family living in or near Buxton, ever.

As Peter was riding back to the parsonage, it occurred to him that Miss Chetwynd's family might be visiting friends in the area, or perhaps they were traveling through Buxton on their way down to Caverswall to visit the Bethertons again. Consequently—while it seemed rather an unlikely possibility, since The Dove Inn was some distance from the glade where he had all but stumbled upon Miss Chetwynd—Peter rode out to inquire at the only inn close enough to use. And there, in as stirring an Irish accent as any, the innkeeper answered Peter's question, "Off to Liverpool they were, very *aearly* this morning."

Her family left neither a forwarding address in Liverpool nor a permanent residence location. So, if Peter chose to count their first meeting in the guest study and their second visual contact at Sylvia's wedding, Miss Chetwynd had now either slipped away or been spirited away from him a total of three times, and he was frustrated.

Lord, is it that You have another plan for my life? Pray, forgive my boldness, but if so, could You not be more clear in communicating it to me?

Peter got up and walked over to his bookcase. He sifted through his atlases until he found the one he wanted. Then, he laid it out on his desk and, withdrawing two sheets of paper from the top drawer, he placed them over the open pages. Next, he removed the wax seal on Miss Chetwynd's picture and, unrolling it gently, wedged it into the atlas's binding between the two papers.

Forgive me yet again. You are gracious and kind, and I am truly grateful for Your many blessings, the greatest of which is Salvation. Everything else, including a wife, is only added grace I do not deserve.

Peter gazed at Miss Chetwynd's face. *And thank You for permitting me to keep her sketch. You know I was loath to return it. I am also indebted to You for allowing me to discover she is presently on her way to Liverpool. Those two things are more than I knew—more than I hoped to know—even yesterday morning. Give her and her family a safe journey, and allow that I can see her again soon. I'll leave the rest unsaid for now. But grant me wisdom and understanding regarding her faith.*

Peter closed the atlas, grabbed his satchel from the floor beside his desk, and placed his Bible and the atlas inside of it. Then he threw the strap over his shoulder and headed for the kitchen.

And guide me as I speak with Father. I cannot see why he would call me away when I have only just begun. Nor can I imagine what I would do if I could not serve You.

"Hello, Mrs. Striklin, is supper ready?"

"Yes." She handed him a bundle. "Here's a shepherd's pie, two big apples, a half loaf of rye, and a flask of Cook's ale. I figured you would want to get goin', so I wrapped it up."

"Thank you. As you are well aware, I will be in Caverswall for the celebration these three days. But if, for some reason, I have not returned by Saturday afternoon, tell Clifton to give the sermon in my stead."

"Mrs. Clifton, that old hoot owl, givin' the sermon? Saints'll be rollin' in their graves!"

Peter laughed. "Not the matron, Mrs. Striklin. Her husband, *Mr.* Shannon Clifton. I have already arranged with *him* should I not make it in time."

"Praise the Almighty."

"Indeed. But be careful. It would not do for Mrs. Clifton to hear what you think of her."

"Don't worry yourself. She knows exactly what I think o' her. We grew up together."

"Well, good day then, Mrs. Striklin. I will be on my way."

"Safe journey, Pastor Adsley."

Peter spent the next three and a quarter hours praying while he and Archangel blazed a trail from Buxton down to Caverswall.

Chapter 27

Providence

Caverswall Manor
Staffordshire, England
10 June 1795

The massive stone edifice with its graceful columns and balustrades came into view. Peter studied the striking architecture with its elegant portico and Palladian windows. Caverswall Manor was the exemplar of aristocratic wealth and power that never failed to amaze him.

Archangel cantered up the circular drive, and Peter dismounted in front of the entryway. Within seconds, a groom emerged from the ground floor and led Archangel around to the stables.

Peter ascended the stairs to the entry door, which opened before he could touch the large brass knocker. Mrs. Alyece Adsley, his much-loved stepmother, welcomed him with open arms.

"Oh Peter, you've come early. I thought you might wait until Friday, before the ..." Tears glistened in her eyes.

"Yes, but what is this? You are crying, Mother. Are you unwell?" She stepped away from the embrace and wiped her eyes with a lace handkerchief.

"I'm sure everything will be settled now that you are here."

"Your coat, sir?" Peter's manservant appeared beside him.

"Yes, of course, Giles." Peter removed his coat, hat, and gloves. "It is good to see you again, my friend. Have you been well?"

Before Giles could answer, Mrs. Adsley spoke up. "Please, son, you ought to come in and rest yourself before Mary Hope, ah . . . You must be hungry after your long ride." She turned away from Peter. "Giles, please send for tea and cakes."

"Yes, my lady," he said and bowed himself away.

With his stepmother's uncharacteristic interruption and hesitation over his younger sister's name, an onslaught of alarming scenarios flooded Peter's mind.

"Mother, you seem rather out of sorts today. Do tell me, what is the matter? Is it something to do with Mary Hope? Is she ill?"

"No. She is fine. But I shall explain everything later. You must refresh yourself now."

"There is plenty of time for that. Can you not speak to me now? You appear to be overcome by something very serious, and I have many questions regarding the business of my parish. Father's message was so perplexing. What has happened?"

Mrs. Adsley's face wilted into her lace handkerchief again, and Peter felt like his heart was being torn apart. He must not make such demands of her. Certainly, she could not be blamed for his being recalled from ministry.

"Forgive me, Mother. Perhaps I should have waited to see Father on these issues."

"No, Peter." Mrs. Adsley's voice tightened as she gripped his arm. "Your father cannot ... is unable to see you at this time." She sighed and probed his eyes as if to pass vital information without using words.

His mother had always been direct. So Peter changed his tactic to lighten the mood.

"So be it then, my dear lady," he teased as he took her hand in his and tucked it into the crook of his arm. He led her toward the staircase. "If you wish to torment me—even after a long journey—you must at least permit me some of my favorite almond cake and the tea you promised. I would also like a hot bath. But for now, let me accompany you to the Rose Room where I can wait for these amenities."

Mrs. Adsley laughed. "Thank you, son. Tea will be quite agreeable. And I'm sure Giles has already set about preparing your bath."

"Peter, wait." He heard Mary Hope call from down the hall as she rushed to meet him.

"I've missed you so terribly," she cried as she hugged him around the neck.

"And I've missed you too, my dear, but why this uproar?" *At least she is standing here and appears healthy. That is a relief.*

Peter unclasped her hands and searched her tear-streaked face. She was twenty-one years of age, but her matted auburn hair, swollen eyes, and pink blotchy skin made her seem younger.

"Has Mother told you yet?"

Peter looked to his stepmother, but Mrs. Adsley avoided his gaze and linked her arm around his sister's waist.

"Hope, my dear, you must try to contain yourself. Your brother has only just arrived. Give him time to refresh himself. I've ordered tea and will explain everything as soon as he's settled. Now go upstairs and have Sophie attend you."

"Yes, Mother," she sighed. "I'm sorry, Peter. I hope I haven't spoiled your return."

"Nothing of the kind, sister. You needn't worry yourself. Whatever it is, I'm sure we will manage." *But if this current distress has anything to do with a suitor of yours, I will not hesitate to call the man out.*

"Thank you, Peter. You are always so good." She gave him another quick embrace, and then ascended the stairs ahead of them.

Following their ascent, his mother led the way down the richly carpeted hall to her private drawing room. Peter stepped ahead to open the door to the Rose Room, then followed her inside. With its beautiful arrangement of mauve roses centered on the table by the windows and white lace curtains fluttering in a breeze, the room was the same comfortable sanctuary it had always been.

They had just seated themselves when the housekeeper entered with the tea service, which she placed beside Mrs. Adsley.

"Will you be needing anything else, my lady?"

"No, Mrs. Worthington. This is fine, thank you."

"You are welcome. I'll see that you are not disturbed." She nodded and left the room. Mrs. Adsley began to pour tea, but Peter's patience had all but expired.

"Please, Mother, I insist. You must explain what has happened."

She looked a bit confused as if she was unsure how to present the situation. Then she set the teapot down with a clatter and forged ahead.

"Peter, your brother …" She took out her handkerchief again. "Richard is dead."

Chapter 28

Inconvenienced

Once again, Sir Steven Likebridge dragged his travel trunk from the guest chamber closet over to the chest of drawers. He threw open the lid, pulled the top dresser drawer out, and dumped its contents into his trunk. Cravats, handkerchiefs, stockings, a night shirt, and a few other unmentionables landed topsy-turvy in the trunk. This was the third time Steven, who was back at Caverswall at Richard's invitation in order to celebrate his birthday, had determined he must leave the Manor immediately.

He started pacing in front of the fireplace, moving to the window for a moment and staring outside. He poured himself a glass of brandy from the service on the table, drank a sip of the amber liquid, and started pacing again. He glanced at the fire and then at the crystal glass in his hand. If only he could smash that glass against the inside of the fireplace, but such a noise would draw too much attention, and he did not need any extra of that right now. It was not part of his plan.

He always orchestrated his malevolent schemes from the shadows, where no one knew or could see how he was involved. But this time, his dear half-brother, Richard Adsley—heir to both the Adsley and Betherton estates—had ruined everything, the miserable drunk.

Just over forty-two hours ago, at about eleven o'clock Monday night, Richard had accepted his wager to jump his horse over a series of new hedges set up in the equestrian center. That was not part of his plan either; the venture was just for sport.

They were together with a few old club mates who had come out to the country a week early to celebrate Richard's twenty-sixth birthday. Of course, they had been drinking when Steven had thrown out the wager just to see if he could pick up a little extra coin.

The full moon was bright. Everything had gone well on the first two jumps. But when it came to the third, the horse balked at the last minute and threw Richard. He flew over the hedge and landed on his head, instantly breaking his neck.

Mr. Adsley—Steven paused for a drink—Richard's and his father had taken the news very poorly. Indeed, upon seeing the dead body of his heir, the old man cried out like a raving maniac, ordered Likebridge and the others to maintain silence until his second son, Peter, arrived, and then sequestered himself in his chamber. Steven had not seen him since, the wretched coward.

The entire affair was rather disturbing—what with so many guests out for the birthday celebration—and now Steven was embroiled in a most delicate family matter, instead of maintaining his distance.

It was not that he was saddened by Richard's death. He was planning to kill him anyway. It was the blasted publicity, a deuce of an inconvenience for a man who liked working behind the scenes. And he could not very well leave with the birthday, now turned funeral. It would be highly improper. It was a good thing the other chaps had taken to their rooms. Next thing he knew, he would be required to comfort Richard's widow, or perhaps his sister, Mary Hope.

Steven set his brandy down and walked to the window. Perchance she was in the garden. He had often seen her there this week. He gazed out and spied Miss Mary Hope Adsley, with her unique auburn hair. She was walking amongst the roses. He watched the delicate curve of her arm as she ran her hand over the roses. She bent to smell a red blossom, and one of her curls caught in its thorns. When she smoothed it away and raised her face toward Heaven, something clicked inside of Steven. If things were different . . .

They had spoken on two occasions this past week. Her very words and the gracious way in which she spoke touched him. They had danced one evening too. Perhaps they could speak again right now. The possibility soothed his disquieted soul.

"Jackson," he called, and the splintery twig of a man sprang to his side with his collar undone and vest hanging open.

"Yes, Mr. Slike? How may I be of service?" His spidery voice matched his physique.

"Do not call me that. I am Sir Likebridge here."

"Yes, sir, Sir Likebridge." The man bowed.

"Stand up and stop fawning about like a beggar. Now, tell me, how might a man go about—?"

"Finding relief, sir?"

Steven stared at his servant.

"If you're speakin' of your masculine urges, I've developed some connections with one of the scullery ma—"

"Imbecile!"

The man cringed as if waiting to be struck. "I could make some inquiries—"

"You will do no such thing. I was thinking of . . . Why am I consulting you?"

"But I thought—"

"Enough, Jackson! Forget I even asked. Have you set up your miserable cousin somewhere close by? I want someone watching Mr. Peter Adsley from the moment he arrives. And make sure someone keeps his eye on the father. There can be no mistakes now. Do you understand?"

"Yes, sir. I've offered Cousin Ives as a man of all tasks. He's building the coffin now."

"Good."

"See that he stays on at the estate. I want to be informed of both Adsley men's every move. And have my things packed and loaded. I will depart directly following the funeral. I have urgent business in Liverpool on Friday."

"Yes, Mr. Sli—I mean, Sir Likebridge."

"And fix that livery. Here, you are a gentleman's man, not a back-alley barkeep."

"Yes, sir."

Chapter 29

Widow

Peter's footsteps reverberated off the walls of the deserted salon as he walked to the eastern wing, where Richard only a week ago had occupied rooms with his bride. It was a haunting sound that toyed with his resolve. This meeting with Sylvia would be their first since the wedding, and he was uncertain what to say.

Richard's untimely death was overwhelming. It unequivocally destroyed Peter's plan to minister to his congregation in Buxton. And lest he consider it to be a solution for his failed attempt to obtain Sylvia's hand in marriage, English Canon Law prohibited a man from marrying his brother's wife.

Nevertheless, a tiny sort of hope had begun to push its way up through the mired wreckage of Peter's thoughts.

Lord, if Sylvia had … Well, to be frank … Peter cringed at the indelicacy of the notion but proceeded. If Sylvia had conceived a child, their circumstances would be far more agreeable, even pleasing. Perhaps God intended to save his ministry through a child. *Please let it be.*

Actually, an heir from Richard would be a victory for everyone, a reason to rejoice. Despite her loss, Sylvia would have attained her most precious desire. Peter's father would have a grandson to inherit the estate. Sylvia's parents would be happy knowing their estate would go to their own grandchild, and Peter could continue in his ministry. Of course, Peter would have to run the estate and make decisions and investments until the child came of age, but that would be a blessing in view of his present circumstances.

"Oh Lord, let it be so."

Doubt gripped Peter as he entered the corridor that led to Sylvia's suite. But what if there was no child? Might referencing the possibility make matters worse? Perhaps he should leave it to Mother.

Outside of her door, Peter quietly knocked and inclined his ear to hear her response.

Nothing.

He knocked again, a little louder this time. He hoped she was not asleep; he really wanted to see her.

"Come in." Small and quiet, as if from miles away, Peter heard her voice. He twisted the knob and entered the sitting room, closing the door behind him.

Sylvia, a dark silhouette against so many bright, diamond-shaped window panes, sat in a chair facing the afternoon sunlight. It appeared she was putting on a long pair of gloves.

"Good afternoon, Sylvia." He drew up a chair from the tea table nearby and seated himself facing her.

"You needn't have come, Peter." Her throaty whisper sank its teeth into Peter's heart. "I am quite all right." She glanced at him. "Truly, I am."

The dark circles beneath her eyes and the pale skin drawn across her cheekbones told a different story.

"I am still your friend, indeed, your brother now."

Peter's eyes drifted to her hands. Putting on gloves had never seemed to take so long.

Sylvia abruptly stood up and retreated to the window, standing with her back to him.

"The weather is quite lovely today. You must have had a wonderful ride."

He followed Sylvia to the window.

"I hardly noticed. I see you are struggling with your gloves, though. The right one is still rather rumpled." Her eyes dropped to it. The glove was twisted. "May I be of some assistance? The other one is in similar disarray and uncommonly tight around the wrist. Perhaps our laundresses lack training on caring for a lady's gloves."

"Oh, Peter, stop. It has nothing to do with cleaning, and you know it."

"I do, but you seemed resolute in skirting, or perhaps covering the issue."

"Splendid. Now you are trying to charm me into telling you." She looked at him. "Well, it will not work unless you can assure me you will not bother yourself with it. You worry far too much."

Sylvia's words struck him hard. What had Richard done?

"Do you understand? Under no circumstances are you to worry, Peter. I am quite well."

He nodded, but said nothing as he followed her back to their chairs, and she started peeling off the right glove.

Greenish yellow splotches appeared on her slender forearm. She laid the glove on her lap and started peeling the left one. Equally aged bruises marred her left arm, and her wrist was tightly bandaged.

"My wrist is broken, but there is no permanent damage. The doctor says it will be as good as new in a few weeks."

Fury boiled up from some dark place inside. He remembered how Richard had grabbed Sylvia by the arm and how he shoved her against the post in the barn that stormy Thursday before they were married.

"He mistreated you."

"But he is gone now."

Her voice was a quiet whisper in a storm of Peter's anguish. He stood up and began pacing. If only he had asked her sooner. If he hadn't gone to Buxton, he could have proposed and saved her from this. If only …

"Look at me, Peter." He felt her grasp his arm and forcibly pull him down beside her.

"I know what you are thinking, and I will not have it. That is why I was trying to hide my arms in the first place. In a few days, the bruises would have disappeared, and you would not have been the wiser. But you asked me, and I told you. Now you must keep your promise and not worry. It was my choice."

"And what has it gotten you?"

"That is none of your concern." Her eyes softened, and her tone changed. "Forgive me. I should not have spoken that way. But if you must know, it has helped me grow. And I must ask you to do the same."

"Grow?"

"We have always viewed the world from a safe distance, you and I. Now, I have experienced it, and my faith has been strengthened. Soon, you will have to grow as well."

Peter stared at Sylvia in amazement.

"Do not worry about me. I still have my parents, and I have you as a brother. And believe me, you will never be rid of me, even when I am old and gray and doddering around Caverswell like . . . like the ghost of Lady Macbeth."

"Ghost of Lady Macbeth?"

Sylvia's eyes grew round, and a quirky smile curled her lips. "I'm teasing, Peter."

"Oh."

"Come now, Peter. Tell me about Buxton. I want to hear about your ministry, for as long as it lasted." She reached out and held his hands.

Peter tensed for a moment, but then the story began pouring from him, beginning with Mistress Hoot Owl and her daughters and ending with his father's demand to return home.

"I am truly sorry. It is a shame, Peter."

"Indeed. But I must . . ." He swallowed hard and wiped his face on his sleeve. "I must trust in God's plan."

"We both must. He will not disappoint." She took out a handkerchief and blew her nose. "But do tell me more of your attempt to clear a field with a shovel. I simply cannot imagine."

As they settled into less serious conversation, Sylvia poured tea.

"Shall we have a toast then, brother?"

"Indeed. What would you have us celebrate today?"

She took a deep breath and let it out slowly. "I rejoice in God's provision for you, Peter. You will take proper care of Caverswall and its people."

"But I know so little about running an estate."

"God will do His work in His time. Now raise your cup, and let's drink to His perfect plan, whatever it is. " She smiled as she clinked her cup against his. "And may all of *your* children, especially your heir, be ever as caring and constant as you are."

"Amen," he sighed. A conversation with Mother would not be necessary. Sylvia had made it clear that Richard had left no heir.

Chapter 30

Shadows

St. Peter's Church
Staffordshire, England
12 June 1795

Peter had witnessed Richard and Sylvia's wedding in this very chapel. Now he sat in the front pew beside Father, watching thin black smoke ribbons trailing up from candles posted behind Richard's roughly hewn coffin. His eyes drifted from the long wooden box to his father.

Mr. Charles Adsley, once the picture of masculine superiority and aristocratic pride, sat stoop-shouldered and pale, staring at his folded hands. His cheeks were hollow, and his characteristic air of self-assurance had been vanquished. Accepting the loss of his eldest son was a calamity from which he would not soon recover. It had been a major accomplishment for him to leave his chamber to attend this funeral.

Reverend Sharpe stepped forward and began the service while Peter bowed his head. He had a few objections of his own.

Lord, now I shall inherit everything, but I have no idea how to oversee it. I do not know the extent of Father's properties, which now include all of Betherton's properties. And so many people rely on me. How will this work?

Peter left off praying and looked up at Reverend Sharpe, who continued mumbling from the *Book of Common Prayer*. He listened for a little while, and then prayed again.

I cannot do this alone. Forgive me for what must seem to You constant droning.

Peter dropped his head in his hands. *Oh Lord, help me. I rely on Your promise 'that all things work together for good to them that love You, to them who are called according to Your purpose ...' Please give me the strength, despite my longings. May Your will be done in Your name and for Your glory. Amen.*

Peter raised his head as the reverend signaled the pallbearers forward. He got to his feet, took his place among the other men, and scanned the audience. As was the custom, no women were present, but Peter recognized many of their tenants. Some of the house staff sat with Giles, and other friends from the neighborhood huddled in the pews. Even some of Richard's mates, who had come early to celebrate his birthday, stayed on for the funeral.

When Reverend Sharpe finished speaking, Peter and the other pallbearers lifted their burden and carried it down the aisle. Just before they exited the chapel, Peter faltered, and the other pallbearers stopped. A recognizable, yet unknown, gentleman sitting mid-row in the middle section nodded at him.

Peter adjusted his grip and moved forward, pondering the exchange. He was the one who had escorted Miss Chetwynd out of the rain the day of the wedding. His black hair and tan skin—although it had since faded—were unmistakable. Who was he, and why had he come?

⋀

After the burial, Peter joined the other mourners for their somber meal; the mysterious gentleman did not, however. Peter was thankful, but he would not soon forget the look of the man's gray eyes. They were smiling.

Chapter 31

Bewildered

Caverwall Manor
Staffordshire, England
24 June 1795

Less than a fortnight after the funeral, Peter, his father, and the steward, Marcus, surveyed the Adsley estate, including the newly-acquired Betherton property, to acquaint Peter with its condition and particulars. It had taken an entire week to explore and to meet with the tenants and, having returned, Peter and Marcus were discussing repairs when Mr. Adsley entered the study.

"Good afternoon, Peter. Marcus." His father nodded as he wandered in and perused the property maps, sketches, and opened account books spread over the desk. "I see you gentlemen are hard at work today."

"Yes. Marcus is assisting me with plans to recover the flooded acreage in the western corner. Do you care to have a look?"

"No, I am certain he will manage well enough. However, I have come to inform you that we will be leaving for a tour on Saturday, the eleventh of July."

Peter composed his face and responded with as much respect as possible. "A tour? Meaning a visit to the Continent?"

"No. You need a proper introduction to our most profitable holdings. You will be accompanying me to the Colonies, where our most lucrative enterprise continues to expand."

Peter was stunned. All combined, the Adsley estate, not to mention the shipping company, was of great consequence—with The Manor and Betherton Hall here in the country, two city houses—one in London and the other in Liverpool—and, of course, some additional property in Derbyshire where he had taken his position at the Buxton parish.

"Business in the Colonies? Do you mean the United States? Why have you not mentioned it before?"

Mr. Adsley's eyes hardened. "Don't be absurd. There was no need to speak of it. Your brother was …" He glanced out the window and cleared his throat.

"Yes, I understand." Peter bowed his head. "But you might have—"

"Enough. The expedition has been arranged for some time. Richard was to accompany me, but things have changed now, so you are going. Marcus will see to the acreage and any other projects on which you have decided." He turned to Marcus. "Is that clear?"

"Indeed, it is, sir. I will take care of everything."

"We also have some business in Liverpool—changing the will, touring the warehouses, and so forth—before our official departure. So be ready to leave Thursday next, the second of July, I believe it is."

"This is a tremendous undertaking. I imagine we shall be gone for some time."

"Six months, give or take a couple weeks, including a stop along the Trade Route and the time we will spend at the Colony. We will be sailing aboard the *Terona* with Captain David Bledsoe, a longtime business associate of mine."

"But what of Mother and Mary Hope?"

Mr. Adsley narrowed his eyes. "Marcus and the staff will see to their needs. My solicitors, who have extensive practice in managing the needs of my family while I am away, will also see to them when they go on their annual pilgrimage to Beverley in Yorkshire later this summer. Or has your memory failed you regarding my travels throughout your youth?"

"I did not mean to imply—"

"Simply because you were not aware of it, does not mean I have not seen to every detail."

"My apologies."

"Blast your penitence! Adsley heirs do not express regret. We are entitled to lead because we have succeeded, and you will do well to remember it. You are the heir now, and it is your singular purpose to know this estate and its business exclusively. So if you have any affairs to which you must attend, consider this your notification to do so immediately. Good afternoon."

With that, Mr. Adsley took his leave.

Frustration was not a strong enough word to describe Peter's reaction to his father's revelation. Yet, as a gentleman, Peter would not discuss his dissatisfaction with the steward.

"If you will excuse me, Marcus, I have other business to which I must attend. Perhaps we can continue later this evening."

"Of course, Mr. Adsley."

Peter strode out of the room, down the corridor, and up the stairs. When he finally reached his room, he went straight to the desk where he kept his Bible and another important book. He sat down and flipped through the pages of the large world atlas where Miss Chetwynd's portrait was hidden. The dimple to the left of her smile, her laughing eyes, and the cheery look on her face caused Peter to smile. He could not help himself; the sketch was so perfect. But that pleasure faded as he considered the impossible distance a trip to the Colonies would put between them.

What if some other man claimed her while Peter was away? Had she not told him her mother was planning for her to come out in society at the end of November?

"July, August, September, October, November . . . That is not quite five months, but the tour would take. . . Lord, in Heaven, You must have heard him—a voyage for six months, and he believes my sole purpose in life is to know his estate inside and out? That is most assuredly not the case. I will do my best to Your glory, Lord, since You have seen fit to provide this opportunity. But I still desire a wife. The estate will be here, but . . . "

Peter bowed his head. *Can You not stop this ill-begotten voyage before it starts? I so desired to find Miss Chetwynd and speak with her father.*

Peter raised his head, slid her picture out, and studied it again. *Since You have made a way for me to go to Liverpool when I least expected it, I must believe I will see her again. Therefore, I pray You will give me an opportunity to speak with her of spiritual matters.*

As much as Peter hated doing it, he carefully folded her sketch and slipped it between the pages of his Bible. "I commit her and this entire situation to You. Please help me to submit to Your will, whatever it is."

Chapter 32

Hope

Woolton Hall, Liverpool
Merseyside, England
10 July 1795, Friday

Three times prior to their departure for Liverpool, Peter attempted to speak to his father about Miss Chetwynd, but to no avail. Preparations for the journey and good-byes were far more important.

On the way to Liverpool, Peter had hoped to take advantage of the long coach ride, but Father did not care to discuss such a trivial matter as finding a wife. And between visits to the solicitors, finalizing arrangements for their departure, and tours of the company's warehouses, ships, and business offices—not to mention analyzing ledgers containing records of his father's investments in the Birmingham munitions factory, which had nearly tripled in value in the last ten years—Peter abandoned the idea of presenting his case at all.

So now, as they sat in yet another coach on their way to Woolton Hall's annual End-of-Season Ball, Peter was astonished when his father brought up the topic.

"Do not concern yourself over a wife. As long as she is healthy and has proper breeding, she will suit the purpose well enough."

"I do not—"

"Liverpool's finest will be here tonight. Examine what's on the market, identify two or three that suit your fancy, and I will see to the matter as soon as we get back."

Their hired coach jolted over a bump in the road, and Peter readjusted his seat on the lumpy cushion.

"And see to your manners. You cannot be overly religious. You are the heir to my estate, not a common cleric."

"I am aware of that."

"Your face does not reassure me. Let me make it clear. If you cannot abide such luxury, as Nicholas Ashton has seen fit to offer, then pretend you are at the Lord's Table partaking of *His* bounty."

"Father, you needn't remind me. I am well aware of how to perform."

"Splendid then. Seek out a daughter of the Pattens or Eryes. An alliance with either family could enhance our position. Of course, the Blackburnes and the Ashtons are also some of the most influential people in Liverpool and, therefore, in the Parliament, and I suppose they have daughters. If you could lay hold of one of those little fillies, the next three generations of Adsleys would be set, and you would have a seat in Parliament for certain."

Peter clamped his mouth shut.

A loud knock sounded on the coach door. "Gentleman, Woolton Hall, if you please," the footman announced.

"Indeed it is," Mr. Adsley said as he exited. Peter maintained his silence.

⋀

Regardless of what little hope Annette had for doing anything more than watching on the sidelines when the dancing began, she was thrilled to be at Woolton Hall. Hundreds of beeswax candles illuminated the luxurious rooms, marble statues, and Greek revival paintings. Servants mingled among the stylish guests, offering champagne, which sparkled in the most exquisite crystal glasses she had ever seen. And copious arrangements of peach and white roses, purple-tipped violets, and other exotic flowers adorned the tables and golden candelabrum.

Having already toured the fabulous gardens with their sparkling fountains, the outdoor conservatory with its magnificent collection of exotic violets, and all the rooms available for a guest's perusal, Annette sat down at a window seat overlooking the entryway. She was studying the visitors as they exited their coaches while Papá was conversing.

Suddenly, her heart leaped. A gentleman whose determined stride and wavy brown hair reminded her of Mr. Peter Adsley was passing beneath her window. She peered out and noticed the royal blue ribbon with which he tied his hair. There was an older gentleman, perhaps his father, with him as well, and by now they were both in the Hall.

With her heart aflutter, she sought her father. Placing her hand on his elbow, she waited for just the right moment to speak.

"Papá, do let's go downstairs. I would like some refreshments."

"Is that so?" He beamed and nodded to his companion. "Well, that is my signal, sir. I must escort this young lady away for now. Perhaps we shall speak more later. Enjoy the evening."

Annette led her father through the crowd.

"Well, poppet, I imagine I shall have to accompany you the entire evening, what with your mother indisposed and Miss Haack attending her."

"I hope it is not too much trouble, Papá. But it was the last ball I could attend before we leave Liverpool, and I—"

"You are absolutely right. I am happy to escort you, though I cannot dance. What say you of this grand mansion? Is it not magnificent?"

"Yes." She looked over the balustrade down to the main floor.

Annette moved toward the circular staircase, searching for the gentleman with dark, wavy hair and a royal blue ribbon. As they descended, she thought she saw him and his companion near the French doors, beside a table with a carved ice dolphin in the midst of various fruits and plates of cheese. She honed in on that place, schooling her reactions as she went. She must be prepared in case it was not Mr. Adsley.

"This way, Papá." She weaved along the fringes of the crowd toward the refreshment table.

"You must be starving, my girl. I've not seen you so intent on getting to a refreshment table since you were a child. Are you well?"

"Yes." She laughed. "Only I do not wish to get caught at the end of a long line."

The two gentlemen Annette sought stood a few feet from the refreshment table. And at that moment, the older gentleman moved away from the one she hoped was her pastor.

Her heart danced. It was he, less than ten feet from her, here in Liverpool.
She said a quick prayer of thanksgiving and then spoke to Father.

"I am going to take my refreshment on that settee over there by that matron in the green velvet gown. Do you see her?"

"Very good, my dear. I shall scout the area for some of my colleagues."

Annette took a plate from the end of the table and quickly turned her back. She did not want Pastor Adsley to see her yet. Having selected some red grapes, she seated herself beside the matron and began to consider her next move.

"Why, Adsley, is that you?"

The older gentleman who was with Pastor Adsley turned to Annette's father.

"Wonder of wonders, it is! How are you, Old Man?"

Annette tried to maintain her composure as she watched and listened to another miracle unfolding.

"My God, Chetwynd, how long has it been? Ten, fifteen years since we were in business?"

⁂

A huge gong struck in Peter's thoughts when he saw his father offering a hand to the gentleman named Mr. Chetwynd.

"I cannot say how good it is to see you, Adsley." The jovial man embraced Peter's father. "And here at Woolton Hall, no less. I never thought I would live to see the day when the Ashtons would invite the likes of us to one of their assemblies."

Both men laughed, and Peter stood amazed. Could he be related to Miss Chetwynd?

"We must talk over dinner, Charles, and you must meet my daughter." Mr. Chetwynd glanced at Peter. "I see you have a young gentleman with you as well. Will you not introduce us?"

"Absolutely. This is my son, Mr. Peter Adsley." His father's face dulled for a second, and then he continued. "He has recently taken up estate affairs. Peter, my longtime friend and former partner, Mr. William Chetwynd."

"Pleased to make your acquaintance, Mr. Chetwynd." Peter offered his hand, and his father's friend shook it vigorously.

"So you are trying to keep your father honest, are you?" Mr. Chetwynd teased. "I wish you the best in that. As I recall, he was a most cunning investor, and I venture to say he will want to teach you a few trade secrets if you can . . . Well, let's leave it at that. It is a pleasure to meet you, young Adsley."

"Quite right, Mr. Chetwynd." Peter was not exactly sure how to respond.

"Now gentlemen, please excuse me a moment while I retrieve my daughter. You must make her acquaintance." Mr. Chetwynd turned away.

Lord, he must be her father. Her disposition is so like his. Praise You doubly much, and thank You for Your endless grace.

Peter turned to his father to subdue his excitement. "What good fortune to meet an old friend. You must be very pleased."

"It is a pleasant surprise, but remember what I told you. No crusading, I do not want you getting him started."

"What do you—?"

Mr. Chetwynd's overwhelming happiness spilled over the rest of Peter's question. "Adsley and young Adsley, here she is. Make my daughter, Miss Annette Chetwynd's, acquaintance," he said with a flourish.

Peter's mouth went dry, and the buzz of his chaotic thoughts almost prevented him from hearing the rest of the introduction.

"She is a great comfort to me in my old age, and quite amiable, if you can abide her impish habits and tireless wit."

"Father, do be careful," she chided, "you will ruin my chances by revealing such faults. Do speak of my other more pleasing accomplishments."

"My dear girl, there is no chance of that. You know I could not part with you so soon. Now let me make the introductions. This is Mr. Charles Adsley, an old friend and business partner, and his son, Mr. Peter Adsley."

Peter's heart pounded as he absorbed her very presence.

"It is a pleasure to meet you, sir." She smiled and curtsied to Peter's father.

"I am delighted to make your acquaintance as well, Miss Chetwynd." His father gave a gallant bow, and then whispered from behind his hand. "And let me say, you needn't distress yourself over your father's slapdash introduction overmuch. Nothing he says can be taken seriously; in fact, he is probably halfway in his cups by now."

"Why Mr. Adsley, you are simply scandalous." She snapped open her fan and started fluttering it along with her eyelashes while Peter's father laughed. Then she turned those gorgeous eyes on Peter.

Flickering candlelight cast a golden halo over her porcelain skin and the twinkling stars in her eyes as she offered him her gloved hand.

"Pas . . . Mr. Adsley."

"I am honored to make your acquaintance, Miss Chetwynd." Peter bowed.

Just then, a breeze from the garden wafted through the French doors and across her delicate, white gown, delivering him an enticing whiff of her alluring orange blossom scent. He closed his eyes and inhaled its intoxicating fragrance while lingering over her wrist.

"As I am yours," she said aloud. Then she whispered, "And do give me back my hand before they suspect something."

Peter immediately registered her concern, released her hand, and straightened up, turning his attention to their fathers' conversation.

"Chetwynd, why do not you come to the library with us? I understand they are discussing some of Parliament's most recent decisions. I am . . . My son and I are most interested in how they will affect the trade. It would be interesting to hear your perspective. Join us for dinner too, if you will."

"I would be pleased to. There is an impediment, however. You see, my daughter's companion is attending my wife, who has taken ill. Therefore, it falls to me to chaperon her tonight."

I am disappointed to hear of your wife's illness, but I certainly understand where your daughter is concerned." Mr. Adsley eyed Peter. "Might I offer a possible solution?"

"Of course."

"My son, who has recently been pastoring one of our parishes, is a most reliable and respectful gentleman. Perhaps he would be willing to assist if you would permit him."

Peter's heart skipped a beat as Mr. Chetwynd turned to him.

"So then, 'tis the Church for you, is it, young Adsley?" Before Peter could answer, her father plowed ahead. "What do you say then? May I count on you to chaperon my daughter this evening? She is a bit young, but you could do worse."

"It would be my privilege, Mr. Chetwynd."

"Then 'tis settled." He turned to her. "Annette, I am placing you under *Pastor* Adsley's care. But be wary of inflicting him with your countless questions, and not too much dancing either. He seems fit enough, but you mustn't cripple him."

"Yes, Father." She gave him a coy little smile.

"Well, Adsley, let's to the library then."

"We will find you later before dinner, son, outside perhaps," Mr. Adsley said. "With all the hot air flowing, doubtless we will need to refresh ourselves."

With that, the two gentlemen left Peter and Annette standing together as the dance music began.

"Bach's Minuet in G, if I am not mistaken. Will you do me the honor of dancing, Miss Chetwynd?" Peter offered his arm but kept his eyes riveted to his elbow. She had already bewitched him, but he mustn't appear too enthusiastic. He had much to discover . . . and much to tell.

She gave no reply and made no move to accept his invitation or arm. Detaching his eyes from his coat sleeve, Peter directed his gaze to hers. As if that was precisely what she desired of him, she rewarded him with an exuberant smile and the answer to his question.

"Certainly, Pastor Adsley, nothing would please me more than to be your partner."

Chapter 33
Enchanted

Gently grasping her delicate fingers, Peter led Annette through the minuet as if she were a marionette. Her lithe form was most graceful. He also noticed when she stood still in front of him, her head would rest against his heart, making for a very comfortable embrace in which he could rest his chin perfectly atop her head.

"Pastor Adsley, may I ask you a question?" She opened conversation as she passed beneath his arm, and his heart sank. *Pastor, again.* He must tell her the truth.

"You may," he responded on the next turn.

"Were you able to resolve matters with the man whose frightening roar startled me back in the forest at Buxton?"

"Yes." *But I am no longer a pastor.*

She gave him an incredulous look. "If you answer so briefly, how shall I ever carry the conversation?"

"I am sure you will manage." He meant to tease her, but it did not come out right.

She grimaced, circled, and then returned. "That was unkind."

"I . . . A pastor cannot reveal one's private concerns."

"I understand, but was my encouragement useful to him?"

Now she was fishing. "I can assure you, the man is thankful for your exhortation."

"What an amiable response."

"As was yours when you . . . managed your father's . . . very distinctive introduction." He tried not to laugh.

"You do not say."

"I do. It is doubtful whether anyone could produce such a pleasant rejoinder after being called an imp with tired wit." He recognized his error immediately. "I mean—"

"Why Pastor Adsley, you should be ashamed of yourself. Papá said I had impish habits and tireless wit."

"I beg your pardon, but I . . ."

Although he enjoyed dancing and was ordinarily quite skilled at it, Peter lost his count and missed a step. He caught up again and, grasping her hand at just the right moment, continued, "Do forgive me. I find myself rather challenged at the moment."

"Indeed. Dancing is often complicated by conversation. I much prefer sitting or walking for the mental demands of a forthright and coherent discussion."

He squelched a laugh and almost missed another step.

"Are you well, sir?"

"I fear the minuet is becoming quite tedious."

"Or has my tireless wit gotten the better of you?"

As they moved in opposite circles, Peter followed her with his eyes. A growing sense of longing gnawed at his heart. He wanted to stay with her, to listen to her, to talk with her more, and to learn everything he could about her. He must find out if they shared a similar faith, not to mention explaining the change in his circumstances.

She returned to face him.

"If you will excuse me, but I would rather not engage in the customary social interactions and flattery an event such as this often necessitates."

The twinkles in her eyes vanished. "Then you no longer desire to dance with me?"

"No. I mean. . ." Another turn demanded his attention. "We may dance as much as you like. I was speaking of shallow flirtations."

"Then you prefer we do not speak?"

"On the contrary, I would converse with you for hours, but I haven't the time. Would you consent to a forthright conversation like the one in the glade at Buxton and in Sylvia's study?"

The question hung in the humid air surrounding them. What kind of mannerless lout would she think him? They moved away from each other again, bowed, and the minuet concluded. He studied her face, which remained completely unreadable.

"Would you care for something to drink, Miss Chetwynd?" He attempted to restore order with etiquette.

"Some punch would be nice."

He escorted her to a refreshment table and selected a glass for her.

"It has grown rather warm in here, and I understand there is a beautiful prospect overlooking the fountains from the promenade. May I escort you outside?"

She murmured assent, but the playful, impish young lady had been replaced by a demure debutante who would not even look at him.

They walked through the French doors, and he guided her around a corner into an alcove where a curved wrought iron bench overlooked the fountains. Then, he leaned his shoulder against the stone wall beside her and turned his attention to the magnificent fountains lining the center of the avenue.

A few other couples meandered up and down the avenue or sat in close conversation on benches placed along the gravel pathway. When she finished her punch, Peter tried a non-threatening opening.

"May I take your glass?"

"Yes, thank you."

"I shall be back momentarily." He left the alcove, placed the glasses on a tray near the French door, and within seconds, returned to her.

"Pastor Adsley—" The firmness of her voice surprised him. "Would you please be seated? I find it rather disconcerting to have you hovering about without speaking."

Cool air ruffled her curls and soothed his heated skin as an avalanche of relief blanketed him. Was that it? After their private interactions in Miss Betherton's study and the forest at Buxton, he was making her nervous? He had no idea.

He looked down at the curved bench. It would not allow him much space. "My apologies but the bench seems rather small."

"There is room enough." She re-situated herself and patted the space beside her. "Now do be seated, and talk to me."

"Thank you, that is much better." But he wondered for whom since it would take considerable effort on his part to keep his right thigh from touching her left one.

"Now, have I understood you correctly? You do not wish to engage in any flirtations or other conventional conversation this evening?"

"Yes." He sighed. Their seating arrangement was somewhat of a distraction.

"How shamefully roguish." She tapped his arm with her fan. "I never thought to hear such a provocative idea from you. Are you not the staid gentleman I met at Miss Betherton's home some months ago?"

"Indeed, I am. Nevertheless, it appears that some of your—How shall I say it?—penchant for . . . unusual behavior has attached itself to me."

"Then my purpose has been fulfilled." She grinned at him.

"Purpose . . . fulfilled? What . . . ?"

"I am not at liberty to say, so you needn't ask. But why have you so little time? Did I not hear you say you would converse with me for hours but for your lack of time?"

Ah, the dreadful tour. He had no desire to think about it, much less waste a single minute discussing it. But he could not just disappear from her life for six months, or more, without some explanation. She must also know of his change in circumstances.

He studied her expectant face. The twilight sky bathed her cheeks and neck in a lavender haze, which tinted her white gown with a bluish hue. Her eyes sparkled like the glittering water droplets splashing from the fountain across the promenade, and his heart rattled inside his chest. Another breeze wafted over her hair. He inhaled, and all rational thought evaporated from his mind.

His eyes drifted to her lips, which she pressed together to moisten, and he stretched his arm out along the back of their bench. Leaning toward her upturned face, he hovered, studying the stars in her eyes. With lips a whispered breath away, he savored their closeness and sighed.

Orange blossoms perfumed the air, and yet he lingered. This would be his first kiss, a memory to last a lifetime. He did not wish to rush the affair. His pulse deepened and a blazing heat burned in his chest. She would be his now. At nearly the last second, he felt his own lips part, and tilting his head slightly to the left, he closed his eyes and moved a hair's breadth forward to—

"Will you answer my question, or am I to be held in suspense?"

Peter instantly turned aside, grazing his cheek against her curls. "Pardon?" He cleared his throat and sat back.

"Really, Pastor Adsley, do keep up. I asked why our time together is so short and you . . . Well, you . . ."

God forgive him, she must have realized what he was about to do. He got to his feet and offered her his arm. "Shall we walk then, Miss Chetwynd?"

"Absolutely." She stood up and snuggled her gloved hand in the crook of his arm. "Walking is said to promote forthright and coherent conversation."

"Excellent, very good then." He covered her hand with his. "I must inform you of the change in my circumstances."

Chapter 34

Calculating

Sir Steven Likebridge, who also made it a point to attend the Ashtons' ball, laughed as he watched his remaining brother—the pastor, no less—and Miss Chetwynd from the shadows.

How quickly he had maneuvered her outside. It would be interesting to see what he would try to get from her before he left on the "grand tour." Pastor or not, he was still a man, and the prospect of so many months without female companionship might prompt any number of desperate behaviors, even from a duty-bound fool like Adsley.

Likebridge remained in the shadows, skirting the crowd until he reached the French doors. He needed just the right vantage point to see this. And though it might have been nice to trade places with Peter, remaining on the fringe of the crowd better served Likebridge's purpose. Foregoing the chaste little kiss he might have forced from Miss Chetwynd was nothing compared to the more vigorous entertainments awaiting him at his customary haunt near the docks. In the end, she and her fortune would be his anyway.

And speaking of endings, the first half of Likebridge's scheme was complete. The original Adsley heir was dead, though fate had deprived Likebridge of actually killing him. Now, it was time to initiate the second half.

Every fiber of Likebridge's being pulsed with anticipation. His years of painstaking machinations and patience would finally pay off. Tomorrow would be the beginning of the two Adsley men's inevitable end. Mr. Charles Adsley and his new heir would sail on Likebridge's ship, and somewhere along the way, they would both end up dead. Then he would take what was rightfully his.

Everything was perfect.

Yet hold. One irresistible option for a bit more torment presented itself in the form of the connection between Miss Chetwynd and his remaining brother, and he must take advantage of it before he left Woolton Hall. Such a delicious little treat would flavor his magnificent plot for revenge with another shade of misery, rather than preclude its inevitable outcome, and it might also provide a bit of amusement for their long voyage.

Likebridge signaled, and his man approached.

"Jackson, I have need of paper and a quill."

"This way to the study, sir."

Once inside, Likebridge sat down at the large polished desk and thought for a moment. The precise wording was so important. He needed the exact nuance for this communiqué. He picked up the quill and wrote on a paper bearing the Ashton crest.

"That should suffice." He melted wax for the seal, and then stamped it with the Ashton insignia. He took a second sheet of paper and composed a lengthier message that he sealed with his own ring. He glanced at his seal—a snake wrapped around a rose. As counterfeits went, it was nicely done.

"There now, Jackson, it seems that our young Mr. Adsley has developed an interest in my future wife, and we cannot have that. Can we?"

"No, sir."

"Deliver this message to Mr. Peter Adsley at the end of the ball, within ten minutes of the time he returns Miss Chetwynd to her father's care." He rose from his seat. "And tomorrow morning, deliver this second letter, instructing my solicitor to submit my offer of marriage to her father no later than Wednesday next. If he accepts the arrangement, inform them to write up the settlement agreements on my behalf. When I return from this voyage, I will sign the contract."

Likebridge stepped away from the desk. "And make sure Cousin Ives keeps a watch on both Adsley men for the rest of the night. After his time with Miss Chetwynd, Mr. Peter Adsley may have a change of heart. If he makes the slightest attempt to circumvent the trip, I want Ives to thrash him. Tell your cousin to make it look like the mugging happened at their Merseyside warehouses, and then get him stowed in the first mate's cabin on the *Terona*." He pulled the man close. "Do you understand, Jackson?"

"I do, sir."

"Good. Because if I do not find both Mr. Charles Adsley and Mr. Peter Adsley on my *Terona* tomorrow morning before we sail, you and your cousin will pay."

"Yes, sir."

Sir Likebridge smoothed Jackson's livery collar. "Of course, if everything goes according to plan, you and Cousin Ives will live a very long and comfortable life in my service."

"Very good, sir."

"And do not fail to get word to me if Ives actually does beat Adsley. I shall inform Mr. Charles Adsley of the problem myself."

"Yes, sir. I will. I promise."

Chapter 35

The Speech

A full moon illuminated the gravel walkway along the avenue beside the fountains. The constant wash of the cascades falling into the pools created a rhythmic song that calmed Peter's nerves as he and Annette strolled toward the gardens.

He wondered if they had the same effect on her. She seemed to have borne the news of his departure tolerably well.

"It has been four months since we first met, and they have passed quickly enough. Papá will also be home for a while. Time goes so much faster when he is with me. And I have my sketches." She grinned. "You will have plenty to do and see while you are traveling, and six months will have disappeared before long."

"You are very optimistic, Miss Chetwynd."

"Yes. But there will be so many plans to discuss with your father. You will have maps to study, a crew of men to whom to minister, and you shall have time to read. Perhaps you could study a challenging theological issue, and prepare a few sermons about it. Surely, there are complicated topics you have wanted to explore, but could not for lack of time."

"You are astonishing, Miss Chetwynd. I told you I was no longer a pastor."

"What of it? You may continue studying and writing. Is there not some controversial issue to explore? For example, what would the Scriptures say about this statement? 'Reason is, and ought only to be the slave of the passions, and can never pretend to any other office than to serve and obey them.'"

Peter recognized the statement from David Hume's *A Treatise to Human Nature*. But how could she know of—even memorize—such foolishness?

"I can tell you despise it. The view prevails in society, though. Refuting it would make for a splendid debate, would it not? And tell me what you think of this? A rough paraphrase, I know, but the potential is endless: Since the universe's design is rather like a very large machine with many hundreds of other small machines running inside of it, and if there is truly a designing intelligence—God—behind it, then that divine designer is rather like a man, except with far greater capacity to create, because men can already create machines."

Peter drew her around beside a tall hedge of white roses.

"You cannot believe that."

"What makes you think I do?"

"The ease with which you speak."

"I have read Hume's work. His *Dialogues Concerning Natural Religion* was most interesting."

"Now I see why you offered to discuss religious philosophy that night in the study."

"You are disappointed."

"Not exactly." *Disillusioned, concerned. What else would you expect from a man who truly cares about you?*

"I am sorry. I meant only to prove there is a variety of topics you may investigate in order to pass the time while on your voyage."

"You need not be concerned."

"Because I am a woman?"

"No. Sylvia and I discussed philosophy as a matter of routine."

"But you are still bothered."

"Not with you." *It is your familiarity with such a worldly perspective.*

"What then?"

"This situation merely goes to show we must become more thoroughly acquainted. However, because of this absurd voyage, we have to wait an additional six months. On that note, I can no longer delay. I must confess."

"A Protestant pastor turning Catholic and confessing to a young lady?" She laughed. "That would make for an interesting study. Perhaps I will look into it while you are away."

"I have lost my parish." His somber tone melted her smile. "I am no longer a pastor."

"I believe you have already informed me of that."

"My older brother, Richard—the *true* heir to the Adsley estate—is dead. He fell from his horse and broke his neck. My father called me away from my parish to take over the role of heir the same day I met you in the forest at Buxton, though I did not know it at the time. And just now—though I am no longer a pastor—he led your father to believe I am. I apologize for any inconvenience this may have caused. Now, if you will, please allow me to escort you back to your father."

"I will not."

"I beg your pardon?"

"I fail to see how remaining in my father's company would aid us in furthering our acquaintance." Her brows knotted and her eyes sparked. "I also fail to comprehend how your brother's death, as tragic and unexpected as it must have been, has destroyed your ministry."

Peter's eyes widened. She was truly irritated.

"If my opinion offends you, I am sorry. But you are profoundly mistaken. While you may no longer serve a flock in Buxton, Mr. Adsley, make no mistake about it. You will always be a pastor. Scripture—Romans, I believe—teaches God's 'gifts and calling' are irrevocable. Furthermore, as the heir of the entire Adsley estate and its thriving shipping company, which may or may not suit your tastes, your Christian legacy will reach halfway around the world. Therefore, it appears to me that your ministry and your pastoral responsibilities have not been taken. They have been multiplied exponentially. 'O ye of little faith!'"

At that precise moment, as he stood gazing down at her radiant face, Peter fell in love.

Lord, I could take her in my arms and kiss her forever. Instead, he reached behind her and plucked a rose from the hedge. "Then I . . . I stand corrected, and in the most satisfying manner I could ever imagine possible, Miss Chetwynd. Will you take this rose as a token of my eternal gratitude?"

"Thank you, *Pastor* Adsley. It is beautiful."

"Now that that is settled, what shall we speak of next?"

↟

Resisting the temptation to tuck one of her errant curls back behind her ear, Peter clasped his hands behind his back and watched her make the adjustment herself.

"How about your coming out? Though I know you loath to speak of it, perhaps there is a chance I might return in time to attend. When is it?"

"Annette, dear girl," Mr. Chetwynd's voice jarred Peter, and he turned to find both of their fathers coming across the lawn. "There you are. I did not see you before."

"I am here. Look at this glorious rose Mr. Adsley picked for me, Papá."

"Magnificent."

"How were the debates?" she asked.

"Stirring, as usual. But it was monstrous hot inside, so we opted for some fresh air. Have you enjoyed your evening?"

"I have. Thank you."

"Has she exhausted you with dancing, young Adsley?"

"No. It was quite invigorating."

Annette chimed in, "We were just discussing the benefits of filling one's time with a variety of useful employments."

"A safe enough topic though rather a dull investigation. Would you not prefer a more risqué subject, say perhaps, the slave trade?" The mischievous sparkle in Mr. Chetwynd's eyes mirrored his daughter's.

Peter glanced at his father.

"I had not thought to destroy your friendship by speaking in public. You have only just renewed it." She turned to Peter's father. "I assure you, Mr. Adsley, I do not wish to distress you with my chatter."

"It is quite all right, Miss Chetwynd. We just came from a blistering debate that could destroy a family. From what your father says of you, my son and I would be most interested in your discourse."

"Well, Adsley?" Mr. Chetwynd questioned. "Will you permit her to speak?"

Peter's father appeared to consider the question while Miss Chetwynd's father drew her aside for a moment.

Typically, a young lady's accomplishments in the arts, proper deportment, a pleasing appearance, and music, drawing, or needlework recommended her to a man like Peter's father. Accepting an offer to share her opinion on such a provocative topic in his company would do nothing to commend her. The fact that she even held an opinion would be beyond imagination, and based on her last two opinions, Peter was uneasy about it.

"As a boon to you, old friend, let us hear what your daughter has to say. It could not be so terrible. She is only a young lady, after all."

"I would not hold that against her. Her education is equal to that of any young man. I have seen to that."

Peter sighed. He was certain his father would disapprove of her.

"Have you, Chetwynd? Whatever for?"

"It was my pleasure, and she is very persuasive. Right, my girl?"

"Yes, Father. But would you and the Adsley gentlemen be seated? I shall stand here by this statue of Diana. Then, when they wish to pelt me with rotten eggs and mushy tomatoes, I shall be able to escape," she teased, and they all laughed.

"There now, are you ready?" She cleared her throat and adopted her public speaking voice. "Very good then, I will begin.

"Gentlemen, we English pride ourselves on being the pinnacle of the civilized world, but we are little more than a greedy mix of opportunists and flailing citizens of enlightened conscience, trying to sort out a dilemma that has ensnared our society for decades.

"On the one hand, we have industry, which rests on the slave trade. Indeed, this marvelous city with all of its inhabitants would fail most profoundly without this trade. On the other hand, we have insistent abolitionists: Wilberforce and Wedgewood—even Chief Justice Mansfield though I do not think he would admit it. Remember, he ruled in favor of a fugitive slave from Virginia—James Somersett, I believe his name was—saying that 'the act of walking on English soil freed him.' That was only three years ago, in '92."

Peter watched the wrinkles forming on his father's forehead.

"Those who make it their business to sell Negroes away from their native lands must consider them to be animals, or how else could they do it? Yet, in the eyes of the Creator, 'There is neither Jew nor Greek, there is neither bond nor free, there is neither male nor female,' according to the third chapter of Galatians and verses in Colossians.

"That means, in words which echo Josiah Wedgwood's sentiments, I am a sister of those poor wretches. But do you or I even know how they are treated? Do any of us know what it means to be owned by another person? We enjoy these privileges . . ." She swept her hand toward the fountains as she spoke. "Yet, we are entirely ignorant of their true cost in terms of human life. However, if any one of us or our family members were to be treated the way a Negro is treated, we would fight.

"Some may say we are doing our Christian duty by bringing salvation to the savages, but that is a ruse. We are taking advantage of them. We must stop the flesh mongering of the slave trade. We must be forerunners in supporting our weaker brothers and sisters and giving them a voice in society. That will be their salvation.

"We must not allow people to fuel our excesses with their lives. If our cities fall, so be it. The empire progressed for centuries before this vice blossomed into what it has become. We are inventors, scientists, explorers, hard-working persistent seekers. We will find better ways to kindle our industrial fires. It will be a monumental challenge, but we must accept it. We will be safer and more blessed to live in a country that has broken the vise-like grip of greed, than to be, as Jonathan Edwards so aptly put it, 'sinners in the hands of an angry God.'"

Spellbound, Peter stared. She spoke with more passion than many of his former schoolmates who supported the cause could ever muster. She was obviously well-acquainted with the Wilberforce movement and the legal debates surrounding the issue. Her gentle, yet determined, voice added all the more strength to her words. And using Jonathan Edwards' quote to conclude penetrated his very soul. Surely, she must be a true believer. How else could she speak so convincingly, and even use Scripture so effectively?

Peter noticed his father adjusting his coat.

Mr. Chetwynd took his daughter's hand and kissed it. "Thank you, my dear. You have spoken most eloquently."

"Yes, Miss Chetwynd," Peter's father added. "A most profound speech, not unlike those I have heard from my son."

"Thank you, Mr. Adsley." She turned to her father. "Will you allow that I stay with Mr. Adsley a while longer?"

"The evening is for you, remember?"

"Yes, and I am quite content."

"Fine then. We shall go in. Join us for dinner in the next quarter of an hour or so."

"Thank you, Father."

"You are most welcome." Mr. Chetwynd turned to Peter's father. "Well, Adsley, there you have it 'out of the mouth of babes.' The Wilberforce movement has infiltrated our women's circles and our nurseries. Neither he nor his ideas will soon disappear."

"Well, Mr. Adsley?" She offered a questioning smile. "Have you nothing to say?"

"Plenty. However, my capacity for selecting the correct words is rather diminished."

"But you know me better now, I think."

"Yes."

"Then what do you say to a forthright and honest discussion about your plans for the week or so following your return to Liverpool sometime in late December?"

"It appears I needn't say a thing."

She gave him an impish grin. "I will be out in society by then."

"Indeed."

"Then perhaps it would be a good idea to . . ."

"The banquet awaits us." He offered his arm. "May I escort you inside, Miss Chetwynd?"

"It would be a pleasure to dine with you, Mr. Adsley. And I shall confine my comments to the weather, the food, and the size and elegant nature of the party, as usual."

He smiled at her. "I dare say you will not. But hearing you endeavor to try will be most interesting."

Chapter 36

Agreement

Servants entered the large dining room with sumptuous courses of Salamongundy, Macaroni Pye, and cut beetroots, followed by the main courses of Welsh Rarebit, roasted goose, and partridge with beefsteaks and shallots. Annette was in heaven, but not because of the food. In fact, she was so excited, she could hardly eat. She glanced to her left to reassure herself he was really beside her.

She took a bite of beefsteak and studied him as she chewed. Warm candlelight poured over his chiseled profile. His sun-warmed cheeks made for a striking contrast against his blazing white cravat. No more workmen's garb or drab pastor's clothes for him, at least for this event. Now, he was lord of the manor, and he was dressed as such.

She bowed her head and closed her eyes.

God, You have outdone Yourself. I am so very grateful he is here, and so many wonderful things have happened. But he is leaving tomorrow. Can You not prevent that?

What a dimwit I am. Of course You can, but will You? I know I am only just making Your acquaintance, and I do not want to presume too much of Your friendship, but please let him stay. As I promised, I will study my Bible every day, and I will pay better attention in church. Well, I would do that anyway, or else he would surely be disappointed.

Annette's shoulders sagged. She should be ashamed of herself for trying to bargain with God. And studying the Bible as if it were some competition—it was downright shameful. She hung her head even lower.

God, I am a wretched slug. How can You stand to listen to me, much less answer my prayers? But I lack a true and deep knowledge of You. And I need Your forgiveness so badly. Please forgive me.

In closing, I want Mr. Adsley to stay, but if he must go, please keep him safe. I could not stand losing him for real. And show me how I can repay You for all Your kindness. Amen.

She glanced at Peter. He looked uneasy.

"Are you well, Miss Chetwynd?"

"Yes."

"For a moment, it seemed as though you might faint."

Annette laughed. "I was praying."

"Splendid." He smiled. Truly he would be happy to know she had been praying, but what if he knew how weak her faith was?

As was the custom, after dessert the women began excusing themselves while the footman brought out the port to ease the gentlemen's more serious discussions.

"If you will excuse me, Mr. Adsley."

Peter jumped to his feet and pulled Miss Chetwynd's chair out for her.

"Thank you, though you know I would rather not leave."

"I would you could stay as well, and you are most welcome." He bowed and his gaze followed the gentle swish of her gown as she moved to the exit across the room. Port wine, cigar smoke, and bickering over politics held little interest for him. He had so little time remaining and so much to say.

"Young Adsley—" Annette's father spoke up. "Are you still standing? Go after her, man. She mustn't be left alone. Her mother will have my head."

"I shall continue my vigil then."

"Perhaps it would be better for me to call it a night." Mr. Chetwynd ran the back of his hand across his brow and rubbed his left bicep.

Peter waited.

"I am getting rather tired."

"As you wish, sir, though I have escorted her thus far and have yet to suffer a dull moment."

Her father laughed. "You are a good man, Adsley. Sometimes the little imp can be quite peculiar. But it is my fault. I wanted her to have an education, and she drinks it up twice as fast as your father downs his port." He nodded to Peter's father, who lifted his glass and smiled.

"It is my privilege to serve as her companion." He directed a questioning glance at his father. The last thing Peter wanted was more trouble from him.

"Go on, see to the girl." Mr. Adsley glanced at Chetwynd. "If you are staying."

Peter took out his pocket watch. "It is just after midnight. What do you say I meet you back in the salon in about an hour?"

"Very good then," Mr. Chetwynd responded. "I am not up for much more than that tonight." He mumbled something else, but Peter did not hear him well.

"Pardon?"

"Ah, 'tis nothing, young Adsley. You are a good man for asking, though. Just take care of my daughter for me."

Chapter 37
An Understanding

Bedazzled ladies gathered in small groups, glided around the salon, or sat chattering together along the walls, but Peter did not see Miss Chetwynd. It occurred to him she might have gone to refresh herself, but after checking and rechecking the stairway leading to the guest rooms upstairs, he changed his mind. Perhaps she had gone out of doors.

Weaving amongst the guests, Peter made his way to the exit. It was cooler than before and light from the full moon illuminated everything, from the smallest drop of water hovering on the leaves of the rose bush beside him, to the cool marble balustrade across the promenade.

He glanced at the couples sitting on wrought iron settees and strolling along the promenade. He walked over to the carved marble railing overlooking the fountains and leaned against the cool surface while scanning the avenue, but he did not see her anywhere.

Then, the soft rustle of silk and the scent of orange blossoms alerted him to her presence. She leaned on the rail beside him. His eyes dropped to her gloveless hands, but he forced himself to look back at the avenue of glittering fountains.

"So you managed to escape the men," she commented.

"Yes, but there were complications."

"What do you mean?"

"Nothing really, only some reference to your being a peculiarity or something of that nature. Your father was making excuses for your education."

"Was he?"

"Yes, but it is of no consequence. However, I have a question that is of much import."

"May we walk as we discuss it?"

"Yes." He smiled and offered his arm. "Let us take a turn in the garden this time."

"So what is your question, Mr. Adsley? I am armed and ready."

"You sound as though you are fortifying yourself for battle."

"One can never tell, these days." He could hear the smile in her voice and glanced at her as they descended the stairs toward the gardens. It was a rather odd statement, but then again . . .

"You did a splendid job with your discourse on abolishing the slave trade. I was particularly impressed with how you used the Scriptures to support your position, and your closing reference to Jonathan Edwards's famous sermon was sublime."

"Thank you."

"So are you as well-versed . . ." He grinned. ". . . in the Scriptures as you appear to be?"

Annette's heart nearly stopped. She knew he would ask something like this. What pastor, who was truly a man of faith, would not? But she must be careful how she answered. She did not want to lose him.

"Well-versed. I like that, though it is a rather *pun*ishing attempt at humor."

He laughed.

"On a more serious note, I have not studied the Scriptures as well as I ought. Of course, I know the Gospel and quite a few verses by memory, as you have seen. But I am not as well-versed as I should be. But is that not the case with all of us? He is faithful, but we are not?"

"Indeed, it is," he responded. "We constantly abide in Him and draw from His strength in order to grow in our faith."

"That is in the fifteenth chapter of John where Christ also speaks of laying His life down for his friends. Remember, when we first met and I asked you . . ."

"Whether I was sacrificing myself for my friend or just martyring myself for another good cause? How can I forget?"

"Even then, I knew my question would stay with you. Might I suggest a joint study, something we can examine together while you are away?"

"That is a splendid idea." His eyes brightened. "What do you say to examining five chapters per day, starting tomorrow with the first chapter of Matthew and proceeding through all four gospels? And once we do that, we can study the book of Romans, if you would like."

"And we can discuss our notes when you return."

"Agreed." How he wished he could take her in his arms. "I look forward to hearing everything you have to say."

"As do I with you. Now, imagine if you will, how this conversation would have gone had you invited me to debate the validity of David Hume's belief that passions must rule over reason."

His laugh was rich and wonderful.

"What a tremendous waste of time that would have been."

"Indeed. And we have so little time." He saw a glimmer of sadness in her eyes before she diverted his attention. "Look, over there." She pointed.

"The conservatory, I believe."

"A breathtaking picture, is it not?" she asked. "May we go? The Ashtons have a spectacular collection of exotic violets, and I would love to see them."

Peter scanned the building and its surroundings. Were there no other guests about? They had passed a small group of people meandering along the avenue of fountains and one or two in the gardens, but this quiet retreat appeared to be free of spectators.

He felt a bit relieved. It was less likely someone would see them, or so it seemed. The only problem was his heart. It beat like a drummer signaling attack. He took a deep breath and exhaled quietly. He was having trouble managing a mental skirmish as well.

On the one hand, he was pleased with her answer regarding her knowledge of Scripture, though she had not given the simple answer for which he had hoped. Conversely, he was sailing tomorrow. Perhaps he should refuse to go. One needn't visit a business to understand how it was run. He had only to examine the account books, and those could be requested any time. After this ball, once his father had fallen asleep, perhaps he could leave the Goree Piazza warehouse apartment where he and his father were staying to avoid traffic tomorrow morning. He could move into their Liverpool residence, and begin his research.

Amidst these considerations, another part of Peter's mind cataloged all the prohibitions society had developed for young men and women: No use of Christian names; no correspondence; no driving in carriages alone; no private conversation, or exchanging gifts, and absolutely no intimate touching. Miss Chetwynd and he together had either literally broken or broken in spirit every one of those rules. Now, the one for which he longed—although it was impossible—was to taste his first kiss from her lips. So much for him being a safe choice of chaperon.

They reached the conservatory, and she tried the door. "It is open. We must go inside."

He held the door, and they stepped into a jungle of exotic plants, trees, and ferns.

"This way to the violets."

His fingers tingled when she took his hand and led him around the large, marble, urn-shaped fountain, which stood in the middle of the room, gurgling up a constant stream of laughing water. Glowing torches mounted here and there in iron torch holders along the walls lit a cobblestone path.

He nonchalantly pulled at his neck wrap and surveyed the room as they wound deeper through the wild bouquet of color and fragrance to a secluded back corner sitting area with a bench. It was a good thing the transom windows lining both sides of the building were open. The cross breeze offered much-needed relief from the humid air.

"Here they are." She turned a most disarming smile on him and gestured towards the purple-speckled beauties. "Are they not the most exquisite flowers you have ever seen?"

Peter examined a deep purple blossom. "Very fascinating."

She ran her thumb over the leaves of the plant. "You must feel its texture. They are as soft as a kitten's paw."

"So botany is another of your interests?" Peter asked as he touched the leaf.

"Violets are my favorite flower."

"I see."

"And you have grown quiet again." She studied his eyes.

"Perhaps we should return to the house."

"Have I done something wrong?"

"No. But it grows late."

"Are there not a few minutes more? I could listen to you dispute Hume's ridiculous statement about reason being slave to passions." She gestured toward a marble bench. "Do be seated. Mr. Adsley, please."

"Sitting in the presence of a lady is highly—"

"May we not simply be ourselves without the formality?"

"Yes, of course." He seated himself on the bench while she stood. "But my training is so deeply engrained, I cannot stop so easily."

He laughed to himself as Giles's face came to his mind.

"What is it?"

"Nothing. I was only thinking of my man. He is a friend—like a father, really—yet no matter how many times I tell him to stop calling me "sir," he still persists. I guess my habits are not so different from his."

"I see." She tilted her head and smiled.

Conversation waned. He watched the firelight from a nearby torch bathing her skin and hair in golden hues.

"Shall we—" Both spoke at once, and their words jumbled together.

"Please. Go ahead, Miss Chetwynd."

"Thank you. I was going to say I have very much enjoyed renewing our acquaintance this evening." She lowered her eyes as she rubbed a violet leaf between her finger and thumb.

"As have I."

How he longed to take her in his arms, lift her chin, and encourage her that six months apart would not be so long. However, now that they had found each other again, the time would seem interminable, at least to him. And God only knew when and if he would ever see her again.

"Mr. Adsley?" Her hand dropped away from the plant. "I wonder if I might ask a small favor of you."

"Nothing would please me more."

"Would you—?" She looked away.

"Please, Miss Chetwynd." He inched forward on the bench. "I haven't much time before I must go. Tell me how I might be of service to you."

"It is nothing, really. You needn't bother." She held up her hands as if to keep him at bay, but Peter captured both and held them to his heart.

"I am at your command, even for the smallest thing. Please tell me."

With one knee almost touching the ground, he was a knight paying homage to his lady. He maintained his petitioner's pose as his stomach flipped. Would this stunning creature, who captivated him one moment, and in the next nearly drove him to distraction, become his wife? Her penetrating eyes and the silken smoothness of her skin teased his senses. His pulse pounded in his ears, and his ability to string logical thoughts together seemed to have evaporated. Suddenly, losing all grasp of propriety, Peter lifted her hands to his mouth.

"I would do anything within my power for you," he whispered and pressed his lips to the back of her right hand.

The trickling sound of water bubbling up from the fountain in the middle of the conservatory faded as he trailed kisses across her knuckles and wrist. She slipped her hand away but said nothing. He focused his attentions on her remaining hand. After some seconds, he turned it over and placed a kiss deep in her palm.

"Mr. Adsley, I would like . . ." The gentle pressure of her fingers cupping his cheek, lifting his face to her, and the whisper-soft tones of her voice brought him away from his feast. She ran her fingers tentatively along the unruly clump of hair falling across his forehead, attempting to smooth it back. Tingles ran down his neck, tightening his throat and challenging his breathing when she traced her fingertips down the side of his face. He swallowed hard. Then she withdrew her hands and moved away from him.

"Forgive me. It was wrong of me to even think it."

He was on his feet in a second. "Miss—"

"I would like to . . ." She caught up his right hand and, drawing it to her lips, spoke against his knuckles. "I want to know . . ." She struggled to get the rest of her sentence out. Then her voice dropped to a whisper. "I long to feel a real kiss."

Her wish—or perhaps it was the frantic plea in her tone—struck an equally hungry chord in Peter's heart. He stepped closer, and extracting his hand from her hold, lightly rested his hands on her shoulders.

"I understand. Truly, I do." He gently tucked a stray curl behind her ear. "But we are not at liberty to indulge such fancies." He hated saying those words.

"Would it be a sin?"

"It would alter our friendship. And if someone was to discover us . . ."

"There is no one here."

Her words hung in the air. She moistened her lips and glanced at his. Their gazes locked again. The luster in her eyes mirrored the same intoxicating force presently flowing through every fiber of his being. No matter what happened next, from this moment on, there could be no turning back. He was responsible for her reputation.

"Ah, Annette," he groaned and gently drew her forward, touching their foreheads together. "What has become of me? I can no longer think."

Silence.

"More terrifying things could happen," she sighed.

"What?"

"Well, they could." She tilted her head away from his and stepped back. "For example, if someone was holding your head under water, you would not be able to breathe."

Dumbfounded, Peter stared at her, and she glared right back.

"You are so serious, Mr. Adsley. You complicate the simplest matter. I was only curious about a kiss. And it is not like I can simply ask anyone about it. Can you imagine what it would be like for me to ask Miss Haack? What if I asked my brother, Gerald? I would never hear the end of it."

"So you have chosen me?" He could hardly keep a straight face.

"Well, I cannot very well ask my footman, can I?"

Tension slid out of Peter like an egg out of its cracked shell. He broke down laughing so hard he had to sit down. Some seconds later when he was able to breathe again, he took out his handkerchief, wiped his face, and looked up at her. She stood with her arms tightly crossed over her chest and scowled at him.

"Miss Chetwynd, forgive me. I did not intend to laugh, but you are so—"

"You mean to continue mocking me then?"

"I was not mocking—"

She started to walk away.

He rushed forward and gently caught her arms from behind. "Miss Chetwynd, Annette, dearest, please don't go." He stood, breathing in the fragrance of her hair and running his fingers along her shoulders and down her arms. "Listen to me."

"Why should I?"

"Because you are the most extraordinary young woman I have ever met."

She leaned back against him.

"And, I find that I could easily come to love you." A profound sense of peace wrapped itself around Peter. "Only with this dreadful voyage, I haven't any time to follow proper conventions for courting. And we must learn more about one another."

She turned around, and he traced the tips of his fingers along her cheek. "And a kiss might make matters worse."

He savored every nuance of her face: her luminous eyes with their elegant lashes; the arched line of her brows; her little, sloped nose with tiny freckles sprinkled across it, and the incandescent glow of the torchlight on her skin. He must remember every little detail of her.

"I know it is disappointing. Trust me, I do," he whispered as he smoothed a diamond tear away with his thumb. Then he bowed his head so their foreheads met again. "But it is not the right time yet. Do you understand?"

"I love you too, Peter," she whispered as she wrapped her arms around his waist.

Dazed, he felt his own arms enfold her in the embrace. For the rest of his life, he was likely to feel slightly off balance. It was rather a good feeling, though, one to which he could easily succumb.

"Then you know a kiss is not such a simple thing." He breathed into the curls crowning her head. Their orange-blossom scent was toying with his resolve. He buried his nose in her tresses and inhaled deeply. He must take this part of her with him too.

The vise grip around his waist loosened and her hands crept up his torso to grasp his coat lapels. "Nor is it a sin."

He paused to accommodate the new rush of emotion, but she leaned so far into him, the only thing he felt was the last bit of reason draining from him. He searched her eyes for some small trace of apprehension, but found none.

"Lord, forgive me. I can no longer help myself." Her took her face in his hands, and closing his eyes, bent forward—

Crunch! The gravely clank of pottery scraping on the cobblestone path startled them.

A soft cry escaped her lips, and Peter involuntarily hugged her to himself, concealing her face in his cravat.

Holding his breath, Peter listened to the circular wobble of a potted plant, which had been knocked over, finally coming to rest. The intruder's confident footsteps—virtually daring Peter to give chase—followed. Then the conservatory door opened, and whoever it was strode into the night.

Chapter 38

To Court

"I apologize. I . . ." Peter thought he heard shame in her voice. "I did not mean to . . . Do you think the person will tell anyone?"

"I have no idea, but it does not matter. I am willing to do the proper thing to protect you."

"So we have an understanding then, have we?"

He could feel the smile tugging at his lips. "Yes, Miss Chetwynd, so it would seem. Shall we discuss the details of it?"

"No." All the joy had drained out of her.

"Is there something amiss? Have I displeased you?"

"No. Only one hopes ..." She reached into her reticule and snatched out a handkerchief. "Forgive me." She sniffed and attempted to control herself. "Everything has happened so quickly, and in such an unusual manner, and now someone has discovered us." She melted into his arms, and he spoke through her curls.

"Annette, please, you must try to manage your tears. It is likely nothing will come of our observer. I will speak with your father tomorrow morning to make certain everything goes well."

Extracting herself from his embrace, she wiped her eyes and blew her nose. It made the same little trumpet noises he recalled from their meeting in the forest, and he smiled.

"I believe we have also arrived at a solution for your mother's tedious conniving while at the same time relieving me of this dreadful voyage."

"We have?" She perked up.

"I will write to your father, expressing my desire to court you, and as soon as an appropriate length of time has passed, I will state my desire to marry you."

"Papá has met you, and he knows your father. If he believes your intentions are honorable and that I am willing to entertain your suit, perhaps your idea will work."

"It is settled then. I shall write it tonight, actually . . . " Peter took out his pocket watch, glanced at the time, and returned it to his pocket. "It is nearly one o'clock. I will write the letter later this morning, and then I will personally deliver it to him in a few hours before it is time for my father to set sail. We will have some time to discuss my interest further if your father wishes. After all, to him it appears that I have only just met you."

"True, but what will you say? Surely, you cannot mean to tell him everything."

"Indeed, I can." Peter smiled. "I will speak of a brief interaction at your cousin Sylvia's birthday. She could vouch for that, if necessary. And Miss Haack, your vigilant chaperon, can vouch for our meeting at St. John's parish in Buxton. I can also explain this visit to the conservatory. He is aware of the violets you wanted to see, is he not?"

"Yes. He told me about them."

"Then all is well. Remember, I am the clergyman who assisted you with your paint supplies, and I even saw you at Miss Betherton's wedding. I cannot help it that I am now the heir to my father's estate."

"Yes, that is good. Those meetings combined with this evening's *chaste* interactions will be enough to convince my father of your sincerity."

"Where are you staying?"

"Number 75 Bold Street about three blocks up from St. Luke's. Father should be ready to receive you by nine o'clock."

"So be it. I shall be by with my letter shortly after nine. Then your father and I will speak to my father. And if he decides to go the voyage alone, that is his decision. No matter what, I will stay here with you."

The tilt of her head and her longing smile urged him to take her in his arms and complete the unfinished business of their first kiss.

"As much as I would like to pander to that inviting look of yours, Miss Chetwynd, I find I must decline your tantalizing offer. We are but courting now, so we may only speak while walking, and that must be with a chaperon."

"But ..."

"Yet, take this instead, my alluring little minx."

Peter took her face in his hands, leaned down, and planted a kiss on her forehead. "'Til next we meet, dearest Annette," he whispered. Then he released her and took out his pocket watch. "Now, so I might keep at least one of my promises to your father, we must go."

"What do you mean?" she asked as she took his arm and picked up her pace.

"I was to be your chaperon, remember? There are many unspoken promises—"

"Oh, I understand." She laughed as they exited the conservatory. "Whatever were you thinking when you agreed to take on such a task with an alluring minx like me?"

"I am not at liberty to respond to that question right now."

Chapter 39
Danger

Peter entered through the French doors, scanned the salon for their fathers, and guided her across the room to where they stood near the entryway.

"Your timing is impeccable, Mr. Adsley." Annette's father complimented him and turned to Annette. "He has been good company for you, has he not my dear?"

"Indeed, Papá. He has many rare and promising qualities."

"Thank you, young man, for looking after my daughter."

"It was my pleasure, Mr. Chetwynd. And on that note, may I call on you later this morning before the ship sets sail?"

Peter's father eyed him. "What's this? We are sailing at eleven o'clock."

"That gives us plenty of time, Adsley. I am up by eight and would see your son at nine o'clock." Mr. Chetwynd smiled and slapped Peter on the back. "In fact, why not come along, Adsley? We will have a decent breakfast before you are condemned to that floating prison."

Peter noted his father's knitted brows. "Thank you, but there are always last-minute arrangements."

"Very well then, I will see you later this morning, young Adsley."

"I look forward to it."

Mr. Chetwynd turned to his daughter, "It has been a long day, my dear. Say your goodbyes to these gentlemen, and we will be on our way."

She nodded; then turned to Peter's father. "It was a pleasure to make your acquaintance, Mr. Adsley, and how nice of you to spend time with my father. I am sure he has thoroughly enjoyed your company."

"Thank you, Miss Chetwynd. You are quite an accomplished young lady and orator. I'm honored to have met you." He glanced at Peter. "And imagine that I shall have the privilege of seeing you again when my son and I return."

She turned to Peter. "I am delighted to have made your acquaintance, Mr. Adsley. You have my most sincere thanks for a pleasant evening." She extended her hand as she curtsied.

"You are quite welcome ... dearest," he whispered as he bowed over her hand. "I am happy to have been of service to you," he said aloud.

Then she and her father disappeared into the crowd, and Peter's father turned to bid good night to another guest.

Peter took out his handkerchief and wiped his damp forehead. The scent of orange blossoms lingered on his fingers. He stuck the cloth in his pocket and checked his watch: quarter past one o'clock, Saturday the eleventh of July. Approximately ten hours from now, his father would be forced to depart for the Colonies without him. Peter swallowed hard and adjusted his coat. How would he ever mend that rift? And would his letter and the meeting be enough to convince Mr. Chetwynd of his honorable intentions?

God, please guide me in these plans.

"I beg your pardon, sir." A footman addressed him. Peter slipped his watch back into his pocket. "Do I have the honor of addressing Mr. Peter Adsley?"

"Yes."

"I have been instructed to give you this letter."

"Oh?" Peter accepted the folded paper. "Thank you."

"You are welcome, Mr. Adsley." The footman bowed and left.

The seal was unfamiliar, but Peter opened the page and read:

> *Adsley, slave driver that you are,*
> *when you tire of that luscious little tart,*
> *do me the kindness of letting me know.*
> *I would like to have a go at her myself.*
> *SL*

Aberrant phrases flowed through Peter's mind as he stared at the monstrosity. How dare the man who penned this outrageous message? When Peter got ahold of him ...

He wheeled around to find the footman as he shoved the note in his pocket. Pushing through the crowd, he went after the man. Lumbering guests offered glazed stares as they wandered toward the front door.

"Halt, footman, I say." Peter grabbed his arm. "Stop! I must speak to you."

"Excuse me, sir?" The footman turned in shock, and Peter's heart sank. He was not the right man.

"I beg your pardon; I am mistaken."

"May I be of assistance?"

"Have you seen ...?" Peter glanced around the room. An army of footmen with their powdered wigs and matching liveries mingled among the departing guests. "Never mind."

"Are you certain? I could call the master of the ball."

"No, that will not be necessary."

"As you wish, sir."

Peter had to think. The revolting message was on Ashton paper and signed SL. Who was SL? Had he seen them in the conservatory? He must find the same footman who had delivered it. Perhaps he knew who had written it. Yet, how could Peter find the messenger? He rubbed the bridge of his nose. He must find her father now.

Lord, help me. I must inform Mr. Chetwynd. She must be protected.

Gripping the rail, Peter mounted the nearby steps and looked down over the guests. Men helped their wives with their shawls. Tired couples yawned their good-byes while the debutantes' mothers packed them up to leave, but Peter did not see them anywhere. He choked back a groan. It was too late.

"Peter, come now." His father motioned and called from below. "Stop wandering about. I am tired. And I needn't remind you of our voyage."

"Father, I must find Mr. Chetwynd." Peter descended the stairs two at a time. "Did you see which way he went?"

"No. He must be at his coach by now. They are all lined up in front." Mr. Adsley tossed a good-bye to the hosts, shook hands, and exited. Peter thanked them and sped out the door after his father.

"Surely, it can wait a couple hours," Mr. Adsley muttered as he trotted toward their coach. "You will see him soon enough. Tell him then."

"I must alert him to a communiqué concerning his daughter."

"Regarding?"

Peter climbed into the coach after his father. "It's the vilest, most repugnant affront I have ever had the misfortune of reading. And on my honor, I must inform Mr. Chetwynd of it."

"Get ahold of yourself. What are you saying?"

"This note!" Peter waved the paper in front of his father. "Mr. Chetwynd's daughter is in danger. We must inform him. I must be assured of her safety."

"I can hardly read it; the light is too dim. But why are you so upset? She cannot mean much to you. You have only just met her."

Peter's anger flared. "She is a decent young lady, and your friend's daughter, and she is in danger."

"I am exhausted and my head aches." He leaned against the cushioned seat. "Ah, stop bothering me now. Inform him later this morning. You are calling on him at nine. And consider carefully: might you have exaggerated the meaning of this message?"

Peter fought to keep the rage out of his voice. "I shall be wary of that possibility."

Chapter 40
Tragedy

Inside their dark coach, Annette's father leaned his head against the cushion of his seat and tried to situate himself. She heard him mumbling in the darkness, but did not think much of it. Coaches were always uncomfortable. But then he started fidgeting again. It was hard to see, but apparently, his left arm was bothering him. He was massaging it quite vigorously.

"Would another pillow help, Papá? I am not using mine."

"No, keep it. I'll be all right."

"Are you certain? I could ..."

"No. I'll be fine."

His tone was short as he obsessed with his left arm. But soon enough, he appeared to have settled once more, and all was quiet again. She listened to the jangling horses' harnesses and the creaking coach noises for a few seconds. Then she leaned her head back and closed her eyes.

Immediately, Peter's face appeared before her. Hugging the memory of his promise to herself, she raised her fingertips to her cheek and relived the touch of his hand against it. Tonight had been the happiest night of her life.

"Ahhh," her father groaned.

Annette sat up. He was struggling again. "Papá, are you well?"

"Just a bad cramp, nothing ... ahh ... nothing a good night's sleep won't mend. Rest yourself, my dear."

His words waved her off, but his voice was wrought with discomfort. She pulled the window curtain open, hoping to use moonlight to see him better.

"AHH ... My Lord," he gasped and jolted forward. Pain warped his brow, and a hoarse cry hardly escaped his lips before he started clutching at his waistcoat and cravat.

She held him by the shoulders. "Papá, *please,* what's wrong?" His only answer was sobbing.

"Papá?"

Another surge of pain sounded in his cry, and impossible torment perverted his dear face. She scooted over to the cushion beside him and tried to help him loosen his shirt, but he would not hold still. He writhed and gripped at his throat and chest as if he were choking.

"Papá let me help!" Tears blurred her eyes. *"Please, PAPÁ!"*

More groaning and tearing at his clothes; now wailing.

"Miss Chetwynd, what is it?" Bright moonlight washed over her father, and someone was pulling at her arm. "Miss Chetwynd, move aside, please. Let us help."

She jerked her arm away and glanced over her shoulder. Three men. Somewhere in the back of her mind, they registered as the coach driver and two footman—apparently, the coach had stopped—but she was not about to leave her father.

"No!" she cried, turning back to him.

"Papá let me help; what can I do?" She tugged open his vest and dried his sweaty face with her gown as he gasped for air. He took a few more labored breaths, and for a moment it appeared as if the pain had lessened.

"Ah, *ma poupée*, sweet girl," he whispered. Tears glistened in his eyes, and he raised his hand to her cheek. "Forgive me, I didn't mean to hurt you."

She found his other hand and, with quivering lips, kissed it. "You never hurt me, Papá."

"Yes ... away gone ... too much ... should have been home. I'm sorry," he breathed in a ragged whisper, and his hand fell from her cheek.

The next wrenching spasm was so powerful his fingers dug into her wrist, and he crumpled onto her lap.

"Oh, Papá, there's nothing to be sorry for. I love you." Rivers of tears flooded her face. More crippling agony.

"Papá. Papá!" Annette cradled his face in her hands. "It's going to be all right. These men can help. Please Papá . . ."

His desperate eyes entreated her, and his pale lips moved, but no sound came. She leaned her ear close to his mouth.

"I love you too. Keep faith . . ." He reached for the gold chain of the locket he had given her. She pulled it out for him. "I'm with you." He fought the pain, and with his last breath pushed out the words, "Adsley ... godly man. He'll take care of you." Then his head fell limply to the side, and he was silent.

"*NO PAPÁ! Please don't leave me!*" She gathered him close to her. "Oh God, please don't take him from me. I need him. *PLEASE.*"

Chapter 41

Setback

Goree Piazza near Wapping Basin
Liverpool, England
11 July 1795, Saturday morning

Between his anger and his anxiety, it took Peter a solid two hours to settle. And when he finally succumbed to sleep, he faced a nightmare of his own.

First, he was gazing at Annette, who was warming herself in front of a crackling fire. He could not help but notice the pleasing lines of her form through the delicate fabric of her gown as she tilted her head and started pulling the pins from her hair. He approached her, meaning to bury his face in the glistening fall of orange flavored tresses tumbling down her back, but the scene shifted and they were transported to a ballroom.

The orchestra began the opening strains of a forbidden waltz, and she gave him a mischievous smile. He extended his hand, inviting her to dance, despite the ban. She took it, and they began gliding around the luxurious room in an outburst of rapturous laughter until the cadence of the dance became so rambunctious that the joyful expression on her face melted into one of abject terror.

He enfolded her in his arms and held her close as darkness closed in on them, and the room began spinning.

Next, they were standing on the deck of a ship during a terrible storm. She was cradling his cheeks in her hands and attempting to speak, but the rain pelted her face, and he could not hear over the howling wind. Suddenly, the deck shifted, and she fell to her knees. Peter dropped, attempting to close the gap between them, but an iron collar and shackles instantly snapped in place around his neck, wrists, and ankles, preventing him from reaching her.

He reached his hands as far as he could strain against his chains, but the vessel tilted still further and she slid dangerously close to the edge of the deck. Grasping and clawing at anything she could reach, shredding her fingers and splintering her nails on fragments of wood protruding from the deck, Annette cried for help, but he could not save her.

Then, as if the power of his sorrow rendered him some mercy, his chains lengthened, and he found himself clamping his hands around her wrists, just as she slid over the side.

"*Hold on, dearest. I'll save you!*"

And there he remained paralyzed on the deck, sobbing, choking, and struggling to breathe while grasping her slender, wet wrists. For though his chains had been lengthened enough to catch her before she fell to her death, the collar around his neck was cutting into his throat so he could hardly breathe, much less find the strength to pull her back onto the deck.

"Be happy for us both," she cried, and he felt her hands slip through his fingers.

"NOOooo!" His wail echoed across the space of minutes, and suddenly he was awake.

He blinked, but saw nothing. Then his mind registered. Instead, hanging over the edge of a ship's deck, he found himself hanging over the side of his bed. Righting himself, Peter wrestled free from his tangled sheets, which were drenched in perspiration. He massaged his forehead.

It was a hideous nightmare. He was in the upstairs chamber at his father's Goree Piazza warehouse near Wapping Basin in Liverpool. Peter remembered it well enough, and Annette was in town. More than that, she was his.

Peter allowed the memory of her orange blossom scent and the warmth of her delicate form nestled against his chest to caress his belabored thoughts.

"Please, Lord, free me of this wretched dream that I might focus on writing the letter to her father. I need Your wisdom; guide my words. I cannot bear losing her, not now. And, permit her father to be receptive to my plan. In Your name and for Your glory, Amen."

There was more about which he must pray. Someone had seen them in the conservatory and the wretched note. *"Slave driver that you are . . . "* What could it possibly mean? And the insult to Annette—a detestable reminder that all was not well.

Peter groped the nightstand for his pocket watch. Moving to the window and drawing back the musty curtain, he made out the time by the first rays of dawn: half past five. Only three and a half hours until his meeting.

He stoked the fire, moved to the washstand, and filled the bowl with water. Then he washed and shaved as best he could by firelight, and was soon enough ready to go.

Glancing out the window, Peter noted the docks awaking to another day of business. Dockworkers, like so many ants coming out of their holes, began loading and unloading cargo, produce, crated animals, and gigantic bales of bound sheep skins and cotton, as well as all other sorts of barrels and parcels. Street sellers put out their wares, and the baker a few doors down opened his doors.

Fresh bread sounded good. Peter grabbed his frock coat, checked his money purse, and quietly exited the room. Slipping through the common sitting area, he paused a moment to listen for movement in Father's chamber. All he heard was the rhythmic sound of his snoring.

Good, he would never know Peter had left. And though he would be furious when Peter did not board the *Terona*, he could do nothing unless he chose to remain in England too.

Quietly opening the door leading to the warehouse offices downstairs, Peter slipped out. He planned to purchase some fresh bread and milk from the baker, and then he would go to St. Luke's Cathedral for a time of prayer before composing his letter. After that, he might have a look at the windmills at St. James and thence to 75 Bold Street where he would call on Annette's father to embark on a lifelong journey with her.

Peter smiled as he reached the last step and entered the ground level office. He glanced at his pocket watch: ten of six, plenty of time.

Briefly, as he pocketed his watch, a movement in his periphery caught his attention. Moving to the windows that separated the offices from the warehouse, Peter looked out into the larger storage area. Light from the high transoms at the east end of the building shone on the towers of neatly stacked crates and boxes labeled for shipment, but there were too many shadows to see clearly. Perhaps it was a rat. The docks were infested with such vermin.

Peter stepped to the door, leading onto the warehouse floor. His stomach rumbled for food. It would not hurt to take a look around. There was plenty of time. He turned the knob and took a couple steps into the dusty warehouse when—

SLAM!

Pain tore through the back of Peter's head as the force of the blow thrust him headlong into a large wooden crate. The left side of his face collided with it, and flashes of white light pulsed behind his eyes.

CRASH! Another bone-crunching blow to his side. Red blinking lights now and a ringing sound in his ears.

Someone grabbed him by the coat collar, and a second assailant pummeled his midsection, planting one, two, three punches deep in his stomach. Bile surged in his throat. He could hardly marshal a breath, but he got up and raised his arm to block any further assault.

"Well now, would ya look at that, Jackson? 'E's tryin' to stand up to us, even after I laid 'im low. Looks like we've got ourselves a fighter. Can I take another shot at 'im? Knock the fight out o' 'im, so to speak?"

"He's a big enough fella—looks like he can take quite a bit more without killin' over," a third assailant quipped.

Peter reached up and caught the speaker by the collar, quickly maneuvered him around, and raising his knee, buried it in the scoundrel's groin. Then Peter shoved him whining and moaning into the first attacker, and they both landed in a scuffling mass.

"Get off of me, Ives. You idiot!"

The rogue pushed him off, jumped to his feet, and rushed into Peter like a rabid dog. A powerful blow to the left jaw—Peter's head lashed back and pain arched through his neck and chest. He returned a punch to the right, but it was poorly placed. Another strike to the chin with additional blows to the stomach and side. Peter tasted blood, and the room started spinning. He tried to catch a breath, but a spasm overtook him, and he dropped to the ground.

"That'll do, Scurvy," Peter heard the man named Jackson saying. "He's nothing to us dead. Remember, both Adsleys need to be *alive* an' on that ship this morning, or we're dead. I need to get the letter posted, and tell Slike we caught this one trying to escape."

"But how do we know he were tryin' to escape?"

"I said so, Ives. Now get him packed up for the trip. I'll tell Mr. Slike so he can get to the father before he starts to worry."

"It'll be easier to load 'im if 'e be full out. Mind if I send 'im over the edge?"

"As long as you don't kill him," were the last words Peter heard before slipping into oblivion.

Chapter 42

Imposter

Mr. Charles Adsley's pulse hammered in his left temple, and his stomach churned. Too much wine last night, no doubt; the stench of sweaty bodies and the dock noise might also have been to blame. He and one Mr. Slike were caught in a throng of human traffic on the decrepit drawbridge between the Old Dock and the Duke's Dock, where the *Terona* was awaiting their departure.

Closing his eyes, Peter's father gritted his teeth. He had no desire to humiliate himself by disgorging the contents of his stomach. However, the constant shouting of dockworkers relieving merchant ships of their treasures and the clanging of ships' bells were tremendously taxing to his nerves. He was also vexed about this incident involving Peter, an attack of some sort. At least that was the story this Slike fellow—the ship's doctor, he said he was—had given after breaking into the warehouse and dragging him out of bed. They were heading for the *Terona* two hours ahead of schedule, but something did not seem right.

Mr. Adsley felt himself growing light-headed, and for a moment, he was glad the crowd was packed so tightly. If he lost consciousness, it would hold him up. If only he could rid himself of this dreadful headache and the gut-rotting stench of these docks.

Notwithstanding his present difficulties, Mr. Adsley's thoughts were plagued with questions. How had this Mr. Slike discovered the attack in the first place? And how had he known who Peter was and that he would find their rooms at the Goree Piazza warehouse? From the sound of it, Peter was unconscious and would not have been able to speak.

Mr. Adsley slipped his hand into his pocket and felt the leather binding of Peter's Bible. He had snatched it from the nightstand before being rushed out of the warehouse. Peter never went anywhere without it. That one thing he knew of his second son. And why had he been up so early? That annoying little meeting over the Chetwynd girl was not until nine. More importantly, who was this Mr. Slike? He did not appear to be much more than a common crew member, though he claimed to be a surgeon. What connection could he possibly have with Peter? Mr. Adsley hated uncertainties, but what did they matter if Peter was in danger? He was Mr. Adsley's only remaining heir.

"Curse the heat and this pitiful communication between these docks. Why hasn't the harbor master improved this muddle?"

"They are finishing the Queen's Dock now. Perhaps, the Duke's will be next. But you needn't worry, the *Terona* is in sight. You will be by his side momentarily."

A modest breeze tiptoed through the humid air. Mr. Adsley inhaled, then suppressed a gag. Tar, pitch, and the putrid stink of the green water sloshing against the hull of the nearest ship was revolting. *Breathe through your mouth,* he told himself as their group surged forward. The bridge whined and creaked under the weight of the oozing mass of humanity as it propelled both men onto the Duke's Dock.

Mr. Adsley shoved his way to the rail and leaned over, but that did not do his stomach much good. A gull standing on a floating piece of wood entangled with soggy paper and rotten hay picked out the eye of a dead fish and gobbled a portion up. The remaining segment dangled from the side of the bird's beak as it tilted its head and eyed Mr. Adsley.

Peter's father held his breath, loosened his cravat, and tried to concentrate. Liverpool docks had most definitely changed for the worst, but they would not get the better of him.

"Tally ho there, Mr. Adsley. The *Terona's* gangway is the next drawbridge up—a minute more and we will be there."

"Splendid."

Halfway up the rickety gangplank, Mr. Adsley snatched out his handkerchief, covered his mouth, and pinched his nose. Merciful Heaven, was that the stench of raw sewage emanating from the *Terona's* belly?

Lord, what have I gotten us into?

A motley crew of seamen gawking from the rail howled with laughter. Five steps more, and they were aboard the *Terona,* just in time to hear Captain Bledsoe spewing crude threats and cracking his whip like a slave master, scattering the crew like rats in high water.

"Welcome aboard, Mr. Adsley. It's good to see you again," the captain commented as he wound up his whip and strapped it at his side. "But you're not lookin' your best."

"It's the wretched traffic and this reeking stench."

"You'll get used to it soon enough," Mr. Slike said. "We all do."

Mr. Adsley studied Mr. Slike. With his lean physique and sun-bleached blond hair, he did not look like any different from the others. But something in his bearing and a certain conceit in his eyes did not quite match.

"Slike?" Mr. Adsley questioned. "What kind of name is that? I've never heard—"

"Ah him, don't worry about him, Adsley," Captain Bledsoe broke in. "I've known him since he was a youth. Found him beaten to a pulp one night about ten years ago out back of Gail's place when I was makin' me rounds. Took him under my wing, I did. 'Cause he reminded me of meself, and I couldn't stand the thought of them dirty navy pressgangs pickin' him up, chainin' him to an oar in the bottom o' one of their ships, and leavin' him there to rot. Happened to me once, you know. That was the beginnin' of my career—"

"I know, Bledsoe. And it happens all the time." Mr. Adsley spoke impatiently.

"The name's short for my given and surnames together," Mr. Slike said. "It's easier for the crew."

"That's right, Adsley," Captain Bledsoe added. "No time for fuss at sea, exceptin' for you and your son, that is."

"I'll take Mr. Adsley to see his son now, Captain," Slike said.

"Yes, please," Mr. Adsley declared.

"That's a good man, Mr. Slike. And get him a spot o' rum too. He's lookin' a bit green, he is," Captain Bledsoe bellowed as he clapped Mr. Adsley on the back. "Your lad'll be just fine, Adsley. I took a look at him meself, and Slike's got some of the finest doctorin' skills around. Lucky thing the doc happened by him this mornin' when he was pickin' up some last minute supplies or your lad might not o' been takin' this trip today."

"Yes, well, let's get on with it. I would like to see my son."

"Of course." Bledsoe turned away and roared. "Turtle!"

"Aye, Cap'n." A skinny, little urchin of a cabin boy appeared as if from nowhere.

"See the doc and our guest to his son, and get him a mug o' ale, and whatever else he needs, or I'll have you swabbin' the decks."

"Aye, Cap'n. This way, sir." The little fellow scurried toward the passageway. Mr. Adsley and Mr. Slike followed. When Turtle reached the cabin, he threw open the door.

"He's sound asleep in the bottom bunk."

Mr. Adsley's spirit sank. The trunk-cluttered cave, which he and his son would occupy during the trip, reeked of tobacco smoke. A series of grimy, square windows illuminated streaks on the dark paneled walls. It seemed like someone had attempted to scrub the oily film of dust and brine, but without success.

Mr. Adsley dismissed Turtle by tossing him a gold coin. It was obvious to Mr. Adsley that neither he nor his son would spend much waking time in this dank grotto—once Peter recovered—but one never knew when he might need something from a little fellow like this.

"Thankee, sir," he said as he bit the coin.

"You are welcome. Now off you go for that rum. I'll have it on deck with the captain."

There was scarcely enough room for one man to stand at his full height without hitting his head on a hurricane lantern—a fact Mr. Adsley discovered the hard way, as he scooted around the trunks to the narrow beds that were shelved one above the other.

"Blasted ..." Peter's father sat down beside the bunk and rubbed his head. "Damnably tight in here, Slike. Is this the best you've got?"

"Yes, sir. As far as space goes, with the trade going so good, every inch is used for cargo. Fact is, most slave ships are fitted out for carrying so much cargo there's hardly enough storage for food, let alone boarding passengers."

"So what's your business with Bledsoe? Those smooth hands and clean-shaven face don't quite fit around here."

"Bledsoe told you how I got started, and now I love the sea. Before that, I worked . . . well, let's just say, the ladies prefer smooth cheeks. So when I'm in port, I shave off the beard."

Mr. Adsley eyed the doctor. "Oh, I see. Before I married, I sailed the trade route myself. But enough of that now, let's see about my son."

Peter lay in the lower bunk. Gauze was wrapped around his head and his left cheek. He had a blackened eye, and his swollen, purple mouth was smeared with ointment.

"Lord, what happened to him?"

"Left side of his face was whacked pretty badly, and he has a gash on the back of his head. Two broken ribs on the right side and three on the left. He's lost some blood from that gash on his head, so he's weak, but I cleaned and stitched the wounds and wrapped his ribs. The blow to the head worries me most."

"Is he going to be all right?"

"I've got all the supplies we need. In fact, I picked up some extra this morning when I found him. I'll keep an eye on him. The most important thing is keeping the wrappings clean."

"Should I postpone this trip, and get him to a real physician?"

"I've done the same as any other physician would. He just needs rest."

"Well, do what you must to get him back to health." Mr. Adsley pressed a pouch of coins in the doctor's hand. "And make certain you have whatever supplies you need before we leave. Spare no expense. Do you understand me?"

With that, Mr. Adsley took Peter's Bible out of his pocket and wedged it between the bunk and the mattress, where Peter would find it when he awoke. Then he made his way around the trunks, ducking as he passed under the lantern.

"Slike, one more thing: how did you know I was his father and where to find me after you found him?"

"He's got a pocket watch on him, and it's carved with your name. I showed it to Bledsoe as soon as I got him back here, and he said you would be in the warehouse apartment."

"Thank you, Mr. Slike. Keep an eye on him and keep me informed. I'm going to have that rum now."

Mr. Slike slipped the money pouch into his pocket as Mr. Adsley left and glanced down at Peter. "Best take your rest now, brother. It's the last time you'll have any peace."

CHAPTER 43

HOSTAGE

On the *Terona*
Between England and Africa
14 July 1795

Meaning to turn over in his bed, Peter attempted to move, but pain racked his torso, and his head throbbed. Grasping the rough woolen blanket covering him, he took shallow breaths and waited for the torture to subside.

Cloaked in darkness, the world swayed to a constant rhythm, but he kept still and listened, waiting for the pain to stop. Boards creaked with a similar cadence, and the smell of salty brine pitch permeated the air. And there was a wretched noise. He cringed at the sour notes. Was someone playing Mozart on a pianoforte? Worthless instrument though it was, one could hardly tell, it was so far out of tune. Where was he? Peter wondered. A storeroom of some back-alley pub on the wharf?

Peter slowly raised his hands to his head and found it wrapped in thick bandages. No wonder everything was dark. He ran his fingers over the wooden platform on which he lay and found a book shoved between the mattress and the wood. He slid the book free and felt its smooth cover. Ah, his Bible. How odd though. The last time he remembered reading it was in the upstairs chamber at the Goree Piazza warehouse where he and his father had been staying. But this miserable excuse for a bed with its musty straw mattress was certainly not his.

Bits and pieces of recent events tumbled through his mind: the ball, Miss Chetwynd . . . Annette . . . their conversations, a letter. He was supposed to write to her father, and there was another thing. . . a terrible message, and . . . an assault . . .

Peter sat up, smacking his head against something. Pain ripped through his head, neck, and sides as he fell back against the thin straw mattress.

"Oh Lord, no," he pleaded. "No, please. It cannot be. It must not. Please."

The words caught in a broken sob. They must have abducted him, and now he was on a ship. He could feel it rocking. "Oh, God of Heaven, no! She will think I have deserted her."

His throat tightened, and another type of pain rose from deep within. Had Father ordered the attack to make certain he took this voyage? Surely the man was obsessed! No one else knew where they were staying, and the attack happened inside the warehouse. His father must have posted guards to watch him.

"OH God . . . no." He covered his bandaged face with his hands and cried. "God, she's in danger, and . . . and she will think . . ." Tears flooded his face. With each breath, his broken ribs stabbed him, perhaps even tearing at his heart. "God, I trusted you. But . . . how . . .?"

"I know the thoughts that I think toward you, saith the Lord, thoughts of peace, and not of evil."

"Jeremiah the twenty-ninth chapter, I know. But not this! How can this give either of us any hope or a future? She is home, and I am here." Peter raged.

Chapter 44

Turtle

On the *Terona*
Between England and Africa
16 August 1795

Peter looked away from his Bible, to the endless stretch of waves glinting in the sunlight. *"Though he slay me, yet will I trust in him."* He sighed. "Lord, if I could have but half of Job's faith, I would be a better man. Nevertheless, give me the courage I need to do what I must."

When Peter had been well enough to get up and speak with Captain Bledsoe, he calculated how long it would take to get to Ouidah on the African Gulf of Guinea, where they planned to stop for more supplies. Six thousand miles from Liverpool at approximately twenty knots per hour in good weather took about five weeks. And the weather had been beautiful.

The second this floating prison docked, Peter was sailing back to Liverpool to ask Miss Chetwynd's father for permission to court her. But he must not obsess over it now. He did not wish to alert anyone to his plan.

Lord, what of Mother and Mary Hope? By now, they must be readying themselves for their trip to Beverley.

Mother anticipated visiting the market town each year. She and Miss Jane Arden, who ran a boarding school in Beverley, had known each other since they were girls. Mary Hope loved to visit with Miss Arden because of Jane's connections with Mary Wollstonecraft, not to mention the pleasure of attending the famous horse races.

Bless them with a safe journey, Lord.

Peter turned back to his Bible. As much as he hated being here, he must acknowledge that his internment aboard the *Terona* was not without benefit. It offered time to read the Scriptures, to pray, and to explore the issue of what he truly wanted. Naturally, he hoped God's provision included marriage to Annette. Indeed, he prayed for it daily. But, the last few months had taught him God's will demanded that he trust God far more than he actually did.

"Though he slay me, yet will I trust in him."

Peter shook his head as he turned to the third chapter of Mark—the passage he believed Annette would also be reading today. He fingered the worn edge of the folded parchment she had torn from her sketchbook just over two months ago. His vision blurred for a moment as he recalled that he had once thought of burning this treasure. How grateful he was to have it now.

Peter unfolded the page, carefully opening it along the weakened creases, and gazed at the faded drawing. He could still make out the lines of her wondrous eyes and the clever little dimple to the left of her impish smile. This drawing kept her real. When he read his daily passage, he looked at the drawing and prayed for her.

The monstrous note he received the night at the Ashtons' ball plagued his thoughts, and he worried about how she perceived his absence. But he did his best to entrust those things to God. He bowed his head.

Lord, nothing happens but what You oversee and permit, and I believe You have plans that will give us both hope and a future. Help my unbelief.

"Afternoon Mr. Adsley, sir. Wanna orange?"

Peter turned to the little cabin boy whose toothy grin covered half his face as he held out the fruit.

"It be the last one 'til we get ta port."

"Have we not spoken of this before, Turtle?"

"I didn't steal it, promise. Cook was lookin' right at me when I pinched it, and he'd be yellin' if he minded. Don't hear any yellin', do ya? Besides, it were for a good cause."

"A gentleman asks first."

"I remember." Turtle looked down at his big toe, which he was pivoting in a knot hole in the deck.

Peter closed Annette's sketch in his Bible. "Well, tell me about this good cause. I am anxious to know what is more important than being a gentleman."

Turtle perked up as Peter put out his hand for the orange. "You, sir! And the betterment of our friendship so you'll take me home with ya when we get to England."

"But, I told you—"

"Oh, please, sir, don't say no." Turtle dropped to his knees. "I promise I'll stop pinchin' stuff—except for fruit. Like I told ya, 'cause it keeps a body safe from dyin' o' gut rot when you're stuck too long at sea. But everything else, if only you'll take me—"

"Stand up. Quick, someone might see you and guess our secret."

Turtle scrabbled to his feet. "So you'll take me?"

Peter dug his thumbnail into the dimpled orange peel, causing a spray of citrus to perfume the air. He inhaled the sweet smell. "I will consider it."

"Not again," Turtle sighed as he got to his feet.

"But I thought you wanted—?"

"I do. I do." Turtle's eyes sparkled, then clouded. "But you're droolin' over your orange like it were a lady's hand."

"What do you mean?" Peter popped a segment in his mouth.

"Every time ya have an orange, ya close your eyes ta smell it, and ya get a weird smile on your mouth." Turtle tipped his head to the side, fluttered his eyelashes, and presented a dazed smile.

"When you put it like that, it does seem rather odd."

"Yah. And I doubt you're thinkin' o' your dear mother or sister." Turtle knitted his brows and took on a more serious tone. "If any of the crew saw ya . . . Why do ya do it, sir—get all silly when ya eat oranges?"

Because even looking at an orange reminds me of her, Peter thought. "I guess I cannot help it, but since this is the last one, I will not do it anymore. Here now, sit down and have a slice with me."

"Thankee, sir." He bit down on the slice and juice dripped from the corner of his mouth, which he wiped with the back of his hand. "So, what were ya lookin' at before?"

Peter followed Turtle's gaze toward his Bible and Annette's sketch peeking out from between its pages.

"A sketch."

"Ya draw? Can I see it?"

Turtle was a good fellow, but Peter was not sure he wanted to reveal this secret.

"No."

"I can't see it, or ya can't draw. Because I promise I won't tell if ya show me."

"My lady drew it."

"The one ya think about when you're droolin'? I wanna see."

"Have you nothing better to do than harass your passengers?" Peter caught Turtle in a headlock and rumpled his hair.

"Mercy, sir, please." Turtle giggled and squirmed. "Please, I won't tell anyone."

Peter let him go, at which point, Turtle tumbled down on the deck to catch his breath. "Well, can I see? I promise I won't even touch it. Ya can just hold here in front o' me face so I can get quick look."

"All right, but you mustn't speak of it again. Do I have your word as a gentleman?"

"Aye, sir. Ya do. I promise I won't tell a soul. I won't even ask her name, and if we ever need ta talk about her again—which I'm sure we won't—I'll call her the orange lady."

Peter eyed Turtle; then set aside the orange and slid out the sketch for Turtle.

"Bless me, she's a pretty one."

Peter eyed him.

"And that'll be all I'm sayin' about her."

"TURTLE!" Captain Bledsoe shouted from the other side of the deck. Turtle shuddered when he heard the snap of the captain's whip.

"Aye, Cap'n, sir!" Turtle shouted. "I'm off, but I got me an idea about when we can start your pinchin' lessons, Mr. Adsley, so ya don't get sick. Will ya hear it?"

"Any time, Turtle. Now, hurry along. I do not want you getting in trouble."

"Aye, sir." Turtle saluted, then scrambled away across the deck and disappeared behind the mast. Peter folded his sketch between the pages of the Bible and glanced out to sea again.

Chapter 45

Music

Wicked laughter broke out some distance from Peter. He noticed Mr. Slike, who had stopped his knife throwing practice, conversing with a crewman named Scurvy. The two appeared to be amusing themselves with a paper—some contemptible pictures no doubt. Peter turned back to his study, but could not maintain his focus.

Seeing both men together was a rather menacing prospect. Scurvy, with his foul mouth and equally repugnant odor, was one of the vilest men aboard, while Mr. Slike tended to keep to himself, yet seemed suspiciously familiar.

Mr. Slike had treated Peter's injuries and provided medicines for the dreadful headaches and bouts of dizziness with which he periodically contended, but there was nothing else Peter could say to recommend him. The fact that there was something familiar about him served only to increase Peter's suspicion.

Peter must finish the third chapter of Mark, and then he must speak to Father. Mr. Adsley's habit of spending hours in the captain's quarters and drinking—God only knew how much rum—was taking its toll.

They had both agreed to keep their circumstances private during the trip. However, Father had taken to blasting forth estate matters over meals with Captain Bledsoe and Mr. Slike as if he were seeking their approval. And whenever Peter suggested he be more circumspect, he became angry, accusing Peter of prying into affairs that had nothing to do with him. Clearly a ludicrous statement, since Peter was the heir now.

Annette had helped him adjust his perspective about the far-reaching nature of his ministry responsibilities, and he wanted to learn everything he could about the estate and people who depended on the Adsley family. Involving the captain and a ship's doctor seemed ridiculous though.

On the other hand, there was likely no harm in sharing the details of their trip with Captain Bledsoe. He was only an old seadog who had started a love affair with the sea after he finally got over the injustice of being pressed into service nearly thirty years ago, was it?

Bledsoe told the story so often Peter stopped listening, but he had not forgotten how it all came about. Apparently, one of Bledsoe's employers found young Bledsoe, who was a piano tutor, of all things, in an unseemly position with his daughter. Consequently, he had Bledsoe beaten and pressed into service on one of his majesty's naval ships.

The young lady—Lizzie, he called her—remained the love of Bledsoe's life. He sang about her, talked about her, and of all the truly bizarre things, still played for her on an old pianoforte he had confiscated from a French sloop and bolted down in his bedchamber. When Peter observed the captain playing, the story seemed just a bit less extraordinary, but not much.

Nevertheless, music exuded from his face and fingers alike. And the entire crew, which he ordered on pain of death to listen to his music every night for half an hour before supper, sat mesmerized while he played.

"It be time for some civilized entertainment before supper, gentlemen," Bledsoe shouted as he dragged his pegged left leg across the deck. "Scurvy, take your seat on the deck with the rest of the rabble. Mr. Slike, Mr. Adsley, and you there, young Adsley, you are in me cabin with me and the other chief officers."

He headed to his quarters with his "chief officers" licking their hands and smoothing their hair down as they shuffled behind him.

"Are you coming, Peter?" Mr. Adsley asked from across the deck.

"Soon."

"Well, hurry along. Slothfulness irks the captain."

"I am studying." Peter looked at his Bible. It no longer mattered. He could not concentrate anyway. He closed his Bible, slipped it into his coat pocket, and headed for the captain's quarters.

"Good evening, young Mr. Adsley," Bledsoe called from the pianoforte when Peter slipped into the chair nearest the open door. "Would you have Mozart or Bach this evening?"

"Bach's Minuet in G, if you please, Captain." Peter leaned back in his chair and closed his eyes. He would attempt to think of Annette and their first dance at Woolton Hall.

"Excellent choice," Mr. Slike whispered. "For a priggish ballroom dance with a proper young lady like Miss Chetwynd."

Peter jerked his head up. "What do you know of it?"

"She's the money pot I've had my eyes on for a while. What may be lacking under that bodice is more than covered in the bank. Why, what's she to you?"

"Do not speak of her, or we will handle matters outside."

"A duel with the doctor who saved your life? That isn't very kind."

Peter stared at him, and suddenly he remembered those ruthless, gray eyes. He had seen them at his brother's funeral. Mr. Slike was the arrogant guest sitting in the middle of the pew that day—only he had black hair then. A wig.

"Who are you, and what do you want?" Peter's pulse throbbed behind his eyes like the sour notes of Bledsoe's music pounding in his head. It was all he could do to remain seated.

"Her. But don't let it bother you, Adsley. There will always be another woman. One's as good as the next. Take it from me. I've had more than my share, and this one's nothing to risk your life over."

The last note of the minuet clanged, and the room exploded in clapping. "Many thanks, gentlemen. Many thanks." Bledsoe bowed. "Now, let's get some food in our bellies. We've lots more to do before we hit port."

"When will that be, Captain?" Peter's father asked.

"Two days at most if the weather holds."

Mr. Slike nodded to Peter and left. It was a good thing too. Peter's tolerant façade was slipping.

Chapter 46

Family Plot

Chesterfield of Taddington
Derbyshire, England
17 August 1795

Gerald, Annette's older brother, sat eating toast and drinking his coffee while seeming to read the paper. He had missed his morning ride because Mother had asked to speak with him. As the new head of household, he was now the authority on everything and must hear her request.

There was one bit of good news though. He took a bite of toast and stared at the page. With Miss Haack's help, Annette appeared to have begun living again. She had taken her meals with the family for the last three days.

But the transition after Father's passing had not been easy for her. To put it bluntly, Gerald suspected Mother was jealous of Miss Haack's ability to work with Annette. This early morning meeting must have something to do with it. Why else would she awake so early? She hardly ever rose before ten.

Gerald sipped his coffee and tried to imagine what plan she had devised for his sister.

"Good morning, Gerald." Mrs. Chetwynd swept into the breakfast room.

"It appears to be. Did you sleep well?" He was not particularly interested in her answer. He made an effort at pleasantries, however.

"Yes. I am quite refreshed." She selected a piece of toast and some apple butter, and then poured herself some tea. "Pass the sugar, please."

He passed it and took another bite. He had no wish to open conversation. The idea of being the final authority also troubled him. If only Father had not . . .

"Well dear, what have you to say about your sister's situation?" She looked at him with as much anticipation as a child waiting for a sweet.

"Situation? It is my understanding you make the decisions regarding that."

"Indeed, I do. However, there are developments that require your attention."

"Regarding her difficulties after Father's passing or her unwillingness to submit to your authority? I understand Miss Haack has done an exceptional job at smoothing over both complications."

"How absurd. I haven't the slightest concern about Annette's friendship with her nurse. I directed Miss Haack see to her every need while she reconciles herself to her father's death."

"Then why have you asked for this meeting?"

"We must discuss Annette's future and the final component of her proper education before there is any permanent damage to her prospects."

Gerald set down his coffee cup with a clatter. "Damaged prospects? What do you mean?"

"These hysterical fits and her recent refusal to eat or get out of bed. I hardly know what to make of them. Miss Haack seems to be of assistance, however."

"What is the trouble then?"

Her face reddened, and she raised her chin in a defiant manner. Gerald halted her looming attack. "Settle yourself, Mother. I do not wish to upset you. I am merely trying to ascertain the problem, so I can offer an appropriate solution. For example, if you believe her mind is somehow affected, that would require a different tactic than if you felt she might need a change of scene to renew herself. You see my meaning, I'm sure."

She crossed her arms in front of her and eyed him the way a cat studies its prey.

"What say you? I have business to which I must attend."

"Gerald, you make a very good point."

He recognized the cold shrewdness of her voice.

"I admit I have not supported Annette as a more conventional mother would, but I do not see any trouble with her mind, at least not yet."

"If you have done what you think is best, what more can I offer?"

"I have done all I can think of, Gerald. Doctor Mayfield has visited many times. I have asked Miss Haack to do as much as she can to help, but if we do not act quickly, Annette may lose this opportunity for a good match."

Now, the truth was out, and it nauseated him. "A good match, what has that to do with anything? Father mentioned nothing of an arrangement, and you have worked hard to keep her from the public eye. Of whom do you speak?"

Mrs. Chetwynd took a letter with an impressive seal on it from her pocket and slid it across the table to Gerald. "I received this letter in Liverpool some hours after your father died."

Gerald opened the letter and read. "So there is no engagement yet."

"No, but Sir Steven Likebridge is an excellent candidate, as you can tell from his offer."

"This letter indicates he is away on business in the Colonies."

"Yes. But that works in our favor. It will give me time to prepare Annette. By the time he returns, she will have moved past this challenging period. Your suggestion of a change of scene is an excellent idea."

What a farce! His suggestion of a change of scene, as if she had not already thought of it.

Mother continued, "I think it best she go to a boarding school for these few months before he returns. There she should convalesce without distraction from these surroundings."

It was just as Gerald suspected. His mother wanted to rid herself of Annette. She probably never wanted her to begin with, a child in older years and that child an ailing daughter. Then to have her husband dote on the girl as if she was the only precious thing in the world; no wonder Mother cared so little for his sister.

Gerald glanced at the letter again. "I am not familiar with the name Likebridge. What do you know of him?"

"Your father and I met him some months ago at Cousin Sylvia's wedding. It turns out he had a connection with Mr. Richard Adsley, God rest his soul. He and your father began discussing the demand for fine china in the Colonies. They had just become partners in business when . . ." Mother wiped her eye and sniffed. Then she took a sip of tea.

"What says Annette of this Likebridge? Does she fancy him?"

"She agreed he could call on her here at Chesterfield, but she is young and uncertain about marriage. Your father made the introductions at the wedding."

"Mother—" he drew his brows together, "I will not arrange a marriage with a man she does not like."

"Understood. We must move slowly then, and that is another reason for boarding school. She will associate with other young ladies who may face similar circumstances. They might give her a new perspective. Later, when Likebridge returns, he can present himself as a suitor."

"Do you have a place in mind?"

"I was thinking a French—"

"Absolutely not. France is too dangerous."

"Jane Arden's Ladies Boarding School in Beverley of Yorkshire has an excellent reputation. I have heard Annette speak of it."

"Yorkshire is quite a distance. Is there not something closer?"

"It comes highly recommended."

"It says in this letter that Likebridge will not return until late December or early January. That is over four months away. What of her coming out? It was to be at the end of November, was it not?"

"I assure you, Annette would be pleased to forego it. And what is the point of putting her under such pressure with Sir Likebridge's offer?"

"Go ahead with the arrangements then. She may attend Jane Arden's school in Beverley. See that you send Miss Haack along with her. She must not be sent away alone."

"Agreed. Oh, but this is all so exciting. An alliance with a title would do very nicely, would it not?"

Gerald stood from the table. "Whatever you say, Mother, as long as Annette agrees. I will not have her forced into a loveless marriage."

"Yes, of course." Her eyes sparkled. "If Likebridge does not suit, perhaps she will attract a viscount or baron while she is in Beverley. I have heard members of the peerage frequent the horse races there." She bit into her toast and glanced out the window.

Gerald shook his head. She was already strategizing. "I am off to the stable now, Mother."

"Splendid, dear. Enjoy your ride."

Chapter 47

Wounded

Gulf of Guinea
Ouidah, Africa
18 August 1795

The *Terona* arrived in Ouidah, Africa, thirty-seven days after having set sail from Liverpool, and not a moment too soon for Peter. After the musical interlude with Mr. Slike, he had been at his wit's end worrying about Annette, trying to understand how a common crewman could have any connection with her or her family. Yet, as long as Mr. Slike was headed for the Colonies and Peter was returning to Liverpool, it did not matter much. Peter would speak with her father about courting before Mr. Slike reached the western hemisphere.

Feeling like a Noah of sorts, Peter sauntered down the gangplank with his father close behind. The ground dipped and swayed with each step, but he did not care. Soon, he would be on the first ship back home, and Father knew nothing about it. He supposed they were going exploring.

Captain Bledsoe advised them not to roam too far from the dock. He could not vouch for their safety, and it was no wonder. The docks were teeming with activity. Hordes of people swarmed back and forth. Peter, who had only recently seen a Negro in Liverpool, marveled at the entire waterfront town pulsing with the inhabitants of Ouidah.

"Now, Peter—" Father spoke over the crowd. "Recall, we mustn't go too far."

"Yes. But it has been weeks since we have even seen solid ground. So I mean to walk on it."

"Slow down a bit. We must talk first."

"Cannot it wait? I would like to have a look around."

"Well, I suppose, but . . ."

"Let us go then," Peter said as he waited for his father.

As they moved through the crowd, across the dusty road, to the offices and shops along the wharf, a strange cacophony of noise competing with the dock traffic compelled Peter to listen.

"Son, let us sit for a moment under those trees." Mr. Adsley gestured towards the palms.

"Why, Father you're—?" Peter immediately noticed his father's distress and offered Mr. Adsley his arm. "Yes, to be sure. What is wrong?"

"My stomach . . . it has been bothering me. Feeling a bit dizzy too—lost my land legs on the trip."

"Right away, then. This way." Peter seated his father. "Do you want something to drink? I could find you some fresh water."

"No. Only sit with me a while. Then we can talk."

"You do not look well. I am getting you some water."

Peter heard his father calling after him, but did not stop. He went to the nearest shop. They had none, but sent him to the next one. The one after that sent him to the next one after that. Peter's frustration grew. He could feel it in his bones the same way he felt the droning noise, which he had originally dismissed as ceremonial chanting, ever growing in dissonance and drowning his very thoughts.

"Mercy! What is that racket?"

When Peter rounded the corner, the appalling source of the clamor loomed ahead in all its infamous shame. There, just up the dusty hill, stood a cattle stockade and system of huge wire-fenced cages. Only, instead of herding cattle, uniformed men were pushing, prodding, and even dragging Negro men, women, and children out of them. The victims cried out in undeniable misery as their captors separated them from each other.

Peter stared in horror as a black man and woman, amidst a surge of anguished wailing, were literally torn from each other's arms. It was an epic struggle of grasping hands, broken beads, and scuffling feet kicking up clouds of dust, ending with the uniformed white man dragging the woman away by her hair, and an African overlord clamping an iron collar around the man's neck.

The man, who must have been her husband, tried to go after her. But with one jerk of the chain leash, he was yanked back to his captor's feet and beaten with a stick. The two helpless Negros were then shackled at the ankles and wrists, shoved into their respective lines, and attached to all the other Negroes who crouched along the dusty road, stoop-shouldered and beaten down in terror.

Scanning the entire thoroughfare, Peter gasped as both white and black men wielding whips forced their prisoners ahead toward the wharf.

"To the harbor with these filthy savages, the *Terona's* here for another shipment." A familiar voice shouted from behind.

Peter turned to find Slike mocking him with his reptilian smile.

"Yes indeed, Mr. Adsley, we are here to restock the *Terona* with black gold and just enough food and water to make to Jamaica, where we sell our cargo for three times the price we pay their enemies to capture them."

With mouth agape, Peter stared in speechless horror.

"What do you think of those fine females over there? They're my own special breeding stock. Every trip, the men set a few aside for me. Go ahead now, Adsley, have a look."

Peter refused to turn his head.

"Blast all, Peter. You left me sitting there." Mr. Adsley stepped up beside Slike. "I was going to talk to you about this."

Peter met his father eye-to-eye. In that single revolting moment, everything came together. All the negative comments about Wilberforce and the anti-slave trade movement; the frustration with slave revolts on the other side of the world; even Richard's insults against Peter's manhood and his father's obsession with the French pirates who had captured Mr. Betherton's ships. It all led to this.

Mr. Charles Adsley had finally introduced his heir to the real family business—flesh mongering. And the chosen system, who knew: a tobacco plantation in the Colonies, or perhaps a sugar plantation in Jamaica? Peter did not care. Suddenly, words from the wretched note flashed in his thoughts: "*Adsley, slave driver that you are . . .*"

"My God, Father! What have you done?"

Mr. Adsley clasped his son around the shoulders. "Now, Peter—"

"Remove your hand from me, sir."

His father's face contorted, but he dropped his arm. "How dare you take that tone? They are just as much yours as they are mine, and you will inherit every one of them sooner than you think."

"Why did you do it?"

"Why shouldn't I? They're savages, mere animals; there for the taking."

"NO! They are human beings created in God's image, and you have no right to do this."

"I earned the right by working to build my shipping business for the last thirty years, and sailing my ships down here to do it. And you will do the same thing—you and your children after you, or everything will be lost. Caverswall will fail."

The Negroes' wailing resounded in Peter's tearing heart. His jaw muscles tightened, and he swallowed hard. Sylvia, his parish, and his dream of settling down to a simple life of ministry—even Annette; he had been forced to yield everything he had ever wanted for this moment, and it was about to kill him.

"Then so be it! Caverswall will fail. I care nothing for your estate. Its foundation is that of men's blood and sweat mingled with the tears of hundreds of women and children. I will not have it!" Peter turned his back and strode away from his father.

"Stop! No son of mine runs away from his responsibilities."

"I am not your son!" Peter shouted over his shoulder, then turned his back and headed toward the dock.

Suddenly, white hot agony ripped through the back of his left thigh. It was nothing, though, nothing compared to the searing pain of his heart being skewered on behalf of these poor natives.

Refusing to acknowledge either stinging reminder of his ridiculous ignorance, Peter kept moving, hobbling now. He did not care what happened to him. His life, his ministry, his love for Annette, all of it was funded by blood money.

He took another step and jerked. Stabbing pain again—it felt like fire, actually—ripped through his right side. Tears streaming down his face cooled his fevered cheeks as a breeze whispered through the hot air. He staggered to a halt and reached his hand rather clumsily behind his back to feel a knife protruding from it. Tugging the blade out of the wound, Peter let it slide from his fingers and drop. Then he looked down at his stomach.

A circle of blood was forming on the front of his shirt. He took one more step and staggered to the ground.

✦

"Blasted Slike, using my son as a target! How dare you?"

"Would you rather I let him disappear into that crowd?"

Mr. Adsley glared at the next wave of human traffic being driven toward the dock.

"You and your wretched trade—as he would likely call it—mean nothing to a gentleman of his ilk, especially now that you've destroyed his ministry."

"Filthy low-breed, that is none of your concern." Mr. Adsley slapped Slike across the face. "I'll have your head for this!" Then he marched down the dusty road to examine his son.

For the second time in as many months, Mr. Adsley was worried. He had purposely concealed this source of his wealth because . . . Well, he was not sure exactly how to tell Peter without losing him, and now he had done just that. It had been challenging enough to extract him from the Buxton parish after Richard died.

Of course, the sugar plantation, Good Hope, was a necessity. It supplemented Caverswall's waning income. But Peter would not care. He was, after all, an abolitionist and a pastor, and not one of those self-righteous, political extremists with his own agenda. His son was a man of faith who truly cared about the plight of the Negroes.

But now, because Mr. Adsley had delayed, Peter discovered the truth as the slaves were being loaded onto the very ship on which Peter was sailing.

And Richard—God rest his soul—had not done much better. After he saw Good Hope's ledgers, he turned to the bottle, and where did that get Mr. Adsley?

God, I was a fool. I should have told him . . . should have told them both, when they were boys. Then none of this would have happened.

"Peter, son, I am here." Mr. Adsley crouched down to examine Peter's injuries.

"Leave me," Peter whispered. "I want nothing to do with you and your vile ambitions."

The thigh injury seemed simple enough; perhaps a cleaning and some stitches was all it needed. But the wound through Peter's right side was another story.

"Mr. Slike!" Damnable wretch, but he was still a doctor.

"You needn't shout," Slike responded as he picked up the knife Peter had discarded. "So now you need me?" He removed his second blade from Peter's thigh.

"*He* needs you!"

"He is your heir, and said, it seems, he wants to die."

"Impossible. Too many people depend on him."

Peter groaned.

"Apply pressure to that leg." Slike tore off a section of his shirt, rolled it over his hand, and knelt beside Peter. "I am doing this for their sakes, Adsley, not yours. And I won't make any promises."

Slike applied pressure to Peter's stomach wound. Then he called out in what must have been the natives' language, and a Negro boy ran off in the opposite direction.

"What did you say?"

"I told him to fetch a surgeon."

"If Peter dies—"

"At this point, it appears you are both going to die. In fact, our whole crew could die."

"Wha—?" Mr. Adsley felt faint. The heat must be getting to him, and his stomach was starting to bother him again.

"If we cannot stop the bleeding, your son is gone. And you could fall to dysentery, the scourge of the tropics, as I call it. Have you taken the chamomile tea I recommended? Three times daily for your stomach complaint, remember? "

"Blast your miserable tea. I am well enough. But if he does not make a full recovery, I will have you hung."

"Suit yourself. Your symptoms seem much like the early signs of dysentery to me."

At that moment, another cramp overtook Mr. Adsley. He hunched over while still applying pressure to Peter's leg.

"I think the surgeon is coming now." Slike nodded, and Mr. Adsley glanced as he directed.

Two soldiers escorting a man wearing a white tunic and carrying a black bag were coming toward them.

"Go sit down under those palms."

"No."

"If you insist on staying, the locals may have you quarantined."

Mr. Adsley groaned as he stood up and made his way to the shade.

↟

Slike turned his attention back to Peter's wound. It appeared to be clotting.

The doctor and two officers arrived.

"What happened here?" the first lieutenant asked. "Why is this man bleeding?"

"A gambling debt, I suppose, or perhaps a woman," Slike answered. "But he needs a surgeon now or he is going to die."

Slike lifted his hands so the surgeon could inspect Peter's wound.

"Get him to the table," the surgeon commanded. Slike and the two soldiers immediately hoisted Peter up and carried him to the same table where Mr. Adsley was seating himself.

"Thank you, officers. Now, can you escort this man to the *Terona*? He is one of our passengers—both men are, actually—and he has heat stroke. I am the closest thing they have to a doctor on that ship, so I will see to both of them as soon as I finish assisting the surgeon."

"Do we need to call the authorities? It looks like foul play."

"No. If the surgeon can stitch him up, I think everything will be fine. The debt was between them, and it has been paid, more than adequately as you can see."

The soldiers looked at one another and back to Slike and the surgeon. "They are English. Therefore, they are your captain's concern. Inform us immediately if there is more trouble."

"I will."

Slike watched the two soldiers escorting Mr. Adsley back to the *Terona*. If he had dysentery, in a matter of hours he would be vomiting. In a few days, he would lose control of his bowels, and sometime after that—when they were well on their way to Jamaica—his tongue would turn black, and he would die.

For a moment, a smile slithered across Slike's lips. He was pleased about his father's pending death. There were only two problems, though. First, Slike had miscalculated with his knife and might have hit one of Peter's arteries. That was unfortunate because he needed Peter's signature. The second problem was somewhat more irritating. If Mr. Adsley had truly contracted dysentery, the entire cargo and crew could be lost. Then, all of Slike's plans would be useless.

He watched the surgeon's steady hand sewing Peter's injury as he recalibrated his plan, adding quarantine for Mr. Adsley. He was too close to the end. It would never do to fail now. Mother and Charlie would be so disappointed.

Chapter 48

Banished

Chesterfield of Taddington
Derbyshire, England
1 September 1795

"No! Please!" Annette's cry rang out from the second story gallery as she groveled at her brother's feet. "Please, Gerald. Do not let Mother do this. I want to stay."

A whirlwind of grief, panic, and complete loss of security threatened to destroy what little peace remained in Annette's shattered heart. If she was forced to leave home, even for a boarding school she had once desired to attend, she would be separated from everything familiar. And the thought of leaving without Miss Haack was beyond her comprehension.

"Annette, stand up. Please." Gerald grasped Annette by the arms and gently lifted her to her feet. "It will not be so terrible as all of that."

"But Miss Haack," she whispered. "I cannot bear to leave without her."

Gerald leveled an angry look at their mother. "I told you Miss Haack must accompany her. Why have you led her to believe otherwise?"

"I had not gotten to that point yet," Mrs. Chetwynd smirked.

"Annette, listen to me. All is well. Miss Haack is going with you. Please, calm yourself, dear sister. It will be a pleasant time away with her. You will have so many new things to explore in Beverley."

Involuntary shudders racked Annette's body as she struggled to compose herself, but her mind raced ahead, and pushing away from her brother, she turned to Mrs. Chetwynd.

"Are there any other arrangements you failed to mention?"

"None of which to speak. You have only to prepare yourself for the journey to Yorkshire and focus on your recuperation."

Annette wiped her face as she studied her mother's inscrutable gaze.

Annette and her nurse left Chesterfield in one of the family's crested coaches five days later. It was a somber occasion, with only Mother and Gerald standing at the front door to see her off. There was not much to say either.

Miss Haack had packed her trunks with suitable dresses and all the necessities. Annette had personally seen to her sketchbook, her letters from her father, and the locket around her neck. Now they sat across from each other inside the coach. It would be a long journey to Jane Arden's Ladies Boarding School in Beverley, but the trip was all properly arranged. Her mother had seen to that.

Annette leaned her head back against the cushion and closed her eyes. She thought to occupy herself with memories of Papá, but . . .

Oh, God. She caught her tears with her gloved hands before they spilled over her cheeks. Reaching into her reticule, she pulled out Peter's embroidered handkerchief and wiped her eyes and nose.

I am sorry, Lord. Please forgive me.

Though she had tried to push Him away, she could not. Sometime over the last few weeks—since the banquet at the Woolton Hall, actually—He had come into her starving heart, and in some unique way had satisfied her. She was desperately hurting, of course. He had taken Papá. Yet, every time she thought of Papá, she would remember what he taught her: God is love, and everything He permits is because of love.

I never should have spoken against You. But I could not help it, just like I cannot help loving Peter. But he never came back for me, and You did not save Papá. I don't understand.

Annette's prayer drifted into a rambling haze of dreams mixed with reality as the coach jolted and bumped along the road.

Sometimes she was in the conservatory on that last night with Peter, reliving their intimate exchanges. Then she was with her father, talking and laughing over the smallest thing. Then she was back in the coach with Miss Haack, having to stop and change horses or unpacking and repacking their necessities, while each day moved her farther and farther away from the familiar.

Three days later, when they finally reached the Jane Arden Ladies Boarding School in Beverley of Yorkshire, Annette exited the carriage a forlorn wreck of travel weariness and dismay. She did not know where she was and hardly cared with whom she would stay. She only wanted a quiet room and a comfortable bed in which to sleep.

"Good afternoon, Miss Chetwynd. It is so good to have you with us."

"Pleased to meet you." Annette sighed. "This is Miss Haack. And please, call me Annette, if you will. I do not desire such formality."

"Splendid. Once proper introductions are made, we favor using first names as well, rather like a family. Now, come inside. You must be exhausted. I will show you to your room, and after you have had time to rest, perhaps you both would care to join us for tea. I have special guests from Caverswall, your part of the country, if I am not mistaken."

"Caverswall is about a day's journey from Chesterfield. My uncle and aunt live there."

"Then perhaps you know my friends, Mrs. Alyse Adsley and her daughter Miss Mary Hope Adsley. Mrs. Adsley is formerly of Beverley, but she visits each year about this time. Do you know of the Adsleys of Caverswall?"

Annette felt a wave of nausea overtaking her, but she managed a response. "I shall be pleased to make their acquaintance."

"Miss Arden," Lucy spoke up, "if you will show us to our room, it would be most helpful."

"Yes, of course, right this way."

↟

Later that afternoon, Miss Arden made the introductions between Annette, Miss Haack, and the Adsley ladies, and Annette wanted to cry. Though Miss Mary Hope Adsley's straight, auburn hair bore no resemblance to Mr. Adsley's dark, wavy mane, her brows arched the same way his did, and she had the same smile.

"I am pleased to make your acquaintance, Miss Chetwynd, but have we not met before?" Mary Hope asked. "You seem so familiar and your name, I believe I have heard it."

Annette wanted to lie, but sooner or later they would discover the connection.

"Indeed, you have. My uncle and aunt, the Bethertons, are your neighbors. I attended Sylvia's birthday ball and . . ."

"Why yes, of course," Mrs. Adsley chimed in. "I remember you from the wedding too. It rained both days, and . . ."

Annette felt her chin beginning to wobble. This sweet woman might have been . . .

"Well, let us simply say few people enjoy rain as I do." Mrs. Adsley's smiled broadened. "And you must be one of them."

"I am relieved to hear you say that, Mrs. Adsley."

"I understand," she responded with a laugh.

"Mother, do let's have some tea," Mary Hope coaxed. "Miss Chetwynd—Annette, if you will—I would love to know how you came to be in Beverley at Miss Arden's, if you will join us."

"Thank you, Miss Adsley, Mary Hope. I would like that."

Chapter 49

Middle Passage

On the *Terona*
Triangular Trade Route, Atlantic Ocean
Mid-September 1795

The Middle Passage left an indelible mark on both Adsley men. While Peter's wrath festered in him like the infection caused by the two knife wounds, Mr. Adsley remained quarantined in his room, struggling with dysentery.

When Peter, now a wild-haired, bearded skeleton of a man, finally emerged from sickbay for the first time, he had the misfortune of witnessing what a cat-of-nine-tails could do to human flesh as a "troublesome" Negro was forced to exact punishment on the back of an innocent Negro youth.

The next day, in addition to the poor Negro boy who received the beating, Captain Bledsoe informed Peter that thirty-two of the three hundred eighty six Negroes imprisoned in the belly of the ship had also died. Apparently, it was common to lose that many within the first three weeks, and he was doing the rest a service by sending his men down to dig out the corpses.

Peter watched in sorrow as each of their pitiful, bodies was tossed over the side of the ship. The bobbing, canvas-wrapped bodies did not fade from Peter's memory, however. They, along with feelings of guilt and rage, combined with his physical pain and became food for rampant nightmares that plagued Peter's sleep and contaminated his thoughts. So by the time the hurricane hit, he was ready to give up.

↟

Nearly senseless from being tossed about like a rag doll in sickbay, Peter staggered up to the deck and begged God to spare him and the Negroes any further suffering by sinking the *Terona*. At that moment, the wind and waves calmed long enough for Bledsoe to reassure Peter they would not sink, whereupon he ordered Scurvy and the crew's tattooed Negro hulk to tie Peter up so he would not get swept overboard.

He also ordered the crew to lighten the load before they left the eye of the storm.

Bewildered, Peter watched as the crew ascended from the bowels of the ship with crates, barrels, and fifteen to twenty of the weakest specimens of so-called "black gold." The poor creatures, who were still chained together, could not stand, but rather crawled and tumbled about the deck, clutching their captors' feet, crying out, drinking in the rain, and inhaling the clean air.

Then Scurvy, even he, reached down to lend a hand to the poor man latched onto his leg.

Peter sighed. Apparently, mercy may yet be had on this God-forsaken ...

"NO!" Peter's heart suddenly felt as if it were being ripped from his chest. He fought the binding ropes, squirmed, and kicked trying to escape. "STOP, please!" But to no avail.

Scurvy, who had unlatched the gangplank gate, opened it, and catapulted the trusting slave toward the deep.

The unspeakable sight and sound of human beings grasping, clawing, and shrieking as the weight of the first slave dragged the others across the ship's rain-drenched deck shredded the frayed remains of Peter's ravaged soul. He tried to avert his gaze, but could not, not before he glimpsed the horror in those innocent Negroes' eyes, bulging as they were jerked over the side of the ship and swallowed by the sea.

Then lightning split the sky, the wind started screaming again, and Peter wailed, *"WHY GOD?"*

In a frenzy of despair, he wriggled free of the rope and sprang for the side of the ship. But Mr. Slike caught him by his injured leg and prevented him from launching himself into the watery abyss. Then he and two other crewmen dragged Peter to the mast and, yanking his arms backwards around the wide pole, secured his wrists with shackles. Then, for good measure, Slike pummeled his right side.

Fire shot through his body and exploded in his head; then everything went dark.

⚜

Peter and the *Terona* survived the storm. But Mr. Adsley's health never returned, and some days before they completed the accursed voyage, Peter's father died.

Feverish, hardly able to stand, and devoid of any emotion, Peter demanded to watch the crew bury his father's body at sea. They dumped his corpse overboard with eight other corpses. A fitting departure, Peter reflected, as he watched the floating canvas-wrapped bodies. He was unable to distinguish between his father's body and those of his would-be slaves.

Then he started to feel faint, and before he knew it, his knees buckled. He felt his forehead smack against the deck in an explosion of white light and a ringing noise.

The last thing he heard was someone shouting, "Slike, we need a doctor up here!"

Chapter 50

Victory

Slike smiled as he stood in his cabin, admiring the Adsley family signet ring with its ruby encrusted rose seal. Before wrapping his father's corpse in a canvas burial sheet, he had slipped it from Mr. Charles Adsley's cold, dead finger.

He put it on the fourth finger of his right hand. It fit perfectly. Then he opened the top drawer of the chest sitting on his dresser and took out his gold pocket watch with its dog's head charm. He glanced at the inscription on the back of the watch: "For my beloved C.A." The ring and the watch were two of the three keys on which his future, and that of his family, depended.

His family! He was finally in a position to help his family.

Time slowed as Steven Likebridge studied the watch his mother gave him when he was young. Then his mind drifted to his sweet Lani. Was she well? Had Fontaine kept his promise? In a matter of days, he would know. His heart leaped in his chest. He would see her again, and he would be able to keep her.

Steven held his breath at the prospect. Was he a father now too? He remembered the possibility of a child. Mother and Charlie would be so happy.

Steven bowed his head. It had been so long in coming, but his plan was nearly complete. Perhaps God was finally pleased to assist him too—finally, after all these years. The Adsley men—the two who were dead—had both died of natural causes.

Captain's second bellowing demand for Mr. Slike thundered down the hall.

Mr. Slike . . . Mr. Slike

Shaking his head, Steven returned to his present circumstances and his patient's injuries.

Those injuries, not to mention the emotional anguish to which the younger Adsley had been subjected, were taking their toll. Perhaps he had grown faint while on the deck. Any further exertion would prove detrimental to his full recovery.

But that was exactly as it should be, Mr. Slike reasoned. The last male Adsley should die of natural causes; then he would be free and without fault.

However, if Peter had somehow sustained a more serious injury, there would be no way to obtain his signature on the death certificate, and Slike needed that signature or he would have to resort to another more painful backup plan he had already settled, in case something went wrong.

Slike dropped the watch back in the open drawer and placed the ring beside it, then rushed out of the cabin and up the stairs. When Captain Bledsoe shouted for the third time, Mr. Slike presented himself.

"Here, Captain."

"Mr. Slike, it is good of you to join us."

"Indeed. What is the concern?"

"Your charge has fainted dead away and broken his head on the deck."

"Has he?"

"Clear the way, you miserable varmints." Captain Bledsoe cracked his infernal whip and shouted at the crew. "Let the good doctor have a look."

Slike noted the blood pooling on the deck around Peter's unconscious form and rushed to his knees.

"Blast it! Bandages! Fetch some now!"

Within seconds, torn cloths like a flock of limp seagulls dropped on the deck beside him. He wadded one into a thick compress and placed it over the gash above Peter's right eye.

Curse the misdirected fool; it was exactly like him to risk his own health to support another man, even one who had wronged him and was now dead.

But why should he? Their father, the rotten coward, had treated Peter abominably.

He knitted his brows together. The irony of an abolitionist pastor being compelled into slave ownership had not escaped Slike's notice. Indeed, every shred of humanity he yet possessed railed against it. Mr. Adsley should have prepared him ahead of time—way ahead. He might have trained both his sons about the way of things much earlier in life. If he had, it would not have gone so poorly.

Slike ground his teeth. Curse Charles Adsley! He had ruined all their lives.

When he threw aside the first blood-soaked cloth to apply another, Steven caught a glimpse of his young brother's graying face, and his throat tightened.

Peter seemed peaceful, almost relieved.

Steven looked away. His brother was a good man, a truly caring man, and an honorable pastor. He did not deserve this wretched end. Had things been different, he would have been in his parish and they might have been broth . . .

Slike swallowed hard. He could not afford this daydreaming, not now. He must focus on the facts.

Peter Adsley's body could not withstand any further trauma, and if he died before Slike obtained his signature on the proper death certificate he had acquired from a legitimate Liverpool physician, his plan would fail.

Slike must have that signature. It would match the one on the latest will and inheritance transfer their father had drawn up and filed in the barrister's office in Liverpool. With the signet ring, Slike knew he could pass himself off as the Adsley heir. Few people, most of whom were women, he could manage later, knew anything of Peter's physical appearance. But there was no way Slike could reproduce Peter's signature to match the official documents, and if he did not have it when he finally chose to return to Liverpool, the authorities would be suspicious.

Clenching his teeth and clamping his arm around his brother's head, Slike planted himself on the ship's deck and pictured his future. In less than a fortnight, with all the Adsley men dead, he would present himself at Good Hope as Mr. Peter Adsley, the only remaining son of his recently deceased father, Mr. Charles Adsley. He would dine in comfort. He would see Lani again and . . . perhaps their child. It was nearly unfathomable.

But he must stop this bleeding so he could get that signature.

All at once, maiming his own right hand—the last sacrifice he would make to forever excuse himself from having to reproduce writing like the true Adsley heir's—seemed less daunting a task than preserving Peter's life.

⚔

Outside Mr. Slike's cabin, Turtle peeled himself away from the corridor wall. He was about to deliver fresh water when the door swung open, and the doctor exited, leaving it ajar.

"Thankee the mighty Damballah, God, and the hail Mary, for gettin' him out of me way," Turtle whispered.

He hated Mr. Slike, and he hated making deliveries to his cabin. Not that the man had ever done anything to him, but the way he eyed Turtle caused the boy's skin to crawl. The rest of the crew noticed it too. They steered clear of him, except for Scurvy. Scurvy was another brutal beast, but Turtle didn't want to think of that right now. He had more important things to do.

Turtle started to go into Mr. Slike's cabin, but then thought better of it. He was not going to change Slike's water out now. If he did, Mr. Slike would know Turtle had been in there. It could not hurt to have a little look-see, though. Maybe he would find a voodoo doll, some signs of black magic or a lonely coin or two lying around. Turtle set down his water bucket and crept into the dim room.

Light from the passageway seeped inside, and Turtle's eyes began to adjust. The bunk with its folded blankets and pillow was neat. A locked trunk stood at the foot of the bed. A signed parchment with a decorative seal on it lay on the small desk where a candle flickered in its lantern. Turtle held the light close to the document to get a better look. He could not read so it did not do any good, but he could tell it looked important. Turtle moved to the dresser.

The small chest on Slike's dresser caught his eye, or rather the red sparkle of a gemstone did. Turtle drew closer. Then his heart skipped. Beside Slike's pocket watch lay Mr. Adsley's big ruby ring. Turtle had seen it on his finger every day since the first day Mr. Slike had brought him aboard. What was Mr. Slike doing with it?

Suddenly, Turtle froze as voices carried along the stairway.

Oh, mighty Damballah, God . . . Turtle shook his head. *Mr. Adsley's ring? Voices? No more pinchin', except for fruit.* He didn't have time to think.

Squeezing his eyes shut, he let his fingers grab the ring and shove it in his pocket. Then he darted out of the room, clicking the door shut behind him. Next, he picked up his water bucket and headed straight toward the voices. If he ran away, they might suspect him, especially if he sloshed his water. But if he moved about his business of delivering water along the corridor the same way he always did, they would think nothing of it.

"Careful now. He must be held still," Mr. Slike commanded as three crew members carried the injured man down the steps.

"You, Scurvy, hold his other leg while Mr. Reed moves around behind me."

"Mr. Slike, you got the Turtle behind you. Want to send him ahead to sick bay?"

Slike glanced over his shoulder. "You heard the man. Put that water down and go open the door down there. We need to get Mr. Adsley back in bed."

Turtle immediately obliged.

"Wait. Take the water too; then get up to deck for the rest of the bandages. I need them right away."

"Aye, sir, Mr. Slike." Turtle moved down the passageway as quickly as he could with the water bucket.

Oh mighty Damballah, God, and hail the Mary, please keep Mr. Adsley safe. I need him ta get me off this ship.

Chapter 51

Pressure

Some hours after Mr. Adsley had fainted, Turtle sneaked down to check on him. His friend lay so pale and quiet in the bunk that Turtle figured he would be gone by morning. But Mr. Adsley lived.

A couple days later, Turtle saw Mr. Slike and Captain Bledsoe visiting Mr. Adsley in sick bay, but he did not hear much of anything, and they were in there again.

Turtle spread himself as flat as he could against the wall outside of sick bay. What did they want from Mr. Adsley?

"There's no reason to delay signing."

Strange. Mr. Slike sounded like he was desperate.

"It merely proves you have witnessed your father's death. Nothing will come of it."

"If it is not serious, why should I sign now?" Mr. Adsley's voice was weak, but firm. "Can it not wait?"

"It is a minor task. You can complete it lying down; then we need not bother you again."

"Captain Bledsoe, if you please," Peter said, speaking more firmly, "kindly escort the doctor out. I am weary of this impasse."

"But Mr. Adsley—"

"Mr. Adsley is not well, Mr. Slike." Captain Bledsoe opened the door to the cabin, and Turtle slid back around the corner. "We will take it up later, when you are better, Mr. Adsley." Then he moved Slike out the door and closed it behind them.

"I need that document signed, or the whole plan is ruined." Mr. Slike was angry.

"What is your hurry? We are not due to reach port for a few days."

"I've lost the blasted ri—" Mr. Slike's voice became knife sharp. "That is not your business, old man. Just see that he signs, or I'll be forced to use more persuasive techniques."

"Fine." Bledsoe scoffed. "Now, outta me way. I've got me ship to sail."

With that, both men left the passageway, and Turtle let out a breath. His fingers tightened around the hidden pocket where he kept Mr. Adsley's ring. Mr. Slike was fuming mad that he lost the ring. The last time he brought fresh water to Slike's room it looked like a hurricane had hit it. But Slike couldn't tell anyone about it, or they would know he took it. Well, it served him right for taking it.

But why was he ordering the captain around? And what did Slike mean by "more persuasive techniques" he wanted to use to get Peter to sign a paper?

Turtle was confused and frightened as he crept back around the corner and leaned his head against the door of the sick bay. If Mr. Adsley had been feeling better, Turtle would have spoken to him about it, but he did not want to disturb his friend. So Turtle stepped into the alcove across the way where he slept so he could be closer to his friend and began repeating his chant to the mighty Damballah.

Chapter 52

Friendship

Jane Arden Ladies Boarding School
Beverley in Yorkshire, England
1 October 1795

"So Annette, is there a particular gentleman for whom you have . . . ? Well, you know what I mean."

Annette sipped tea across from Mary Hope Adsley. She did not wish to reveal her connection, if it could even be called that, with her new and very dear friend's brother. The subject was too painful. As a matter of fact, it had taken some time for her to adjust to living in the same boarding house with the two Adsley women, those whom she might have called Mother and Sister if . . .

Annette could hardly bear to think of what might have changed Peter's mind, and she so desired to hear what they knew of him. But she was afraid to ask. Yet, they were both so kind that Annette found it impossible to resist their friendship.

"Come now, Annette, you needn't be shy. We have spoken of everything from the abolition of slavery to *A Vindication of the Rights of Women*. We have even compared David Hume's philosophy of the first cause—though Mr. Hume is completely ignorant of what the Scriptures say of God and His work—to the Lord's plan for our salvation. You can tell me his name."

"There is." *And I so want to talk to you about him. I have so many questions.* "And some day, I will tell you who he is."

"Annette, you must tell me."

"I cannot, not today." *Oh, Mary Hope, your brother promised he loved me, but he left. And there was no letter. Your brother promised to write a letter to Father, but he left on the Terona, a known slave ship bound for Africa. Martin found out for me. Can you tell me how that is possible?* "I have spoken all day thus far. Now it is your turn. Tell me more about your brother. Have you had any news from him? Does he still support Wilberforce and the Movement? I recall him speaking against the slave trade at Betherton Hall a couple years ago."

"Yes. He's an avid supporter, and I remember the exact day at your aunt's garden party. Peter was appalled. He told me he had to leave or else make a scene, and he would never do that." Mary Hope sighed. "I was finally able to speak with Sir Likebridge that day." Mary Hope reached for Annette's hand. "But that is an entirely different matter."

Annette stared at Mary Hope. Had she some feelings for the man?

"Well, then—" Annette set her teacup down and held her friend's hand. "We shall both keep our secrets a little longer then. But let us walk into town now; it is such a beautiful day."

"Agreed." Mary Hope offered Annette her hand. "But I shall expect to hear of him soon."

"And I shall tell you."

Chapter 53

Scurvy

On the *Terona*
Middle passage almost complete
4 October 1795

Turtle woke to the sound of clanking chains and shouting crewmen. They had begun resurrecting the living cargo from their hellish prison. Soon they would reach Falmouth Harbor, and the crew had to get the human cargo organized for inspection.

Now that about fifty slaves had been assembled, he commanded the crew to wash them with fresh water and give them as much food as they could handle. Once their bodies were accustomed to eating more again, they would be given as much as they wanted. Not only would they be given more food than they had during the entire crossing, but the crew would also properly clean and dress any injuries or wounds the slaves may have acquired during the voyage.

The whole thing was a lie, and Turtle hated it. No one really cared about the Negroes. They just wanted the money they would fetch. He had seen the auctions. A healthy slave, at least those who appeared to be healthy, would bring anywhere from £90 to £272.

Turtle stayed hidden in the shadows of the stairwell a few minutes longer just to make sure Mr. Slike was occupied. The cabin boy could not risk getting caught helping Peter, but he must at least see him.

Finally satisfied that everyone would remain on deck, Turtle skittered down the steps to the gallery. He snatched out the empty rum bottle he had hidden under his shirt and dunked it in the fresh water barrel. He replaced the lid of the barrel and was off again through the passageways and deeper into the belly of the ship. One more turn and he was at sick bay. He looked both ways. The passageway was clear, so he lifted the door latch, ducked inside, and closed the door behind him.

A sickly yellow candle burned in the lantern on the wall. Turtle deposited his water bottle on a wooden chair and then turned to his friend.

"Oh, Mr. Adsley, what happen—?"

Instead of lying in bed, Peter was perched on the edge of a crate opposite the door with his ankles and wrists twisted back and chained to mounts on the wall.

Turtle rushed to Mr. Adsley, but then stopped.

There was a scuffling sound outside in the passageway. Then someone was fumbling with the door latch. Terrified, Turtle grabbed the water bottle and dove into the corner behind an old crate. Holding his breath and wishing he could disappear, Turtle turned toward the intruder entering the tiny room. Pressing his face as close to the corner of the old crate as possible, he took a quick peek around to see who it was.

"Oh, God and hail the Mary, you're a good ship. It's Scurvy! I be a prayin' ta whoever be there: please sir, ya know that besides Slike, Scurvy be the foulest man alive. I do beg ya, if ya'd hide me now and keep me friend, Mr. Adsley, safe, I'll do anything I can for ya."

"Wake up, ya miserable whelp!" Scurvy growled. Turtle watched him grab a handful of his friend's hair and yank his head up. "Doc Slike says it be time for a li'l more encouragement to 'elp you sign that paper o' 'is."

Turtle flinched. Peter's left eye was swollen shut, and the bandages covering his wounded head were encrusted with blood and dirt. Suddenly, Scurvy drew back his fist and catapulted it forward. There was a loud crack as Scurvy's fist smashed into his friend's left cheek. The force of the blow slammed his face into the wall. It bounced off and flopped down like a dead fish. It appeared as if Peter had not even tried to brace himself. Scurvy yanked Peter's head up again, and blood poured from his mouth.

"Some broken ribs and a black eye ain't enough, 'ey Gov'nor? Now ya 'ave a split lip to go with 'em."

Peter's good eye fluttered open, but he said nothing.

"You were a fighter back in that Merseyside warehouse, ya were. That were the first time I 'ad a go at ya, and lookie 'ere. I'm doin' it again. Aye now, there we 'ave it. Got your attention, did it? I wonder if ya'd do any better knowin' that the pretty li'l Chetwynd filly ya met at Woolton 'all were Doc Slike's betroth'd?"

Peter groaned and pulled at his chains.

"Now that be more like it." Scurvy smiled and rubbed his fist with his hand. "Ya know, if ya'd just sign that paper o' 'is, 'e might put off the li'l rendezvous 'e's plannin' for 'er when 'e gets back 'ome. 'E said you'd know what I meant if I recited a poem 'e wrote at that fine gatherin' with the Ashtons. Let me see now, 'ow did it go? 'When ya be tired . . .' Nah that ain't right. It were like this—'When you tire of that luscious little tart, do me the kindness of letting me know. I'd like to have a go at her myself.'"

Scurvy slapped his knee and broke out laughing. "Ya liked that, did ya? See 'ow the 'know' and 'go' matches together in a rhymin' fashion? That means it be good poetry. Bet ya didn't know our own Mr. Slike were a poet, did ya?"

Peter gasped, sputtered something, and then his head lulled off to the side and he was quiet. Turtle must do something or his friend would not survive.

"SCUURRRVY!" A roar and the unmistakable sound of Captain Bledsoe's wooden leg scraping against the floorboards came closer. Turtle squeezed his eyes shut and tried to disappear into the corner. Seconds later, Captain Bledsoe nearly yanked the rickety door off its hinges and rushed in.

"Well, ya bloody cur, be he ready to sign?"

"No, Cap'n. But 'e's payin' proper attention now."

The captain stepped further into the room, and it was quiet for a few seconds until . . .

"AAARRRR, ya filthy wretch! Ya killed the lad. Young Adsley's dead. He's not breathin'. Why ya . . ."

There was a scuffling sound, a number of well-placed punches, and some smothered gasps as the captain pounced on Scurvy.

"You've ruined Mr. Slike's plan, not to mention I'm in a fury. That lad was me friend's only livin' son. And to top it off, he was one of God's own servants, a preacher, you idiot. So I'm thinkin' Mr. Slike, I, and the good Lord himself will be after you." Captain Bledsoe cracked his whip. "Now, get your grimy carcass out o' my sight, and hide as best you can."

Scurvy whimpered as he dragged himself out of the room.

"The next time I lay eyes on you, I'll kill you meself," Captain Bledsoe called out the door, but there was no response.

Turtle held his breath and waited for Captain Bledsoe to leave, but he sat down in the rickety wooden chair. "Well, Turtle, you feisty runt, how long do you think you're goin' to get away with this?"

The hairs on the back of Turtle's neck stood on end.

"I can smell you. Now get your skinny little hide out here and have a listen."

Figuring death was on his heels anyway, Turtle crawled out and faced Captain Bledsoe with hands shaking and lunch on its way up from his stomach.

"So, you want off me ship, eh?" Bledsoe asked.

"No, sir."

"That's a whale of a lie if ever there were one." Bledsoe raised his hand.

Turtle closed his eyes and held his head high, waiting for the death punch. The only thing he regretted was not being able to help his friend.

The punch never came, though. Squinting open one eye, Turtle ventured a look at the captain, whose face was now eye-level.

"Now, tell me honest, Turtle. I may be an old sea dog who lost his lovin' Lizzie and wasted his life away in slavin', but I know a boy lookin' for somethin' new when I see one. You've been achin' to get off me ship since you found a friend in Mr. Adsley here. Am I right?"

Turtle bowed his head. "That be the truth, sir. But now he's dead."

"Listen to me, son. He's not dead, at least for the moment." Turtle's eyes brightened, and his heart began to sing. "But Slike's a snake, and he's out to get our Mr. Adsley."

"Aye, sir, I know it."

"But it isn't right, and I won't have it. Killin' my old friend's only heir, and takin' his God-given inheritance. It's plain wrong. So we're goin' to have to work together to get Mr. Adsley back to England safe and sound. You understand me, boy?"

"Aye, sir."

"Now, here's what I need you to do . . ."

"Have you lost your wits, old man? He was practically dead!" Slike shouted. "How could he escape?"

"I have no idea. Scurvy might have taken him. I haven't seen that filthy vermin 'round for quite a while, and one o' the skiffs is gone. Or maybe he flew away."

"How dare you toy with me, you pitiful excuse for a pirate. I could wring your neck this instant, and no one would care."

Turning his back on Slike, Captain Bledsoe sat down at his pianoforte. He fingered the broken ivory keys of the dilapidated instrument. "I care not what you do, you shameless maggot, with your schemin' on how to rob a good man o' his fortune. I should've put a stop to it long ago."

Bledsoe began playing Bach's French Suite No. 3 in B minor. If the fiend was going to kill him, it would be a relief. Bledsoe would die content, listening to the last strains of the only meaningful accomplishment of his entire miserable life—his music—and knowing he had saved Mr. Peter Adsley.

"Well, on with it. Do your dirty work, and let's be done. I'm weary of bein' your lackey."

"You're mistaken, old man." Slike came up beside Bledsoe. "You will continue to do as I bid, and to sail the *Terona* as long as I say, or I will pay your dear old Lizzie—Miss Elizabeth Alexander, should I say—a little visit."

Bledsoe's fingers stumbled across the keys. How did he know Lizzie?

"I've hit a sensitive note, have I, Bledsoe?" Slike jabbed his finger into the soft tissue between the captain's neck and collarbone. "Or perhaps I was bluffing."

Bledsoe shifted his body away from his instrument, toward Mr. Slike's granite stare. With the mocking promise of information and a threat about Bledsoe's only love, the captain cursed the day he had found Slike mangled in that back alley in Liverpool. The only reason he helped the young man those ten years ago was because he reminded Bledsoe of himself when he had been beaten and pressed into service after Lizzie's father had found them together.

Though Slike had been gratified that Bledsoe had helped, and they had developed a working relationship of sorts, Slike was far from being his friend. As Bledsoe had said, he was no longer willing to be Mr. Slike's slave.

"Well, Captain, get moving. Find Mr. Adsley or I will pay your Mrs. Chetwynd . . . My goodness, did I let her married name slip?" Slike covered his mouth with his hand and acted modestly surprised. "How very dull of me. Now that you know her name, you might be tempted to see her. She is a widow, so that may not be a bad idea." Then his face turned dark. "But do not even think of it. Simply find Adsley and get us to Falmouth. If you do not, the second we reach port, I will write and have her killed."

"As you wish, Mr. Slike." The captain bowed his head, and Mr. Slike turned to leave his quarters.

"Steven, dear boy, would you be willing . . . ?" Bledsoe spoke in a plaintive voice.

Slike whipped back around. "I told you never to use—"

Bledsoe swung the most potent blow he had in years, and Mr. Slike was out cold on the floor. The captain stepped over the body and opened the door. "Mr. Reed," he shouted to his first mate. "Get me some crew."

Within seconds, three men were at his door.

"Yes, sir, Captain, sir." All three sang out as they saluted.

"Get this man out of here."

"Overboard, sir?"

"No, to the brig. I need not another sin on me head, but I have no wish to see or hear him for the remainder of the trip."

"Yes, sir."

They hoisted Slike up and carried him away.

Chapter 54
Rescue

Trelawney, Jamaica
Port of Falmouth
8 October 1795

The steeple of Falmouth's newly-constructed St. Peter's Anglican Church rose like a gleaming sword as the *Terona*, which had docked early that morning, disgorged its crew and every last one of the slaves, who were being herded into the stockade behind the auction block.

Turtle sat on top of a barrel, watching the whole endeavor and waiting for the moment he would deliver Mr. Slike's last meal to the brig. As soon as he did that, he was to help Peter collect his things and get off the ship. Captain Bledsoe, who had decided his reason for returning home was far more important than sailing a slave ship, had already secured passage on the first of His Majesty's Royal Navy fleet departing to England. The three of them would return together.

"Well, I'll be a pocket pinchin' . . ."

"Turtle." Peter cautioned as he stepped up to the barrel.

"I'm about blown over, Mr. Adsley. Ya look a sight, but at least you're on your feet again." Turtle jumped off the barrel. "For a while there, I was pretty worried."

"Thank you, Turtle." Peter started to smile but stopped instantly to prevent the wound on his upper lip from splitting again.

"That eye looks pretty bad too, sir. Do ya s'ppose I should raid some of Mr. Slike's ointments and potions? He won't be needin' them for a while. And if you're headin' back ta England ta see the oranges lady, you'll need all the help ya can get. Ya should get that mop of yours cut too. It's crawlin' with lice."

Peter felt his matted hair. "Aren't you full of ideas?"

"That's what friends be for, isn't it?"

"True enough. Now, how about some of those ointments?"

"Aye, sir, but not 'til I see ya snatch a couple o' those limes out o' that barrel over there. We never got to your pinchin' lessons and no one's here but me."

"I cannot just—"

"Ya have ta. We're goin' inta unfamiliar waters, and we might run out. Please, sir. No one's goin' ta mind or miss 'em and you're too close ta dyin' for my comfort."

"All right."

Peter slowly stepped over to the barrel, grabbed four limes, two in each hand, and quickly slipped them into his pockets. Then he stepped back to Turtle. "Are you satisfied?"

"Yes, but ya need more practice. I saw ya do it."

Peter shook his head.

"I got ta go feed that snake, Mr. Slike, and pinch me some of his ointments, but I'll be back."

"You really should not—"

"I know. I need ta be more respectful. Ya told me that already. But he's just so mean. How can ya still be so . . . ? I just don't follow it, sir."

"I don't either. But we'll have plenty of time to discuss it on our return trip."

"Aye, sir, Mr. Adsley." Turtle nodded his head and smiled. "And time for ya ta practice your fruit-pinchin' skills too: one fruit in each hand for every sermon I have ta hear."

Peter lunged at Turtle, but the little fellow laughed and skittered off across the deck.

Chapter 55

Relief

Jane Arden Ladies Boarding School
Beverley in Yorkshire, England
5 November 1795

Annette, Miss Haack, Mary Hope, and Mrs. Adsley, along with two other young ladies lately arrived at the Jane Arden Ladies Boarding School, finished their excursion to the market. Having perused the fabrics and wares at the mercantile, enjoyed tea at the coffee house, and slipped into the Beverley Ministry to hear Mr. George Lambert practicing the pipe organ for Sunday services, they were now entering the house.

"Annette, see here, there is a letter for you." Mary Hope smiled. The chattering group of ladies thrilled with excitement when they heard, but Annette felt a sinking feeling as she took it.

"Are you well?" Mary Hope asked, and the ladies quieted themselves. "Certainly it will be good to hear from your family, or perhaps it is your Cousin Sylvia. You have told us so much about her."

"Yes, thank you, Mary Hope. Perhaps, you are right. I shall go read it now." Annette turned to her nurse. "Lucy?"

"All right then, we're off to the drawing room." Miss Haack adopted a pleasant tone as she shooed the rest of the party along. "Anyone for a game of whist?"

"Would you have me sit with you while you read?" Mary Hope asked.

Annette's heart sank. "It is Mother's writing. But why so early? We agreed I would return in mid-December for Christmas."

"Listen to me, sweet friend. I see you are distressed." Mary Hope put an arm around her, and Annette rested her head on her friend's shoulder. "Do let me help you to your room where you can have some privacy."

"I am sorry, Mary Hope. I know not what to do."

"Well, go upstairs with me, and then decide." Her friend guided her to the stairs. "Perhaps, you should read it before worrying. It may not be as dire as you think."

"It is; I know it."

"Come inside; we can work it out together. Or, if you prefer, I will leave you."

"Please stay. I have so much to tell you, but I fear you will hate me once you know."

"I could never hate you, Annette. You are my friend, and as such, I love you. But do not be so anxious. Whatever it is, the Lord loves you, and He will accomplish His purpose for this. And no matter what, I will still be your friend."

"But—"

"No excuses. You have been hurting too long. Let go of whatever you have been harboring. And if the letter holds more pain, we shall deal with it together."

They sat on the bed while Annette calmed herself by breathing deeply.

"Dearest Annette, you fume about slavery, and you dream about the freedom to choose your own path, but you are so bound by doubts. Let me help you. Or at least let me show you a verse in Romans that has helped me. You said your father taught you about the Scriptures. Let us see what they say."

"All right, but I must tell you something first."

"Anything you like."

Annette folded her handkerchief in such a way as to present Peter's initials to her friend. "I received this handkerchief from a gentleman whom I have no doubt you know."

Mary Hope touched the initials and stared at Annette. "Indeed, I do. These are my brother's initials. I stitched them myself. How did you come by this?"

"When I was last in Buxton, near St. John's parish, I met your brother again."

"Again?"

"Yes. I met him before that on the night of my Cousin Sylvia's birthday celebration at Betherton Hall. I believe you were there too. It was the night of your brother, Richard's engagement."

"I was there. And you have known Peter since then? Why did you not tell me? Mother and I would have . . . I am sorry. I did not mean to interrupt. Go on. I am most astonished, but nothing you say will cause me to hate you."

"Let me show you something else then." Annette went around to the other side of the bed and dug under her mattress for her sketchbook. If she were going to tell this story, she would share everything.

Chapter 56

Confession

Returning to Chesterfield of Taddington
From thence to Liverpool in Merseyside
16 November 1795

The fateful letter mentioned nothing of a suitor or an arrangement as Annette had feared it would. It did, however, inform her that her convalescence had come to an end.

Annette looked across the coach at Miss Haack, who was sleeping, despite the jangling chains, galloping hooves, and constant rocking of the coach. Then she gazed out the window at the crystal waters of the Derbyshire Lake District.

As usual, Mother's letter left no room for debate. And to be frank, Annette no longer cared to have one. Revealing the truth about her understanding with Peter to his sister and his mother, followed by their faithful reassurance that Peter would never lie about such things, had helped Annette recapture some of the hope she had lost. Mary Hope had also helped her with grief over her father's passing.

Tears clouded Annette's vision whenever she thought of him, but just as Mary Hope had taught her, the twenty-eighth verse of Romans chapter eight readily came to combat the pain.

"And we know that all things work together for good to them that love God, to them who are the called according to his purpose." Annette repeated the verse two more times.

Of course, it did not promise all things were good, as well she knew. But no matter how much she hurt because of her losses, and no matter what Mother had in mind, God promised He would use it for the good of those who love Him.

Annette hugged herself and bowed her head. *Lord, thank You for giving me Mary Hope. I cherish this promise she showed me. Please help me remember it, and help me to love You as I should. I will certainly need it with Mother and her schemes. Please keep Peter safe too.*

Raising her chin, sitting up straighter, and turning her head to the right and left, Annette assumed the air of conceit she knew Mother considered to be proper. Mary Hope and she had decided the best way to avoid conflict with Mother was by giving her what she wanted— at least the exterior appearance of it. And if Annette was going to do it correctly, she must start practicing now.

⚜

The coach stopped, the door popped open, and a footman offered Annette his hand. Tilting her head to accommodate her hat, Annette stepped out of the coach. She paused for a moment, and with head high and back arrow-straight, she nodded at the line of servants assembled at the stairs.

There was a bit of shuffling amongst them, but she chose not to notice. They immediately recovered their stiff poses and curtsied as she passed without even glancing in their direction. To them, it would appear that Mr. Chetwynd's daughter—the impish little darling they knew and loved—was gone forever. But Annette knew better, and someday she would tell her friends what she was doing.

Inside the hall, she removed her hat. Her hair was arranged in a rather severe, yet very modern Grecian-looking upsweep with a couple honey-colored curls stuck into place on her temples. A servant took her hat, traveling coat, and reticule. Mrs. Chetwynd took her hand and paraded her in a circle for inspection.

"The hair is right, but the dress is rather plain. We shall see to that soon enough, though." Her mother dropped her hand. "How was the journey, my dear? Did you find your accommodations comfortable?" Mrs. Chetwynd did not wait for an answer. "You look rather pale. How is your health?"

"I have been traveling for three days, quite a task. But I have managed well enough."

"Indeed, you have." Her mother almost smiled. "And you must be tired. Rest for a while before supper; then we will talk. You recall from my letter we are off to Liverpool next week. I have made your appointment for a fitting. We must get your wardrobe in order."

Turning to Miss Haack, Mrs. Chetwynd started in, "See that Annette has a hot bath and lay out some fresh clothes for her. If she needs some refreshments before dinner, fetch her some almond cake. Cook just baked it this morning."

"Yes, Mrs. Chetwynd." Lucy curtsied and headed for the kitchen.

"Annette, your stay at Miss Arden's school appears to have worked wonders." Her mother's eyes once again surveyed Annette from head to toe. "You have a suitable air of confidence about you. With just the right wardrobe, you will be a great success."

With that, Mrs. Chetwynd walked away. "I will be playing the pianoforte if you need me," she called back over her shoulder. "Do enjoy your rest."

Chapter 57
Questions

Liverpool
Merseyside, England
21 November 1795

HMS Swiftsure, under the command of Captain Charles Boyles, was true to her name, and just over six weeks after their departure from Jamaica, Peter, Captain Bledsoe, and Turtle were approaching Liverpool.

"Are ya well, sir?" Turtle sat down beside Peter, who was looking out across the sea. "Ya look rested enough, but for your eyes."

"And what is wrong with my eyes?"

"They make me think your heart hurts. Is it 'cause I turned ya into a thief by teachin' ya the fruit pinchin'?"

Nightmares still plagued Peter's sleep and turmoil over his slaves haunted him daily. And that horrible darkness of the hurricane still echoed in his thoughts. He was so ashamed, and now that he was home again . . . What about Annette?

He sighed. "You are quite observant, Turtle. But the Lord and I are working on it."

"Good. Ask Him ta help ya work on that servant thing too then."

"What?"

"Just now ya called me a servant, but ya promised I wouldn't have ta be one if I stayed with ya here in England."

Peter thought for a moment then sighed. "I said you were *observant*. It means sharp-eyed; watchful, always alert—not a servant."

"Sorry, sir. I didn't mean ta—"

"It's all right, Turtle."

"I got a bigger question, Mr. Adsley."

"Go on."

"It's about when ya said we are a miserable lot of vermin compared ta God's bein' perfect and hatin' sin."

"I said nothing of us being vermin."

"I know, but it's my word to help me remember how bad we are. Remember, Cap'n Bledsoe used ta call Scurvy a vermin. It also helps me understand how big God is and how He could stomp on me if He wanted ta. Anyway, why did He love us so much if we're just a bunch of wretched sinners? Why would He let his only son die? I wouldn't give up me boy if I had one."

"Well, that is the difference between us. We are selfish, but God isn't."

"I got some more questions then."

"You have the deck. I will do the best I can."

"I got ta thinkin' 'bout God some more. He's really different from what I learned on the island 'bout the Mighty Damballah and the hail Mary."

"Yes."

"But what I really want ta know is . . . How will your father's men know ya? You're a sight better looking than ya were before, what with the haircut and shave, but ya aren't all rich and fine as ya were. Do ya s'ppose we'll ever see Mr. Slike again? I really don't—"

"Slow down, Turtle. Everything will be fine."

"Remember when Mr. Slike wanted ya ta sign that important paper? What if he just signed it himself and beat us back here? He mighta said ya were dead, just like your father. If he got ta your father's men before us, we won't have a chance."

"Turtle, settle yourself. Everything will work out. It might have been a little easier if I had my father's signet ring. But I know these men, and I can prove who I am with my signature."

"What kinda ring is a signet?"

"It has my family's insignia or seal engraved on it. There is only one like it. A man uses it to identify himself and approve documents. Normally, a father passes it to his heir when he is too old or ill to oversee an estate. But my father's is at the bottom of the sea, I imagine."

Turtle started digging around in the waist of his pants. "Is this it?"

"It is, thank Heaven! How did you get it?"

"Well, sir, that is a real good story, but do I have t' tell ya now?"

"Yes. And, stop calling me 'sir.' You, Captain Bledsoe, and I have been fellow travelers these six weeks; we could even be called friends. Now, how did you get my father's ring?"

"I pinched it from Mr. Slike's cabin the same day they buried Mr. Adsley. Couldn't stand him havin' it when he were so hateful ta ya."

"Why did you wait 'til now to show me?"

"I don't know. Guess I kinda wanted ta keep it for meself in case things didn't work out. Ya know ya were pretty bad off for a while. I wasn't sure ya were goin' ta make it."

"Well, God has seen fit to allow me to make it, and now I have my ring. God will take care of everything, Turtle. I've been praying about it. We just have to be ready to follow in the direction He leads. In the meantime, the first thing we are doing after we get to shore is to get a bath and some more clothes."

Turtle cringed.

"No excuses, Turtle. You need it as much as I do."

"What 'bout Cap'n Bledsoe?"

"He will too. We are going to have a decent meal as well. After that, I will find my lady."

"What if Mr. Slike's already got her?"

"I doubt that is possible. We left Falmouth the very same day we arrived while Slike was still chained in the brig. All the crew was in town drinking and carousing after weeks at sea. I doubt anyone would return to the ship, and if they did, it is unlikely they would go down to the brig and find him. Also, it takes a while to reload the ship. Slike would never leave without his precious merchandise. No, Turtle, we needn't worry about Mr. Slike too much. All is well now."

Chapter 58

Declaration

Annette and her mother left Chesterfield for Liverpool a week after Annette's return from boarding school, and since then, life had become a whirlwind of social calls, shopping, and fittings. Mrs. Chetwynd had also obtained an invitation from her friend, Hannah Mary, wife of Mr. William Rathbone IV, to their annual Harvest Ball at Greenbank, which was to be held two nights hence, on Annette's birthday.

In addition, maintaining her façade by allowing Mother to control everything was becoming a challenge for Annette. She missed Mary Hope and Mrs. Adsley, and she still had no clue as to why she had been called away from Jane Arden's school. Most importantly, Annette was growing weary of today's last-minute trip to the boutiques.

"Oh, Annette, see that jeweled fan in the window? I must have a closer look." Her mother released her arm. "You go on ahead to Suzette's shop. I shall meet you in a moment."

Annette plodded along the boardwalk as if in a fog. One, two, three steps . . .

All of a sudden, right there in the middle of the walk, she stopped. Her eyes dropped to her feet, and she stared at them. She simply could not take another step without knowing why her mother was doing this.

Suddenly, someone—a gentleman—collided with her and she felt herself falling backward. Her hands flew out, and she grasped his coat lapels, pulling him toward her. His hands wrapped around her waist, and the world stood still.

"Pardon me, Miss. I was not . . . not paying atten—Annette." He whispered her name from his soul, and his face lit up.

"Oh, Peter." Her hands sneaked up around his neck, and his strong arms drew her closer. "Peter, you're home. I can hardly believe it." She melted into his arms.

"Dearest, Annette . . ." He breathed into her curls. "I cannot begin . . ." His words faded, and she could feel his body shuddering.

Suddenly, remembering where they were and that Mother would certainly see them, Annette pushed away from him. "Yes, oh yes, I know. But here, take my handkerchief, quickly." She gazed into his eyes as he quickly wiped his face. He was truly here.

"Annette!" Mother's call echoed across time, and she felt herself sinking back into the world of shopping.

"You, sir, who are you? I'll have you arrested for this."

"Forgive me, Madam, but I . . . we—" Peter shoved the handkerchief, which was actually his already, into his pocket.

"Well, speak up. I am her mother, and I expect an explanation."

"Mother, stop this. I started to fall, and he caught me. He has done nothing wrong. He is a pastor, for Heaven's sake, and very nearly family to us."

"I beg your pardon?"

"This is Mr. Peter Adsley of Caverswall Manor. He is brother to my Cousin Sylvia's late husband. There is no impropriety here. He was helping me."

"Well, 'tis a good thing because I could have him jailed for assault."

"Mrs. Chetwynd, I—"

"Mr. Adsley, my daughter and I have an appointment now. We must be off, but thank you for your assistance. If you wish to call, please save yourself the trouble. We will not be available 'til next week. However, you may find us at the annual Harvest Ball at Greenbank two nights hence, if you care to join us. Now, good day to you."

"Thank you, Mrs. Chetwynd. I will see you then." Peter tipped his tall hat and gazed at Annette a moment longer. "Good day, Miss Chetwynd." Then he stepped around her and continued along the walk.

"Annette, I say. What was going on with that man?"

Annette detached her hungry eyes from Peter's retreating form and found her words. "Nothing, Mother, nothing. When I looked down to check my boot, I lost my balance, and he assisted me. That is all."

"Well, he should have known to release you. A public display such as he made is entirely unacceptable. How obtuse, and him being an Adsley of Caverswall. He should know better. I suppose he is the new heir, and that is why he thinks he owns the place. But what does it matter? We have resources of our own."

"Whatever you say, Mother."

"Excellent spirit, my dear."

⚜

With thoughts adrift, Annette sat in the dressmaker's parlor, staring as her mother poured over fabrics and patterns with Suzette, their dressmaker.

Suddenly, Annette jumped to her feet. "Mother, these fittings, the clothes, all these new things . . . Why are you doing this?"

"Goodness, what do you mean?" Mrs. Chetwynd laid the embroidered piece of muslin on top of the other bolts of fabric. "You have just returned from boarding school. Your birthday is in two days. Expanding your wardrobe is nothing so serious."

"You needn't pretend." Annette eyed her mother. "I know it is more than that, and I want you to tell me now. Or I am leaving."

"Pretend? Leaving? Of what do you speak?"

"You will give me the truth, or I will walk out of this room, and you will never see me again."

Mrs. Chetwynd's face reddened, and she turned to the seamstress. "Suzette, darling, we need some time alone. I will call when we are ready for your assistance."

"Certainly, Mrs. Chetwynd." Suzette bowed out of the room, closing the double doors behind her.

Mrs. Chetwynd walked to the window. "No longer the naïve child, I see. And you want the truth, do you?"

"I do."

"Well, it is about time. The world does not favor the innocent for long."

Annette waited while Mrs. Chetwynd shook her head as if to rid herself of a distant memory before turning to Annette. "To be precise, we have received an offer—quite an exceptional one, actually—and your brother and I have decided to accept it."

"Without asking me?" Her stomach turned, even as her throat tightened.

"Why should we ask you? You would only decline it, and it is the best you are likely to receive."

"Because it is my choice; I have the freedom to choose. Papá said."

"Your choice, freedom? Ha! Have we women ever a choice or freedom of any kind?"

"We do, Mother. Listen to me: we do. When I was away in Beverley, I learned—"

"You have learned nothing." Mrs. Chetwynd's voice grew cold. "You may have read about it and debated the topic with your father, but you haven't the slightest understanding of what a woman's life is."

"But Mother—"

"Silence. You will hear me out, and then you may leave, if you like. We are only as valuable as our dowry is rich and our reputation is pure. Once we have used them to attract the man with the highest position we can hope to obtain—and we have produced his heir, and at least a spare—we may live a fairly comfortable life. It is a gamble, of course, finding a man you can tolerate while bearing the burden of his children. But once you have accomplished that, you will be free."

"That is not freedom."

"You think you know what freedom is? You haven't the slightest idea. But I have, and it was the most unbearable experience of my life. I was once like you, though I know you will not believe me. Like you, I was gregarious, romantic, beautiful, and as accomplished at the piano as you are at your drawing and painting. And my mother allowed me all the freedom I desired."

"What are you saying?"

"You have wondered why I kept you so close since the garden party incident. It is because my mother paid no attention to me. She let me do as I wished, to associate with whomever I chose, hoping I would attract a good match. Well, I did. I fell in love with a devoted man who adored me. But he was not good enough."

"But—"

"Wait. We were children, David and me, thoughtless and carefree children. He had no position, no connections, and no real means of making a way in the world. We planned to run away and give concerts in Vienna. And we would have done so, except my father found us together and put an end to everything. He even ended my music. He chopped my pianoforte to pieces with an ax as I watched. And I never saw my tutor again.

"Perhaps Father paid David to leave—or he had him murdered. I will never know. And when I could no longer hide my condition, Father sent me to the country with my sister, your Aunt Claire, so I could give birth in secret while all of society believed I was in France.

"Do not look so surprised. It happens all the time. A young lady supposedly goes on tour or visits some relatives in a remote part of the country but gives birth to a child. It is quite common, I tell you."

"You had a child?"

"Yes. But I never saw it. They took it as soon as I delivered. Some time later, they told me it died. I do not even know if it was a boy or a girl."

"So you want me to have what you think you missed?"

"Indeed."

"But I have no need of it. I want what you shared with David: love. A Season and the trappings of wealth are meaningless."

"Oh, you say that now, but wait 'til you are older, and you have no means of providing for your children."

"But what of Father? How does he fit in?"

"Your father, God rest his soul, was a good man. He was some years older than I, but we became friends while I was with my sister at Betherton Hall. He was a business partner of Mr. Charles Adsley, who bought Caverswall Manor just a few months before I arrived at your Aunt Claire's manor. When I was well enough, I played at Caverswall and other local assemblies. Mr. Adsley introduced your father and me. I especially remember a masked ball when your father came disguised as King Arthur."

Tears collected in Mother's eyes. She brushed them away and continued.

"He loved listening to my music."

"Did Papá know your story?"

"Yes. That is what I meant when I said he was a good friend. I told him the whole story, and he still accepted me. He told me if the Lord could forgive him of his sins, then he could certainly forgive me mine.

"He believed he had allowed greed and growing his business to overtake him when he should have been supporting his family. He was a widower; his first wife died in childbirth."

"Gerald?"

"Yes. Your father was a romantic old fool. Based on his income, he could have chosen anyone, but he did not want to buy a wife. He said he needed a mother for his heir, and he wanted a friend to share in a platonic relationship. If that suited me, he guaranteed no one would ever discover what I had done.

"So we wed. He loved me in his own way. I loved him for the chance he gave me. Our lives were complete for a long while, especially with his business travels. Then one night, after one of his longest ventures—nearly eight months, I think—I made a mistake and allowed him into my bed. You were the result of that decision, a child of his advanced years. He was overjoyed.

"From the moment he saw you, he loved you the way I love music. When we discovered your condition, he was heartbroken. But you continued to thrive under Miss Haack's care. Apparently, she let you suck on sugar cubes whenever you looked poorly. As you grew, your father denied you nothing, not even the education that could, in due course, devastate your chances. But I stepped in, and now you are an accomplished young lady with an excellent match."

"I do not want your excellent match. I want to marry the man I choose, one who loves me for who I am, not what I can give him."

"So beautiful, yet so blind." Mrs. Chetwynd sighed. "Men only want us for what they can get from us."

"That is not what you said about David."

"Do not speak of him. He never came back for me."

"I am sorry, but I will not accept this match."

"Oh yes, you will. And you will forget this foolishness about women having a choice. Even your beloved Mary Wollstonecraft, who penned those worthless essays about our rights and freedoms, attempted suicide just this past June—or perhaps it was May, I do not recall—because the father of her by-blow would not marry her.

"Obviously, the fact is not widely known. I only happened upon it because of your desire to attend Miss Arden's boarding school. I knew of Jane's association with that woman, and to ensure their connection would not affect your reputation, I had to research further. And that, my dear, is why Gerald and I have made this arrangement, to protect you and your secret."

"Protect me and my secret? What secret?"

"Your health, of course, what else? If anyone discovers it—and I mean anyone—they will gossip. Suitable gentlemen will hear it, and your chances will be more bleak than mine were before your father saved me. One cannot hide a fainting disease as easily as I was able to hide my confinement. We can only hope your blood is not tainted. But even if it is, by then it will not matter. So many infants die, it will not seem unusual. At least one will survive, and hopefully that one will be a son. Then you will have fulfilled your obligation."

Annette could not speak. Rage, grief, shock, and despair battled inside.

"I am leaving, Mother."

"Leaving? Where could you possibly go?"

Annette's heart sank, and suddenly she knew she must never tell Mother about Peter.

"You look pale, my dear. Do you need some refreshment?" Annette saw her mother reaching for her, and jerked away.

"I am fine, but it is time to go."

"There is no reason to rush. Come, let us take our luncheon at the Water Street Inn while we are here. It was always one of your father's favorites."

Did her mother expect a *Yes Mother; do let us take some tea together?* Well, it was not going to happen that way. Annette was uncertain about how to even comprehend the situation, let alone respond to a lunch invitation. So she carefully put her façade in place.

"All right, but after that we are going home to Bold Street. And right now, I am stepping outside to take some fresh air." Annette stood up and headed for the door as her mother called for the dressmaker.

"Suzette?"

"Yes, Mrs. Chetwynd, how may I assist you?"

"We are finished for today. Save that embroidered muslin there, the lavender satin, and the printed cotton. I would also like . . ."

🔺

"Thank you, Suzette. We will be back soon," Mother called as she closed the door to the dress shop and joined Annette.

"That's much better, my dear." Mother attempted to take her arm, but she moved away.

"I will walk on my own, Mother."

"Of course, the inn is only a couple of streets up."

They walked separately along the boardwalk. And then came the question.

"Would you at least like to know the gentleman with whom Gerald and I have been speaking? Certainly, you must be a little curious, even if you intend to decline the offer."

"No, Mother. I do not care to know. I have made a discovery, however, and I would like you to confirm it."

"What is it?"

"I believe I finally understand about the missing portrait."

"Of what portrait are you speaking?"

"When Sir Charles Alexander, your father, died, Aunt Claire brought a portrait of him into her gallery. You recall the painting of my grandfather in hunting dress with his dogs. But we do not have one at Chesterfield, and I always wondered why. I suppose I no longer need to ponder it."

"To be sure. I was glad to be rid of him."

Chapter 59
Providence

"Cap'n, Cap'n!" Turtle darted up the stairs of the Adsley warehouse in Goree Piazza where Peter and his father had spent the night before leaving on the *Terona* back in July. "Mr. Adsley just saw his oranges lady and her mother when he was out walkin'. I went ahead of him ta get a look at some candy in a shop window, but then he came and got me, and showed me the oranges lady and your Lizzie. They were drinkin' tea at the Water Street Inn."

"What's this, you're weavin' yarns again? You little spider. I should box your ears."

"No, please, 'tis true. Tell him, Mr. Adsley. I saw his Lizzie and your oranges lady."

Peter closed the door of the upstairs room. "He did, indeed, Captain, if Lizzie is truly Mrs. Chetwynd."

"That's what Slike called her back in Jamaica just afore we got off the *Terona*. He bragged, sayin' he knew her as that."

"Then I believe she is my lady's mother, and we just saw both of them," Peter said.

"Tell me about her, Turtle. Is she as fine a lady as I recall?"

"She is that, with feathers and lace and lots o' jewels, but she's not as sweet as her girl is."

"So what do we do next, young Adsley? I'd like to see me Lizzie, but can't let her see me, not yet anyway." Peter saw the captain look down at his peg leg.

"In two days, the Rathbones are holding a ball at Greenbank. Mrs. Chetwynd invited me to attend. Perhaps you should come along. You and Turtle can be my coachmen and then have a look around. There is bound to be a way to see Mrs. Chetwynd without her seeing you."

"It's a plan. We will keep an eye out for Slike, too. Just in case. In his other life here in Liverpool, he makes it a point to appear at these high society shindigs."

"I doubt it will be necessary. He could not have beaten us here. I do not expect to hear anything from him for another week, if even then."

"Aye, lad. I'm hopin' on it, but Slike can be a tricky one. And the *Swiftsure* weren't near as fast as the *Terona*. They coulda passed us in the night, and we'd never o' known it."

"So I'm gonna be *your servant*, or *odservan*t. What's that word ya were teachin' me?"

"You mean observant?"

"Aye, that be it, sir. I'll be observant while the Cap'n watches for Slike and his Lizzie. Then you can talk ta your pretty miss. So what do I do if I spy the snake?"

"If you see the beast anywhere's about, Turtle, you let me handle him. Don't be botherin' Mr. Adsley and his lady. They have got some catchin' up to do." Captain Bledsoe winked at Peter.

"Aye, aye, Cap'n."

Peter smiled. What would he do without these two?

Chapter 60

Charade

Greenbank of Toxteth Park
Liverpool, England
27 November 1795

Peter had no interest in the splendor of Greenbank and its prominent guests. He was at the Harvest Ball to see Annette. He moved from room to room, studying the crowd, until he noticed her standing with a small group of ladies. Leaning against a large marble pillar unobserved, Peter drank in every detail of her.

A rose-colored blush whispered across her cheeks. Decked with a string of pearls and with amethyst gems woven into her curls, she was the picture of style in her lavender gown. But where were her passion and that natural charm he so admired? He noted her stiff posture and that beautiful yet reserved smile which seemed to be held in place by the determined force of her will. She appeared to listen with respect and added comments as needed, but her eyes held no luster.

After running into her on Water Street, Peter hoped, indeed prayed, they would be able to reestablish their connection—following his very necessary explanation, of course. It was her birthday tonight; it seemed as though she had been happy to see him just two days ago, and he loved her. But something appeared to have changed.

Suddenly, she glanced in his direction, and their eyes collided. Shock—no panic, or perhaps a look of regret—flashed in her face. As quickly as the dismay appeared, it was replaced by the impervious mask of perfection she maintained with the ladies.

Peter moved out of the shadows when she excused herself from the knot of women and wound her way around the refreshment table to the exit onto the terrace.

God, I know naught what she thinks of me, but it cannot be much. Without doubt, she is hurting. Comfort her, and give me the words she needs to hear.

Peter's heart was pounding as he wove along the outer edge of the crowd to the refreshment table and the French doors. After one hundred thirty-three abysmal days of torture, he would be with his lady again. Yet, how to begin?

He paused to think and noticed the linen-covered table decked with red grapes, cantaloupe, pomegranates, oranges, all variety of cheeses, as well as a large punchbowl and glasses. Yes, of course. He smiled to himself. It was perfect: she might enjoy some punch, and he would have a story just for Turtle.

Peter did a quick survey of people in the vicinity of the table then walked up, pocketed a bunch of the red grapes, and picked up two cups of punch. Then he moved outside.

This time, there was no searching for her. Annette stood with her back to him, leaning on the balustrade overlooking the Green.

"May I interest you in something to drink, Miss Chetwynd?"

"Thank you," she answered with an aloof smile that never reached her eyes. "However careless you are in essentials, you manage the details reasonably well."

Lord, help me with her pain.

"You have returned sooner than I expected, though late enough." Her eyes sparked, and she set her cup down without drinking. "But do let us get to more serious matters, Mr. Adsley."

"As you wish."

"While I am pleased you are yet living, I would like to know if you are still in the habit of making promises you do not intend to keep. Or shall I expect excuses tonight?"

Clearly, she had no desire to receive well-wishes for her birthday, at least not from him. He must try a different approach.

"Provocative questions." Peter set his cup beside hers and offered her his arm. "Would you walk with me, Miss Chetwynd?" She took it, and he guided her away from public view.

"Interesting that you should describe my questions as provocative. They have been my grim companions these last four and a half months since Father died in our carriage on the way home from Woolton Hall, not more than half an hour after you gave me your pledge."

God in Heaven, the agony must have been unspeakable. From but one evening of observing them together, Peter recognized the depth of their bond. Nothing he could say would suffice. Yet he must try.

"I cannot begin to imagine your grief, Miss Chetwynd." He stopped their progress and studied her hostile eyes. "Your father was an exceptional man. You have my deepest condolences, though I earnestly regret having been powerless to offer them sooner."

"Earnestly regret? Powerless to offer condolences?" Her face melted, and the pent up rage she had masked so perfectly burst forth in a flurry of pounding fists and heartrending sobs. "What are you saying? Where were you? Papá is dead, and you were not there." She could hardly get the whisper out. "Why?"

Stunned and sickened at having caused her pain, though indirectly, Peter tried to calm her. But to no avail. Tears streamed down her cheeks, and she beat his chest, pulling at his coat and crying all the while. "Why didn't you come? I waited and waited, but you did not come. Why?"

He glanced over his shoulder. He saw no one at the moment, but guests were everywhere. He must shelter her from them. At his wit's end to contain her despair and to protect her, Peter caught her wrists with one hand, buried her face in the folds of his cravat with the other, and whisked her around behind a hedge to the side of the house. Then, leaning his full weight against her and pressing her back against the wall as much as he dared without hurting her, he took her face in his hands and stopped her mouth with a kiss.

She groaned, and fire shot through his entire being.

"Listen to me," he whispered against her lips and kissed her again. "Please give me a chance to explain." He gently brushed her lips with another kiss and enfolded her deep in his arms, resting his cheek on her head and holding her close, waiting, praying, and working to control his own emotions.

Finally, she began to settle. He took a deep breath and sent up one last prayer. Then he spoke.

"You have suffered so very much, and I was not here to help you. It will haunt me daily." He kissed her forehead and the curls at her temples, then leaned his cheek against her head again. And thus he stood for a bit longer until she relaxed, and he felt her arms slip around his waist.

"But I had no intention of leaving you. Please, Annette, you must believe me. I would never do anything to hurt you." He loosened his hold on her and leaned back just enough to see her face. "Even so, can you ever forgive me?"

"Yes, I can and do," she murmured. "But what happened?"

Still holding her with one arm, he smoothed away her tears with his thumb. "Since even before our last extraordinary night—which I now know to be a very tragic one as well—I have cherished you as I cherish life itself. So I decided to stay with you instead of taking the voyage with my father. Nevertheless, that morning, before I could write my letter and meet your father, I was abducted."

"Oh, Peter." She gently fingered the scar on his upper lip. "I knew it. Something must have happened, or you would have come. I am so sorry. My behavior has been atrocious. I should never have reacted the way I did." Tears glazed her eyes as she touched his wound. "Can you ever forgive me?"

"Yes, always." He gently grasped her fingers and kissed them.

"Thank you," she whispered. Then she cupped his face in her hands, drew him close, and time stood still as their kisses mingled with words of affection and tormented tears.

"Shh. . . please, dearest." He pulled back from her. "No more crying. There must be no more sadness now. I am recovered." He kissed the top of her head. "And I have returned." He kissed her forehead. "And all is well."

She looked up at him and sniffed. "Would you happen to have a handkerchief then?"

"Indeed I do." Though he was loath to break their embrace, Peter released her and pulled one from his pocket. "You may keep it when you have finished."

She smiled and blew her nose. "I usually do."

"Indeed."

"But what of this abduction? Oh, Peter, how did it happen, and why? And what of your father—did you sail with him? My footman told me you were on a slave ship: the *Terona*. I don't understand."

She sniffed and buried her face in his cravat.

"Sh ... dearest, please. You needn't cry. All is well now. But when I first discovered what had happened, I nearly went insane. I thought Father planned it, though he did not. Finally, after committing myself and my abysmal circumstance to God, I studied your sketch so much the paper has fallen apart. I also followed our reading plan for the gospels. Did you?"

"But did you figure out who abducted you, and why? And how did you escape? Are you still in danger?"

"Sh. Annette, please, too many questions. Let us not worry over them now. I am home again, and we are at Greenbank. We should be dancing."

Peter felt a sharp tap on his shoulder.

He stepped back from her but saw her flinch. Whoever was behind him, she recognized. Then she masked her feelings and extended her hands to greet the unwanted guest.

"Good evening, Sir Likebridge. How good of you to join us."

Peter's jaws clamped together. Sir Likebridge? Was it possible? He turned around, and sure enough—

"This is Mr. Adsley, a friend of my late father's." She continued with the introductions as pleasantly as ever. "Mr. Adsley, this is Sir Steven Likebridge, a business associate of Father's."

"And her betrothed husband," Mr. Slike added with a knowing smile.

Annette and Slike! Despicable slaver and conniving rake! Fire shot through Peter as his torso tightened with rage.

"Hold there, Mr. Adsley." Slike locked his fingers around Peter's bicep. "Wouldn't want you cracking your head again," he whispered.

Peter yanked his arm away from Mr. Slike, who was now donning his black wig and the ever-stylish garb of Sir Steven Likebridge.

"What have you done?"

"Me? I have done nothing, nothing that was not already arranged by this young lady's mother."

Peter followed Slike's gaze to Annette.

"Ah, Miss Chetwynd, you needn't look so surprised. It has been planned for nearly two years, since that little affair at your aunt's garden party. Surely you remember? The rain, the chapel . . ."

"But Mother said—"

"You?" Peter's brows knitted even as his fingers curled into fists. "You are the scoundrel who assaulted her?"

Annette stared at Peter. "How do you know about . . ?" She covered her mouth.

"What a delicious surprise, is it not, brother?" He turned to Annette. "It is a shame your mother meddles so. If she had left well enough alone, you would be free of me and could have him. He's quite the catch too, now that his father is dead. Being the new owner of a sugar plantation with some fifty or sixty slaves, he must bring in over thirty-thousand a year."

Peter felt sick as he watched Annette's eyes widen.

"If you will pardon me, gentlemen. I find I am rather exhausted." She started to leave.

"I will do no such thing. You are not excused. Mr. Adsley and I are taking a walk, and I require your presence, my dear."

"I am overly tired for a walk just now. I will have a bit to eat and retire for the evening."

Slike grabbed her arm, and Peter lunged. But the distinctive *whish* of a knife being pulled from its sheath stopped him instantly.

"You may dine with me on the wharf if you like, Miss Chetwynd. But for now, I would advise you to do exactly as I say."

Moonlight flashed across the blade of a dagger Mr. Slike held pointed upward under Annette's chin. "Mr. Adsley, you will control yourself, or this luscious little tart will be of no use to either of us. Understand?"

"Yes."

"Come along then, my dear. We have a little trip to take."

He moved forward, and she followed as best she could with her head held high to avoid the point of Mr. Slike's knife.

Chapter 61
Revelation

Peter's emotions constricted his soul. *God, here he is again. What am I to do? I love her, but she is his,* he shouted inside as he strode down the hill. *Of all people, HIS! Why? Finding her; losing her over and over; being abducted only to return and find her then lose her again, WHY? Why this constant struggle? I only wanted a wife. Is that so complicated?*

"Being found in fashion as a man, my Son humbled Himself and became obedient unto death--even the death of a cross!"

At that precise moment, Peter stepped on the uneven grass, and his ankle gave out. He quickly recovered his balance, but a large part of him shuddered at that response.

"Mind your step, Adsley," Slike smirked. "You're no longer an invalid."

Peter refused to acknowledge him, but glanced at Annette and stepped ahead. She did not look at him.

Indeed, Lord. I am nothing without your beloved Son and his sacrifice. I have no right to even speak. Yet, forgive me once again. And . . . He gulped begging that his circumstances would never come to this, and then proceeded. *And please give me but an ounce of Job's strength when he said, "Though he slay me . . . (and even her), yet will I trust in you."*

🔺

Stars twinkled in the haze that was closing in on Annette. The pace was too fast. Her head had begun to float. But the relentless jabbing knife under her chin forced her to move along.

She had passed right beside a fine refreshments table minutes ago. Peter had even given her a cup of punch. But she was too angry to eat. Why had she refused to yield? She was truly ill, though it pained her to admit it. And now she would have to . . . Oh, why was she so stubborn? She had had so many opportunities in so many different realms of life, but now—

The ground bounced as she lurched along. Now, it was almost too late.

God, I am truly sorry.

Even if He chose not to help her now, Annette believed He was there and that He cared for her. And if it were the last thing she did, Annette would tell Him. She could do that much, at least.

I was wrong . . . so stubborn . . . so full of pride. I cannot begin to understand . . . Mother. . . this horrible man . . . even my health. And Peter has slaves? God, everything changes, everything except You. You love me. You gave Your Son for me. Peter said He loves me too, and I deserve none of it. Thank You for everything You have done for me, and forgive me. I yield myself to You, for what little I am worth. And I trust You.

Annette felt her shoe catch in her hem. Then she was stumbling forward. Pain like fire screamed under her chin and she—

"Steady, Miss Chetwynd." Sir Likebridge yanked her arm upward and stopped. "Let me have a look at that."

Whimpering, she attempted to tilt her head. He grabbed her chin and forced it further back. Now the stars swirled above her, and she felt her knees weakening.

"Straighten up, Miss Chetwynd. It's just a scratch, not so bad. Here, my handkerchief, press it against the wound. The bleeding will stop soon enough."

"For God's sake, man. Why not carry her?"

"Get ahold of yourself, Adsley. It's not much farther. See down there?"

Annette took the handkerchief and urging herself to look, she turned in the direction Sir Likebridge indicated. Moonlight revealed a coach some yards down the slope.

"Then let me help her."

"No, I can manage." As much as Annette hated saying the words, she pushed them out. "If you will but give me your arm, Sir Likebridge."

"There you have it. The lady will walk with me, Adsley."

If she fainted inside the coach, so be it. But if the Lord would grant her strength, Annette would take his hand before allowing this beastly man to discover her condition by fainting at his feet.

Lord, please help me.

With the last bit of her strength, she held the cloth to her chin, took his arm, and pushed ahead to the coach. And soon enough, they were at the door.

"Here we are then. Open her up, Adsley. Have a look inside."

Annette felt her knees melting and rested against the coach.

"Isn't that charming, though, riding accommodations for two, complete with shackles for wrists and ankles? A friend of mine had her outfitted for his own diabolical purposes, but never mind that. Climb in, Adsley. Miss Chetwynd will follow."

Annette watched Peter duck his head into the coach.

"Fine. Now fasten the irons into place."

Annette listened to the clanking chains as her vision blurred. They sounded so far away, almost in another world.

"Say there, Adsley, you did so well with that. After our venture on the *Terona*, I can't say I'm surprised, though I was astonished to discover you knew nothing of them beforehand."

"Miss Chetwynd—?" She felt his hand cupping her cheeks and tried to focus on his eyes. "I did not mean to offend your abolitionist's sensibilities, but it is only right that you should know of Mr. Adsley's status as a new slave owner before entering the coach. Is that not so?"

She could not speak.

"Is there a problem, Miss Chetwynd?"

She shook her head. He must not see her faint.

"You look rather ill-at-ease, my dear. You needn't let the slave master bother you. He's still our same old Pastor Adsley. Our father, Mr. Charles Adsley, God rest his soul, just recently introduced the good pastor to the family business as we were loading the slaves onto the *Terona*."

Annette heard Peter groan.

"Yes, Adsley, I said *our* father. You needn't be so disturbed. We will speak of that later." Slike took out his knife again. "Oh, and another thing, I stabbed him with this very knife, if I am not mistaken. So, Miss Chetwynd, if Peter mentions it, you can trust him."

Nausea assaulted Annette, and the moon began swimming while little yellow and red stars danced across her vision.

"But let's get you in the coach so you can take that little rest you wanted." Slike's fingers snaked around her ribs. "Up you go. That's right. Get yourself situated opposite Mr. Adsley. You needn't be so close to him. Would you like me to clap on the handcuffs for you?" He ran his fingers along her arm. "No, I think not, wouldn't want to bruise those delicate wrists. Only the ankles, for tonight."

He lifted her gown and grabbed first one and then the other of her ankles, locking the cold iron cuffs into place. Then his hands roamed up her legs, and her stomach turned.

"Please, sir. Stop."

"Ah yes, your precious reputation; I had to pay a pretty penny for that. Very well then, I will spare you for now."

Slike dropped her gown back in place and turned to Peter. "We have a bit of a drive ahead, so perhaps a sermon on a wife's duty to submit to her husband would do."

With that, Slike snapped the door shut, and the world went dark.

↟

"Cap'n, Cap'n, come quick. Ya gotta see this. Are me eyes failin' me, or be that Mr. Slike down there by that coach?"

"Don't know, Turtle, but tell me what you saw."

"Well, I were watchin' Mr. Adsley and his lady talkin'. It looked like she were kinda mad at him." Turtle looked down at his boots.

"Go on. If that be him—"

"Well, for a second I looked away at those . . . It was fine though. I saw Mr. Adsley and his lady walkin' down that hill toward that coach at the bottom—"

"You sure it was Mr. Adsley and his lady?"

"Yes. And then they were gone, and now I saw a lady gettin' in that coach and a gent lookin' all fine and dandy climbin' up ta drive it. See there? Could it be Slike?"

And you're sure they were walkin' to that coach?

"I am, and no mistakin' it with this big moon glarin' down. I can see everything."

"Let's go, Turtle. I'll not be takin' chances. We will follow them in Mr. Adsley's coach."

Chapter 62

Freedom

"Annette, can you sit up?" He attempted to lean toward her, but the shackles around his wrists were not long enough. "Annette, please. Can you hear me?"

The coach lurched forward, and he was thrust back against the seat. His fear was confirmed. She had fainted, just like the time when he had rescued her from Slike.

Lord, how can You possibly listen to me again? Ashamed and broken, he closed his eyes. *I am as inconstant as the sea; a wave tossed in the ocean. I am praying for Job's faith one minute and begging Your help the next. Forgive me. Strengthen me with Your spirit, despite my weakness.* He could hardly bring himself to say the next words. *But must You take her for lack of a little bit of food? That's all she needs. God, I beg—*

His eyes flew open. "Grapes! Lord, I pinched them to show Turtle . . . Oh, praise You!"

The coach went over a bump, and his teeth slammed together. *But curse this wretched road!* With chains binding his wrists, Peter maneuvered enough to reach the grapes in his pocket.

"Annette! Sit up!"

When she did not answer, he nudged her leg with his knee. Still no response.

"God, this is my nightmare all over again. She is slipping away, and I cannot reach her."

If he could get her to lean forward, he might tip her onto the seat beside him. Then he could move her onto his lap and feed her the grapes. But he had to get her to move first.

"Annette, lean forward! I have grapes," he shouted over the road noise.

Nothing.

"We have not come thus far to lose her, Lord. Please move her."

The coach's momentum increased, as did the noise of jangling harnesses. "Come now, you must sit up, Annette!"

Suddenly, the coach jolted over what felt as if it was a trench in the road. Peter's teeth chomped down on his tongue, but Annette launched forward, bumped against the cushion beside him, and rolled across his knees.

Peter closed his eyes for a second. "All right, I praise you for the road as well."

Then, with the iron cuffs cutting into his wrists, he went to work lifting her across his lap and leaning her against the wall of the coach so she could swallow without choking.

"Here, dearest, have some juice." He parted her lips and squeezed a grape so the juice would trickle into her mouth. It dribbled from her lips.

"Annette, you must swallow the juice. Come now, we must try it again."

He popped the smashed grape in his mouth and squeezed a second one for her, but the juice spilled again.

"No! I refuse to let you go." He re-situated her and adjusted his own seat, even as the chains tore at his arms. Then he slapped her cheeks. "Forgive me that, my lady, but you must swallow this juice now." He squeezed the third grape.

The coach creaked and swayed, making it nearly impossible to see if she was swallowing.

"Swallow it up." He patted her face again. "I said swallow, now stop this teasing and do it. I am giving you some more now." *God make her swallow.*

He ate the third smashed grape, and when she sputtered, he laughed in relief.

"I told you. Now, look what you've done, drooling all over your gown. What will Miss Haack say?" He wiped off her mouth. "Let us try this again, dearest."

He squeezed a fourth grape into her mouth, and she swallowed.

"Very good. Keep going." He repeated the process over and over. "I'm giving you a whole grape next. You will need to chew it."

Her jaw was moving.

"Splendid. I'll have another right away."

As she continued to chew, tears streaked his face. "Thank you, Father. Whoever she belongs to, Lord, I am ever grateful for her life."

He continued feeding her grapes, praying, and encouraging her to eat as the coach sped along. Some time later, Annette spoke.

"Slaves. You own slaves."

Peter's heart sank, and he leaned back into the corner of the coach. "To my utter disgrace."

"And you just learned of it?"

"I knew nothing of it until we reached Ouidah. It is not my doing, though. You must know that, Annette, I had no idea."

In the darkness, he tried to contain his emotions, but to no avail. "It was a ghastly scene, atrocious, actually. I saw a Negro man and his wife . . ." His voice cracked. "They were literally torn from each other's arms. And a youth . . . no, no, a child less than twelve years of age perhaps . . . A slave judged guilty of mutiny was ordered to beat the boy . . . He died. Back shredded with a cat-o-nine-tails. Then, during a hurricane they attached stones to . . . Oh, Annette." He could no longer speak.

Annette cupped his face in her hand and smoothed away his tears. "But you are not to blame."

"It was unspeakable. And I own them. Human beings uniquely created by God Himself, for His pleasure and in His image, and I . . . I have lived my entire life in luxury while they . . . they—"

"Shh. Oh, Peter, you mustn't do this to yourself." She took him in her arms as best she could and held him. "I know, Peter, I know. It is appalling how the world works, but things will change. They will. The change has already begun."

She held him and waited.

"How?"

She loosened her hold to look into his face. "You care so deeply for your people. Perhaps you are meant to liberate them in both the spiritual and physical realms. You are a pastor, after all."

He gazed into her eyes but could not speak.

"I never knew before this night, Peter, but you saved me from dire consequences in both areas."

"That is quite another matter. Slike was attacking you."

"Nevertheless, if you had not been there or heard him, or whatever it was that caused you to be there at that time, all aspects of my life would be different."

"I had not thought of that."

"I have not stopped thinking of it."

"I am no longer a pastor."

"Have we not spoken of that before? Your influence now reaches halfway around the world, Pastor Adsley, and I expect you to use it."

He laughed. "As you wish, Miss Chetwynd."

"Much better. Now, I have been meaning to ask, why do you call that beastly man Slike?"

"Sir Likebridge, as you know him to be called, used that name for himself when he sailed on the *Terona* with Father and me."

"The *Terona* with you? How?"

"He is not the man you know him to be." Peter stopped. Something in that idea did not sit well, but nothing in the entirety of their circumstances suited him. So he filed it away with the rest of the disturbing muddle. "*Ah,* Annette, how can you abide this . . . this whole shameful situation? You are his; and he is a slave trader. I love you, but now I am a slave owner."

"Because I know you will do the right thing."

"What do you mean?"

"You own slaves and have the right to do with them as you please. So free them. It has been done. France abolished slavery last year—the fourth of February, I believe. And the revolt on Saint Dominique led to freedom."

"After a terrible massacre. The struggle continues to this day."

"But many are free. Some own and run their own plantations. If it can be accomplished in such turmoil, certainly we can deed your slaves the plantation without violence."

"You speak as though you are at liberty to help me."

"I . . ."

Peter knew he must tread lightly, but he had to broach the topic. "You were so different on Wednesday when we first met. And then tonight, you were so cold. When did you hear of the arrangement?"

She groaned. "Just now, as far as to whom I have been sold. But Mother announced that an arrangement had been reached minutes after we collided on Water Street. I was so angry, I refused to even hear his name. Seeing you gave me the courage to tell her I would leave if she forced me."

"What of the agreements? Are they signed?"

"I know naught. Is he really your brother, well half-brother that is?"

"I suppose it is possible. Father might have . . . But it is of no consequence."

"If he is trying to steal your inheritance, it is." Annette grew more serious. "Think of it, Peter. First Richard died; then your father. Do you not see? Might Mr. Slike, or whoever he is, be planning to kill you too? Then he could take everything."

"Yes. But if there is one thing I have learned over the last few months, minutes even, God will direct His own plan. Tell me, you seem so much better now. How long will the effects of these grapes keep you in health?"

"If God directs his own plans, does it matter?" She turned away from him.

"Annette, what's wrong? Look at me; tell me."

"You know so little of me."

"Then I desire to know every detail."

"You worry about your slaves, my arranged marriage, my health, and you pray all the time. I am certain of it. But I have so little faith."

"A lack of faith, after what you just said about my ministry reaching around the world?"

"It is true."

"With your knowledge of the Scriptures and our study of the Gospel? You even challenged me to reconsider my reaction to losing Sylvia with a powerful argument from Isaiah. Was it all a sham or a device to ensnare me?"

"No. I was afraid."

"Afraid?"

"You were a pastor and I . . . Well, frankly, I doubted God's very existence, and if you knew it, you would never have wanted me."

"I see. Yet, you speak of it as if it is in the past."

"Father taught me the Gospel. I questioned how it could be possible: God sacrificing his Son to pay for our sin? Whoever thought of such a thing? Sin is not mentioned in church, and I did my Christian duty. I was not even sure if I was sinful. So I turned to philosophy, the classics, science, and whatever else I came across."

"Plenty of Rousseau, no doubt."

"And Mr. Hume, as you know. But after I met you, I began a new acquaintance with God by praying—for selfish reasons, I admit, but it was an attempt. You listened to me and conversed with me like Father did. And, I wanted to see you again, more than that, actually.

"When we met the second time at Buxton, my faith grew. By the time we met at Woolton Hall, I wanted to study the Bible as a means of repaying His kindness while preventing you from discovering my deficiency. So I devised the study. But that night—though I begged Him not to—God took Papá. I was furious and closed my heart again. When you did not come, I locked it."

"From what little I do know of you, Miss Chetwynd, you tend towards impulsiveness."

"So you have noticed." He heard the smile in her voice.

"But spontaneity has its benefits. And your heart seems to be open again."

"Mary Hope helped me."

"My sister?"

"We met when I was in Beverley. I will tell you more when this is over."

"I anticipate hearing it."

"My ankles are hurting. I must move back now." With chains clanking, she settled on her side of the coach and bent down to rub her ankles. "So there is the story of my faith, which is nothing compared to yours."

"You know naught of what you speak." Moonlight sneaked in to reveal her glistening eyes. "I am a weak and imperfect man by far. I cannot even tell you my shortcomings, let alone confess them with such honest humility as you just displayed."

"I have not asked."

"Still, I can tell you this. When we were caught in that hurricane, I begged God—nay, even commanded Him—to sink us so I would die rather than face another day of suffering."

"You did?"

"I am ashamed to admit it. Wallowing in fear and self-pity, I allowed my pride to prevail over my position and betrayed my Creator. At one time or another, we are all a Judas of sorts."

"I know. I always felt like a traitor, but still I chose to go my own way."

"Much to our shame though He is the Sovereign Creator and we but mere creations, we all run astray and judge God's plan—despite the fact that He loves us and gave us His Son."

"Peter, you are so— I cannot even explain it. But I love you for it."

"And I cherish you as I cherish life itself."

"I cannot respond to that now, but the coach is slowing. We must be nearing Slike's . . .?"

"Challenge?"

"Yes, and it frightens me," she whispered. The tremble in her voice did not escape him.

"Here, give me your hands, and I will pray. Lord of Heaven: protect us, guide us, and give us wisdom so we may prevail against this evil and continue to serve you in faith."

"Do you have something else? Anything? A verse, perhaps? Reciting it will help me."

"Two things: One—" He held up his finger. "He knows the plans He has for us both, plans to give us hope and a future. That's from Jeremiah. And two: in the midst of his trials, Job said of God, 'Though He slay me, yet will I trust in Him . . .' With His help, I have committed myself to trusting Him thus. Will you trust Him?"

She squeezed his hand and prayed. "Lord, thank You for Peter, and for saving him for me just as I asked before I even cared to know You. The least I can do, as I said before, is offer my life back to You. So like Job I confirm: Though You slay me, Lord, yet will I trust in You. Amen."

Chapter 63

Coercion

Dock near Wapping Basin
Liverpool, England
23 November 1795

When Mr. Slike opened the coach door, boisterous noise and the muggy stench of brine engulfed them. Peter's heart sickened—the docks. Nothing good could come of this.

Yet, I trust you.

"My lady, if you please." He raised her gown. "Off with the shackles, and out you go." Annette did not answer but took his hand to exit.

"Splendid. The rest has done you well, I see. But stand there beside Cousin Ives while I see to Mr. Adsley."

In a second, Slike was back in the coach at Peter's throat with a knife he produced from who knew where. "Remember Adsley, no heroics or she will suffer." Then he bent to release the shackles from Peter's ankles. "We're keeping the wrist bracelets on, in case you forget." Slike backed out of the coach, pulling Peter by the chains binding his wrists. "Ives, step ahead, man. We have business in the tavern."

"Come Miss Chetwynd, move along."

Peter ground his teeth as Slike placed his hand in the small of her back and propelled her to the door.

"You needn't be afraid. They are a friendly lot."

Peter leaned close to Slike. "If anything happens to her, I will exact payment from you."

"As inviting as your threat sounds, I can scarcely comprehend why you would address it to me. Her fate depends entirely upon you."

Vigorous laughter, the tinkling noise of a harpsichord so far out of tune it rivaled Bledsoe's poor instrument, and the oppressive reek of sweat and spirits spilled from the tavern when Cousin Ives opened the door.

Instantly, the crowd inside silenced themselves. With mouths agape, they stared as Annette lifted her lavender gown and stepped over the threshold. She took two more steps, and it parted like the Red Sea. Then a provocative whistle split the air.

"Say there, Mr. Slike, sure got a pretty one for tonight. Do we get the privilege of knowin' 'er better too?"

Rage boiled in Peter's chest, but he held his peace.

"It's not for me to say."

Peter heard the smile in Slike's comment, and his fists tightened.

"But when I'm finished, I'll let you know."

A lusty roar broke loose, and the entire company returned to its vulgar pursuits.

"Why 'ello there, Mr. Slike." A painted female latched onto his arm and whispered in his ear loud enough for Peter to hear. "I wouldn't mind a round with this fine-lookin' gen'leman 'ere. 'E's up for a bit o' fun too, isn't 'e?"

"Could be. I'll see what I can do, Bessy." Slike squeezed her cheek. "Now, leave us. If I need you, I will call."

"If you say so." She pouted as she wedged herself back into the motley group.

"Up the stairs and turn right, Miss Chetwynd. Then down the hall, the first door on the left."

Proceeding through the crowd, Annette lifted her gown, mounted the rickety steps, and made her way to the door of which Mr. Slike had spoken.

"Here we are." Slike swung open the door, pushed her into the sparsely finished room, and followed. Peter was at his heels. "Welcome to my humble abode!"

"Good evening, Mr. Tarlton." Slike greeted a man who sat at the table beside the fireplace. A single candle illuminated his small round glasses and the gag tied in his mouth. "Thank you for joining us."

"Miss Chetwynd, do be seated here, at the foot of the bed." He glanced back at his man. "Ives, wait outside. But stay close." Then he closed the door and turned his attention to Peter. "Sit there, beside Mr. Tarlton, and put out your hands." Slike attached Peter's shackles to an iron ring on the floor.

"Mr. Tarlton is an associate of yours, is he not, Mr. Adsley?"

"He is one of my father's . . . my solicitors. Why is he here? You have no business—"

"If I were you, Mr. Adsley ..."

Slike nudged a chain and iron cuffs under the foot of the bed on which Annette was seated. Then he glanced to the wall behind the bed. Peter's eyes bounced from the floor to the wall where he saw two additional shackles hanging, one on each side of the bed.

"Need we complicate matters with impoliteness, Mr. Adsley?"

Peter glared at Slike.

"I thought not. Now then, to the business at hand. This lowly chamber, with its peeling paint and cracked walls . . ." He stretched his arm out as if to display the room. ". . . is not much, I agree. But it has been mine these many years since our father, Mr. Charles Adsley, put Mother out. I regret that she is not here to welcome you herself, but—"

At that moment, an odd sort of howling wind echoed through the room, and Slike ceased his introduction with a shiver. He bowed his head and closed his eyes. Peter watched his jaw muscles working and noted his hands curling into fists. He glanced at Mr. Tarlton, who drew his brows together as he shook his head.

Peter looked back at Slike, whose forehead wrinkled in such a way as to suggest he was suffering some tremendous pain. Then, quite abruptly, Mr. Slike jerked his head up, and with glistening eyes, which seemed to look right through Peter, spoke.

"I am to inform you that Mother is dead." Great sorrow compounded by something Peter could only describe as a gaping hole of emptiness seeped from Slike's eyes. "She and Charlie are both dead." He sighed heavily. "Some thirteen years ago, she died of consumption six months after being beaten and left for dead right there." Slike motioned with his foot to the floor under Annette's feet. She jerked her feet up. "My six-year-old brother, Charlie, followed her in the same hour."

The dark emptiness in Slike's eyes melted into smoldering rage. "They will never know I was finally able to save them. Nor will they see me gain what is rightfully mine, Mr. Adsley. But you may take comfort in knowing tonight you will, once and for all, correct the grievous injustice brought upon my family and me by your father."

"Sir Likebridge—"

"Ah, the lady speaks? Shall we hear her?" Slike's demeanor changed as he sauntered over and stood beside Annette. He traced his finger along her jaw and over her lips. "I think not. I haven't the time now. You shall have to wait, Miss Chetwynd."

"Well, let's get on with it then." Peter ground out his comment. "What do you want? How shall I resolve this problem?"

"We are going to make a trade."

"What kind of trade?" Annette asked, and Mr. Slike seated himself beside her. Peter clamped his jaws shut and watched her shudder as Slike ran his fingers down her neck and across her bodice. When he bent his head, Peter started up from the chair, scraping it against the floor and sending his chains into frenzied clanking.

Slike stood up. "Mind what I said, Adsley. Below stairs, a shipload of hearty sailors awaits the pleasure of her acquaintance."

"To the point then; what kind of trade?" Peter ordered.

Slike moved to the table. "A triangular trade, of course. What better type than one that reflects our business route?"

Fire burned in his chest, but Peter did not answer.

Slike unrolled a large parchment and spread it across the table in front of Peter and Mr. Tarlton. "This is a transfer of title deeding your entire estate to me. Mr. Tarlton was kind enough to write it up for me."

Peter looked at Mr. Tarlton, who nodded.

"Your signature on this document will spare Miss Chetwynd the unpleasantness of the *intrusions* I have just mentioned. It will set to right everything regarding my inheritance. Mr. Tarlton will witness the signing to make it official. In short, Miss Chetwynd leaves here as pure and fresh as the driven snow, just as she came in. I take my rightful position as heir of the Adsley estate, and you—having been relieved of your estate—property for which you have no taste anyway—return to your quiet life of ministry in the Church. As I said, a triangular trade, a rather comfortable arrangement for everyone involved if you think about it."

"No, Peter. You mustn't sign," Annette implored.

Peter's heart sank. Had she any clue what Slike was insinuating with those sinister intrusions and introductions to the sailors below? How could she? She was thinking of the slaves and their plan to free them. Yet Slike had made his plan for Miss Chetwynd abundantly clear. Peter must sign the document to free her. His heart twisted inside, but he reached for the quill and ink.

"Please, Peter. You cannot sign it."

Peter's jaw and neck muscles hurt as he looked at her. Tears glistened on her ghostly pale cheeks, and she shook her head, repeating her plea. "Please, Peter. You mustn't. They need you. Please."

Peter ground his teeth together. He knew what Slike would do with the plantation, the entire estate and shipping company: more slaves, more and more sugar. Profit. Blood money. And all of this would be Peter's fault if he signed away his inheritance. Oh, why had he let this happen? He should have been careful. He should have paid attention to what his father was trying to say. He should have fought for his slaves and his property even though the idea was repulsive. Now, they would be condemned to live under the heavy hand of a greedy master.

Peter could never permit Annette to undergo such treatment, though. He loved her. She must not suffer anymore, not this way, not anyway. Even if he could never have her, if she were destined to be Slike's wife, Peter could at least save her from the unspeakable evil Slike had prepared for her downstairs.

He looked into her eyes, even as tears gathered in his own. "Dearest Annette, I love you. Therefore, I cannot permit you to undergo this torture, not for all the slaves in the world."

With that, he dipped the quill in the ink and signed his name with a flourish. The estate was Slike's, and she was safe.

Annette bowed her head and wept.

"Thank you, Brother. Now, Tarlton, you may take your turn. Sign as witness."

Mr. Tarlton signed his name. Slike picked up the page and blew on the ink.

"Splendid. Mother and I have waited so long for this." He carried it across the room and smoothed it out on top of the dresser, resting two books on each side. "We shall have to celebrate."

In the two seconds it took to walk from the dresser to the table, Slike whisked out two separate knives. Stepping up behind both Mr. Tarlton and Peter, he placed each of his blades sideways against the gentlemen's throats and addressed Annette.

"Now, it is time for your part of the trade, my dear."

"What could you possibly want now?"

"How kind of you to ask. I want that we should wed in the same church in Caverswall—the family parish, St. Peter's Church, I believe it's called—where your cousin Sylvia married my brother Richard, God rest his soul. The ceremony will be held on Thursday, the tenth of December. You will also conduct yourself as a willing and happy bride from this point onward, carrying on your usual life as if this meeting never happened. If you do not agree to this, I will kill Mr. Adsley here and now and have his body tossed out to sea with Mr. Tarlton's."

"What assurance have I that you will not kill him after I have made the agreement?"

"Clever little chit, isn't she?" He looked at Peter. "No wonder she interests you, Brother." Slike returned his attention to Annette. "As a wedding gift to you, Miss Chetwynd, I guarantee Mr. Adsley and Mr. Tarlton shall live aboard the *Terona* until such time as it reaches Good Hope. That's the name of the family's plantation, by the way. I cannot very well have them walking the streets of Liverpool, can I? Upon arrival at Good Hope, they will be in God's hands and will reside on our family's property. And if Mr. Adsley succumbs to disease or death by any means over the next twenty years, let's say, I will see that you are informed."

"But you said he would have his ministry back."

"I did. I made no mention of its location, however. To God, one soul is in as much need as the next. So it makes no difference where a pastor serves. Is that not so, Pastor Adsley?" The blade at Peter's throat made it challenging to respond, but he murmured assent.

"How dare you speak of God?" Annette's brows knitted as she spoke. "You know nothing of Him or his work."

"On the contrary, I know far more than even our pastor would expect. Many a caring soul ministered to both me and Mother while we struggled to survive in this squalor."

Annette turned to Peter. "What am I to do? I would not have you dead."

"Trust Him. Though he slay me, yet . . . Trust Him." Both times Peter emphasized the *Him*, praying she would remain strong.

"But the *Terona* again, and Jamaica? You might—"

"I will manage."

"May he not stay and earn a living somewhere in the South Country or on the Continent? Surely, that is far enough away."

"No negotiations. Now make your decision or they both die this instant." Slike pressed the blade into Peter's throat. Surely he was drawing blood. Mr. Tarlton groaned, and Annette's eyes widened.

"I would that they should live," she whispered.

"What is that, my dear? I could not quite hear you."

"Let them live."

"Then you agree to my terms?"

"Yes!"

Slike removed the knives.

"I'm sorry, Peter." She fell to her knees at his feet. "I could not lose you again."

He cupped her face and whispered. "Trust Him. God works when we are weakest."

Mr. Slike bent down and took her arm. "None of that, Miss Chetwynd. We have an agreement. And if there's one thing I am, it is a man of my word. Now get up." He pulled Annette to her feet and guided her toward the dresser.

"Where are we going?" she asked.

"Back to the Greenbank, of course. We've an announcement to make, and what better place than a ball?"

"But what of Mr. Tarlton and Mr.—?"

"Mr. Tarlton is none of your business. As for your precious pastor, he will stay here until I install him on the *Terona* tomorrow."

"But—"

Slike took out his knife, strode to Peter, and grabbing a handful of hair, yanked Peter's head back. "You agreed to my terms. If you care to change your mind, I will adjust my plan accordingly."

"No. There is no change."

"Very good then." He put the knife away. "Let's be off."

"You will not get away with this, Slike." Peter ground out the words as he pulled against the chains.

"I already have," Slike responded as he looked at the deed to his new estate. Then he folded it and placed it in his inside coat pocket. "For over half my life, I have been planning it, and finally Mother is avenged, and I have what is mine. It is finished."

He proceeded to the door, opened it, and spoke to Ives, who stood outside.

"Hold these keys, Ives. No one goes in until I return. In the meantime, get Bessy up here. She will keep our friends company while I'm gone."

⚔

Captain Bledsoe knew the shady wharf tavern Slike called home. So there was no difficulty in following Slike's coach to the establishment.

"Look, Cap'n, they're comin' out." Turtle pointed and whispered from their hiding spot on the deck of a docked ship across from the tavern. "Wonder what he's gonna do with her."

"Not a blasted thing, Turtle. He's got to get her back to her Mamma, safe and sound, or there'll be trouble."

"What kinda trouble?"

"Never mind. But it's the kind our cagey viper doesn't welcome. Now, let's get back to the plan. I'm goin' 'round back. Slike's most likely got our Mr. Adsley cooped up in his room. You get down to the end of the wharf where Mr. Adsley's coach is and have our new friend, Martin, drive it up."

"Will you be long, Cap'n?"

"Nah, they all know me here. I'll just tell 'em Slike asked me to transport the baggage he left. That should get 'em a good laugh. You goin' to be all right here?"

"Aye, sir."

⚜

Smiling to himself, Captain Bledsoe hobbled up the rickety stairs to Slike's room. The bawdy crowd could not care less about his presence in the tavern. He turned right at the top of the stairs and ran into Cousin Ives, who appeared to be guarding the door.

"Well, Ives, me man, how you be? You're lookin' a mite thirsty to me."

"Could always use a drink, Captain, but I got to guard me some prisoners."

"Prisoners? You mean the miserable baggage Slike told me to pick up?"

"It weren't no baggage, least not to Bessy Blue. She's lookin' after two blokes in there."

"I know, me man. Slike just told me to come and get 'em cause they're takin' a ride on the *Terona* with me. Now, give me them keys so I can haul 'em out."

"Well, Captain, I'm real sorry, but Slike told me to keep 'em 'til he's back."

"Blasted, Ives, I'm the captain, as you just said. Stop with your foolishness, and hand 'em over while I'm still happy to see you or soon enough I'll be takin' my whip to your stinkin' hide." Captain Bledsoe fingered the leather coils he kept ready at his waist, and Cousin Ives's eyes widened as he gave up the keys. Then Captain Bledsoe flipped a gold coin in the air. "Now, get on down there and get yourself a drink."

"Thank you, Captain." Ives' eyes brightened as he caught the coin.

"Keep the change too. Might as well get a little extra out o' this while you can."

"Yes, sir, Captain, sir." Ives saluted and headed downstairs.

Bledsoe opened the door to Slike's room and surveyed the situation. "Now Bessy Blue, me Lass, I wouldn't be doin' that if I were you." He chuckled as she looked up. "The man whose lap you are perched upon is a pastor, you know."

"What?" She bolted to her feet.

"That's right. You've been ministerin' to a pastor, and a noble one at that—a true believer, not a greedy bird in a robe."

"No I wasn't, really. I was just getting ready to. I didn't do anything wrong."

She skidded to her knees at Peter's feet. "I'm so sorry, Pastor," she cried. "My mother taught me better than that. But I didn't know who you were. Can you forgive me?"

"I forgive you, but that won't keep you safe forever. You need God's forgiveness."

"Ah now, Bessy, see what you done. He's gonna start preachin'. Quick, get up girl and get on your way. Take this for your trouble." Bledsoe handed her a gold coin. "And don't you be tellin' Slike a thing, except he didn't want you. Understand me?"

"All right then, Captain," she said as she bit the coin and checked for a teeth mark. Then she turned to Peter. "I'm real sorry, Pastor. Can you ever forgive me?"

"I already have," Peter responded. "I am not the One you have offended, however. See if you can attend services Sunday next, and talk to God about it."

"Yes, sir." She curtsied.

"That's right, Bessy, clean yourself up and get to church like the pastor says," Bledsoe added.

Bessy groaned and ran out of the room, slamming the door behind her.

"Thank you, Captain. And thank God you came when you did."

"Adsley, you are the strangest man I've ever met. But I like you. So let's get goin'." He unlocked Peter's handcuffs. "Are we takin' this fella too?"

"Yes, he's my witness. Mr. Slike has been impersonating a gentleman of rank. He has committed extortion against me, and Mr. Tarlton is going to help me get him arrested."

"Extortion?"

"Yes, he now owns my entire estate."

"Good Go—"

"He is indeed, but we must get moving."

"And what of your lassie? He has her."

"She's safe, for the moment. But according to the triangular trade he just negotiated, they will be married in less than a fortnight."

Mr. Tarlton spoke up. "Therefore, we may also add distressing a lady to his charges."

"That's right," Bledsoe added, "you could send that fiend back into the hell from whence he came on that charge alone."

"Let us not wander too far afield, gentlemen," Peter commented. "Mr. Tarlton, you are in danger until you report these things to the authorities. Do so immediately tomorrow morning, and then direct them to Caverswall for the arrest. They must make it before the tenth of December—before the wedding ceremony, you understand—or Miss Chetwynd is lost. I will tell them as well, but I must be off to Caverswall before Mr. Slike arrives, in order to prepare my family and staff. This is no simple business. We must be very careful, and we are all in danger. Slike's men are everywhere."

Chapter 64

Duress

Betherton Hall
Staffordshire, England
4 December 1795

Except for the astonishing flow of conversation between Sir Likebridge, Mother, and Miss Haack, of all people, the carriage ride from Liverpool back to Betherton Hall was uneventful. When they arrived, and Sir Likebridge made the announcement, the pace of life increased considerably, however.

Upon hearing the news, Aunt Claire immediately set to work planning the event with Mother. And while Cousin Sylvia was hesitant at first, for Peter's sake, Annette encouraged her and acted the part of the eager bride-to-be with such enthusiasm, Sylvia's doubts appeared to have subsided.

Everything was falling into place for Steven. For the first time, he appeared to be happy. Annette could see it in his gray eyes. They were no longer cold. Instead, they laughed and sparkled with joy. His abrupt manner had changed as well. He seemed thrilled to speak with everyone, especially Mother, but also with Mr. Betherton and even Miss Haack. He was making great strides with Aunt Claire too, until she took him on a tour of the house. When they reached the second-floor gallery, something changed.

Having ascended the grand staircase, Aunt Claire, Sir Likebridge, and Annette stood gazing at Annette's grandfather's portrait—the one Annette had been studying since she was a child.

"And this . . . this is . . ." Aunt's voice faltered. Annette looked away from the remarkably lifelike hounds at her grandfather's feet to Aunt Claire.

Aunt's skin had gone pale. She glanced from the portrait to Sir Likebridge and then back again. "Why, Sir . . . Why, you are so like . . ." She whisked out her handkerchief and wiped her cheeks then cleared her throat. "You must excuse me, please."

She turned her back and began coughing.

"Aunt Claire." Annette was at her side in an instant. "Are you well?"

She inhaled deeply and straightened up.

"You both must forgive me." Aunt resumed her elegant manner. "I hardly know what came over me."

"If you desire some rest, Mrs. Betherton, surely the tour can wait." Sir Likebridge was genuinely concerned.

"Yes, of course. Thank you. But I am quite well now."

Annette watched as Aunt Claire addressed Sir Likebridge. "This is a portrait of my father, Sir Charles Alexander, and his hounds. Is he not striking?"

Likebridge looked up at the portrait. "Indeed. He was a fine gentleman."

"Sir Likebridge, do you have the time?"

"Certainly, Mrs. Betherton." He retrieved a shining gold watch from his surcoat pocket and flipped it open. "It is ten of four."

"What an interesting timepiece, Sir Likebridge." Annette noted her aunt's increased attention. "Wherever did you get it?"

"My mother gave it to me. Before that, her father gave it to her, and so on." He slipped it back into his pocket. "Shall we continue later, or stop for a bit of refreshment? Some tea, perhaps? We can always tour another day."

"Yes. Tea. That sounds quite lovely."

"Would you like me to call for it, Aunt?" Annette asked.

"No, dear. It is quite all right. You and Sir Likebridge be seated there by the window overlooking the lake, and I shall have the tea sent up for you."

"Will you not join us?"

"How kind you are, Sir Likebridge. But I have just remembered some arrangements for the wedding banquet to which I must attend. You enjoy it with your beautiful bride." Aunt gestured toward Annette, and she smiled on cue. But it was obvious, at least to Annette, that Aunt Claire could not wait to get away. What had changed?

"Yes, Sir Likebridge, do join me." Annette looped her hand around his elbow and motioned to the chairs. "The prospect of the lake is quite extraordinary from here."

"Thank you, my dear. And Mrs. Betherton, thank you for the tea."

"I will see to it right away." Aunt smiled, and then she was gone.

⁂

Aunt Claire paced beside the window of her private sitting room, working her handkerchief back and forth. Would he make it in time? She had sent a footman to Caverswall Manor. It was just down the road. A horse could get a man there in less than five minutes. But could Giles leave his duties on an instant's notice? And would they both get back in time—the time it took to prepare a tea tray?

"Oh, please. Please let him get here in time."

Guilt mixed with a roiling fear taunted her. She had hoped and prayed this would happen. For years she had prayed. Yet, now that it had, she did not know what to do. She needed help: help to soothe her broken heart, help to set matters right, and help to protect her beloved niece from pending disaster.

Yet, perhaps she needed nothing at all. Might it simply be a figment of her overactive imagination? Surely, Giles would know. She must speak with Giles. How she wished he had stayed with them. He had served as her husband's valet when they first were married some thirty-two years ago. Or was it thirty-one? At the moment, she could not remember. But he could not stay, not with memories of his daughter surrounding him.

Mrs. Betherton sighed. She musn't worry about that now. It was long in the past, and Giles was only down the road at Caverswell. He could still help her figure out what to do. She just needed a little patience.

A quiet knock sounded at the door. Or was it simply the noise of a creaking floor? Aunt Claire stopped pacing to listen. There. It sounded again. She rushed to the door.

"Oh, Giles, good afternoon. Do come in."

"Mrs. Betherton." Stepping into the room, he removed his hat and waited. She darted to a chair beside the fire. "Here, Giles, please be seated."

"Thank you, my lady," he responded in a gravelly voice, then shuffled to his seat. She seated herself across from him and drew her chair closer to his.

"It is good to see you, Giles." She fiddled with her handkerchief.

Giles spoke in a flat tone. "Has the day come?"

"Yes." Another rush of guilt. "I fear . . ." She sniffed and wiped her eyes.

"I mean no disrespect, but could there be some mistake?"

"Yes. I mean no. Oh, Giles, I am uncertain. I need your help." She blew her nose. "But the resemblance, it is so striking. You will recognize it. And he has the watch."

"The watch? He has it then. You have seen it."

"Yes. I asked for the time, and there it was, right in his pocket. Giles, I saw the dog's head coin."

"Have you spoken to Mr. Betherton?"

"No. There has been no time. They only arrived yesterday with my sister and her party, and it was late. I was scarcely able to see them to their rooms and have a meal prepared."

"And what are the circumstances of this unexpected arrival?"

"He is to marry my niece on Thursday next. Oh Giles, you must help me. Surely, there is something we can do. If only Mr. Adsley were here. We could consult with him."

Mrs. Betherton broke down yet again.

"Dear lady, if you will pardon me. But please, do calm yourself. We need to keep a clear mind for this."

"Yes, Giles. I understand. I will do my best." She wiped her eyes and cleared her throat.

"Well then, I would like to meet this gentleman for meself. Might I see him up close?"

"Yes. He and Miss Chetwynd are in the small drawing room off the gallery, overlooking the lake. You may carry up their tea. I ordered it exactly when I sent for you, hoping you would make it in time. And you did, oh thank you. They are expecting it by now. Come along. We must get to the kitchen."

"As you wish, Mistress." Giles got to his feet and followed Mrs. Betherton out of the room.

Giles found his target exactly where Mrs. Betherton said he would be. "Tea is served," he said as he carefully placed the tray on the table beside the young lady.

"Thank you," she responded. Then she turned. "Would you care for some tea, Sir Likebridge?"

Giles gasped. Then he started coughing and felt himself folding over. It was the name. Yes, that name. He had not expected to hear it ever again.

"For goodness sake, sir!" In an instant, Giles felt her arm around his shoulders supporting him. "Please, Sir Likebridge, can you help him to a chair? I'll get him something to drink."

Strong arms lifted him away from the young lady and carried him. In a matter of seconds, Giles was resting on a chaise lounge and both of them were staring at him.

"Can you manage some of this tea?" she asked as she held up a cup.

"Thank you, Miss," Giles mumbled and leaned forward to take a sip while doing his best to study the man beside her. He had not planned it this way, but it worked well enough.

The watch, the name, and now the face: there was no mistaking the man's identity. His nose was different—of course it wouldn't be a perfect match—but there was no mistaking those icy gray eyes, the strong cheekbones, and the ball of a chin. Few people had such distinctive features, and since he had the watch and the name, there could be no question.

Mr. Likebridge had most certainly returned to his birthplace, but did he know his family?

Chapter 65
Solution

Caverswall Manor
Staffordshire, England
5 December 1795

Having hitched a ride with the post-coach, Peter, Captain Bledsoe, and Turtle arrived at the outer edge of Caverswall Manor under a full moon. With their breaths coming as puffs of smoke, they hiked down from the main road to the back stable and sneaked inside. Peter had no wish to alert the staff to his presence, at least not yet. He had no clue what Sir Likebridge had told them or if he had even arrived yet.

"Look at the size o' this place, and it's only for horses," Turtle whispered. Said horses whinnied and clomped their hooves in the darkened stable.

"That is correct, Turtle, and I will be happy to show you more of it soon. But for now, I need you to stay quiet. You and the captain must hide out here until I can get a place ready for you. I do not want anyone to know you are here, especially if Slike is around."

"I'll take care o' the boy, Adsley. You just get inside and find a place where we can warm up."

"As soon as I can, Captain."

⯅

What a strange thing, having to slink about into one's own house, Peter thought, as he made his way from the kitchen up the back servants' stairs. Yet, it was no longer his, not according to Slike's deed.

Peter must speak with Giles to ascertain what changes, if any, Slike had made.

The step creaked, and he froze, listening for any hint that might suggest someone had heard him, but the house was quiet. He continued up the stairs until he reached the landing.

He glanced both ways. No movement or noise. Quietly stepping ahead, he made his way down the hall and past his former bedchamber. Ordinarily, a man's valet would have a room in the servants' quarters. That would have been much easier on this occasion. But due to his age, Peter had seen to it that Giles's room was down the hall from his. Just a few feet further, and he would be there.

Peter let out a breath when he reached the door. All was well. He knocked and listened for movement. Nothing. He knocked again, a bit louder this time; and then he heard some grumbling.

"Livin' saints awakin' me in the middle o' the night! What could ya possibly be about?" Peter smiled. It was good to hear his friend's voice again.

"What's it ya want now, ya—?" He opened the door and held up a candle. When he squinted up at Peter and his whole countenance changed. "God bless me. Be it you, me boy?"

"It is."

"Well, come in, come in. What're ye doin' standin' in the dark?"

"Thank you, Giles. But we must be quiet. No one can know I am home yet."

"Step over there by me fire," he said as he closed the door. "And let me have a look at ya." Giles grasped his arms. "You're lookin' mighty thin to me. How was the trip?"

"There is much to tell, but before I do, I have two friends hiding in the stable. Will you see to them?"

"Indeed I will, and to you this very minute. Are ya hungry? Can I get ya somethin' to eat?"

"Hold a moment, not yet. They are settled for now. I must ask though, have there been any changes here at Caverswall? Has a man named Sir Steven Likebridge arrived?"

Giles eyes darkened. "I saw him over at the Bethertons' today. What do ya know of him?"

"Has he been here yet?"

"No, why should he be?"

"He is the new owner of the estate."

"Merciful God in Heaven," Giles groaned. "And he is plannin' to expand his holdin's with a dowry from Mrs. Chetwynd's daughter. But it mustn't be."

"Precisely. I will not allow it, Giles."

"Then ya know of his connection?"

"He forced me to forfeit my property or the lady's life. He planned to use her as . . ." Peter's voice cracked. "It was revolting; unspeakable. I could not allow it, not for all the slaves in the world."

"So ya know nothin' of his circumstances or relations."

"What do you mean?" Peter stared at Giles, and the old man smiled. "This is no time—"

Peter bowed his head in his hands. "God, how can this be happening? This cannot be your will. So many lives at stake: my family; my friends, and . . . God, I love her."

"Calm yourself, me boy." Peter felt a strong hand on his shoulder.

"The Lord has already provided the solution."

"What?" Peter looked up.

"There is work to be done, most certainly. But there's no use to troublin' yourself over it. He has already settled the matter. Now, let's see to your friends in the stable."

"But Miss Chetwynd . . ."

"You needn't worry, me boy. Trust me."

Chapter 66

Crisis

St. Peter's Church
Staffordshire, England
10 December 1795

Steven glanced in the mirror to check his cravat one last time. Then he stopped. Something, or perhaps someone, demanded his attention.

He studied his gray eyes. No longer cold and hard, they reflected a light he rarely observed in himself. Joy? Anticipation? Relief? A sense of freedom and closure? He could not describe it. However, his purpose was accomplished—well, nearly so.

He smiled, but his eyes turned misty. He had not had time to find Lani. Between freeing himself from the brig, auctioning the slaves, loading the *Terona*, and chasing back to England after Peter, there was not a minute to spare. And had he attempted to visit her, none of this would be possible. He swallowed hard. But there would be other visits.

Steven wiped his eyes and sniffed. Then he glanced at the signed deed that lay on his dresser. "Well, Mother, today I wed. You would love to be here, I know. When I take my rightful position—I will make the announcement today after the ceremony—you and Charlie will come home with me."

Home in Caverswall, a wife, and his family with him here in Caverswall. Might there be others? The thought struck him oddly. It followed that there could be. Mother may have had family before she left.

He shook off the bizarre sensation the thought caused, folded up the deed, and slipped it inside his coat pocket. Quickly wiping his eyes again, he adjusted his coat and cleared his throat.

"There is nothing to worry about, Mother. Heaven has finally smiled on us."

⚔

In his coach on the way to church for another wedding, Peter sat tall and straight, confident in God's provision for the day. By God's grace, he would present the evidence against Mr. Slike, and Miss Chetwynd would be free of him forever. Yet, what would become of her after this scrape with notoriety? And what of her mother? The prospect was not entirely pleasant. Her mother would be more willing to hear his suit, though.

Peter looked across the coach at Captain Bledsoe and Turtle, the curious pair who had become his friends. *Thank you, Father, for these caring souls. They have laid down their lives for me on more than one occasion, and today they stand with me again. Bless our efforts as we move against that treacherous fraud.*

"*The Lord is long suffering toward us, not willing that any should perish, but that all should come to repentance.*" The tone was too firm to deny, and Peter responded accordingly.

"Forgive me. I meant no disrespect, though he deserves—"

"*For all have sinned and come short of the glory of God.*" Peter raked his fingers through his hair. "Indeed, but I . . ."

"*For by grace are ye saved through faith; and that not of yourselves: it is a gift of God: not of works, lest any man should boast.*"

"Mr. Adsley, are you talking to God again?" Turtle asked.

"As a matter of fact I am."

"Well, it seems to me like you better start listening instead."

"*Out of the mouth of babes . . . thou has ordained strength . . .*"

"Thank you, Turtle. I appreciate your insight."

Peter took out his pocket watch. It was fifteen minutes after nine. Slipping the watch back into his pocket, he looked out the window. Whitewashed houses with their thatched roofs appeared here and there along the road. Within the hour, the present conflict would finally be over.

↟

The footman opened the door, and Peter, Captain Bledsoe, and Turtle stepped out.

"Do we go now, Mr. Adsley?"

"No Turtle, we must wait for the exact moment. I will tell you when."

"Aye, sir." Turtle saluted, and Peter had to smile.

"In the meantime, keep an eye out for Mr. Tarlton and the authorities. I had word they are on their way up from Bradley." Peter caught Captain Bledsoe's eye. "Are you ready to do this?"

"Indeed, I am." With a wicked smile, he drew his coat aside and displayed his ever-ready whip. "And I got the biter with me too."

Peter glanced at it and sighed. "Then so be it."

Peter led them to the back door of the gray stone chapel and leaned close to listen. Reverend Sharpe was wheezing his way through the lines, approaching the part Peter awaited.

". . . in prosperity and adversity. Into which holy estate these two persons come now to be joined. *Wheeze* . . . Therefore if any man can show any just cause, why they may not lawfully be joined together . . . *Wheeze* . . . let him speak now, or else hereafter forever hold his peace."

Peter's back and neck muscles went taut. "Forward, our time is now, men." He threw open the doors with a loud bang.

"I must speak." His voice boomed, and the witnesses, indeed, the building itself gasped. The Reverend, Miss Chetwynd, and Mr. Slike, as well as Mrs. Chetwynd, Miss Haack, Cousin Sylvia, and Mr. and Mrs. Betherton and the other guests turned with wide eyes and mouths agape.

Peter strode down the center aisle with Captain Bledsoe and Turtle in his wake. "This union is unlawful and prohibited by God's and man's laws alike."

"That's right," Turtle shouted. "She's his sister!"

The audience's second collective intake of breath was so deep, it might have drowned the whole lot, had they been near any form of liquid. Marshaling her shock, Mrs. Chetwynd got to her feet and responded.

"That is ridiculous!"

The Reverend Sharpe started wheezing, and the rest of the group—save Miss Chetwynd—broke into various levels of hysteria. Mr. Slike instantly produced a knife, took aim, and—

CRACK!

Captain Bledsoe sent the tail of his whip hissing through the air and twisting around Mr. Slike's wrist, knocking the blade from his hand and bringing him to his knees. Whereupon the captain strode forward, grabbed the groom's other wrist and wrapped the remaining length of his whip around both Mr. Slike's neck and wrists together. Then he clamped his hand around the back of the prisoner's neck and forced him to kneel right there in front of everyone.

"Steady, scoundrel, or I'll finish the job here and now."

Peter stepped up. "I say this marriage is prohibited. She is his sister, and I have proof."

Chapter 67

Exposed

"Miss Chetwynd, you may be seated if you like." Steven heard the words, but—

"Thank you, Mr. Adsley," she whispered, and Steven was alone, again.

"Now, Mrs. Betherton, if you will, please stand."

Steven's pulse hammered in his ears as the lady, who was quite obviously shaken by the entire affair, got to her feet. Her husband stood beside her, while another old man, who had been out of sight until now, stepped to his accuser's side.

Miss Chetwynd, his sister, what rubbish! He was the Adsley heir, not the Chetwynd heir. But why so many witnesses standing with Adsley?

"Mr. Adsley, I demand to hear your statement," Mrs. Chetwynd spoke up. "How dare you insult me thus, and disparaging Sir Likebridge's character? I could have you drawn and quartered. I am the mother of but two children, both of whom you see here."

"Would you care to discuss this matter in a more private environ?" Peter asked.

Steven's breath came in short bursts, and for the first time in years he felt a tremor of apprehension. Its nibbling anxiety picked the same spot until the ache boiled into fear—fear like a master craftsman feels when he sees a tiny fissure in the solitary mold of his finest masterpiece.

"Indeed." Reverend Sharpe cleared his throat. "An allegation of this magnitude . . . May we not adjourn to my personal study?"

"I will hear it right here, right—"

"Sister, do consider." Mrs. Betherton spoke in a quiet voice. "At least permit the Reverend to ask our guests and that urchin boy to wait in the foyer."

"Yes," Mr. Betherton confirmed. "We have suffered enough. A disgrace of this sort could ruin us forever."

"Very well then." Mrs. Chetwynd yielded.

Steven fought the dread. He was the man of information. His plan was perfect. He had studied every feasible circumstance. He knew the deepest and darkest secrets of some of the most influential people in Liverpool. What could these country folk know that he did not? What indeed? He dredged up the catechism his mother had taught him over twenty-five years ago. *I am the firstborn son of Mr. Charles Adsley of Caverswall Manor. I was born on the first of April in the year of our Lord, 1767. I am the firstborn son of Mr. Charles Adsley of . . .*

His knees hurt, his head throbbed, and the leather tail of Bledsoe's whip cut into Steven's neck. Nevertheless, the room was clear of everyone except the people of interest: Mr. and Mrs. Betherton; the old man beside Peter; Mrs. Chetwynd and his future brother-in-law, Gerald, and Miss Chetwynd, of course.

I am the firstborn son of Mr. Charles Adsley of Caverswall Manor. I was born on the first of April in the year of our Lord, 1767.

"Mrs. Betherton, have you the portrait at hand?"

"I do."

"I will see to it for ya, Mistress."

"Thank you, Giles," Peter said as the old man turned to exit the side door of the chapel.

So that was his name. But he could offer nothing. A servant's word did not signify.

"Mrs. Betherton, are you ready to present your account?"

"I am, but I must address my sister first."

Mrs. Chetwynd, his would-be mother-in-law, wrung her hands and smoothed her gown. She did not make eye contact with her sister.

A chink developed in the armor surrounding Steven's heart as he pondered the reason for a lack of visual communication between them.

"Elizabeth, dear sister, I must beg your forgiveness. Truly I am sorry, but I thought it for the best."

"Please share your story, Mrs. Betherton," Reverend Sharpe coaxed.

"Yes, I fear I must." She wiped her eyes, raised her chin, and began. "Some twenty-nine years ago, my father sent my sister to join me here in the country."

Mrs. Chetwynd groaned, and Steven held his breath.

"Yes, Sister, I know. But I must." She turned to the larger group. "Mr. Betherton, Giles, even my sister's husband, God rest his loving soul, were all privy to the circumstances—though Mr. Chetwynd learned of them after the fact. Of course, Father and Mother also knew, but it had to be done. On the night of the first of April, 1767, she delivered a child, a boy."

Another crack in Steven's meticulously constructed world of plans and schemes traced its way to the dark corner of his soul where he concealed and repressed all things contrary to his purpose.

"Of course, there was no way for her to keep the baby. We could not simply dispose of him either. His birth was no fault of his own." Mrs. Betherton broke down.

"Enough, gentleman, my wife has nothing more to say." Sitting her down, Mr. Betherton encircled her in a comforting embrace as the side door of the chapel opened.

"I have the portrait, sir."

"Yes, Giles. Can I aid you in moving it?"

"If you will, sir."

Peter went to assist, and in a few moments the sheet-covered painting was leaning against the pulpit.

"Giles, Mrs. Betherton has shared her part. Please tell us yours."

"Yes, sir. I'll begin by sayin' me surname's not Giles. When I came to work for the late Mr. Adsley some eight and twenty years ago, I asked that he use me Christian name in place o' me surname. What with me poor girl's ruination, it was all I could do to find work and keep the rest of my family fed, without the world knowin' all me family's business. Me true name is Likebridge."

The fracture that tore through the foundation of Steven's reality pierced his heart and touched his soul. He felt a cry escape his lips, but he heard it as if from outside of himself. Then, a tiny spark brightened in his soul—a grandfather. A moment later, the spark died. Impersonation: Steven would hang for it. Men, even children, were hung for less every day.

"Earlier the same week that Mrs. Chetwynd birthed her son, me own Abigail, God rest her soul, brought her babe into the world, a boy as well. You see, she was a chambermaid at Betherton Hall, and when she came to be with child, they ousted her."

"We never knew the father, though. She refused to give him up. To the point, though, me girl's babe died a few hours after his birth. But instead o' tellin' her, since she was in such a bad way already, I went to Mrs. Betherton to see if we could resolve the problem together."

"And so we did," Mrs. Betherton spoke up. "I gave Elizabeth's son to Miss Likebridge to rear as her own, and I told my sister her baby was dead."

Giles added, "At least he'd have a Ma that loved him instead of bein' killed, as they sometimes are."

Steven's reality splintered. Yet, for as much anguish as the truth about his birth inflicted upon his poor mind, the tortured shout he gave was nothing compared to Mrs. Chetwynd's deafening wail.

"NO! My baby died. You told me it . . . it . . . he died. I loved my baby. Claire, I loved ... You told me . . . ma babe. . . " Her mouth drooped to the side, and she crumbled to her knees. "Ma babe . . . ma babe." Her words slurred as she repeated them over and over; then she tipped to the side as if to faint, teetered and—

In that instant, the whip around Steven's neck went slack, and he fell chin-first at Peter's feet. From that peculiar angle on the floor, Steven watched Captain Bledsoe slide to his knees and catch Mrs. Chetwynd before her head hit the wood floor.

"Ah, Lizzie, me lass. I'm here." With tears streaming down his cheeks, Captain Bledsoe gathered Mrs. Chetwynd in his arms and sat patting her cheeks, kissing her forehead, and rocking her. "It's all right me darlin', Lizzie, I'm here now. Everything's goin' to be all right."

Steven stared at the unlikely pair and then gasped. By this calculation, he must be . . .

Choking and retching all at once, even as the group gathered around Mrs. Chetwynd, Steven finally knew who he was. His eyes saw the chaotic scene: people calling for help to carry her out, her first love--David Bledsoe--beside her, and Mr. Betherton directing the lot, but none of it meant much.

He felt his mind calculating, recalculating, and attempting to reconcile his life's purpose with the truth. It came up short. His entire existence was meaningless. Worse yet, he had been a blight from the moment he came into being. The mother of his birth should never have had him. His servant mother's life was ruined by taking him. His debauched youth was a travesty of shameful acts perpetrated for the sake of . . . Of what?

"Is she breathing?" someone asked.

Steven had little will to listen. He had spent nearly half his life plotting against a man and his entire family to gain an inheritance that was not his. His actions might even have led to the family's destruction. Steven had destroyed Richard Adsley by introducing him to women and strong drink. Mr. Adsley died on his *Terona*. He had taunted, even brutalized Peter Adsley, a true man of God. And what had he planned for Miss Chetwynd, his own sister? God forgive him. What had he become?

Steven's reason tilted further toward oblivion. Mrs. Chetwynd, his mother? Captain Bledsoe, his father? And what of his friend, his sweet Lani? He had sold her.

Despair threatened to destroy him. Shame like a constrictor squeezed the last bit of sense from him. From that odd angle lying on the floor, he did, however, spy the knife his father had whipped away from his hand just minutes ago.

There, under the first pew. A glint of sunshine crossed the blade, and he saw his beautiful, cinnamon-cheeked friend again. But she was angry. *Beast. Wretched, depraved monster. Betrayer. Judas. Hopeless, vile . . .*

Steven rolled himself toward the knife, snatched it from beneath the pew, and kissed the blade. Then he faced it toward his own stomach, raised his hands above his head, and plunged it—

"AHHhhh!" He cried as his fingers crunched under a boot.

"That is not the way." Peter Adsley bent down and removed the knife from between his broken fingers. "You will be held accountable, Likebridge. But you will not dispatch yourself without the benefit of time. God is not willing that any should perish; nor am I."

"What's this?" Reverend Sharpe grumbled.

"I have him managed, Reverend." Peter turned back to Steven. "Now get up. You will hear this out." With that, Peter grabbed his elbow and hoisted him to a sitting position in the front pew. Then he turned to Mrs. Betherton.

"May we finish, Mrs. Betherton? Can you explain why you have brought the painting? Or shall we postpone it for a while?"

"It has been too long; we must have it out. Then I will go to my sister." Mrs. Betherton pulled on the sheet covering the painting to reveal Sir Charles Alexander attired in his red fox-hunting coat and white breeches with his three hounds attending at his feet. Steven had just seen it in the gallery.

"This is Father, as most of you know. If you compare Mr. Likebridge's features—his gray eyes, his cheekbones, and the ball of his chin—you will see the resemblance. It is striking, actually. I saw it the moment we met, but I had to ascertain a bit more information before announcing it. This portrait confirms my findings."

Steven forced his eyes and ears to focus.

"Do you see Father's watch fob hanging from his pocket?" The audience murmured assent. "I will describe it to you as I see it in the painting: a gold chain containing a coin bearing the image of a dog's head."

Steven groaned.

"Maintain your composure," Peter whispered. "It only confirms what we already know."

Mrs. Betherton stood before Slike. "Mr. Likebridge, may I see your watch?" He attempted to oblige her, but with his wrists bound, he was unable to reach it.

Peter moved Steven's coat aside to retrieve the watch and noticed a parchment of particular size and color. He removed both the watch and the document, placing the watch in Mrs. Betherton's hand and the folded page into his own pocket.

Steven eyed Peter but made no move against him.

"Here is the dog's head coin, and if you turn the watch over, you can identify the words, 'For my beloved C.A,' the statement Mother had engraved on the watch for Father, Clarence Alexander. It was a wedding gift from her to him." Mrs. Betherton held it out for everyone to examine.

"When Mr. Betherton and I married, Father gave me this watch as a wedding present, anticipating the birth of a son. We both so enjoyed the hunt, you know. He expected any son of mine would be doubly pleased to receive the watch. But two years into our marriage, which is about the time of the event we have been discussing, I still had no children. So the day she left Caverswall—it was early summer, I think—I gave Father's watch to Abigail Likebridge as a gift for her son, my sister's child."

Steven felt himself fading, folding as it were into nothingness. All the fight was gone; nothing remained but his shame.

Mrs. Betherton seated herself beside Steven. "You see, I would have kept you myself if I could have. Mr. Betherton and I discussed the possibility at length. Alas, it was not feasible." A tear slid down her cheek. "So I gave you a token, a bit of your inheritance, as it were, praying God would allow you to find your way back." More tears washed her cheeks. "And so the Lord has seen fit to bring you back to me . . . Nephew."

Steven bowed his head as she held him close. Even his tears were ashamed to appear. He had wasted his entire life pursuing and ruining an innocent family. Yet, this dear woman, his aunt, refused to let him go. How was it possible? Even Peter denied him the death he sought. It was unbearable. He had found his true family, but he did not deserve them. He could never deserve them.

"Well then." The Reverend Sharpe cleared his throat. "Mr. Adsley, you were correct. The marriage is unlawful according to the evidence—"

Suddenly, a great pounding noise sounded at the back of the chapel. Steven cranked his neck around to see the door burst open for the second time that day, and Mr. Tarlton strode in, leading several uniformed officers down the aisle behind him.

"Be there a Mr. Steven Likebridge present?" an officer asked. "If so, yield him up. He is under arrest."

"Thank Heaven," Steven whispered.

Chapter 68

Promise

Betherton Hall
Staffordshire, England
11 December 1795

The next afternoon, Annette addressed Captain Bledsoe, who sat holding Mother's hand and talking to her as she lay silent in her bed.

"Captain, surely you need some rest, or something to eat, perhaps?"

"No, thank you, lassie. I've been away far too long to leave her now." A knock sounded at the door, and Annette turned to see Peter looking in. "Go along with your Mr. Adsley. I'll take care o' me Lizzie."

Annette went to Peter.

"Are there any changes?" he asked.

"She is sleeping, and the captain refuses to leave her side."

"I am not surprised. You have been up all night too."

"Not nearly so long as that."

"Have you had your meal?"

"I had some cake a while ago."

"Miss Haack commanded me to see that you eat these." Peter offered a bowl of orange slices. "You must look after yourself, or you will be of no use to her."

Annette slipped out of the room. "Thank you." She popped an orange slice in her mouth and studied his eyes. They were somber.

"I was up early too, praying." He paused. "We must speak."

"There is a place in the gallery. I will show you." She guided him to her special haven. When they reached the alcove where her favorite painting hung, Annette pulled the cushioned bench away from the wall. "Sit here."

"Interesting painting."

She seated herself beside him and stared at her loving shepherd. "It was my favorite. I used it to remind me of you."

"Me? How so?"

She turned to him. "After Sir Like . . . After the attack . . . Well, I did not know it was you who rescued me, but I remembered the man had dark hair. I was so ill, I am surprised I could recall even that. So when I found this painting, I could not help but think of him—you, actually. I used to sit here and sketch his face until you came along. That seems so long ago," she sighed.

285

"Indeed."

She looked down at her folded hands. "Much has changed since then."

"It has?"

"But you needn't worry, Mr. Adsley. You are under no obligation. With Mother ill, I—"

"Obligation?"

Annette got to her feet. She could not allow him to see her cry. He mustn't feel obliged or responsible . . . Tears filled her eyes, and she started to leave.

"Miss Chetwynd." He caught her hand, but she attempted to pull away. He stood up. "Please, Miss Chetwynd . . . Annette, stay."

"I find I am rather. . ." She bowed her head into her free hand.

Standing behind her, he gently drew her back against his chest. Wrapping his arms around her shoulders, he whispered in her ear.

"You with your constant prattling. Will you never permit me to speak?" She sniffed, and he took out his handkerchief. "Here, take this. There is nothing more amusing than the sound of your little trumpet nose." Annette laughed and blew her nose. "You may keep it. I have an endless supply, since Mary Hope never tires of sewing."

"I know. I watched her embroidering them daily at Jane Arden's school in Beverley."

"You promised you would tell me about that. Remember?"

"Yes, but not now."

"Precisely. I have much more important matters to discuss. Come then. Sit with me." He leaned down to pick up the bowl of oranges and handed it to her. "And eat these. They will help you listen."

She took it and selected another slice.

Peter's voice turned serious. "Annette, you must know I have been praying for a wife." She nodded. "And God answered that prayer long ago, though I never stopped to listen. Since then, I have come to understand He desires that I wait for the right lady and the right time."

A unique sense of peace pervaded Annette.

"Dearest lady—" Peter took the bowl from her, set it on the ground, and then took both of her hands in his. "Since first we met in the study at Betherton Hall when you answered my prayer, I have admired you." His warm, velvet eyes stirred with sentiment. "Notwithstanding your unreserved passion for testing limitations and speaking your mind, and despite my contrasting inclination toward propriety and decorum, every part of my being yearns for you." He gazed into her eyes. "Nevertheless, I cannot marry you now. It is not the right time."

"I understand." Annette swallowed hard. They were the most challenging words she had ever said, but they came from somewhere deep within her soul, and they were true.

"Annette, beloved, we have faced so many challenges."

"And I have been so foolish. Too romantic in my grasp of the world, of God, even in my responsibilities toward my family." A plaintive laugh bubbled from her lips. "I am surprised you even allowed yourself to be subjected to my antics."

"Do not reproach yourself, for I will not. I have my own flaws as well you know since I revealed my hurricane experience."

"But I see myself another way now, Peter. And I see God in a different light too. Before, I thought He was supposed to prevent bad things from happening, but I have come to understand He uses them to help us grow."

"Well said."

"I must learn so much more. And now that Mother is ... Well, frankly, I need to grow up." She rolled her eyes. "Mother would faint if she heard me acknowledging these things."

He laughed. "I suppose she would." He brushed a curl from her face and traced his fingers along her cheek. "You are so beautiful and sincere . . . and irresistible, much like your mother must have been to Captain Bledsoe."

"What an amazing story that has been."

"Indeed."

"And so disappointing. No wonder she was so adamant about me having a chaperon. But let us not speak of such things. You were talking of our future, I think."

He smiled. "Your boldness never fails to amaze me."

"Well, since that night in the Ashton's conservatory, we are practically engaged. So might I expect to hear something of a marriage, even if it is to be postponed?"

"You might."

"Then I would be delighted to hear your proposal for our future."

"I have a verse for it, one to which I am wholly committed to submitting from now on."

"It is the twenty-ninth chapter of Jeremiah, the eleventh verse, where God promises each one of us he has a special plan that will give us hope and a future, is it not?"

"You are absolutely right." Peter held up a finger, and she calmed herself. "Nevertheless, with so many responsibilities: estate matters, Betherton's financial challenges, understanding the workings of the shipping company, the plantation in Jamaica, and our slaves—" He cleared his throat. "Forgive me, they are my slaves. I must even attend to Mr. Likebridge."

"Peter, you must pardon me for saying so, but it appears that we are equally capable of prattling."

"Are we?"

"Without a doubt. While you are certainly correct in expressing that it is not the right time for such a joyous event as a wedding, you are thoroughly mistaken when you, a minister of God's grace, think that you are not prepared to overcome the present turmoil."

He raised an eyebrow. "And you must point out this flaw because it is in your nature to do so."

"Yes. Do you remember what I said about you having a ministry that would reach halfway around the world?"

"I do. The moment you said it, I knew I loved you."

"Then what is the matter? You have all you need for success."

Peter cleared his throat and focused on her eyes. "I know I must do this. It is His plan, or I would not be in the position. Only I know naught how to do it. It is not a pastor's employment."

She caressed Peter's cheek and ran her fingertip over the scar on his upper lip. "I never thought I would say this, but you are not a pastor. You are a godly man who is committed to serving our Lord. And what He has called you to do He will enable you to do, by the power of His Spirit living in you."

"The task seems so overwhelming. And what of Likebridge?"

"He is Mother's and the captain's son, and he will likely be executed at Stanley Tower in Liverpool."

"You have suffered much of that man, but the captain is my friend. I cannot see his son dispatched without another opportunity to repent."

"I know of no one else who would care, especially after what he did to you and your family. But I would expect nothing less of you."

Peter's brows knitted together. "It is not so much caring as a duty."

"Nevertheless, who would desire to fulfill his duty to such a man?"

"And you would stand by me as I do it?"

"Yes. It is my purpose to help you."

"The matter is settled then." He slid his fingers into her hair and placed a kiss on her forehead. "Though I wish the timing were better."

"As do I," she sighed.

"I have another confession to make." He removed his hands and tucked her curls behind her ears.

"You are worried a new suitor will snatch me away while we wait for a better time?"

"No. I will speak with your brother today."

"It could not be so terrible then. Tell me, and have done with it."

"Back in the Ashtons' conservatory, when I spoke about the nature of a kiss and how it changes a relationship, I failed to mention exactly how it changes one."

"I am not certain I remember, but do tell." Her eyes brightened.

"I cannot."

"Why not?"

"I cannot say, exactly."

"So you purposely misled me?"

"I suppose one could say that, but not with any malicious intent."

"Then why did you?"

"I was attempting to redirect your interest because my own was so strong."

"Mr. Adsley, you should be ashamed of yourself, lying to avoid an innocent kiss. It is unthinkable." She gave him a sidelong glance. "And now it is a moot point, since my curiosity has been satisfied."

"Has it?"

"Not entirely. When my last opportunity presented itself, I was not fully engaged in the activity."

"Talking again?" He grinned.

"You might say that. I do spy a means to remedy the situation, though."

"I just did, by confessing it."

"I meant a way to redress our deficiency." She glanced at his lips then caught his eyes. They seemed to drink in every feature of her face. Peter leaned forward, and their foreheads met. "But we mustn't delay any longer, or they will notice we are missing, and someone might find us."

"Agreed."

He took her face in his hands and brought her so close she could almost feel his smile against her mouth.

"Dearest Annette, I love you," he whispered. "And I would be honored if you would be my wife."

"I will, Peter. You know I—"

Before she could finish, he gently brushed his lips against hers with a tentative touch. Wrapping her arms around his waist and savoring the scent of his sandalwood soap mingled with the taste of the oranges, she returned his soft caresses.

He slid his hands down her neck and around her shoulders, drawing her closer and enfolding her to his heart as he tested and tasted her lips. Then, deepening the kisses together, it seemed as if they were melting into each other.

All the passion and pent-up emotion from nearly a year's worth of missed opportunities and painful memories soon fell away, and Annette knew, without a doubt, that she would someday be the wife of Mr. Peter Adsley, the master and pastor of Caverswall Manor. And she was thoroughly satisfied with the prospect of it.

Author's Invitation & Gift

Dear friend,

Authors are encouraged to write what they know, so I've shared my heart with you. Once in a while, I catch a glimpse of the doubt Annette experiences. Like Peter, I let my focus drift away from Christ, and when I try to control things, I recognize in myself Slike's selfishness and lack of trust in God's Plan.

While these issues show I periodically struggle with applying my belief in God's sovereignty to my daily life, there is still hope, because I haven't the slightest bit of doubt about the Lord Jesus Christ and His amazing work on the cross.

When we truly recognize our weaknesses and accept the fact that we cannot do life alone, we are closer to overcoming them through Christ, and we can begin to know and trust Him more. (For those of you who've never faced these challenges, I am truly happy for you, and I hope life continues to treat you well.)

No matter where you are in your spiritual journey, it would be an honor to get to know you and to share with you on a more personal level. Contact me at janinemendenhall@gmail.com. I would love to hear how the Lord used *Starving Hearts* to touch your heart. And, whether you're a believer or not, I've posted practical ways to grow your faith on my blog, *Hopefuel*, at janinemendenhall.com.

In closing, it has been my pleasure to serve you by providing a few hours of escape with Book 1. I pray the Lord will use it to draw you closer to Him, and I know He will, if you let Him, because no one is ever past Hope.

Sincerely, your friend,

Janine

P.S. Speaking of *Never Past Hope*, that's the title of Book 2. If you can't wait to see what happens next, click http://www.janinemendenhall.com/never-past-hope/ I've posted Chapter 1—The Verdict on my website just for you. And, don't forget, keep in touch!

Made in the USA
San Bernardino, CA
17 June 2017